From the
BEACHES
Iris Rainer Dart

The Stork Club

"HILARIOUS . . . warmhearted and surprisingly genuine in its emotions. . . . The bestselling author of *Beaches* and *I'll Be There* is right on the money with this clever, timely exploration of the emotional turmoil engendered by the brave new world of contemporary baby-making."

—*Publishers Weekly*

"JUICY, FUNNY, SAD, AND TRUE, *The Stork Club* will make you laugh through your tears."

—Connie Chung and Maury Povich

more . . .

"A DOCUDRAMA in which Dart skillfully deals with a very real phenomenon."
—***New York Sunday Daily News***

"AMBITIOUS. . . . A good novel for a lazy rainy day."
—***Los Angeles Daily News***

"VERY CONTEMPORARY, VERY READABLE. . . . A story that's as witty as it is poignant."
—***Anniston Star***

"A HOLLYWOOD NOVEL WITH A TWIST."
—***Seattle Times***

"Entertaining, trendy, and seeping with baby lust."
—***Kirkus Reviews***

"Dart, the author of *Beaches*, writes with such humor and compassion that it's hard to dislike any of these people."
—***Cleveland Plain Dealer***

"Singularly good. . . . With humor and poignancy, Dart probes the challenge of child rearing in the 1990s."

—***Library Journal***

"Timely, topical."

—***Virginian Pilot & Ledger-Star***

"A unique story, eminently readable, that explores material different from that addressed in most novels."

—***San Antonio Express-News***

"Indeed a novel of and for the 1990s."

—***Sunday Oklahoman***

"Dart's stunning new novel . . . develops each individual story carefully and blends them into a viable and provocative tale."

—***Ocala Star-Banner***

By Iris Rainer Dart

'Til the Real Thing Comes Along
The Boys in the Mail Room
Beaches
I'll Be There
The Stork Club

IRIS RAINER DART

The STORK CLUB

WARNER
VISION
BOOKS

A Time Warner Company

To Steve, Greg, and Rachel.
My three miracles.

WARNER BOOKS EDITION

Cover design by Elaine Groh / Jackie Merri Meyer / Diane Luger
Cover photograph by Herman Estevez

This Warner Books Edition is published by arrangement with Little, Brown and Company.

Warner Vision is a trademark of Warner Books, Inc.

Warner Books, Inc.
1271 Avenue of the Americas
New York, NY 10020

A Time Warner Company

Printed in the United States of America

First Warner Books Printing: August, 1994

10 9 8 7 6 5 4 3 2 1

Thank You

Elaine Markson—for being there even when I wasn't
Dr. Melanie Allen—with gratitude for the many hours of your time and the benefit of your gifts in the field of child psychology
Barbara Gordon, MSW—for the unending information and patience you gave to me and to all who need your warmth and love
David Radis—the Zen baby lawyer, whose gentle touch has brought joy into the lives of so many families
Marilyn Brown—Senior Director of the parenting center at Stephen S. Wise Temple, for loving information personal and professional
Dr. Betsy Aigen, director of the Surrogate Mother Program of New York—for insight into the process
Vicki Gold Levy—a wonderful friend, and a new mother at fifty!
Christopher Priestly—my strong and dear man. You know some of this is for you

In memory of the late *David Panich*
With love as always to *Barry Adelman*
Mary Blann—There would be no books without you in my life.
Meg Sivitz—There would be no life in my life without you.
Francois R. Brenot—without whom I would still be using a pencil
Susan Sivitz—for her time and effort and love
Cathy Muske—for sharing her painful ordeal
Mary Kaye Powell—for inside tips
Dr. Jeff Galpin—a technical adviser, friend, and terrific writer
Dr. Pam Schaff—a toddler-group colleague from the early days
Sandi—for friendship and support and laughter through it all
Fredrica Friedman—a wonderful editor and friend, whose loving style makes it easier for me to work hard
All the families in the Mommy and Me groups who shared their lives, their toys, their snacks, and their stories with me
And most of all for the children.

"My baby. My baby . . . !"

"Mother!" The madness is infectious.

"My love, my one and only, precious, precious . . ."

Mother, monogamy, romance. High spurts the fountain; fierce and foamy the wild jet. The urge has but a single outlet. My love, my baby. No wonder those poor premoderns were mad and wicked and miserable. Their world didn't allow them to take things easily, didn't allow them to be sane, virtuous, happy. What with mothers and lovers, what with the prohibitions they were not conditioned to obey, what with the temptations and the lonely remorses, what with all the diseases and the endless isolating pain, what with the uncertainties and the poverty—they were forced to feel strongly. And feeling strongly (and strongly, what was more, in solitude, in hopelessly individual isolation), how could they be stable?

—Aldous Huxley, *Brave New World*

1

BARBARA SINGER couldn't stand Howard Kramer. Especially the sight of the top of his shiny bald head when it caught the too-bright light of the examining room while he sat on a creaking little chair on wheels between her outspread legs and moved his cold, K-Y Jellied speculum inside her. And every time she reclined on the examining table with her upturned feet against the cold hard metal stirrups, she vowed to herself and the heavens above that before her next checkup she was going to find a female gynecologist. A doctor who, as her seventy-year-old mother, Gracie, liked to put it, "knows how it feels because she has the same plumbing."

But the months would rush by, and her life would be busy and frantic. And soon the postcard she'd addressed to herself the last time she left Howard Kramer's office would appear in her mail, reminding her she was due for another routine visit, and she still hadn't found a woman doctor.

For a few days she'd feel the postcard staring at her from her desk and want to make the calls, but she wouldn't have a free minute. Then she'd worry that if she didn't get a checkup soon, by the time she did something would be found festering inside her. So eventually, she'd take the path of least resistance and call Howard Kramer's office again, because she knew that since he was her husband's golfing buddy he'd agree to stay in the office to see her during her rare free lunch break from work.

And once again there she'd be, squinting to avoid the light bouncing from the shiny bald head of Howard Kramer, whose only charm was his lunchtime availability, swearing to herself yet again while he invaded her genitals that after this visit she'd take the time to find a new doctor. Unfortunately, finding the time to take was nearly impossible.

She'd given up manicures completely, hadn't had her hair colored in she didn't remember how many months, didn't ever have a break to eat a real lunch in a restaurant or even at a counter in a coffee shop. Instead she ordered the charbroiled chicken sandwich and a diet Coke from the drive-through at Carl's Junior, and ate it while she nosed her cluttered car through the traffic between her private office on Wilshire Boulevard to the clinic downtown, or from the clinic to the pediatric development unit at the hospital.

And that was why her gynecologist of record continued to be hairless Howie, a physician of such skill and such powers of concentration that at the same time he probed, scraped, and pressed down too hard on everything, he was able to describe the Sunday buffet he'd enjoyed last week at Hillcrest Country Club. Praising the Nova Scotia salmon in the same nasal voice that always grated on Barbara when he looked over her chart and asked the obligatory questions.

"Date of last period? Are they still regular? What are you using for birth control?"

"Exhaustion," she'd answer, hoping to get a laugh, though there was truth in her joke. Her own crazy schedule and Stan's busy legal practice often left them with just enough energy to eat a hastily thrown-together dinner or a meal delivered from the neighborhood Chinese restaurant, read a page or two of the newspaper, and fall asleep.

"Really, Barb," Howard said. "At your age, why fool around and have to worry about it?"

She certainly didn't want to report to the doctor that the way she'd been feeling lately, she wasn't thinking about what a man whose office was festooned with degrees and awards from Harvard Medical School still referred to as "fooling around." Besides, she knew if she got into that discussion it would lead to Howie using terms like *premenopausal*. And eventually he'd ask the question that always sent a jolt of anger through her, which was "Why don't you just let me tie your tubes?"

Tie your tubes. He tossed it off as if he were saying "tie your shoes." As if it were that simple an act, that simple a concept. Not to mention the way the words "at your age" always sounded as if he meant "Why does an old bag like you need any parts that have to do with reproduction?" She was only forty-two, for God's sake. Somewhere, she would laugh to herself, in that gray area between fecundity and a face-lift. There were plenty of women well into their forties who were still having babies.

So what, she thought, if Stan and I started early and our babies are twenty-three and seventeen? I'm not going under a general anesthetic just because Howard Kramer, OB/GYN, thinks I'm too old to have to worry about birth control. And each time he'd offered her that option, she'd made some joke like, "I'll tell you what. I'll agree to a tubal ligation if you have the plastic surgeon standing by. That way when you're finished at your end of the table, he can step right up and do my eyes. As long as I'm knocked out anyway, why not?" But she knew she was wasting the levity on Howard Kramer, who'd never been famous for his sense of humor.

After Howard removed his rubber gloves and made some notes on her chart, he invariably launched into a long story about one of the celebrities he treated. It was appalling to her, the way he could go on endlessly about some anchorwoman's cervix or some television star's sterility, leaving in the names and details, while a too-polite-to-stop-him Barbara sat on the table, a prisoner of his monologue.

Sometimes she'd try rustling the blue paper gown in which she'd been uncomfortably clad for the examination, hoping the sound would bring Howie back from his narcissistic reverie, convey the message that now that her Pap had been smeared, she was out of there. But he never noticed. And that was why, she told herself this morning as she sat at her desk enjoying a rare quiet moment in her workday, she was postponing making her appointment this month. Because being face to face with Howie Kramer, not to mention face to vagina, was never a picnic.

This morning she looked at the most recent postcard from his office sitting on her desk with a coffee ring on it because she'd been using it as a coaster for her mug. No. She'd be damned if she'd fall into the same trap and go to Howie Kramer again. This minute she'd call her friend Marcy and ask about the female doctor who treated both Marcy and her daughter, Pam.

She got as far as putting her hand on the phone, but

something stopped her from making the call. Probably it was the reality that going to a new gynecologist would mean somehow juggling her own time to fit into the doctor's schedule, then sitting in a strange waiting room filling out a clipboard full of forms. So she promised herself she'd worry about the gynecologist decision later, and she pushed the rewind button on her answering machine.

Beep. "Barbara, this is Joan Levine. I'm calling to tell you that Ronald is trying to get out of our session with you today because, as usual, he says he has some business he can't put aside . . . even for his own son. I'd really appreciate it if you'd call him and tell him he has to show up for the sake of Scottie's sanity. This is just another example of how that son of a bitch doesn't give a good goddamn about Scottie and when we go into court, believe me, I plan to use it. I, of course, will be there at eleven as scheduled. Thank you."

Poor little Scottie Levine; his parents were going to keep beating each other over the head with him until he fell apart, Barbara thought as she made a note to call Joan Levine back and tell her it was okay if her estranged husband didn't come in today. Joan and Barbara could use the time to talk about how the parents' problems with the impending divorce were having a damaging effect on Scottie.

Beep. "Barbara, this is Adrienne Dorn. Jacob's mom. Jacob peed on the floor in his dad's closet again, all over my husband's shoes. And he's waking every night and climbing into bed with me when my husband is out of town. Our session with you isn't until next Thursday, and I'm afraid if we leave these problems undiscussed until then, Jack won't have a pair of shoes left to wear."

Jack Dorn traveled for business three days out of every week. Jacob Dorn, age three, probably figured if his daddy's shoes were covered with urine, he wouldn't be able to leave home. Simplistic maybe, but Barbara was sure the problems the little boy was having centered on his father's constant absences. She made a note to call Adrienne Dorn back and offer to see her today.

She could imagine what her mother would say if she heard those messages. "Spoiled West Side parents who think they're buying their children a fashionable indulgence or an emotional vaccination." Gracie had no patience for her daughter's West Side yuppie clientele. Her own background was in cultural anthropology and she wore her disdain for the world of psychology on her sleeve. "I think you ought to drop the private practice completely. Spend all your time with the needy ones, with crucial life problems. That's where the juice is."

At the family clinic where Barbara spent about a third of her workweek, there was a long waiting list of those. Troubled, anxiety-ridden children whose tiny brows were already permanently furrowed as if they'd seen it all, and many of them had. There were days when she looked into the very old eyes of those very young children and ached to see the absence of hope in them.

Some were referred by social workers, like five-year-old Jimmy Escalante, whose father was murdered while the two of them were having breakfast together one morning at a Bob's Big Boy as a robbery took place. Jimmy had survived the shooting by hiding under his father's jacket until the robbers left and the police came. Now he woke up screaming every night. Last week he told Barbara that someday he would "kill the world" to get even for his father's death.

Some were referred by pediatric clinics, and some children were brought in to her by parents who managed to find their way there by instinct. They were the ones who presented their hurting children to her as unsure of what she could do as if they were handing them over to a witch doctor. The way Angel Cardone had with Rico.

"I think somebody at the nursery school is doing something funny to him."

"What do you mean, Mrs. Cardone?"

"I mean, a couple of times he tried to tell me somebody's been sucking his little pee pee."

"You think there's someone at the school who's molesting him?"

"I don't know exactly. But there's lots of people around there. Teachers, helpers, big kids who get paid to work there in the summer. Maybe one of *them* is doing it."

"Have you examined him? Had a doctor examine him? Is his penis red or irritated?"

"No. I mean, that's the thing. It don't look like he puts up a fight about it, 'cause he don't have no bruises."

"Is there anyone at the school you can trust to talk to?"

"There's nobody anyplace I trust."

"Why don't you bring Rico in?" Barbara asked, her mind racing to think of an open time when she could try to get through to the little boy, and wondering how she would approach him. "How about early tomorrow morning, before you take him to school? Maybe I can find out from him what's going on?"

"I can't pay for coming in again."

"Don't worry about paying. You don't have to pay. Will you work with me on this?"

"Yeah. Sure," she said, turning to go. Then she turned back and looked gratefully into Barbara's eyes. "You're a nice person."

Thinking about Jimmy Escalante's cries of revenge and fearing that Rico Cardone was being sexually abused brought nightmares that made Barbara cry out in her sleep. Many nights Stan had to wake her and hold her and assure her everything was all right. But after he'd calmed her and fell back to sleep, she stayed awake and worried with a heart-pounding anxiety because she knew better. Everything was not all right.

"I'm losing it," she told Stan more than once at the end of a workday. "So often I see the parents look at me blankly, then look at the clock, and I know they're thinking, 'When the hell can I get out of here? And what does all this psychological crap have to do with me?' "

"At least those families have found you," Stan would tell her. "That means there may be solutions for them."

At the end of a difficult day she'd let herself imagine how it would be if she let herself live a life in which Stan supported them completely with his law practice. Tried to picture how it would be if she woke up every day and did whatever she happened to feel like doing. Instead of shuttling between the families who had too much and the families who had too little, listening to the painful stories that seeped into her soul.

This morning while she waited in her Beverly Hills office for the red light on the switchplate next to the door to go on, signaling that her first private patient had arrived, she doodled absently on the coffee-stained postcard from Howie Kramer's office. After a while she picked up the morning newspaper and turned to the View section to find her horoscope.

"Even a scientist like you can't resist the magic," Gracie always teased when she caught Barbara checking in with her astrological forecast.

"It's harmless fun, Mother," Barbara would say defensively. But the truth was she *did* feel foolish about skipping the front page and going right to the astrology.

"Not to the countless people who are loony enough

to change their entire lives based on what it says,'' Gracie said, bristling. Bristling was what Gracie did best. But at least she had a sense of humor about herself. ''Now read me mine,'' she'd always add with a mock-serious face.

Today for Pisces, Barbara's sign, the message read: *Unexplored territory offers exciting life-changing opportunity*. Barbara laughed a little burst of a laugh out loud, just as the red light came on. ''I sure as hell hope so,'' she said, then she stood to open the door to welcome her first family of the day.

2

EVERY TIME Stan came home from a long trip he smelled like the inside of an airplane. The odd scent of fuel got into his clothes and hair, and when his relieved-to-be-home hug engulfed Barbara, so did that odor. Usually his eyes were ringed with red, and he'd say something like "I'm not fit for human consumption." Then he'd hurry upstairs to take a shower and put on sweatclothes. Barbara unpacked his suitcase, carried the dirty clothes down to the laundry room, and met him in the kitchen to make him a snack.

It was after those trips when she'd look appraisingly at him and be secretly relieved to see him looking his age, their age. For the longest time she'd been noticing the way her own face was starting to sag a little around the mouth, and wrinkle a little around the eyes. At last Stan's temples were gray and he was getting a pouchy place just under his chin, which, when he spotted it in the mirror, would make him decide to grow a beard.

But after a few days he'd look at the scruffy growth on his face and reconsider, deciding that the gray in the beard would be more aging. With or without a beard, the truth was that to his wife he was looking sexier than ever.

After she made him a sandwich she sat next to him at the kitchen table, watching him eat, and realized she was breathing differently, more easily, because he was back. She always felt safer when he was near. There were days when she had rushes of feeling as mawkishly in love with him now as she'd been at seventeen when they met, and at eighteen when they eloped. An act which had horrified all of their parents. Particularly Gracie, who still had what Barbara knew was a forced smile on her face every time she talked to her son-in-law.

"You don't get to pick, Mother," Barbara remembered saying when her mother had referred disparagingly to Stan's straitlaced style.

Today while he finished his sandwich, he held Barbara's hand, as if to say he felt the same romantic way about her, and she looked down at their two hands together. At the slim gold wedding bands they'd slid onto each other's fingers so many years ago she could barely remember life without him.

"Are you okay?" he asked. That was always the question he used as an opening to check in with her, to find out if she needed anything or wanted to report any new worry, to discuss something about the children, her mother, or her practice.

"Just my usual overwhelmed self," she said, picking up a thin slice of tomato that had fallen out of the sandwich onto his plate and eating it. "I'm worried that I'm working by rote, that nobody's getting the best I have to offer because I've taken on too much. I console myself all the time with the idea of an early retirement."

"No chance of that. I know you. You go through this from time to time, usually after you've had a few weeks of twelve- and fourteen-hour workdays. Then something happens to excite you and you're off and running again. A few months ago you told me you were cutting back. Too many private patients, too many groups, and did you?"

"Tomorrow I meet with a new family, and I'm meeting with another new referral on Friday," she said, feeling like a child confessing a misdeed.

"I rest my case. Sometimes it's like that. All the personalities and needs and pain get inside you and you start living them. I understand, because I do it too. My clients rail and scream and yell, I get involved in it, and then they feel better and *I* walk around with indigestion." They both smiled. "You realize, by the way, that as far as I'm concerned you can quit working any time you want. Take a year to read the classics, another year to putter in the garden. But I say that secure in the knowledge that you won't." Barbara sighed. Probably he was right.

"Of course we could have a baby," he said, putting the sandwich down and taking a big sip of some orange juice he'd poured over a glass of ice. It sounded like a joke, and she laughed an outraged laugh, sure the remark was just his way of getting sexy with her.

"What?"

"Just a thought," he said, and the look in his eye was mischievous.

"A unique one for a couple who's approaching their twenty-fifth anniversary, wouldn't you say?"

"I guess. But there was a baby next to me on the airplane on its mother's breast, and it was so adorable. I forgot how sweet they can be."

"I hope you're referring to the baby and not the breast."

He smiled. "Speaking of breasts, where's our son?"

"I'm curious and not a little bit concerned about how you made *that* linkage," she said, laughing and leaning forward, using the corner of a napkin to wipe a crumb from his chin.

"I mean, if he's out and not due to come back looking for money or food, the only two reasons he ever stops in, maybe I could reacquaint myself with yours."

"I thought you'd never ask," Barbara said.

Upstairs in their bedroom, they slid naked between the cool soft sheets of their bed and moved close to each other. A thrill of familiar warmth passed through her as she felt his chest pressed against her breasts. At first their kisses were tender but soon he touched her in the way he knew would arouse her, and she felt her own passion rise and wanted the release, wanted him inside her.

Just as she was so familiar with his moves when they slow-danced, knowing that a certain lift of the shoulder meant they were about to turn or a certain swivel of his hip meant they would dip, when they made love she knew exactly at which moment he was going to move over her and then inside her, and she opened her entire being to his entrance, feeling the perfectness of their union.

"Welcome home, my love," she whispered.

Once their sex could make her weak with heat. Today as their bodies united it was as if some part of her own person had been away, and by the act of sex had been reconnected.

A baby, she thought. The idea interrupted her reverie. He had to be kidding. But while he filled her insides with his hard self, and kissed her, then kissed her again, as their lips and their tongues collided and then entwined, she was counting behind his back on her fingers to be sure it was late in her cycle. Hoping it was a safe day, so that she could let her mind get lost in the joy of his return. Her love. How lucky it was that after so many years their sex was so delicious and loving and good.

"Ma?"

Barbara and Stan were in bathrobes, had just stepped out of the shower when Jeff got home.

"Hi, honey. Dad's home. Come in."

"Hey, Dad." Jeff pushed the bathroom door open and gave his father something that could be construed as a quick hug. "Can I take the car down to Orange County? There's this game down there some of my friends have been going down to play. It's called Photons and it's really amazing. It's like being inside a video game. You play on teams and you run around this maze in the dark and try to blast the other guys with your light beams."

"Sounds like *my* idea of a good time," Stan joked.

"Why don't you stay home, honey? You haven't seen Dad in over a week. Let's all have dinner together, eat at the dining room table, and . . ."

"Relate?" Jeff said, giving her a sidelong give-me-a-break look.

"Spoken like the son of a psychologist." Stan laughed.

"Can we relate tomorrow night, Mom? I really want to do this."

"I think it's all right if he goes." Stan looked at Barbara and grinned. "This is why people our age have babies."

"You two having a baby? Oh, cool," Jeff said over his shoulder, and he was gone.

Later that night when Stan was turned away from her and she was snuggled close against him, knowing by his breathing he was seconds away from sleep, she said to his back, "How serious were you about babies?"

She was relieved to hear his groggy reply, which was "Not serious at all."

"Scottie, what's going on?"

Scottie Levine, age four and a half, was dressed in a Ralph Lauren shirt, khaki pleated pants, a tan braided leather belt, tan socks, and brown loafers. And his haircut wasn't from the Yellow Balloon or any other kid's barbershop. It was shaped and gelled into some semblance of the haircut of a thirty-five-year-old man. He looked as if he should be carrying a portable phone and talking on it to his broker. Scottie was one of a group of children who had been nicknamed "chuppies" by one of Barbara's colleagues, children of yuppies.

Even his sigh was adult, a strained exhale that sounded as if it meant he was resigned to the fate of being the child caught in the middle of a warring, acting-out couple and forced to be the sane one in the family. Barbara watched him pick up a small black bag of magnetic marbles he'd played with before in her office, spill them out and line them up so he could flick them the way he liked to, one at a time until they hit the molding at the far end of the room.

"Do you go to your daddy's house to be with him?" Barbara asked. He nodded.

"And is it fun to do that?"

No response.

"What do you and Daddy do on your days together?"

"Nothing." He moved the marbles around, rearranging their order into groups of matching colors.

"Do you stay at home and play together?"

"We play Frisbee."

"Oh yes, I remember your telling me how good you're getting at Frisbee."

"I sleep over too."

"That must be great. Do you have your own room at Daddy's?"

He nodded, was silent for a while, then added, "And Daddy sleeps with Monica."

"Who's Monica?"

A shrug. Then Scottie turned onto his stomach, made a circle of his thumb and forefinger, and with a hard ping sent the first marble across the floor, and then another. When all twelve of the marbles were against the wall, Scottie put his elbows on the floor and his face in his hands and said in a near whisper, the way Barbara often heard many of the children she treated state their hardest truths, "I saw her tushie."

"You saw Monica's tushie?" She spoke softly too.

She could only see the back of Scottie's head as he nodded. "In the morning in my daddy's bed. She was sitting on top of him and they were naked."

Now he put his face down on the floor and left it there for a long time, the gel on his hair glistening from the sun that poured in through the office window.

"It must have made you feel funny to see your daddy and Monica naked."

The little head nodded again, almost imperceptibly.

"Was it sad because of your mom?"

No answer. Barbara sat on the floor next to him. He was crying. When the hour was up she opened the door to the waiting room, and Scottie left with the Levines' pretty, Swedish au pair, who had been waiting for him. Barbara called and left a message on Ronald Levine's answering machine asking him to call her as soon as possible.

She was late, due downtown in twenty minutes and it would take her at least half an hour to get there. She was rushing to get out of the office, so when the phone rang she decided to let the machine answer it. But she stood in the open doorway waiting to hear who was calling in case it was an emergency.

Beep. "I'm Judith Shea, I was referred by Diana McGraw, who's in your Working Mothers group. I had two babies by D.I. and I need to talk to you as soon as possible. Here's my number."

Barbara pulled a pad out of her purse and jotted the phone number down, then locked the office door and rushed out to the parking lot to her car. D.I., she thought. D.I., and for an absent minute as she looked at what she'd written, she thought the caller was being strangely coy and giving her the baby's father's initials, but then she laughed at herself as she made the turn out of her office parking lot and realized what the letters actually meant.

3

THERE WAS a kind of glow around Judith Shea as she sat on the floor of the reception area nursing her baby. She was one of those women whose look Barbara always envied. Skin that was a naturally peachy color no cosmetologist in the world could ever recreate, green eyes so bright they might have been ringed with liner, though she wasn't wearing a drop of makeup. Her thick shiny auburn hair was cut bluntly in a perfect bob. Barbara realized with embarrassment that her own unconscious prejudice had made her assume that a woman who used donor insemination to conceive a baby would be homely.

The nursing baby looked over the full round breast at Barbara with eyes that matched her mother's, while her cherubic sister, a toddler girl with red ringlets, was asleep on the love seat. "We got here a little early," Judith said. "Jillian fell asleep. I hate to wake her."

"Don't move," Barbara said and hurried into her inner office to get a pad and pen. "You're my last family of the day, so there's no reason why we can't talk right here," she said, returning to sit across from Judith in a way that accommodated her own straight black wool skirt.

"So let's see. Where do I start? I was thirty-six years old with no boyfriend and not a whole lot of dates either. In fact, my friends at work always kidded me that Salman Rushdie went out more than I did. But I always had a powerful craving to be a part of a family. Maybe because I was an only child or because so much of my own family are deceased.

"I wanted to be a mother. But as independent as I am, it was the only thing I couldn't do alone. And I didn't see marriage anywhere on the horizon." She thought about what she'd said for a minute, then laughed a bubble of a laugh. "Marriage, hell! I couldn't find a man I'd risk safe sex with, let alone the kind without a condom that could make a baby." Her eyes tested Barbara's to see if the psychologist was making a judgment about what she was hearing.

"Go on" was all Barbara said.

"You don't know me yet but believe me, I'm not one of those women who won't buy herself a white couch in case she meets a man who might like a brown couch better. I've got plenty of my own money, a great career, I'm an art director in an advertising agency. Remember that quote from Gloria Steinem? Something about how we've become the men we wanted to marry? Well it's true. I love my life and don't have any enormous need to couple up.

"So I went to a sperm bank, and not only did I buy and use the sperm successfully once, but having Jilly was so much fun that I did it again. And I used the same donor both times, which means that my girls are full sisters, with the same mother and the same father . . . in absentia though he may be."

"How much do you know about the father?" It was not the question Barbara wanted to ask. She would have loved to ask, "Aren't you dying to meet the donor?" or "Aren't you afraid he'll show up someday?" or "Weren't you worried there would be something wrong with the sperm? Genetic problems or God knows what?" But she was working at keeping her professional distance.

"The truth? I know less about the co-creator of my children than I do about the Federal Express delivery man," Judith said, and laughed. "Actually the way these cryobanks work makes it very chancy, because all you get from them is a list of numbers that represent each donor. And all they tell you is his race, blood type, ethnic origin, color of eyes and hair, type of build, and then a one-or-two-word description of his special interests.

"It's funny how rational it all feels when you're doing it, and yet when I describe it to you, I can hear how weird it must sound. I mean, for example, I wanted my babies to have light hair and light eyes, so I picked donor number four twenty-one, and all I know about him besides his coloring is that he likes reading and music."

The baby on her breast let out a happy little shiver of a moan, and Judith gently patted its tiny behind. "I made it a point to buy the sperm from one of those places where the donor agrees to let the children meet him in eighteen years, which means that my kids have a chance of knowing their father someday if they like."

"How do you feel about that?" Barbara asked.

"A little worried. But I've got a long time until I have to face it," she said, then added grinning, "Somehow I get the feeling you probably don't get a lot of people coming in with this kind of story."

"You're right about that," Barbara said.

"For all intents and purposes I'm a single mother. And a hell of a lot happier than if I'd been divorced and had to go through all of the who-gets-custody issues. I mean, it's a very no-muss, no-fuss way to go. Not to mention the fact that you've never once heard any torch singer sing 'The Donor That Got Away' or 'My Donor Done Me Wrong.' "

Both women laughed. Barbara liked Judith Shea's spirit. "How can I help you?" she asked. And as if that was the cue Judith had been anticipating, her front of confidence fell away, her cheeks flushed, and she looked very young and full of emotion. It took her a while to pull herself together. For a long time there was no sound in the room but the *plink* of the numbers on the digital clock as they rolled over.

"Jillian's nearly two and a half, and she's already talking about penises and vaginas and babies. And I realize that pretty soon she's going to want to know how they get inside mummies' tummies. When I think about that I start to panic and I worry about her coming to me and asking, 'Whatever happened to good old donor number four twenty-one?' " She shook her head at her own funny take on the situation. "When I thought about having a baby I pictured going out to buy happy sets and pretty nursery furniture, and then having someone soft to cuddle. But not even once did I plan for what happens when the babies are children who have language and ask tough questions, which will probably be any minute."

"And when they *do* start asking you about their father, which they will, you'll have to give them some unprecedented answers," Barbara said.

"Sometimes at night before I drift off to sleep I think of elaborate lies I can tell them about their genesis. But then I know I won't be able to do that because I think lying to kids about anything is unconscionable. Don't you?"

"Yes," Barbara said.

"I know you have a lot of programs over at the hospital for single parents and widowed parents and working parents, but I also know my problems don't fall into the purview of any of those groups. So what do I do?"

"I don't know," Barbara said honestly. "As you said, this is a new one. But we'll work on it together."

"You see," Gracie said, "it's why I always tell you that you can't predict human behavior by scientific laws. That woman is a product of these times. Sexual relationships are unsafe, infertility is rampant, people are faxing their brains out instead of speaking to one another. And there's no rat in a maze who could have made the kind of emotional decision she made to have those babies."

Barbara and Gracie moved swiftly down San Vicente Boulevard on the grassy medial strip. As usual Barbara was huffing to keep up with her energetic mother, telling Gracie, as she had for years, about what was going on at work. She always left out the personal information to protect her clients' confidentiality, and knew she was leaving herself open for some disdain, like that pointed comment about the way psychologists studied laboratory animals to learn about human behavior. But she was sincerely interested in her mother's always passionate input. Today when she talked about Judith Shea, Gracie "tsked" every now and then as she listened.

"New arrangements, new technologies, in a world that's not ready for them," she said. "The quantifying of human life. Can you believe they freeze embryos, then the couple get a divorce and fight to see who gets custody of the damned things? Frankly it all gives me nightmares about the future."

"Me too," Barbara said. As they approached the open-air marketplace at Twenty-sixth Street she wished they could just stop there for a cup of coffee. Gracie must have received her brainwaves, because just then she stopped walking in front of the open-air marketplace, said, "To hell with exercise, I need caffeine," and turned into the courtyard, where Barbara found an empty table for them while Gracie walked up to one of the stalls and ordered two cappuccinos.

"I think it's interesting," Barbara said as Gracie placed a steaming cup of white froth in front of her, "that she chose to bypass the human factor, obviating the messiness and the awkwardness and the commitment of a relationship. And she seems reasonably comfortable with that."

"Well, *she* may be, but I'm not," Gracie said, shaking her head. "I say marriage is better."

"Mother, you're not exactly a testament to the success of matrimony and the nuclear family."

"But *you* are, so do as I say, not as I do. I made mistakes, Bar, and not working harder on my marriage was one of them, but the older I get the more I believe that a strong and loving family is the basis for mental health. You and your sister were exceptions. You both came out okay, in spite of my divorce because I was such a brilliant mother." The smirk on her face told the truth they both knew.

"Absolutely," Barbara said. "And let's hope the children of this woman will be too." She watched a pigeon bob around the brick patio pecking at crumbs.

"You know," Gracie said, "I'll bet in this crazy city there are dozens like her. Women are buying eggs if they don't have any of their own. Then they're even having other women carry the embryos for them. Have you read about the mother who did that for her daughter?'' She put her hand on Barbara's arm and grinned. ''Honey, I love you, but *that* far I will not go!''

They both laughed at Gracie's joke, and Barbara thought how she loved this crazy loon of a mother of hers. ''Oh too bad, Mother,'' she said. ''I was just going to ask you if you'd mind.''

''So what *about* these people?'' Gracie asked, dipping a *biscotti* in her coffee and swirling it around in the bubbles of milk.

''Families with issues for the new millennium,'' Barbara said. ''Beyond the birds and the bees. I should form a group just for them. To figure out how to break through the technological and get to the human issues.'' When she looked up she saw an unmistakable glow in her mother's eyes.

''That's a hell of an idea,'' Gracie said, then she bit into the now soggy cookie.

''Thank you, Mother.'' Barbara smiled, thinking it was the first time she and Gracie had agreed on anything in years.

''After all, what is it that woman is trying for by having those babies?'' she asked Barbara in the way she always posed questions, making it sound as if she were giving you a test.

''Normalcy,'' Barbara answered. ''Oddly enough she's using high-tech reproductive techniques to create some kind of regular family life, some kind of intimacy for herself, by being somebody's mother.'' This was Gracie's meat. It was socially significant. Bigger than the everyday development problems Barbara dealt with all the time, and she heard the giddiness in Gracie's voice when she spoke.

''There are some interesting ethics involved here too.

I think it's the cutting edge of family practice. What do *you* think?"

"What *I* think," Barbara said, standing, "is that I'll have a croissant," but as she walked over to the bakery counter she felt a little zap of adrenaline she knew wasn't from too much caffeine.

In her office she picked up her mail on the floor where it had fallen through the slot, then pushed the button on her answering machine.

Beep. "Yeah, hi, I'm Ruth Zimmerman, my pediatrician said I should call you. I'll leave you the phone numbers for me at my house and my office and the studio, and my car, because I'm in a state of urgency here. Please try me as soon as possible. I have a two-and-a-half-year-old son and I need to talk about him with you right away. You see, here's the thing about how he was born . . ."

Barbara listened to Ruth Zimmerman talk about her son and the unusual circumstances surrounding his conception. When the message was over and she picked up the phone to call the woman back to make an appointment, she thought about what her daughter, Heidi, always said when things in her own life fell together in a pattern: "Totally spooky."

While she waited for someone to answer Ruth Zimmerman's phone, Barbara tried to remember her horoscope of a few days earlier. What was it? Something about unexplored territory and a life-changing opportunity. It was totally spooky.

4

ON THE WALL of the messy undersized office of Ruthie Zimmerman and Sheldon Milton was a framed needlepoint sign which said DYING IS EASY, COMEDY IS HARD. It was made by Ruthie for Shelly long before they were a successful comedy-writing team, before the series and the Emmys and the big money. Shelly was sure the sign was a good-luck charm, so over the years he took it with them from office to office.

This space in the writers' building at CBS in the Valley was furnished with two back-to-back desks and two old upholstered desk chairs, plus a small upright piano that had spent most of its life in rehearsal halls. In every corner and on every shelf were piles of scripts. Some were written by Zimmerman and Milton, some were written by their staff, and some were written by hopefuls whose agents had begged Ruthie and Shelly to read them and consider the writer they represented for a job on the show. And of course on both of their desks was an eight-by-ten photo of Sid Caesar.

When the phone rang it was Solly, their agent, so Ruthie took the call, and while Shelly waited for her, he did the *New York Times* crossword puzzle.

"Are you kidding?" he heard Ruthie practically sing into the phone. "It's no trouble at all. We'd love to. I'll talk to Shelly about it and call you back." When she hung up he didn't even have to look at her to know what was coming next.

"What did Sol have to say?" he asked, carefully filling in some letters across the top of the puzzle.

"There's no business," she answered.

"I'm praying," Shelly said, "that the next three words out of your mouth are going to be 'like show business,' but I'm afraid it's a faint hope."

"You're right," Ruthie said. "I wasn't doing my imitation of Ethel Merman. I was telling you what Solly told me, which is that the television business stinks, and how incredibly lucky we are to be doing this show instead of being out there in the job market." She watched him fill in a long phrase all the way down the right-hand side of the puzzle with that look of triumph he always wore when he deciphered one of those. "He's right, you know. We're truly blessed. And we can't forget that." Her voice was becoming what Shelly always called "soggy." The way it got when she was feeling awed by how far they'd come in their careers.

"Uh-oh," he said, looking up at her. "When you start sounding like Jerry Lewis on the telethon it means you've just volunteered our services to some fund-raiser so we can prove to the world and ourselves that we're thankful. Which one was it today?"

"The benefit show for the Writers' Guild fund, and they need us right away. It'll be good for us. We're always so busy with casting sessions and network meetings we hardly ever get to sit and write anymore. This'll keep us fresh."

"Can't we just use deodorant?"

"Oh come on," she said, taking the Arts and Leisure section out of his hand. She was glad to have a reason not to go back to looking at some set designer's elevations for next week's show. She much preferred to plop a brand-new yellow legal pad on Shelly's desk and one on hers, divide several sharpened Blackwing 602s between them, and say, "Gentlemen, start your pencils." This was their favorite part of working together. Finding their way to an idea, moving it along, exploring it, turning it every possible way, or as Shelly liked to tell the writing staff, "You take a germ and spread it into an epidemic."

"Okay, let's see," he said, planting his feet on the floor and twisting back and forth in the reclining chair the way he always did. "The Writers' Guild. Here it is. What if a husband-and-wife writing team realize that nobody wants to buy their material anymore, so they decide to make a suicide pact and kill themselves?"

Funny, Ruthie thought. Already it has promise.

"But of course," he improvised, "they have to leave a note. And since they're writers it has to be a great note. So they start to work. The husband sits at the typewriter; the wife paces. Suddenly the husband says, 'I've got it! We'll open the suicide note by saying "Au revoir, heartless universe." ' "

Ruthie knew exactly where he was going and she jumped in. "But the wife sneers and says, 'Are you nuts? That stinks! You can't open a suicide note without saying "Farewell, cruel world." ' "

Shelly was really working it now. "The husband laughs a mocking laugh and says, 'That is so kicked. I've heard it a million times.' "

"Which infuriates the wife." Ruthie put her feet up on her battered old desk, sat back and thought for a minute. "So she turns on him . . . she's always been a shrew, and she says, 'Oh yeah? Well, I happen to think it makes the point better than "Au revoir, heartless universe," which like most of your ideas is completely phony.' "

"The husband is hurt," Shelly said, "but he's going to be a martyr about it, so he gets very tight-lipped and says, 'Fine. Let's go on. We can come back to the salutation later.' "

" 'What later?' the wife shrieks. 'There won't *be* any later! Don't you remember? We're going to be dead.' "

"And he says, 'Yeah? Well, if we open with "Farewell, cruel world," we'll be *worse* than dead. We'll never work in this town again.' Hah!" Shelly laughed a cackle of a laugh at his own punch line.

"Funny," Ruthie said, taking her feet off the desk, sitting forward in her chair and looking pleased. She loved this man. Still found him so entertaining, so clever, so much the perfect counterpart to her that all the years they'd been hidden away in dimly lit closetlike spaces to write and produce shows were paradise for her just because they were together. And she'd felt that way about him since the night they met, eighteen years ago.

It was in summer stock in Pennsylvania when they sat lit by the summer moon on the big wooden steps of the White Barn Theater, where Ruthie was an apprentice and Shelly was a rehearsal pianist. As the crickets of summer throbbed and a yumpy-dump band from the cocktail lounge of the hotel across the way played "I Can't Get Started with You," the two of them exchanged horror stories about their respective Jewish mothers.

* * *

"Mine had a plastic throw made to put over the chenille toilet-seat cover."

"Mine couldn't get a lawn to grow in front of our house, so she cemented over the dirt, then painted the cement green."

"Mine told me if I ever touched myself you-know-where, I'd eventually get locked in a crazy house and she'd never come to see me."

That was when Shelly smiled and took in that kind of deep breath which means, Now I'm going to pull out all the stops and tell you the ultimate Jewish-mother story which you'll never be able to top. And Ruthie, who'd been looking for an excuse to do so all evening, leaned in a little closer.

"Mine," he confided, "made the ultimate sacrifice for me not long ago when I fell madly in love with a creature so magnificent, there are no words to describe the temptation into which I was led by this—and I apologize in advance—gentile." He is so funny, Ruthie thought, and so cute. "This," Shelly went on, fueled by her obvious admiration, "was a lover par excellence, who whispered to me one night in the heat of passion, 'If you really love me, you'll go and cut your mother's heart out and bring it to me.' "

Ruthie giggled, and Shelly tried to look serious. "Naturally," he continued, "I did what any red-blooded American boy would do under the circumstances. I ran home, grabbed the old bag, and not only cut her heart out, but to add insult to injury, I took a Reed and Barton platter out of the silver closet and put the quivering mass right on it. Without a doily." Ruthie would always remember the way the moonlight made it appear as if there were frost on the top of his curly brown hair and the way those hazel eyes behind the horn-rimmed glasses were so alive with glee.

"To say that I hurried back to my beloved's house would be a gross understatement. Unfortunately, blinded by my passion, I didn't notice a branch which lay across the sidewalk in my path, and sure enough the branch caught my foot, my ankle turned, and as I tripped and fell, the heart flew from the tray and landed in the street in a bloody, pulsating pile."

"No!" Ruthie said, grinning as she jumped into the game, loving the delight she saw in his face when she did.

"And as I lifted myself to my feet, my mother's heart spoke to me."

"Really?" Ruthie asked, knowing the punch line was coming, and hoping she was offering the proper straight line. "What did it say?"

"It said," Shelly answered, taking a deep breath before he went on, " 'Did you hurt yourself, honey?' "

No one had ever told a joke that hit home so well with Ruthie, who let out a laugh of recognition, and Shelly laughed with her. So hard he had to take off his glasses and wipe away a tear from the outside corner of his left eye. There are very few things that make two people feel closer than laughing together, but just at the moment when it was clear that Ruthie and Shelly were feeling that closeness, Shelly looked at his watch.

"It's late," he said, patting Ruthie's hand. "I've got to go."

Later, in her cubicle of a hotel room, by the light of a bare bulb in a wall socket, Ruthie changed out of her overalls, dabbed some dots of Clearasil on the eruptions here and there on her face, slipped on her Pittsburgh Steelers nightshirt, and fell onto her bed. Then she reached into the bedside-table drawer for her little spiral notebook, in which she made a list of possible bridesmaids who would precede her down the aisle when she married Shelly Milton.

"What's the thinnest book in the world?" Shelly asked the next night.

"Jewish Circus Performers," Ruthie answered, having no idea where she got that answer. It had just popped into her head. "What's wrong?" she asked him. "You don't remember Shirley the Human Cannonball?"

"I do," Shelly said. "She was a terrible woman . . . but a great ball."

They both screamed with laughter. Soon they had ritualized their end-of-the-day meeting on the steps of the theater, each of them finding the way there after the long hours Ruthie spent building and painting scenery and Shelly spent pounding out the same tunes again and again for the rehearsing dancers. Just knowing they could look forward to the time they spent afterward laughing and mining their creative and bizarre minds enabled them to get through each day.

Ruthie thought it was the beginning of a great romance, though there was never even so much as a kiss on the cheek as evidence. She had the naïveté of the unsought-after girl who had never once felt the front of some eager boy's corduroys, lumpy with lust, pushing heatedly against her, since no boy had ever really desired her. And that was how she came to be nineteen and, with the exception of a few disastrous fix-ups from some of her mother's friends who sent a pitifully too-short son to call or forced a stuttering nephew to take Ruthie to a movie, she had never dated. Undoubtedly it was the fact that she knew so little which enabled her to continue to imagine that someone so obviously crazy about her was simply taking his time about declaring his romantic feelings.

Then one chilly night she woke in her bed at the Colonial Manor Hotel with an overwhelming urge to pee. She had never yet made it through any night in her life without being rudely nudged out of a dream by her full bladder. At home where the bathroom was a few yards away and the floors were carpeted, those nighttime forays weren't much of a problem. But in the drafty old hotel with the cold hardwood floors, the communal bathroom was a long journey down the dimly lit hallway. Thank God, she thought, standing up, that my mother wasn't around to see me having to make this trip.

Groggily she stumbled toward the glow of the bathroom night-light that seemed to be miles away, passing the rooms of the other apprentices, sending a silent little message of love as she passed Shelly's room. Envying Polly Becker, the big-nosed forty-year-old costume designer who wore low-cut blouses and flirted with every guy who walked by, because Polly had arrived at the theater weeks before the others and thereby got to claim the room closest to the bathroom.

Just as Ruthie reached for the bathroom doorknob she heard an odd sound from one of the rooms. It was a long low moan. Somebody must not be feeling well, she thought. And it was certainly no wonder, with the disgusting food they served around here. In fact she'd felt a little queasy herself just last night after the lasagna. But then there was another moan, after which she understood that it wasn't the kind of sound that accompanies illness. She felt flushed, her whole body aroused by the idea of something carnal happening so close to where she was standing.

She was sure the sounds had to be from Polly Becker's room. So the old girl had succeeded in luring someone into her bed. And she was having a hot time of it too. The moans were moans of pleasure, a lot of pleasure, mingled with creaks from the springs of those uncomfortable old metal hotel beds.

"Oh, God. Oh, yes. Oh, God."

They got louder. Ruthie, embarrassed by her own

excitement, wasn't sure what to do. She closed the bathroom door behind her and stayed inside longer than she needed to, splashing cold water on her face to calm herself. She even flushed the toilet a few times to drown out the sounds. Finally she opened the bathroom door slowly, listened long enough to be certain that the hall was now silent, then made her way on tiptoe back toward her own room.

She was looking down at her own chubby toes, which were bent in their effort to keep her from clumping noisily and being heard, so when two big hands on her arms moved her to one side she took in a terrified gasp. When she let it out it was into the handsome craggy face of the company's leading man, Bill Crocker.

He was a square-jawed, well-preserved actor of indeterminate age, who, from what Ruthie overheard while she cleaned the ladies' dressing room, still believed his big break was coming. "Little summer-stock jobs" like this one, he said, were just filling his time until the big call came. The call that would make people stop referring to him as "the bus-and-truck John Raitt."

"Little lady," he said greeting Ruthie now, as if he were reciting a line from a play. He was wearing jeans, and his shirt was unbuttoned to the waist the way he'd worn it the first week, when he played Billy Bigelow in *Carousel*. It seemed as if he had appeared from nowhere, and in an instant he was gone.

Ruthie, whose heart was still pounding from the embarrassment of having the gorgeous Bill Crocker see her in her nightshirt and Clearasil, crept into her room and pulled the covers over her head to go to sleep. But the moment her eyes closed they opened again, because a tingling of realization came over her ears and neck and face. Bill Crocker hadn't come out of Polly Becker's room, and the person who was moaning wasn't Polly

Becker. It was Shelly. Bill Crocker had been with Shelly.

Ruthie was awake all night, trying to force pictures out of her mind that kept insinuating their way back in. When the neon sign went off and the chirping birds announced the morning light, she sat up, feeling a stiffness in her back and neck and the kind of dull headache that comes with lack of sleep. She couldn't shake the heavy sadness, and when she put her feet on the floor, she remembered all the mornings she had been so eager to get dressed and rush downstairs to the dining room to see Shelly there.

She would stand for a moment and watch him reading the morning paper and drinking coffee, and imagine the days ahead when he would be doing that in their own little apartment somewhere. Today the thought that she had to face him made her queasy. In the high-school cafeteria one day, she overheard the boys talking about Mr. Lane, the English teacher. Singing to the tune of "Pop Goes the Weasel," "He doesn't go round with girls anymore, he doesn't intend to marry. He stays at home and plays with himself. Whee. He's a fairy." Ruthie had asked her best friend, Sheila, what the song meant. When Sheila first told her, Ruthie was sure Sheila must be kidding.

This morning she opened her spiral notebook, tore out the list of bridesmaids, and with a match from a Colonial Manor matchbook, put it in the ashtray and set it on fire.

The hallway was empty, and from her open doorway she could see that the bathroom door was open, too. Maybe a hot shower would make her feel less achy. When she closed the bathroom door behind her and locked it and looked at herself in the full-length mirror, her tears finally came.

"Hey, Ruthless," Shelly said to her, putting an arm around her at breakfast. He was using the name he called her when he wanted to tease her. "I've been thinking about all these routines we've been coming up with every night, and it seems to me we ought to put them someplace." As if last night he hadn't ruined her entire life.

"Other than in a porcelain bathroom fixture?" she said, defensive and embarrassed and wishing it weren't too late to switch to the summer job her mother wanted for her, answering phones in Dr. Shiffman's office.

"I mean on the stage. In the lounge of the hotel. When the band takes a break, you and I could perform them. I'll bet we could turn some of our ideas into a comedy act," he said, ruffling the top of her hair in a way she loved. A way that when anyone else did it made her furious. She wanted to say yes to anything he asked of her.

"You mean do them for *other* people?"

"Yeah, do our own little show after the big show, for the people who go over to the cocktail lounge afterward. Most of them are so schnockered anyway they'd never know if we were good or bad. We could be the new Mike Nichols and Elaine May. Think about it," he said.

Over the next few days she hardly thought about anything else. She was much too self-conscious about her appearance to ever display it on a stage. Any aspirations she'd had about show business were about working behind the scenes. She had no interest in being out there in front of people having to worry about how she looked.

But now that marriage to Shelly was clearly out of the question, performing with him was a way to be linked with him and to spend time with him. So after she painted and spackled the scenery until the flats and her overalls were covered with dots of every color, she took out her spiral notebook and wrote a list of ideas for their show. After all, Elaine May had never been married to Mike Nichols either.

The cocktail lounge was seedy and mercifully dimly lit, and after the band played a barely recognizable version of "Misty," the guitarist walked up to speak into the microphone, even though the six people in the audience were two feet away from the bandstand. He told them that while the band was taking a break, some "kids are going to do their stuff." The people, who were on their second round of drinks, chatted loudly to one another through the first few minutes of Ruthie and Shelly's show.

But after a short while, something caught their attention, and soon they were laughing and then applauding in the right places. The act worked so well that when the reviewer from the *Pittsburgh Press* came to the theater to see *Li'l Abner* and stumbled afterward on Shelly and Ruthie's show in the lounge, he mentioned them in his column, calling their show "clever, zany, and witty."

As September drew nearer, the Pennsylvania nights grew brisk and fresh, so that by the time the company was doing the last production, which was *South Pacific*, the big barn doors to the theater had to be closed while the show was in progress. During the last performance when Bill Crocker played the soldier who sang "Younger than Springtime" without a shirt on, Ruthie could tell all the way from the wings that he had goose bumps on his naked chest, and she looked away.

Later, while the actors were drinking champagne in the dressing room downstairs, she slowly swept the stage with the heavy push broom, moving the dust from behind the thick musty-smelling velour curtain downstage toward the sky blue scrim upstage. When she turned from downstage, Shelly was watching her.

"You know about me and Crocker, don't you?" he

asked her. With the big blue background behind him he looked eerily like a character in a dream. She'd been composing speeches in her head all day, knowing they would be saying good-bye that night, wanting to be eloquent when she did. But to be confronted with this subject was too painful. She'd been certain it would be something that would always remain unspoken between them.

"Yeah," she said, "I do," clutching the broom handle hard.

"I love you so much, I can't believe it," he said, moving a few steps closer. She didn't mean to let go of the broom handle, but she did, and it hit the ground with a sharp rap. "You get my jokes, you look at me the way Doris Day looks at Rock Hudson in all those schmucky movies, you're funnier than any five people I've ever known, and I love you."

He'd said he loved her. Twice. No one, not even her parents, had ever said those words to her. She knew what was supposed to happen now. She'd seen enough movies, read enough books to know it was her turn to speak next, to say words she'd practiced saying to her pillow to some generic fantasy lover for years, and had never said to a living soul. But now she did. She looked into Shelly Milton's eyes and said, "Oh, Shel, I love you too."

"Thank God," he said, and they moved together. When they collided, they held each other so tightly that Ruthie could barely breathe. Or maybe she couldn't breathe because it felt so good to feel so good. Her face was buried deeply in the front of his blue oxford-cloth shirt and his face rested on the top of her thick frizzy hair as the laughter of the actors downstairs floated up to the stage where the two of them stood. After a few minutes, they looked puffy-faced at each other.

Shelly wiped his eyes where a tear had formed and

brushed it across his cheek with the palm of his hand, then felt in the back pocket of his pants for a handkerchief. When he couldn't find one, he pulled the sleeve of his shirt across his face to dry it.

"I'm not going back to Northwestern," he told her. "I'm leaving for Los Angeles tomorrow with Crocker. We won't officially be living together, but I am going to stay with him until I can somehow get a job, maybe playing piano and eventually writing." Then he said in a way that seemed to be partly teasing and partly testing her, "Want to come along?"

"My parents would kill me first," she said.

"Mine weren't thrilled. But I convinced them everything would be okay when I told them I had a nice roommate." They both smiled an aren't-parents-dumb smile, and hugged again.

When the dressing rooms had been cleaned out and only the two of them were left in the theater, they sat on the stage, which was empty except for the piano and a work light. Shelly played songs from the summer and songs the two of them had invented for their act. When it was nearly dawn they walked hand in hand back to the hotel. Outside Ruthie's room, he held her in his arms and they swayed, then he twirled her around, and bent her back into the dip they always did in the "Top Hat" sketch. When he pulled her up to both feet he looked into her eyes. "You'll always be my Ginger Rogers," he promised. It was a promise he would never break.

5

AFTER SUMMER STOCK Ruthie moved into the college dormitory with a hole in her heart so big that the cold Pittsburgh wind blowing off the Monongahela River went right through it. All she did was sit in her room like a zombie, longing for Shelly, fearing she'd never hear from him again. She was as obsessed with getting a letter from him as if she were on death row and he were the governor deciding on her pardon.

She registered for classes, but spent the next three weeks never attending any of them. She looked out the window from her pie slice-shaped cell in the cylindrical, architecturally monstrous dormitory, watched the cars go by on the street below, and thought about the summer. Later she wondered how she ever survived those twenty-one days in the dorm eating only pepperoni pizza brought to the desk downstairs by the delivery boy from Beto's on Forbes Street. The only time she left the room was to go down to pick the pizza up, after which she walked to her mailbox and opened it with the key to check for certain, though she could already see through the glass door there was nothing inside.

When the letter came, she read it standing right there with the mailbox door hanging open, and wept openly, her tears of thanksgiving wetting the pizza box, because her prayers had been answered. On her way back to her room she did a little dance of joy that was witnessed with raised eyebrows by the girl on her floor she liked the least and to whom she was happy to offer a gesture she'd only seen others use but whose meaning she now fully understood.

Ruthless,

Enclosed are the lyrics of "Hooray for Hollywood." It is my new favorite song about my new favorite place. I love everything about it. The weather. (It never rains.) The palm trees. The weirdos, or should I say the other weirdos. It truly is screwy and ballyhooey, and there is only one thing missing from my life here and that is you. Every day I wish you were here with me. Drop out of school (Everyone who is anyone *has*, you know!) and come to the land of show business. I'll pick you up at the airport.

Shel

She jumped into the shower where she sang while she washed her hair, then she went to the Laundromat and did three weeks' worth of laundry. When she got back she called her parents from the pay phone in the hall and was relieved when it was her father who answered.

"Daddy," she said, "I need you."

Manny Zimmerman was a Russian immigrant whose grocery store, Zimmerman's Fine Foods, had been on the same corner in the East End of Pittsburgh for thirty years, maintaining its loyal clientele who wouldn't set foot in a Giant Eagle or Kroger's when they could get Manny's personal service. After all, poor Manny and his family had been through so much. People still mentioned the accident when they talked about the Zimmermans, even though it had been so many years.

Ruthie's memories of Martin and Jeffrey were vague and dreamlike. She was only two when they were killed in an automobile accident on the Boulevard of the Allies in a collision with a bus. All she remembered about her two older brothers was the way they used to lift her high into the air to play "see the baby fly." But maybe she didn't remember that at all, maybe her mother had told her about it.

Her parents' grief over the loss of their two sons permeated everything about the family's lives forever. Ruthie would never look at a flickering candle that wouldn't remind her of the two yahrtzeit candles her mother lit every year in memory of Martin and Jeffrey on the anniversary of their deaths. That day when her father walked into the lobby of the dormitory, Ruthie could see he feared the news she was about to deliver was as bad as the news he'd received that night the police came to tell him about Martin and Jeffrey.

She put her arm through his and moved him through the lobby toward a circle of naugahyde chairs, and as they walked, in her mind she went over the words she was going to say. Manny Zimmerman sat, and the sofa squeaked under him.

"You're all right?" he asked her.

"I am, Daddy, and I didn't mean to scare you, but I didn't want to say this on the phone and I wanted to try it out on you before I mentioned it to Ma, but I'd like to drop out of school and move to California."

Her father reached into the pocket of his jacket and pulled out a Marsh Wheeling cigar, peeling off the cellophane, and then by virtue of a custom they'd shared for years, he removed the paper ring and slid it onto his daughter's finger. "After you finish, maybe. But not now."

"I don't want to finish, Daddy. I want to leave school now. To go out there and be with my friend Shelly."

The wood match Manny Zimmerman lit flared against the blunt end of the cigar, and he puffed and puffed until the thick tobacco smell that would remind Ruthie of him every time she whiffed the odor of cigar for the rest of her life filled her nose and eyes.

"Is this Shelly a boy?" he asked, not looking at her, still holding the cigar between his teeth while smoke came out of both sides of his mouth around it.

"Yes, Daddy."

"And is he going to marry you?"

Ruthie stood and took an ashtray from a nearby table and handed it to him. "He's gay, Daddy," she said softly. This he would never understand. Men, big strong he-men, my Martin and my Jeffrey, was how he always talked about her dead brothers. "My Martin could lift a box full of groceries on one shoulder and another one on the other shoulder and make a delivery like Superman." Gay wasn't something she expected him to understand. Nor would he understand the reason she wanted to fly all the way across the country to be with someone who was like that.

"Gay?" he asked. "What's that?"

The term. Obviously he had never heard the term. She would have to explain it with a word he would know, though it felt derogatory to her and she didn't like it. "He's a fairy," she said.

Her father looked into her eyes for a while, saying nothing. She loved his sweet little round mustached face. Whenever she wanted to do something unique or out of step in her life and her mother had been against it, that face would flush red and he would speak up and be on Ruthie's side. He was awkward with her, and she was sure he wondered many times how God could have taken away his two wonderful sons, Martin, a talented violinist, and Jeffrey, so good in science he surely would have become a doctor. They were gone and he was left with only this lump of a daughter.

He had always taken her part. When Ruthie didn't want to be bat mitzvahed, when she wanted to get her ears pierced, when instead of working in a doctor's office she wanted to be an apprentice in a summer theater. She couldn't imagine what her life would be like if he hadn't stepped in and made certain her mother relented. Well, maybe now she could get him to be on her side again.

"A fairy," she said softly, trying again, aware of the giggling, squealing girls who were greeting one another at the dormitory mailboxes as they came in from their classes.

"Ruthie," he said, taking her chin in his hand, and when they were looking into each other's eyes he shook his head and said, "I don't believe in fairies." Ruthie tried not to laugh at what sounded like a line from *Peter Pan*, because he was serious and went on. "Because I'm a man, and men like women, and that's all there is to it. Believe me."

"Daddy . . ."

"And California is so far away," he said in a voice that made her certain that what was coming was a no. So she was surprised when, with the hand that wasn't holding the cigar, he touched her face and said, "But if you want it so bad, and you maybe come back to school in a year or two, it'll be okay by me."

"It will?" Ruthie asked, feeling light with relief and surprised that her father's face was red as if he might cry. "Thank you, Daddy," she said, leaning over to hug him as he quickly moved the hand that had been holding the cigar out of the way so as not to burn her, even though the cigar had gone out.

She was four inches taller than he was, and while they hugged she looked over his head at the gray Pittsburgh day, and in her mind she was thinking the words, "You may be homely in your neighborhood, but if you think that you can be an actor, see Mr. Factor, he'd make a monkey look good." And she realized they were from the lyrics Shelly had enclosed with his letter, from "Hooray for Hollywood."

"You'll do good no matter what," her father said, then turned to go. When he was too far away to hear, Ruthie, who was still watching him, said to his parting figure in the distance, "Thank you, Daddy," and went up to her room to pack.

The day she arrived in La-la, as she and Shelly came to call it, he met her at the airport, at the gate, with a bouquet of daisies, and never said one word about how bad she looked. Just loaded her and her luggage into the beat-up Volkswagen bug he'd bought, handed her a newspaper, and told her to look for cheap furnished apartments.

They found a small two-bedroom in West Hollywood. It was a dive, a dump, a hole in the wall, but they didn't notice because they were together. Roommates, best friends, partners. Their big luxury was an answering service that picked up on their phone line. They told all of the operators to make a note to be sure and pick up on the first ring every time a call for them came in, and to only answer with the telephone number. If the two of them were at home when the phone rang, as soon as they were absolutely certain the service was on their line and talking to the caller, one of them would pick up and listen in to see who the caller was. If it was Shelly's mother, Shelly would say, "Oh, hi, Ma, I just walked in." If it was Ruthie's mother, Ruthie would say that. For a long time, no one but their mothers called them.

They also rented a piano that they squeezed into the living room so Shelly could sit and compose melodies for which Ruthie wrote special lyrics, the way she had in the summer. They took odd jobs. Ruthie worked for a private detective as a process server, Shelly waited tables at the International House of Pancakes. Ruthie was a receptionist at a beauty salon, Shelly worked at the Farmer's Market at the seafood counter, and at night they wrote. First they reworked their act, and when they had it down and were ready to try it out they went to hoot nights at clubs where the audience, who was expecting a guitar player or a band, frequently booed them off the stage.

They put an ad in the trade papers saying they entertained at parties, and were hired to do a sweet sixteen where the birthday girl, who had taken Valium before the party and consumed spiked punch during the party, had to be rushed to the hospital right after their opening sketch. The same ad was responsible for their being hired to perform at the tenth wedding anniversary of Phil and Myrna Stutz, who called them and canceled on the morning of the party because they'd decided that instead of having a party they were going to get a divorce.

Their agent was a guy they met at the Comedy Store who was known as Shotgun Schwartz. Shotgun believed that 10 percent of nothing was nothing so if you were breathing he agreed to represent you, figuring the more clients he had, the better his chances were of making a buck.

The first time he sent them on an interview, they got an assignment to write an episode of a Saturday morning cartoon show about a musical dog, "Rudy the Poodle."

"It ain't exactly a short story for the *New Yorker*,"

Shelly said as the two of them sat down to work on the first script, "but we'll take a shot." They thought of twelve more "Rudy the Poodle" ideas, and sold nine of them before the show was canceled.

Every night no matter how hard a day they'd put in, they went to the Comedy Store and watched the comics try out new material. They would make notes, whisper ideas to each other, and when the show was over, they would ambush one of the comics at the door and beg him to listen to what they had.

"Jerry," they would say. "Have you got a sec?" Leaning on the door of the guy's car so he couldn't get in. Or, "Joey, listen. We've got a whole hilarious run for you." And once they had the comic's interest piqued, they would break into their material, right there on the cold cement, lit only by a purplish streetlight. Sometimes the comic would even pay them cash on the spot. But the stand-up comic to whom they would always give credit for the success of their careers was Frankie Levy, who had no cash that night so he gave them an IOU.

"Hey, kids, I don't have my wallet on me," Frankie said to them, "but I'm crazy about the supermarket run, and I'll pay you for it tomorrow night. Okay?"

Okay! Frankie Levy had once been on the "Tonight Show."

The very next night Frankie performed Ruthie and Shelly's supermarket routine and brought the house down with it. He was happy and very sweaty as he backed off the stage, both arms raised in triumph. For a few minutes he stood in the rear of the club shaking hands and taking the backslaps he knew he so richly deserved. Ruthie and Shelly elbowed their way through the crowd to get over to Frankie, waiting until the others around him had gone back to their seats to watch Eddie Shindler, who was up next.

"Way to knock 'em dead, Frankie," Ruthie said, holding her arms out wide. With the success he'd had with their material, Frankie would surely want to give her a grateful hug. In fact she was so close to him she could feel the dampness coming off his still-nervous body, but he turned on his heel as if he hadn't even seen her and walked out of the building. There was a moment of realization and then Shelly said, "He's leaving for Australia tomorrow, I heard him telling Mitzi. The schmuck is ducking us for the money," and they rushed out the door to stop Frankie Levy, who by the time they got outside was already at the top of the parking-lot ramp.

"Frankie," Shelly yelled, but Levy didn't turn around.

"You owe us money," Ruthie yelled. But Levy was already in his black Cadillac and in an instant he screeched past them.

"You thieving son of a bitch," Shelly yelled, running back down to the bottom of the ramp where Levy's car was stopped at the black-and-white wooden arm that had served as a momentary impediment to his escape. As Frankie was reaching out to get his change, in a move Shelly once saw in a James Bond movie he jumped on the trunk lid of Frankie Levy's car. Then as he stood there, not sure what to do next, Frankie Levy peeled out onto Sunset, and Shelly's moment of heroism was marred dramatically by the fact that he was thrown crashing onto the cement.

At UCLA Emergency the wait is always interminable. Shelly sat in the big windowed room, bruised and aching and huddled close to Ruthie on the couch as they waited for his turn to be examined. It was past two in the morning and there were several other people waiting: a dark-haired heavyset man with a beard, who had his hand wrapped in a tourniquet; a woman who told Ruthie she'd brought her husband in hours ago with extreme chest pain, and he'd only been called in to see the doctor moments before; and a family who were sitting together staring up at a television watching an old Humphrey Bogart movie.

"What happened to your hand?" the woman asked the bearded man.

"I was trying to slice some meat for my wife on the electric slicer, and my hand was in the way," he said.

"Just your way of trying to give her the finger?" Shelly asked. The man laughed.

"How about you?" the woman asked Shelly.

"You'd never believe it," Ruthie answered for him.

Then, almost as a healing process, the two of them told the story of how they came to Los Angeles, and about working on "Rudy the Poodle," and how they spent their nights writing and selling jokes, and about Frankie Levy. Maybe it was the lateness of the hour or the absurdity of the situation that gave them a freedom and a relaxation and a punchiness, but the story was coming out so funny that soon all the assembled patients were laughing loudly. Ruthie and Shelly had never had a more receptive audience.

In fact it was a rude interruption when a nurse opened the door to call the next patient.

"Mr. Lee?"

She was calling for the bearded man, who before he followed the nurse out managed, with his good hand, to pat Shelly on the back.

"My name is Bill Lee," he said. "I'm a producer at NBC. I think I might have a job for the two of you on a prime-time show I'm doing for John Davidson. Give me a call tomorrow at NBC."

On their first day of work they tried acting nonchalant, but it wasn't easy to fool anyone since they'd arrived an hour early. Their assignment, before they even laid eyes on John Davidson, was to write a dialogue between John and this week's guest, George Burns. "We need it by four o'clock," Bill Lee told them.

"Great," they said, but when they closed the door of the little cubicle of an office they'd been assigned, upstairs from a sound studio at NBC, they stared at each other in terror.

"What are we doing here?" Shelly asked. "Some of the best writers in the world have written for George Burns." George Burns had recently been a big hit in *The Sunshine Boys*. It was his first movie since *Honolulu*, a movie he'd made with Gracie Allen in 1939.

"Let's not panic yet," Ruthie said. "You be George Burns, I'll be John Davidson, and we'll see what happens."

Shelly picked up his black pen and held it in his hand cradled between his thumb and first two fingers, the way George Burns holds a cigar.

"Okay, I'm George Burns."

"That's good," Ruthie said. "It's a good start." She felt sick. They weren't ready for this. Couldn't they have started with someone less famous? Less funny? Shelly looked down at the pen, rolling it in his hand the way George Burns always did with the cigar when he was thinking.

"John Davidson," Shelly said, sounding a little bit like George Burns. "You're a nice kid. Handsome kid, too. How old are you?"

"I'm thirty-four," Ruthie answered, playing the part of John Davidson.

"Thirty-four years?" Shelly asked, then with a twinkle in his eye, he added in his best George Burns, "*I* pause that long between pictures."

"That's good." Ruthie laughed. "But let's not get overconfident, let's keep going." They improvised.

They switched roles. They wrote things down, typed them up, tried them again, changed them and fixed them. Tore the whole thing up twice. It was almost four o'clock. At four o'clock on the dot they walked into Bill Lee's office to read it to him. He laughed. He laughed harder. He congratulated himself with a grin that meant, I'm a smart son of a bitch for hiring these two. And he was. Two seasons later they were the hottest writers in television.

6

THEIR NAMES on a project gave it "heat," made it a "go," a "green light," and soon they were writing and producing their own series, and garnering huge consulting fees to come in and doctor the shows of other writers. They had a certain style no one could equal, genuinely funny, with a touch of poignancy and humanity rare in television half-hour comedy, so everyone wanted their work. Fifteen years after the George Burns joke, their popularity was still happening. Their success had made them rich, enabled them to support all four of their aging parents, to travel during their time off and see the world.

The only thing neither of them had was that elusive commodity so idealized by the very industry in which they were thriving, romantic love. Though at some point each of them had tried for it. Ruthie fell hard for Sammy Karp, a black-haired blue-eyed wild-minded stand-up comic who wanted to be an actor. She met him one hot summer L.A. night at the Improv, after his set, when she was standing at the bar with some other writers and Sammy came over to schmooze. When she congratulated him with a handshake for the good work he'd done, he kept holding on to her hand, looking meaningfully into her eyes. Then he said, "Ruth Zimmerman, I love your work. Let's do dinner."

They did dinner at La Famiglia, dinner at Adriano's, dinner at Musso's. Somehow it was understood that Ruthie was the one with money and Sammy was struggling, so she always picked up the tab. When *he* made it, she told herself, he would pay for the dinners. It was also what she told Shelly when he asked. In the week of her birthday she thanked Shelly but passed on his offer to throw a small party for her. Sammy, she explained, was taking her dancing at the Starlight Room at the top of the Beverly Hilton.

No man had ever taken her dancing. While a piano, bass, and drums played "Call Me Irresponsible," Ruthie and Sammy danced close with her arms around his neck and his arms around her waist the way she'd seen couples dance in high school when she'd stood by the punch bowl pretending not to be watching. She ached to have Sammy make love to her. And when he led her to the suite he'd reserved in her name she could barely wait until he unlocked the door to touch him, thanking heaven the champagne she'd just paid for was doing such a good job on her inhibitions.

She was hungry for him, starving for him, and the things they did in bed made her embarrassed the next morning. When she woke up alone in what she saw by the light of day and sobriety was a very grand suite, she walked naked around the room trying to reconstruct in her mind what she'd said and done. Probably she'd been a complete fool. But then she looked in the mirror and saw the Post-it he'd left on her naked breast that said

You're fabulous and I'll call you later and felt gorgeous and sexy for the first time in her life.

That week Sammy called her at the office so often that she had to walk out of the casting sessions four different times to take his adoring phone calls. "How's it going, beautiful?" he would ask her, giving her the chance to babble on to him about the people who were reading for parts on the show. But it wasn't a coincidence that immediately after she told him that the part of the young leading man had been cast, his ardent interest in her seemed to end, because that was the night he didn't show up for their dinner date.

"Giving new meaning to the term 'stand-up comic,' " Ruthie told Shelly while she looked out the window one more time for Sammy's car, and tried to make light of the rejection.

Shelly had a wonderful romance with Les Winston, a beautiful, warm, gifted man in his fifties with white hair who always had a gorgeous tan. Les was a furniture designer whose teak outdoor furniture was sold all over the world. Piece by piece he'd rid Ruthie and Shelly's West Hollywood apartment of the tables, chairs, and sofa he called "early thrift shop," and replaced them. Ruthie loved Les's creativity and sense of humor, and their mutual admiration for Shelly sealed their friendship.

The two men talked a few times about moving in together, and probably would have, but one day Shelly got a paralyzing call from Les's brother saying Les had died suddenly of a cerebral hemorrhage. It took Shelly two long painful years to recover from the loss.

But the one who was the biggest heartbreaker of all was Davis. Lovely Davis Bergman. Ruthie met him one night at some show business party. One of those after-the-pilot celebrations at CBS studios on Radford. He was an entertainment lawyer. A partner in a well-known firm, Porter, Beck, and Bergman. He was Jewish, separated from his wife, they were filing for divorce, they'd never had children, and in the divorce settlement, *he* got the big house in Santa Monica. The perfect man.

"What do you think?" a nervous Ruthie asked Shelly, who'd been standing in the corner at the party talking to Michael Elias, one of the producers of "Head of the Class," when she pulled him away.

"I think he's great. From here," Shelly said.

"Come meet him," Ruthie said. "He's funny. I can't believe he can be a lawyer and be funny too." She dragged Shelly by the hand to where Davis Bergman was standing and introduced them.

"Shelly Milton, Davis Bergman."

"I never trust a guy who has two last names," Davis said, shaking Shelly's hand. They all laughed. Ruthie felt flushed. Maybe it was because of the diet. The strict one she'd been on for six weeks, feeling cheated and deprived and miserable, but she'd lost seventeen pounds, and the healthy eating had made her skin look great too. So maybe this was God's way of rewarding her. Proving to her that good disciplined girls had the Davis Bergmans of the world beating a path to their doors, or at least talking to them at parties.

Davis told Ruthie and Shelly funny stories about being a Hollywood lawyer, and when the party began to break up he looked disappointed, so Shelly—oh, how Ruthie loved him for this—suggested they all go for coffee at the Hamburger Hamlet on Sunset, and Davis agreed. Ruthie, who had come to the party in Shelly's car, rode nervously to the restaurant in Davis's Porsche, looking at Davis's hand as it shifted gears. Wanting to put her own hand on it, but being too afraid.

"Comedy writers," Davis said in the restaurant, as if marveling at the good fortune that had brought these exotic people into his life. "I represent some screenwriters, but they're all very serious." The three of them talked and laughed for hours.

Davis lived in Santa Monica, nearly all the way to the beach, and Ruthie didn't know if he would understand about her living with Shelly, so when they got out to the parking lot at the Hamlet she said, "Shelly can take me home," and Davis looked at her sweetly and said, "Great." As Shelly was about to pull his Mercedes out onto Sunset, Davis pulled his Porsche loudly up to their right, opened his window and gestured for Ruthie to open hers, then he shouted into Shelly's car above the din of his engine, "I've got tickets for a screening at the Directors' Guild tomorrow night. You want to come along?"

"Sure," Ruthie said, hoping to sound nonchalant.

"Pick you up?"

"Meet you," Ruthie said hastily.

"Eight o'clock," Davis said, and was gone.

"He's dating you up," Shelly said in a teasing voice as he stepped on the gas. "Filling your dance card."

"Shelleee," Ruthie squealed. "He is *so* adorable."

"Please! I already hate the son of a bitch," Shelly said. "You'll fall in love and get married and I'll lose a roommate, then he won't want you to work anymore so I'll lose a partner too."

He was teasing and she teased him back.

"Shel, you know I'll never leave you. To begin with, you'll come over constantly for dinner, and for every holiday. After a while Davis will probably get so used to you, you'll probably come on vacations with us. We'll be the Three Musketeers, I swear we will."

The next morning she sent Shelly in to work alone and she went shopping at Eleanor Keeshan. She found a new sweater and some black pants to make her look nearly slim, and a royal-blue-and-black silk shirt that also went with the pants, so she'd be ready with something to wear on the next date, and while the saleslady called in her credit card number, Ruthie looked wistfully through racks of beautiful silk dresses and pants outfits, and at the Fernando Sanchez lingerie.

Tonight her social life was about to experience a personal best. She was actually seeing the same man two nights in a row. Okay, so last night Shelly was with them, but it was still sort of a date. Maybe it was finally her turn to have something real. With someone who would appreciate her. If that was true, and they were to start dating, she would come into stores like this one and try on clothes for hours. Looking at each item and asking herself, Would *he* like this? What event do he and I have coming up that I have to dress for? Oh yes, dinner with his clients, and the lawyers' wives' luncheon.

Davis, please, she thought, walking back to the counter to retrieve her package. When she passed the three-way mirror she caught sight of herself looking chunky despite the weight loss and vowed that for Davis she would starve off at least fifteen more pounds. When she arrived at the office and Shelly was out to lunch she sat down at her desk and did something she hadn't done in years. She made a list of possible bridesmaids.

After the film they went to the Old World on Sunset. Ruthie ordered the vegetable soup, and Davis had an omelet. And just the way he reached over and put his spoon in her cup to get himself a taste was so intimate, it made her feel as if she could probably open up to this man. Davis was what she'd heard the girls she'd lived with in the dorms at Pitt refer to as "husband material."

While they were talking, an extraordinarily beautiful woman walked by their table. Ruthie noticed that although Davis saw the woman, he didn't offer a second glance or ogle her the way a few of the men at some of the tables did. It was a show of respect from Davis for her feelings, and that made her feel even closer to him. By the time the dishes had been removed from the table and she was finishing her second cup of coffee, she had told him all about her life. Even about her two brothers dying when she was very little. She talked about her love for Shelly and explained why they lived like brother and sister.

Davis didn't make any judgments, make any gesture that could have been construed as a negative comment about what she was saying. He seemed to think everything she was telling him was okay. And Ruthie invited him to come for dinner one night, knowing she could convince Shelly to cook.

"Only if you'll let me reciprocate and make dinner for the two of you," Davis answered.

"Of course," Ruthie said, in a voice that she was afraid sounded too loud and too eager. This was the best result she could have imagined. Davis liked Shelly too.

When her mother invited her for Passover, hinting as only her mother could that it might be her father's last ("With that heart, he's liable to croak any minute. He has to stick a heart pill under his tongue just to watch the eleven o'clock news"), she accepted.

The few days she spent sleeping in her old room made her glad she'd agreed to come back. Her father conducted their own quiet little Seder service, and aside from the store-bought gefilte fish, Ethel Zimmerman cooked all the traditional foods Ruthie remembered eating when she was a child. During dinner, in a rare moment, her mother even reminisced about Martin and Jeffrey. "When they were little boys they used to say, 'Ma, when we grow up, we'll have a double wedding. It'll be the biggest party in the world, and you and Daddy will be the king and the queen of the wedding.

There'll be lots of cake and dancing with an orchestra just like at our bar mitzvahs.' "

"But," her father jumped in, "I told them the difference will be that I don't have to pay for it," and then he added, "I was kidding them, because for a wedding, the father of the bride always pays."

A silence fell over the table then as the three of them ate the matzoh ball soup. All of them were thinking the same thought. That in this family there had been no bride.

Davis. Wouldn't her parents love him, Ruthie thought. Okay, he was divorced, or soon to be divorced, but *that* they could forgive. Once they talked to him and he laid on the charm, her mother would melt, and her father would say, "A good head on his shoulders."

"I have a boyfriend," she said quietly. Her mother dropped the spoon into her soup dish.

"Besides that Sheldon?" she asked.

That Sheldon. After all these years she still referred to Shelly as "that Sheldon."

"So who?" her father asked.

"He's a lawyer. An entertainment lawyer. Jewish."

With every word she could see her mother sit up straighter. Maybe this was a bad idea. Premature. Davis hadn't even kissed her yet.

"Divorced," she said.

"Well," her mother said quickly. "That happens."

For a while there was no sound but the slurping of soup, until her mother had a thought she couldn't hold inside.

"Listen," she said, "Molly Sugarman's daughter, Phyllis, didn't have her first baby until she was forty years old, and the baby is perfect."

"Ethel, please," said her father, "first let's meet the guy and then we'll talk babies."

"Why not plan ahead? You think it's so easy to get a party room at Webster Hall? Sometimes you need to call six months in advance."

"Ruthie," her father said, turning to her seriously, "you'll give us notice? And you won't elope?"

"I promise, Daddy."

That night, after her parents were asleep, she lay in her old bed, remembering the other day when Davis drove her to the airport, and hugged her close, saying he would miss her. She had smiled about that for the entire flight. Tomorrow she'd be back in L.A. and things with him would probably start to get serious. God, she could hardly wait.

Just before she turned over to go to sleep she realized it was only eight o'clock in Los Angeles. She probably should call home and see how old Shel was doing without her. She picked up the receiver of the pink phone her parents had given her when she was sixteen and called her own number in Los Angeles.

"H'lo."

"Hi, it's me."

"Ruthie!" Shelly said, in a very loud voice. "Uh . . . hi there, Ruthie." There was noise in the background. "Let me turn down the music," he said, and then was gone from the phone for a while that was too long for just turning down music in their small apartment. "So, how's it going?" he asked her when he got back to the phone.

"Shel, it's so cute," she said, confiding in him. "My parents have really been wonderful this time. They even talked about my brothers tonight, and maybe it's because they haven't been bugging me at all, but I actually told them about Davis."

"About Davis?" he said, again too loud. "What about him?"

"About my seeing him, and how terrific he is, and

how he's so perfect for me. So right away my mother starts talking about somebody she knows whose daughter had a baby at forty. Is that hysterical?"

There was no sound.

"Shel?"

"I'm here."

"You okay?"

"Yeah, yeah, I'm fine. You coming in tomorrow?"

"At two-ten."

"You want me to pick you up?"

"Has Davis called? He said he was going to call you and make sure you were okay while I was gone, and find out when I was coming in. So I thought *he* would probably pick me up."

"I'll tell him," Shelly said.

"Good idea," Ruthie said. "Give him a call, and remind him that I'll be in at two and see if he can make it. If not, I'd really appreciate it if *you* could pick me up." She switched on the pink lamp next to the bed and looked for her purse. When she found it, she pulled out her little telephone book.

"Here," she said to Shelly, "I'll give you his number."

"I don't need his number," Shelly said. "He's sitting right here."

7

BARBARA SINGER looked across the desk at Ruthie Zimmerman. She was certainly not the unattractive girl she kept describing in the story she'd been telling about her life. She was attractive in a funky way. And though she joked through the telling of her story, Barbara, who often used the same device of humor to cover her feelings, recognized it as subterfuge. It all seemed to be leading to something painful and difficult.

"What happened when you got back from Pittsburgh?" Barbara asked her.

"Shelly and Davis met me at the airport and said they both loved me but that they loved each other romantically and they were sure I'd understand. And you know what? I *did* understand. Because I thought both of them were so great, they should be with each other and not me. Kind of like Groucho Marx saying he'd never belong to any club that would have him as a member.

"So Shelly and I kept working together, only he moved into Davis's house, and I bought myself a condominium in Brentwood. I mean basically at that point all we were then was business partners."

"You sound very matter-of-fact about it all. Is that how you felt?"

"Are you kidding? At the time I felt like killing both of them. I hated Davis for using me to get to Shelly. I hated Shelly for taking Davis away from me. I hated myself for being the dumbest woman alive. But I acted like it was okay with me. Shrugged it off and said hey, no problem. Because I just couldn't let go."

"Of what?"

"Of Shelly," she said, and the look on her face made Barbara push the tissue box on the desk closer to her. "I couldn't stand the idea that I could lose him."

One morning they were just finishing a pilot script, working at Ruthie's condo, when their agent called and asked if they wanted to write a movie of the week for Pam Dawber.

"I think you should take it," Shelly said.

Ruthie looked at her watch. "Geez, Shel, it's almost lunchtime and we still don't know what we're going to do for the act break."

"I'm going to stop work for a while," he told her.

"Me too," Ruthie said. "I'm going to pick up my cleaning and get a sandwich. I'll be back around two, and then we have to decide what to do about the second act, and call Solly back about the script for Pam Dawber. You want me to bring you anything?"

"I mean stop for a long time, Ruth. Not do the movie for Pam Dawber or any other project for a while. Because Davis wants me to be around the house more. Work with the architect on the plans for the remodel and—"

No! She couldn't believe this. Now he was going to stop writing with her, too? "And be his wife?" Ruthie flared, feeling as if her whole life was being pulled out from under her. "No, goddammit. No." Shelly didn't flinch. "You mean you'll take over where the former Mrs. Bergman left off? Shel, that's crazy. Don't let him do that to you. You'll end up playing tennis and going shopping every day and not having any self-worth. You can't give up a good career to stay home and just run the house."

Ruthie sat on the edge of her desk, looking out the window. She was tired. They'd been rushing to finish their current pilot, working endless hours, and what she felt like doing now was taking a long nap.

"Hey!" Shelly said, "I like the idea. I've been working all my life, pounding a goddamned piano and writing stupid songs and sketches to make a couple of bucks. I'm just dropping out of a painfully hard business to sleep late, eat great, and redecorate. And in my case it's with someone I love. How bad can that be? Wouldn't *you* take that deal? Goddamned right you would."

That was low, she thought, since they both knew she'd been planning on taking exactly that deal. She left the office and the building, and nearly got hit by a car when she crossed Sunset against the red light.

"Ruuuthie." Davis always greeted her so warmly when she called to talk to Shelly, and maybe, just maybe there was a hint of mockery in the greeting. "How's the funnyness business?" he'd ask, and she didn't have an answer. Sometimes late at night she would just lie in bed, wanting to talk to Shelly, wishing she could go into the next room and find him the way she had for the years they lived together. Then she would picture him at home with Davis.

But she never thought about the sexual part of their

relationship. It was imagining the cozy part that made her envious. Shelly and Davis reading the Sunday paper together, doing the crossword puzzle, playing Scrabble. When it came to Scrabble there wasn't any way that Davis could give Shelly as big a fight as *she* had.

She finished the project for Pam Dawber and was offered a two-year exclusive deal to write pilots for Twentieth Century-Fox TV. They would give her an office and a secretary at the studio, lots of money, and a parking place with her name on it. And all she had to write were a couple of pilots. Shelly was wide-eyed.

"They'll give you how much? They didn't ever offer that much to the two of us."

"I'll be glad to split it with you," she said, squeezing a lemon wedge above her salad and watching the juice spurt. "Just come back to work."

"Can't" was what it sounded like he said, but later when Ruthie thought about it she decided that maybe he'd actually said something else.

One night after Davis and Shelly got back from a trip to Hawaii, Shelly invited her for dinner. Davis barbecued the chicken outside while Shelly was inside making the salad, and Ruthie helped him chop. He seemed upset. Finally he said in a voice that was designed for Davis not to hear, "He's going to be traveling to New York a lot for the next few months on business. I'm going to go berserk without him. I'll probably be calling you every five minutes for solace."

Ruthie was starting to feel annoyed every time she was with Shelly. The way he mooned over Davis, tiptoed around his moods and feelings, made every plan around Davis's whims and schedule. When she got into her car after saying good night to the two of them she decided she didn't want Shelly to call her for solace. And she wasn't going to call him. She was starting to make some friends over at Fox, some other women writers and a woman in casting. She would make dinner plans with them and keep busy, and Shelly would be just fine without her.

Once, years before, when she lived in the dormitory at Pitt, she overheard a girl in the next room crying as she told a friend, "I called my mother and told her that he broke up with me. That he took his pin back from me and gave it to another girl on the same day, and do you know what she said? She said, 'Throw yourself into your work.' Throw yourself into your work? My life is ending and she says, 'Throw yourself into your work'!" The girl's crying had echoed through the walls of the dormitory for hours.

Ruthie thought of that incident while she tried to throw herself into her work. She wrote another movie of the week and got an assignment to write a pilot called "May's Kids," which was about a children's talent agent. One day she realized it had been more than two months since she'd spoken to Shelly. Apparently he had done just fine at home alone during Davis's New York travels. That hurt. It was one thing for him to be too busy for her when he was with his lover, but when he was alone. Not to call. Maybe something was wrong. Obviously something was wrong. Maybe she should call him.

It was ten o'clock at night, not such a great time to call people out of the blue like this. The phone rang ten or twelve times, and Ruthie was about to hang up when she heard a tiny, quiet voice pick up the phone and say hello. Oh, God, she woke them. The voice didn't sound like Shelly.

"Shel?"

"Yeah."

"Shelly, it's Ruthie."

"Hi, Ru," he said. And then he said, "Oh, my God." And it sounded like he started to cry.

"What's wrong?"

"Nothing."

"You okay?"

"I'm okay."

"Then why do you sound so—"

"I can't talk," he said. "I can't. I can't talk to anybody anymore." And he hung up.

Something was very wrong with Shelly. If Davis was at home, Shelly wouldn't be able to talk, so there was no point in calling him back and trying to get him to tell her what the problem was. Maybe she should go over there. It wasn't very far. A light rain was falling. She could see it on the tiny terrace outside the sliding doors of her living room. She'd be crazy to put her shoes and her raincoat on and start looking for her glasses and her keys and schlep over there to Shelly's, just to find out that he and Davis had had some lovers' quarrel.

No. She'd sit down now, make a few last-minute notes on the pilot script. Then she'd take a nice long bath and try not to think about Shelly and his dramatic voice on the phone. The tub was already full when she changed her mind. Somewhere in her stomach where she always knew the right thing to do, she was sure she had to at least drive by that house and check on Shelly. She threw her raincoat over her sweatpants and UCLA sweatshirt, found her old Nike Waffle Trainers under her bed, located her car keys on the kitchen counter, and made her way down to the cold quiet garage in her building.

"Why am I doing this?" she wondered out loud as she was unlocking her car in the cold garage. And again as she drove through the rain-slicked streets. "Why am I doing this?"

Davis's car wasn't outside the house. Shelly's was. Ruthie pulled her car into the carport, turning her lights off, and when she'd turned the engine off she sat shaking her head at what a dumb jerk she was to come running over here. The rain had stopped, and everything was so quiet; maybe she could just look in a window and see if everything was all right.

She stepped slowly out of the car, and carefully closed her car door to try to make the least amount of noise. The freshly wet grass sent up a sweet smell and the moon cast a white glow on the house as Ruthie walked from window to window, looking into each one, first at the pretty country French living room, then the dining room, and now the yellow-and-blue French kitchen, all dimly lit, and all orderly. Davis was away, and Shelly was asleep, and tomorrow he would call her and tell her why he'd sounded so weird on the phone. So why couldn't she stop herself from turning the knob on the kitchen door, which was unlocked, my God, it was unlocked, and pushing it open?

Her Nikes squeaked on the tile kitchen floor, and she was so afraid she could feel the waves of panic coursing through her, but she couldn't turn around. She moved to the staircase, and quickly up the steps, passing the two extra bedrooms, toward the new master suite, the door of which was wide open. No one was inside. Oh, God. Davis and Shelly had gone out somewhere in Davis's car. Maybe they *did* have a fight, and they'd gone out to have a drink and sit and talk it over. Probably they took Davis's car and would be home any minute and find her there. Wouldn't she be mortified? She had to get out of there.

Suddenly she had to pee. So badly that she knew she'd never make it to her car, start it, and then get to a gas station. Never. She'd have to go into Shelly and Davis's bathroom and pee fast then run to her car and get the hell out of there before they got home. She hadn't even seen the master bathroom since it was remodeled. She'd seen the plans a few times, knew how they wanted it to look. This was her chance to see it, she thought, and laughed a little giggle at how ridiculous this story would be to Shelly if the two of them ever sat down alone again to talk. The phantom who peed and stole away into the night.

She didn't dare turn on the bathroom light. Suppose they came driving up and spotted a light on where they'd left darkness? She'd have to find her way to the toilet in the . . . Jesus. What was that on the floor? No. *Who* was it? By the moonlight pouring in the bathroom window she could see now that it was Shelly, curled up in front of the marble bathtub, an empty pill bottle next to him. Dead. Limp. Gone. Dead. Shelly.

A sick, horrifying numbness filled her, and she sank to her knees and put her head on his dead body. As if from a distance, she could hear her own voice begging the lifeless body of Shelly to tell her why he did this. How could he take himself away from her? Hating him, she beat on his skinny unresponsive frame and screamed his name as all of her pulsed with the horror of this loss. Shelly, her love. Dead.

Laying her head on his chest, she wailed, a cry that made her head pound. But then she realized the sound wasn't in her head. It was a heartbeat. A heartbeat! Alive.

"Shelly." She sat up, grabbed his arms, pulled him into a sitting position and shook him. "Shelly, you're alive," she screamed into his slack-jawed face, knowing she was supposed to do something to him, like breathe into his mouth, but she wasn't sure how. She had to find someone who knew what to do, so gently she placed his head back on the floor, ran into the darkened bedroom, slapped around until she found a switch to turn on the light, then grabbed the phone and dialed 911.

When she'd given the necessary information to the

operator and was about to run back into the bathroom again to try to rouse Shelly, she looked on the bedside table, and there, with nothing else around it, in a silver frame, was an old photograph of her. She remembered the day Shelly snapped it. They had gone to ride the carousel at the Santa Monica Pier. She was wearing shorts and a shirt, sporting the first suntan of her life, and holding her arms up in a gesture of pure joy, but still she winced when she saw it. Because to her she looked like a frizzy-haired witch. But Shelly had framed it, and kept it by his bed. Ruthie marched into the bathroom.

"You're gonna live, schmuck," she announced to Shelly's inert body. "I'm here to tell you," she said, kneeling beside him and taking him in her arms, "that anyone who can stand to look at that picture of me every day can live through a stomach pump. For me, Shel. You have to live. For me."

He was in the hospital for two days, and Ruthie stayed there too. She slept in a chair both nights and covered herself with a blanket that a sympathetic nurse brought in for her. Shelly refused to say anything until she took him out of the hospital and back to her condo where she put him in her decorated-by-a-decorator bedroom. And naturally his first words were a joke when he looked around, winced, and remarked, "Either that wallpaper goes or I do." Then he fell asleep.

An odd comfort filled Ruthie as she lay on her new living room sofa, knowing he was nearby. Later, when she brought him some tea, he stared out the window and said, "Davis decided to go back to his wife. She met him in New York, and they were together and he said he wants her back. Told me I had to get my stuff out of his place by the end of the . . ." His voice lost control and he put his face in the pillow.

"Shel, don't!" Ruthie said, sitting down next to him. "You'll get over him. You'll start to work again. You'll work on my projects with me, and we'll have fun again, and soon you'll meet someone else."

"You shouldn't have found me," he told her. "It was a waste of your time. Eventually I'll just do it again. I don't want to be without him. I don't want to go back to work. I want to stay home and—"

"Have babies?" Ruthie said. There was anger in it, and a little bit of a joke, but Shelly looked at her seriously.

"Yeah," he said. "I would like that."

Ruthie laughed. "You're right. I should have let you bump yourself off. You're a wacko." She stood, and touched his hand. "While you were sleeping I threw out every pill and hid everything sharp in the house, so if you want to do it again, you'll have to go somewhere else. I've got a meeting at ABC."

She was already in the garage of her building when the idea hit her with such force that she spun around, rang for the elevator, which was too slow in coming, so she ran up the stairs to the third floor and down the hall to her apartment.

"Shelly?" she said. He was in the bathroom with the door closed. "Shelly, don't you dare try anything," she shrieked at the door, which she discovered when she turned the knob was locked.

"For God's sake, I'm on the john," he said. He emerged a few minutes later, looking haggard and green. "I thought you had a meeting."

"I do," she said, "but this is more important. Shelly, let's have a baby together."

"Oh, Christ," he said.

"We don't have to have sex to do it. There's lots of other ways."

"This I have to hear," he said, but for a second she saw a smile in his eyes that reminded her of the old Shelly.

"Some gay women are even doing it with turkey basters."

That got him. He was smiling, and then he giggled.

"I could get pregnant." She was so excited she was pulling at the sleeve of his pajamas. "With our baby. And after the baby's born if you still don't want to work, I could go back to work, and you could take care of her."

"Or him," Shelly said, seeming to warm to the idea.

"Shelly, say yes. At least say you'll think about it. Can you picture it? A little baby from you and me? We'd name it after Sid Caesar if it was a boy, or Imogene Coca if it was a girl. It would have a great sense of humor. It would come out and say, 'A funny thing happened to me on the way to the delivery room.' Shel, maybe I can't even make babies. Maybe you can't. Maybe you have comedy sperm, like in that Woody Allen movie. But isn't it worth a try?"

Shelly walked out of the room past her and into the kitchen, leaving her standing there alone. Obviously he thought she was so crazy he wasn't even going to talk about it.

Forget it, he was saying. Letting her down easy. It was a ridiculous idea and a stupid time to present it. Three days after a man tried to kill himself over the love of his life, she was asking him to have a baby with her. No wonder she was still single, without a prospect in sight. She didn't have an ounce of subtlety in her entire body. And Shelly was being gracious by pretending she never said any of those things. Just strolling right by her into the kitchen. She would go in there now and apologize for being insensitive, then hurry to her meeting at the network.

"Shel," she said, walking into the kitchen. Shelly had his back to her, and when he turned she squealed and he laughed, because in his hand he was holding what he had just taken out of the top drawer by the sink. A turkey baster.

"You rang?" he answered.

8

"AND THAT'S HOW you conceived Sid?" Barbara tried to keep the astonishment out of her voice.

"That's how," Ruthie said.

"Were you concerned at all in these times about having a baby with a gay man?"

"No. We talked about it, and decided that it was safe, because since his long-ago relationship with Les, Shelly had only been with Davis. And Davis told him he was fresh from a monogamous relationship with a woman he'd been married to for years. So that seemed to be the safest person in the world for him to be involved with." She looked down at her lap when she added, "Davis and I never did have sex.

"Anyway—we went ahead. Sometimes we'd inseminate me, and when I got my period we'd say to each other, 'It wasn't supposed to work. Two weirdos like us have no business trying to bring a kid into this world.' But then a week or so would go by and we'd be working or talking or at the movies and Shel would say, 'So I guess you'll be ovulating next week, huh?' And I'd say, 'Yeah,' and he'd get this look in his eye and I'd say, 'I think the best day would be Friday.' And then we'd try again."

Her eyes were fogging up and she thought for a while then seemed to bring her mind back to the room. "Anyway, one morning I woke up and I just knew I was pregnant. I was puking my guts out. I left work at lunchtime and went to the doctor's. By the time I got home from work at dinnertime, they called to tell me I was preg. I was so excited, I called Shelly and he rushed home.

"We laughed and we cried and we did our versions of what our parents were going to say when they heard." She looked long at Barbara, then said, "Let me tell you something. Heterosexual couples think they have a monopoly on joy, but if you had seen the two of us, you'd have known there were never two happier people in the world than we were when Sid was born. The last two and a half years have been magical for us, even though we've had a few ups and downs in our careers, because we have that boy and he makes everything in life pale by comparison."

Sid, the comedy kid, was born at Cedars-Sinai Hospital. He weighed five pounds eight ounces.

"How small is he?" one of the writers asked Shelly.

"He's so small that when he's naked, he looks like he's wearing a baggy suit," Shelly answered, then passed out cigars to everyone on the writing staff.

"How did Ruthie do in the labor room?" someone asked at lunch.

"Just like you'd expect for a Jewish girl. She said, 'Honey, I'm too tired. *You* push,' " Shelly answered, and ordered champagne for everyone at the table.

The night Ruthie and Sid came home from the hospital to the new house she and Shelly had bought in Westwood because it had a play yard fit for a prince, an entire video crew met them at the door. Shelly had hired them because he was afraid if he relied on his own technical know-how to preserve the historic moment, he would screw it up.

As it turned out, Shelly directed every move they made. Sid with the nanny, Sid with Ruthie, and Sid being adored by both grandmothers, who had been invited to visit simultaneously in the hopes that, as Shelly put it, "While sharing a hotel room, they will get on each other's nerves so much they'll spontaneously combust."

They didn't. They were soul sisters in every way, and at some point, while alone at the Bel-Air Sands Hotel, out of their children's earshot, they must have made a pact that neither of them would mention the word *marriage* for fear of expulsion. And after cheek pinching, toe naming, and tushie biting their grandchild ad nauseam, they waved at the video camera so often that when they watched the replay even *they* couldn't tell themselves apart. ("Look, there's me giving him a bath." "What are you talking about? That's *me* giving him a bath.") And each of them referred to Sid as "*my* grandson."

When the two women left, flying together as far as Chicago ("Isn't it cute? They can't bear to part with each other," Shelly pointed out), Ruthie was forced to admit that she missed them a little bit. It had been fun for there to be people in the world other than Sid's mommy and daddy who thought the baby's every dirty diaper was a work of art.

The day Ruthie got back to work, Sid became a part of the writing staff. If he gurgled at a joke, it stayed in. If he spit up after a punch line, it had to be rewritten.

He became the reason to get the rehearsal over early and the reason to stay home from some dull party and the reason to sit around on a Sunday morning and do nothing. The three of them had become, for most intents and purposes, a happy family, with the obvious and unspoken exception, albeit a significant one, that Sid's parents never had and never would consummate their love for each other. And though to the conventional observer this seemed to be a pitiable loss, Ruthie and Shelly's nonsexual relationship created an unclouded kind of comfort between them that many couples never had.

Ruthie couldn't believe her life had become a Kodak commercial. Joy and love and a family whose greatest pleasure was being together. The morning Shelly stayed home from work saying he was "under the weather," Ruthie didn't think much about it. When she got home, Sid was playing with the nanny and on the dining room table there was a note. It was held down by one of the crystal candlesticks her mother sent her years ago, hoping that if she had them she would light shabbat candles. Now, as the nausea of fear seized her, she had the fleeting thought that maybe lighting candles would have saved her from Shelly's words: *I have to be away for a while. Believe me I'll come home as soon as I can. Just look after our most precious life for me. You are my world. Shel.*

If Sid's arms hadn't been around her legs, and his beautiful little face hadn't been looking up at her, she would have screamed, wept, lost control, because she knew what the note meant and why Shelly was gone. Two weeks passed. Every morning, she woke, fed and played with Sid, then handed him over to the nanny and went to work, where she told everyone who asked that Shelly had a family emergency. It was a description that could cover almost anything. Some nights she was so wrung out with worry she couldn't even sleep, just stared at the phone, begging it to ring and have Shelly on the other end of the call.

Her favorite sleeping position was on her stomach with her right knee jutting out to the side and her right foot sticking out of the covers. It was the way she remembered seeing her mother sleep, and in the past when she woke up and found herself in that position, she thought about her mother and wondered if the positions people slept in were hereditary.

Tonight she maneuvered herself into that position, hoping that just being in it would induce sleep. Maybe she could fool her mind into believing it was time to let go of all the panic she was feeling and ease into dreams. But instead, the silence of the night made the sound of her stepped-up heartbeat all she could hear, and there was no chance that she would sleep.

She probably should get up and write. With Shelly's absence there was so much to do every day at the office that maybe she should get some of it done now. She was wide awake anyway. She ought to use the time to accomplish something instead of lying there worrying where Shelly was, which was all she'd done for the past two weeks.

She turned over on her back and stared at the blue numbers on the digital clock. Twelve-fifteen . . . no . . . twelve-sixteen. She was never going to get to sleep now. She had friends who told her they did their best work at night, when there was no possibility of the phone ringing or the baby crying or an unexpected knock on the door from UPS. Maybe she ought to . . . no, just the thought of getting up and trying to write was so off-putting that after a few minutes of thinking about it, she was back on her stomach with her right knee jutting out to the side and her right foot sticking out of the covers, and this time it worked. She fell into a deep sleep.

The sharp jingle of the phone jarred her awake, and for a second she wasn't even sure where she was. The blue numbers. It was three o'clock. Goddammit. Then it occurred to her that the only calls that came at three in the morning were death calls. Shelly. The phone rang again. She slid on her belly to the end of the bed, leaned toward the night table, and grabbed the telephone receiver.

"Yeah?"

"Howdy, pardner."

"Shelly?" He was drunk, she knew his three-glasses-of-wine voice only too well, and this was it. "Let me just tell you you'd better be calling to tell me you're being held hostage in Iran, you dog, because you left me here with all the work, making up lies to cover for you with everyone including our son, and now you're waking me up to listen to you do a bad John Wayne? This better be good."

All she heard for the next long time was the crackling hush of the long-distance line, then Shelly said, "I've got bad news and I've got good news. Which do you want first?"

Ruthie sat up and put her feet on the floor, feeling around with them for her slippers. She had to pee. As soon as she got off the phone she would go and . . .

"Ruthie?" Shelly asked.

"I'm here, I'm here, and I can't believe you're doing good-news, bad-news jokes at three in the morning, and using me as the straight man. At least you had the courtesy not to call me collect."

"I didn't have to. I punched in your credit card number. So which do you want first? The bad news or the good news?"

Ruthie sighed and wished for a second that she smoked. This would be the perfect time to light a cigarette.

"Gimme the good news first," she said, turning on her bedside lamp.

"The good news," Shelly said, "is that I'm in Texas and I'm rip-roaring drunk, or as some of the folks here like to call it, shitfaced."

"Yeah? So what's the bad news?"

Silence. Static. Then, "The bad news is that I came here to see a specialist because I suspected I was at risk."

It took a moment for the words to get to her solar plexus, and when they did she didn't think she'd ever be able to breathe again. But the news wasn't a surprise. She'd been waiting to hear it since his departure, feeling all the while as if she was hanging from the edge of a cliff by her fingertips fearing the fall, and at last here it was.

"I'm HIV-positive, Ru-Ru," he said. "But there's good news about that. I don't have any symptoms, and my helper cells are at seven hundred and thirty. Ready for more good news? I've managed to convince my mother it's because I'm an intravenous-drug user."

Shelly was doing horrible jokes at three in the morning from Texas. Ruthie's stomach throbbed and a chill raced through her so that she took her slippers off and pulled the bed covers close around her.

"Okay," she said. "It's funny. We can't use it on the show. It's in terrible taste, but it's funny. And I miss you."

"I'm coming home tomorrow. American Airlines flight two twenty, at two o'clock your time."

"I'll pick you up at the airport," she promised.

"Do you remember," he asked her, "the night a few months ago when we were having dinner at the Mandarin, and the waiter brought the fortune cookies, and when I opened mine it was empty? This must be why."

"I love you," Ruthie said, "I love you, and I'll be at the airport waiting for you tomorrow."

After a while, exhaustion forced her to fall asleep again, but she opened her eyes in a panic at the first light. As she got out of bed, the truth ran over her with the force of a freight train and so immobilized her that she had to recite aloud to herself the steps she needed to take to get dressed. "Put on underpants, socks and bra, sweatpants, sweatshirt."

When she was dressed she walked to Sid's room, where the nanny was dressing him.

"Mama, can we go to the park?" he asked, smiling a delicious smile, and there was a look in his eyes that reminded her so much of Shelly that she had to turn away for a beat to catch her breath.

"How about some eggies?" she asked him.

"Yay, eggies, and jelly on toast," he said.

She held him very close as she carried him into the kitchen and instead of putting him on the floor to play, she held him on her hip while she cooked his eggs. Then while he spooned them into his mouth, she told him her version of the "Three Bears," in which there was a Mommy bear, a Daddy bear, and a Sidney bear. When the nanny had taken him out the door to head for the park, Ruthie called her office and said she wasn't feeling too well, made sure the writers knew how to proceed, then sat on the living room sofa, holding the morning paper but not really reading it.

She thought about going to the airport and what it would be like to see Shelly get off the plane, wondering if his being HIV-positive meant he'd be emaciated and sickly. She'd seen him only two weeks ago and he'd looked great. She felt cold and weak, and didn't know how to spend the day waiting for him to come home, so she made an outing of taking the car to fill it up with gas. She took Sid to Harry Harris's shoe store and bought him some sneakers. She made popcorn and ate all of it. Then she took a very long shower, and decided that instead of driving to the airport she would call a limousine service, so she called Davel Limousines and asked for a driver to pick her up at home to take her to and from the airport.

The driver was the same man who had driven Ruthie and Shelly to the Emmys last year and he recognized her and wanted to make small talk, but Ruthie closed the window between the front and backseat, and immediately regretted hiring a limo because the long blackness of it felt so funereal. She would have to be strong and in charge to take care of Shelly now. This wasn't like taking care of Sid, a job for which she had help. Besides, there was a library full of books about what to do with a baby. But Shelly with this virus inside him. This was different.

She realized as she looked up at the television screen for his arrival time that she should have called from home to check because she saw now that the flight from Houston would be late. Houston, Texas. He had gone there to be diagnosed. Afraid that if he went to UCLA he'd see someone he knew there, or be examined by a doctor who would tell someone.

For a while she sat on a bench near the gate where Shelly's flight was scheduled to land, looking out the window at the airplanes. She hated to fly, tried to avoid it by traveling as rarely as possible, as if by remaining on the ground she could trick death into staying away from her. Death. In her mind now, she did what she'd been trying not to do since Shelly's phone call. She ran down the list of all the friends they had lost to AIDS in the last few years.

Then she fished around in her purse for some paper, but all she had was a MasterCard receipt, so she turned it over and on it she wrote their names, sat in the corner of the airport on a bench near the window in the terminal and made an unbearably long list. Brilliant colleagues, cherished close friends, people who were gone too soon. With each name came the memory of the service she and Shelly had attended for that person. Some ceremonies were so dark and gloomy they could barely speak to each other about them later. Some were so filled with the love of the deceased's family, and relief from the pain they'd suffered that the memory felt as light as the balloons they had let fly at the close of the service.

When she finished the list, Ruthie prayed silently to all of them to help Shelly have enough time left so that Sid could get to know and remember him. When she felt someone standing next to her, she looked up, into the sweet face of Shelly.

"Sid's mother, I presume?" he said.

Ruthie stood and threw her arms around his neck. In her embrace his body felt the same as always. Good, healthy, not thin or weak or sickly, but perfectly fine, and she stepped back to look at him again.

"It's me," he said quietly, "and it wasn't a nightmare you had, Ruthless. However, there's a bright side. I'm leaving everything to you. So with your money and mine, you'll be the richest Jew in Hollywood, unless you count Marvin Davis, who is really four or five Jews in a very large suit."

"We missed you so much," she said, hugging him again. He was carrying his suit bag over his shoulder and a duffel bag in his hand, and he didn't have any other luggage so they walked, arms around each other, directly to the curb and the waiting limo.

"Mr. Milton," the driver said, "welcome home, sir," and opened the door. As the car moved on to Century Boulevard, Shelly slid his hand over the black leather seat and took Ruthie's.

"I'm scared," he said.

"Me too," she admitted. "Me too."

"How's Sid?"

"He doesn't sleep, he throws his food, he removes his diaper in the supermarket, in other words he's perfect," she said.

Shelly smiled, a tired smile, and still holding her hand, he fell asleep with his head pressed against the back of the seat. When the car pulled into the driveway of the house, the stop awakened him. The driver carried the bags inside, and Ruthie and Shelly walked in with their arms around each other. When Sid saw his father, he broke away from the nanny, ran to him and threw himself at Shelly, crying long and hard.

"Daddeeeee. Daddeeeee."

Shelly knelt, and spoke gently to him.

"Hi, Sidney. How's my boy? Don't cry, honey. Don't." Then he lifted Sid and held him tight.

After he'd unpacked and presented Sid with some Corgi cars, he got into bed for a nap. Ruthie kissed him good-bye, covered him warmly, changed Sid's diaper and turned him over to the nanny, then she left to keep the appointment she'd made a few days earlier with Barbara Singer.

"The first thing you must do is be tested and have Sid tested too," Barbara said to Ruthie when the painful story had been told and hung in the air between them. She could see that spilling it all out had been good for Ruthie, who seemed to relax in her chair for the first time. When Barbara reached to turn on her desk lamp, she realized she'd been so involved in and intrigued by Ruthie's story that she'd never once looked at a clock. Now it was night, and hours had passed since her arrival.

"When I first made this appointment," Ruthie said, "it was to come in and ask you to help me to help my son grow up in a world where people like his father, who I love more than my next breath, are stigmatized, condemned, and dropping like flies from a disease that must be stopped. But I guess there was always a part of me that feared this day might be coming, and when it did I'd have to face the real dilemma of how to get the three of us through it.

"I told Shelly today that I made an appointment to come over here and talk to you about raising Sid, and what kind of problems we were going to face. Only when I made the appointment I didn't know what I know now. He told me not to tell you he has HIV. We're writing and producing a new television series right now, and the executive producer is a nasty little bigot. Shelly's afraid he'll fire us if he hears about this. But I said you have to keep everything we tell you a secret, right?"

"Right," Barbara told her.

Ruthie took a tissue from the box on Barbara's desk, but her eyes were dry. "I hate to feel sorry for myself because I have had so much in this world where most people have so little, but goddammit, it took such a long time for us to hammer out a little niche for ourselves, after both being odd man out all our lives, and just when it was feeling like we had it together, there's this." Her head hung toward her lap and finally she let the tears come, and for a little while she cried quietly. Then she looked up at Barbara, her face a mass of red blotches, her bloodshot eyes large with fear.

"I'll go get Sid and we'll both be tested right away," she said. "And I'll see if I can get Shelly to start coming in here with me to talk to you. We've got so much to work on, and nobody to ask how to handle it. I mean it's not exactly your run-of-the-mill situation is it?" She smiled an ironic smile beneath her despairing eyes.

"Not exactly," Barbara said. "But I know you and

Shelly and Sid and I can work out a way to handle it that will be right for your family."

"Our family," Ruthie said, liking the sound of that. "We really are a family. Although I'm sure we're not the kind you're probably used to counseling."

"True," Barbara said. "But things are changing." Then she told Ruthie about her idea for the group.

9

THE SENIOR STAFF MEMBERS were all women, and they jokingly referred to their weekly meetings as "the kaffee-klatsch." But after the first few minutes of commenting on the quality of the coffee and asking about one another's families, their meetings were far from social. In fact, they were sometimes so serious that during a presentation Barbara had the same performance anxiety that she used to get at University High School when she stood up to deliver an oral book report.

"As you're probably well aware, there are sperm banks all over the country, selling sperm which has been donated by men identifiable to the purchaser only by numbers, and a few broad-stroke descriptions of their race, religion, and favorite hobbies." One of her colleagues let out a titter of a giggle over that information, and Barbara knew they had to all be wondering what this had to do with their child-development program.

"It's a chancy way to go, but women who want

babies badly are willing to take the risk. Donor insemination obviates the discomfort of dating, awkward sex, and uncomfortable relationships. The irony is that the same women who were freed up by the sixties to have sex without the problems of babies, twenty years later find themselves eager to seize the opportunity to have babies without the problems of sex.

"What's happened with all of the reproductive technologies is that some important issues are being created that will affect us, the child-development professionals. In this era of embryo transfer, in vitro fertilization, menopausal mothers carrying pregnancies for their daughters, and much more, it seems what many of these families may not be considering fully is the psychological and emotional effect the circumstance of these births will have on the people being created.

"And I say it that way because even in our studies here of intact nuclear families, frequently the baby-craving is just that. I mean, there's little thought about what happens beyond the excitement of new babies, when the realities set in. When the babies become children who have language and begin to wonder about their genesis. In my private practice in the last two weeks, I've met with a single woman who's been donor inseminated twice, and a couple in which the heterosexual mother was inseminated by the baby's father, who is her homosexual male best friend. And in both cases the families have toddlers who are very verbal, and the parents are concerned." That got a few "Hmm"s.

"It'll take a long time before there's real data on how those babies will feel when they're adults, but I suspect that the key to making it all work has something to do with creating a loving context for them. To find warm ways to deal with cold realities.

"I'd like to alert pediatricians and run an ad in some publications in order to look for and then begin a group for those special families. I believe the world isn't prepared yet with a new way of thinking to go hand in hand with those newfound methods. That culturally, socially, ethically, morally, and legally, we don't have adequate rules or answers for the exquisitely complicated issues that have already come up around these methods. Nevertheless, we need to find some way for the families to operate now."

Louise Feiffer, the director of the program, was a tall dramatically attractive woman in her fifties, with high cheekbones, ivory skin, and dark hair pulled back into a bun. Barbara was relieved to see her bright-eyed and smiling as she went on.

"I want to conduct this group under the aegis of the hospital and our pediatric-development program, so I'm presenting it to all of you for discussion." She looked around now at the faces of the others. Hands went up, there were dozens of questions, surprise at the statistics, and a fascinated curiosity about Barbara's research.

"It's undoubtedly an exciting new area," Louise said. "I think we should try to work a group like that into our schedule."

An elated Barbara congratulated herself all the way home on the good job she'd done. She was glad to have the meeting out of the way before tonight. The romantic quiet celebration with Stan of their twenty-fifth wedding anniversary. Impossible, she thought. A twenty-fifth wedding anniversary is something that happens to somebody's aunt and uncle. Not two youngsters like Barbara and Stan Singer.

She had sworn to Stan that she didn't want a party. Just dinner, preferably with her family, but when she invited her mother, Gracie said there was some committee meeting she couldn't miss. Jeff apologized that he had to go to basketball practice. Because the anniversary fell in the middle of the week, Heidi told her sadly that she couldn't make it in from San Francisco.

So after a fast shower, the application of some fresh makeup, and slipping into a dress she was proud she could still wear since it was about fifteen years old, she and Stan sat alone in a large booth at Valentino's. Maybe, she thought now, it had been a mistake not putting together a big blowout of an anniversary party. A quarter of a century of marriage was certainly something to celebrate.

Stan seemed unusually nervous. He kept looking over at the door, and postponing ordering dinner presumably because, as he told Barbara twice, he'd eaten a late lunch and wasn't very hungry yet. Now he was watching as a stunning young girl in a tight black minidress was being led across the restaurant. When the maître d' stepped aside and Barbara saw that the girl was Heidi, she let out a yelp of glee, followed by another when she realized that behind Heidi, dressed in a sport coat and tie, was Jeff. And miracle of miracles, behind Jeff was Gracie. She looked great in a silk shirtwaist dress and long dangly earrings Barbara hadn't seen her wear in years.

"Surprise, darling," Gracie said, and Barbara wondered if she was thinking the posh restaurant was excessive.

"Happy anniversary, Mommy," Heidi said, sliding into the booth and giving Barbara a hug.

"You planned this behind my back?" Barbara asked Stan.

"Of course," he said as he grinned, and received a kiss from his daughter.

"I *knew* I liked you," Barbara said.

"Mother, you look fabulous," Heidi said.

"Thank you, honey. I was just going to say that to *my* mother."

Gracie laughed and slid in next to Stan and gave him

a patronizing little pat on the arm. "Good work, kiddo," she said.

Barbara felt warmed by the sight of her family all together in one place. Stan liked to call the need she had to see all of them assembled at a meal her barbecue fantasy. Now if the fantasy came true, which it never did, they would all be happy to be there, get along smashingly well, and leave full of love for one another and better for the encounter.

"Your hair looks totally idiotic," Heidi said to Jeff, and the fantasy went the way of all fantasies.

"That dress is so tight, if you fart your shoes'll fly off."

"Time out, you two," Stan said. "You've been together one hour. Can you stay civil for one more, in honor of the celebration?"

"Classic sibling rivalry," Gracie said. "My girls had it constantly."

"No, we didn't. Not constantly," Barbara flared immediately, knowing as she did it was a mistake to rise to the bait.

"Let's call New York and ask Roz. *She* has a mind like a steel trap," Gracie said.

"Maybe that's why they had sibling rivalry, because you compared them, Grammy," Heidi said.

"I *never* compared them."

"Well, if Aunt Roz has a mind like a steel trap, what does my mom have?" Jeff asked.

"I'm debating whether I should call a waiter or a taxi," Stan said, and everyone laughed.

"I guess no dinner with our family would be complete without tears, insults, hurt feelings, and unfulfilled expectations," Barbara said.

"In other words, we're normal," Gracie offered, then she lifted her arm to hail a passing waiter. "Could we have menus here pronto, dear boy? I'm starved."

"Mother!"

"The real issue you and your family-therapy associates ought to confront is why people jump through such hoops to conceive babies in the first place. All the babies do is grow up and mistreat one another, and *you* in the bargain."

"You can understand why I'm such a shining example of mental health with a mother who has *that* philosophy," Barbara said.

"Happy anniversary, sweetheart," Stan said, patting her hand.

"You know what?" she said, smiling at him. "If we're still around for our fiftieth, let's just go on a cruise."

They said good-bye to Gracie and made their way home, Heidi and Barbara sitting in the back of the car. When Heidi took her hand and held it, Barbara felt a surge of gratitude for being blessed with these two complicated creatures, her children. It was the best anniversary gift she could think of to be able to tuck Heidi into bed tonight in her old bedroom, even though the room now had a desk and a wall unit of bookshelves on one side and had been serving for the last few years as Barbara's at-home office.

"Grammy looked adorable tonight, but she's such a cuckoo," Heidi said. She was turning down the daybed while Barbara stood watching.

"Thank you for coming in for this dinner, honey," she said.

"Are you kidding? I wouldn't have missed it for the world."

Every time Barbara saw either of her children after not seeing them for a while, like the times Heidi came in from San Francisco to visit or Jeff got off the bus from spending a few weeks at tennis camp, she would be gleefully bowled over by the sight of them. Not by their beauty, because she knew she had no objectivity about that, but by the miracle of genes. She would marvel as she gazed at one of her kids, for what they always found to be an annoyingly long time, at the way her own characteristics and Stan's fell together to shape them.

Their carriage, their gestures, their speech, their respective senses of humor, the familiar amalgam of her characteristics and Stan's mixed in with each child's individuality never ceased to amaze her. The same kind of uncontrollable hair she tried to tame on herself in high school by rolling it around orange juice cans and plastering it with Dippity-Do, on Heidi was a wild, wonderful-looking mane caught stylishly in a headband, or worn hanging loose, showing off the girl's personal confidence, which was more than Barbara ever remembered having at that or any age. And the darkness around Stan's eyes, which had always been his least favorite feature on his own face, had been inherited by Jeff, on whom it looked exotic and mysterious.

"Sit down, Mom," Heidi said, and Barbara knew it was an invitation to stay in the room to talk, so gratefully and obediently she sat on the desk chair across the room from the bed, and started the conversation with what she hoped sounded like a casual, not-too-probing question. "How's everything in San Francisco?"

She'd been saving any girl talk for the time when they were alone, hoping she'd get real answers instead of the upbeat facile ones Heidi might give in front of the others. Or maybe she wouldn't get a real answer at all. That sometimes happened too. Usually after Heidi first arrived, there would be a kind of tense feeling-each-other-out time between them, until the familiarity took over and Heidi dropped the exterior of a chic San Franciscan.

"I'm not good," Heidi said, moving some clothes from her duffel bag into a drawer. "I'm in love."

Hmmm, Barbara thought, things are getting chatty a lot faster than I'd anticipated. "But why does that make you not good?" she asked. "I thought that was supposed to be happy news."

"It makes me not good because he's crazy. Because he's thirty-five years old and can't make a commitment. Because speaking of mothers, his did such a job on him that nobody will ever live up to her so he can't get married, can't be exclusive to any woman. And I'm the poor jerk who stays with him, even though I know that all I want in life is to have a relationship like yours with Daddy. But there's not a prayer. Not with this guy. I mean, I know he lies to me and probably cheats too."

"Are you practicing safe sex?" Barbara asked, knowing she would get an outraged answer back.

"Oh, God. Of course!" Heidi flared.

"I'll bet the lying and the cheating hurt a lot," Barbara said.

"Don't shrink me, Mother!"

"I'm not shrinking you. I'm being sympathetic."

"Yes, it hurts a lot, and I'm thinking of moving back to L.A. just to put some distance between me and Ryan. Yikes. Even when I just say his name I get a pain in my chest."

Barbara held her breath so she wouldn't say what she was thinking, which was hooray, yes, move back here, because if she said that, Heidi would probably buy a condo in San Francisco by Monday. Instead she waited for her to go on.

"How did you ever get so smart when you were eighteen to marry my cute daddy? A man you still love after twenty-five years."

"Oh, it was easy, really. Grammy helped me decide."

"She did?" Heidi was surprised by that answer.

"Uh-huh. She said, 'If you ever go out with that

nerdy little tight-ass again, I'll kill you.' Two weeks later we eloped." That brought a laugh from Heidi, a laugh Barbara loved and remembered from all her daughter's years of growing up, a laugh that made her know Heidi was going to be okay in spite of the thirty-five-year-old man and his mother. "And the rest is history," she added, laughing with her, and hurting for her.

You don't get to pick, Mother. Those were words that Barbara had thought and said to Gracie endlessly in battles, not just about Stan, but about everything she could think of over the years. And she knew the same rule applied to her relationships with her own children. After they reached a certain age, they didn't give a damn what she thought.

"What can I do?" she asked.

"Nothing," Heidi said and lay on the bed and pulled the covers up to her neck, looking to Barbara the same way she had when she was six years old. In fact, the fading honey-colored Winnie the Pooh that had been a gift to her at birth and one of her favorite baby snuggle toys still sat on the night table next to the bed, completing the picture. Barbara wanted so much to say something comforting, and the only thing she could think of that might work was something she really didn't believe, but it was hopeful, so she said it anyway.

"Well, maybe he'll change."

In the morning when she drove Heidi to the airport she remembered a story Gracie had told her when she was a little girl, about a turtle who watched the birds fly south for the winter and longed to go with them, but of course she couldn't because turtles can't fly. When two of the about-to-depart birds saw how wistfully their friend the turtle watched them, they offered to take her along. They would, they told the turtle, find a stick onto which she could clamp her mouth, and each of the birds would carry an end of the stick in its mouth. The only caveat was that the turtle had to keep her mouth shut for the entire flight.

The turtle, her mind racing, reminded herself again and again of the perils of speaking, but finally she had something which felt so important to say—Barbara couldn't remember now exactly what it was—that she spoke and of course fell from the stick, and not only didn't make it to the destination, but was never seen again. Barbara and Gracie always joked that the moral of the story was "If you want to go to Florida, keep your mouth shut," but the message was clear, and Barbara frequently felt when she was with Heidi as if she were that turtle.

At least they were sitting in a car, which was a great way to talk about uncomfortable situations, because if you were the driver you had to watch the road and there didn't have to be eye contact.

"I miss L.A. and I miss you and Daddy and Grammy, and even Jeff the brat. I always think I'm going to visit more often, but then I get bogged down with work and . . . and I never think I should leave . . ."

"Ryan?" Barbara asked, realizing she'd just caused the turtle to fall out of the sky.

"Yeah. I don't know what I'm going to do about that. Maybe give myself some time limit in my mind, and if he doesn't come around by then I stop seeing him."

"That sounds reasonable."

"It does, doesn't it? Unfortunately I don't have the guts to really do it."

"Do you have any women friends there?"

"A few. But they're all going through their own stuff, you know? Every now and then I see one of them, and they seem to be in worse shape than I am. At least I have a good job."

They were both silent after that until they got to the curb at United Airlines.

"Want me to park and wait with you?"

"No thanks."

"Whatever you decide to do about Ryan, I love you," Barbara said, and on the way to the office she told herself it was because Heidi was too choked with emotion that she didn't say "I love you" back.

At the office Barbara shuffled through the mail and returned some calls, and just before her first family arrived she took a call from a friend she hadn't seen in years. Lee Solway, a thoughtful, well-respected pediatrician to whom she'd referred dozens of patients.

"Lee. How great to hear from you. How are you?"

"I couldn't be better. Listen, I wanted to advance a call you're going to get from a fellow named Richard Reisman. I've come to know him quite well and he really needs your gentle guidance. Let me tell you why."

As Lee Solway described the referral Barbara listened, then wrote down the name Richard Reisman—and next to it the words *Candidate for new group*. The doctor was right. This man would need all the help he could get.

"Does it sound like it's your bailiwick?" Lee asked her.

"More than you know," Barbara answered. "Have him call me."

10

AT THE MOTION PICTURE Convalescent Home and Hospital, Bobo Reisman was known to everyone on the premises as the Mayor. Maybe it was because every morning, rain or shine, he made his way slowly and carefully, so as not to fall and hurt his hip again like last winter, to the bench outside the front door of Reception. Once he arrived safely, which at his age was a considerable accomplishment, he sat slowly, first putting his hand down behind him, then gently lowering himself into a seated position.

"Good morning, Mr. Mayor," Dr. Sepkowitz said as he passed.

"How's yourself?" Bobo asked him, but by the time he did, the doctor had disappeared into the building, leaving only the thud of the heavy glass door as an answer.

"Lookin' fine, Mr. Mayor," Margo Burke, one of the night nurses, said as she came out the door, and Bobo tipped his hat to her.

On the days when Ricky came to visit from the minute he got off the Ventura Freeway and turned the corner onto Calabassas Road, he could already spot Bobo on the bench and know immediately that his uncle was all right. Most of the time he would bring along a picnic lunch from Greenblatt's, and the two men would sit and share a chopped liver sandwich, which they both knew was bad for them, along with a Dr. Brown's celery tonic, which was also not so great but which they both loved. Then, on sunny days, Ricky would help his uncle to his feet, and they would walk haltingly around the grounds, being greeted by the passersby.

"Morning, Mr. Mayor," people would say to Bobo, then they'd nod to Rick and add a wink that meant, Aren't you nice to come out and spend time with an old guy like that? But Bobo didn't notice the others, because all he knew was that his nephew, his Ricky, was there to ask his advice about the business.

"Your dad couldn't understand why I wanted to do the goddamned outer-space stories. Years before that Sputnik was even heard of, I kept telling him, let's make movies about outer space. And wasn't I right? That's all you see now are those goddamned outer-space movies. The one with the guy with the pointy ears. How many times can they make that goddamned movie again and again? The whole crew of that spaceship is so old they should be moving into *this* place, for Christ's sake. It's like I told your dad years ago, I said, You know why outer space, Jakie? Because everybody wants to know what's out there. Are they people like us, or are they little green guys who are so small they use bagels as tires on their flying saucers? Ever hear that joke?"

"I *have* heard it, Uncle B.," Rick said. It was a scorching Valley day, and he was pushing Bobo, whose foot was bothering him a little, in a wheelchair around the labyrinthine paths of the grounds.

"You have?" Bobo asked.

"Uh-huh." Rick watched a young nurse leaving one of the cottages stop to write on her clipboard then reach back and tug something at her waist, probably the band on her panty hose. "The Martian tastes the bagel and says, 'Mmm. This is good, but it would be better with lox and cream cheese.' "

"Yeah," Bobo said, "that's the punch line. But Jesus, you *shmendrick*, I'm an old man, for Christ's sake. You couldn't maybe have pretended you didn't know the *farshtinkener* joke, and given me the pleasure of being able to tell it again?"

"I've tried that with you in the past, and you always say, 'Don't *yes* me. I know I already told it to you. I'm only old, I'm not crazy too.' "

Bobo laughed, revealing yellowed dentures, and reached his veined and crooked-fingered hand back to pat his nephew on the arm. "Don't worry, Ingeleh, soon I'll be gone and you wouldn't need to schlep out here no more."

"You'll probably outlive me," Rick told him.

"God forbid," Bobo said, reaching back to smack him. "I already got a number. I'm just waiting for somebody to call it. You? You're not even married yet, so you can't die."

"And what does one thing have to do with the other?" Rick asked. They were at that part of the walk where he had to push the wheelchair up a small hill, and he was a little out of breath, vowing silently to start going back to the health club on a regular basis. But by the time they were on the level again he'd forgotten his promise.

"What it has to do," Bobo said, "is why should you be so lucky to get out of this life never having been nagged by a wife?"

"Do girlfriends count?" Rick asked, stopping the

wheelchair next to a grassy area with lawn chairs, stepping hard on the brake, pulling one of the lawn chairs over, and sitting on it. "I get nagged by plenty of girlfriends."

"It ain't the same," the old man told him, shaking his head. Rick was always amazed at how, despite his uncle's wizened face, the man's big brown eyes danced with such life. "No matter what all the current cynical, immoral garbage television programs and movies tell you, my Ingeleh, it ain't the same. Listen, Ricky," he said, his brow under his wild crop of white hair furrowing with concern. "How is it you're in such bad shape for such a young man? Can it be a man your age goes up a little hill and huffs and puffs like that? Maybe you should knock off a couple a pounds?"

"I'm all right, Uncle B.," Rick said. "Don't worry."

"Why shouldn't I worry? I already told you you're in my will. You never mentioned if I was in *yours*."

Both men laughed, and then they sat in silence for a long time.

"You listen to me, Rickinue, it's time to make a life for yourself already. You're a big shot, a *shtarker*. And you date little girls who call themselves actresses, who shake a little *tochis* at you, and leave in the morning before you wake up. Right? Right! So what? You may be bigger in the business than me and your dad were, but me and him . . . at least we had something you don't have. A wife. I had your aunt Sadie, a pistol, a son of a gun, when she said 'Bobo,' I saluted. Whatever she wanted, I gave her, because she was a good soul, and we loved each other . . . what? Fifty-four years.

"And your mother, what an angel. A sense of humor on her, and she was crazy about your dad. I got married on accounta them. I used to watch them smooching when me and your dad came home from work, and I figured that's how it is when you get married. Smooching all the time, so I did it too. Of course, in your generation you get all the loving you want without benefit of a *chuppa*, but believe me''—Bobo was tapping with arthritic fingers on his own knee for emphasis—''believe me . . .'' But then the thought was gone, and he sat quietly again.

''Do you want me to take him back, Mr. Reisman?'' A tall black nurse was standing next to Rick, who realized now that he'd been staring at the water spurting from a nearby fountain for a long time and hadn't noticed that Bobo had fallen asleep. He'd been thinking about what Bobo said, which though he'd heard it many times before seemed to grab him inside today, as if a hand were squeezing his heart. Or was it the chopped liver? We had something you don't have. A wife.

''No, I'll go with you,'' he said. ''I'll come along, in case he wakes up.''

Rick pushed the wheelchair toward the lodge. The pain was just heartburn, he promised himself again. As they got to the door the nurse hurried ahead to open it, and walked with him to Bobo's room. The two of them lifted the old man onto his bed, and Rick covered his uncle's feet with a green-and-yellow afghan he remembered from his childhood, when it used to sit on his aunt Sadie's sofa. As he held the door for the nurse she smiled and said, ''He's very proud of you. Brags about your success around here to everyone. I haven't seen all of your movies, but I did see *A Quarter to Nine*, and I enjoyed it thoroughly, I must tell you.''

Rick thanked her, then excused himself and walked wearily through the hallways leading toward the exit to the parking lot. This is how it ends, he thought. This is where I'll wind up too. If I'm lucky. And when someone stands up to give the eulogy, is it really going to matter if I directed twelve films or sixteen films? He slowed his gait just by a fraction to look at the black-and-white stills of the classic films lining the walls of the building. Bobo, he thought, smiling to himself as he moved toward his car, wishes I was married. That's adorable. Every time we're together he gives me a little dig about it, just like every woman I date. That made Rick laugh, a little burst of a laugh, and when he got into the car and turned his car radio to KKGO FM, the jazz station, Dizzy Gillespie was playing "I Can't Get Started with You."

At home he warmed the dinner the housekeeper had left for him, ate it quickly in front of the television, moved the remote from channel to channel, then he dialed the Malibu number and Charlie answered.

"It's only me," Rick said yawning. The antiseptic smell of the convalescent home was still in his clothes.

"You mean you're sitting at home by yourself on a Saturday night?"

"So where else would I be?"

They were having the conversation they called "two really old guys in Miami Beach." It was part of an agreement they'd made with each other years ago. That when everyone else, lovers, spouses, friends, deserted them or dropped dead (anyone who leaves either one of us should *only* drop dead), the two of them would end up together, in a high rise in Miami Beach. Like *The Odd Couple* or *The Sunshine Boys*. After twenty-five years of marriage to Patty Marcus Fall there were no signs that Charlie would ever be alone. And for Rick there were only candidates. Dozens of candidates.

"No Mona?"

"No more Mona."

"The long talk?" Charlie asked, and Rick smiled and emitted some air from his nose, along with a laugh, which meant, How does Charlie know so much?

"I only know," Charlie said, as if he were reading Rick's mind, "because it's, what? Let's see. Six months? That's usually when it happens. Right? Last night I realized. You met her in October. This is March. I swear, I was thinking to myself, Mona is going to spring the long talk on the poor bastard any minute. And she did. So you said?"

"The usual."

"Ah, yes. 'Don't feel bad, it's not you, it's me. I'm no good for anybody.' So now you're depressed, right? Do I know my customers? Ricky, something's got to give, guy. Maybe it's time, and I say just maybe, for you to think about a little bit of compromise. No one's perfect. Right? You think *you're* such a bargain? So you dump Mona and now you're going to have to go through the whole process of dating again. How do you think Bush is doing? How do you feel about South Africa? And that's only on the rare occasions that you date someone who's even heard of Bush and South Africa. Christ, the thought of those evenings makes *me* depressed."

"Oh, leave him alone," Rick heard Patty say in the background.

"You're right. I'm pitiful, but I'm all I've got," Rick said.

"I don't know how to tell you that if you picked a woman for reasons other than how she was in bed, maybe when you got tired of screwing her and she could speak the English language you'd want to keep her around for more than six months."

"Yeah. Grow up, Uncle Ricky," he heard a voice say on what had to be Charlie's extension phone. It was Charlie's eldest son, Mayer, now how old? Could it be he was twenty? "My dad's right. Anyone can get laid. The trick is to relate to another human being in a loving, nurturing way. Not exploit them. You're becoming a cliché. The Hollywood Bachelor. It's so trite."

"Well, I can't tell you how delighted I am that I called," Rick said, grinning to himself at Mayer's outburst. He'd changed the kid's diapers, for God's sake, and now the boy was a second-year film student at USC, hoping to follow in his father's footsteps.

Now Patty got on another extension and told both her husband and son to "stop nagging Uncle Ricky, and hang up so I can talk to him." Patty Fall. Now there was a gem, a beauty, his favorite woman in the world. He always said if he could find one like her he'd be married. "Can I pin you down for a night to come over and have dinner with us?" she asked.

"Gorgeous, you name it," he said and wrote the night she chose into his planning calendar. Then he hung up the phone, turned off the television and the light, and drifted into his room to go to sleep. Somewhere before dawn, he moved over to the other side of the bed and remembered uncomfortably that the warm body most recently occupying that spot was gone. Mona. That's who it was, only now it wasn't. Oh well, he thought as he went back into a very peaceful sleep until his alarm went off.

He was somewhere on the Ventura Freeway when his car phone rang. He had had the phone installed two years ago and still that muffled eerie sound of it ringing, like a telephone in a nightmare, never failed to startle him. He was sure he would never get used to simultaneously driving along the freeway and talking into the speaker. It felt too much like science fiction. He tried using the handset, which made it even worse, because then he had to drive with one hand while the other one held the receiver, and when he wanted to change lanes or get off the freeway, he had no hands left to move the turn signal.

Once he'd been so involved in a telephone conversation that without realizing, he'd changed lanes too quickly and neglected to signal, and the guy behind him in a truck honked his horn at him, cursing. Rick had managed to hear some of what the guy in the truck was hollering. The part about the turkey in the Mercedes convertible on the fucking telephone. And when the truck driver passed Rick's open car, he shouted a final angry curse and spit out the window into the Mercedes. The spit missed Rick, but the point didn't. Talking on the phone while driving on the freeway in your high-priced car made you a Hollywood asshole.

Today it was Carrie in Nat Ross's office. "Mr. Reisman, are you in for Mr. Ross?"

"If this is what you can call in, then I'm definitely it," Rick answered.

Carrie clicked off, and Nat Ross got on the line.

"Rick?"

"Nathan Ross. Studio boss. How's your high-powered self this morning?"

"Fine, I'm fine," Nat Ross said, and then in a way that was clearly designed to indicate that he was also a nice boy who takes care of his family, he said, "You know, I always mean to ask about your uncle Bobo. I was such a fan of his and your father's. How's he doing?"

"Bobo is Bobo. He's nearly eighty-five, with diabetes, cataracts, an ulcer, kidney problems, and phlebitis," Rick answered. "But," he added, "at least he has his health." His stomach suddenly felt crampy as he wondered what this call was going to be about. He had four projects in development under his deal with Nat Ross's studio. Only one of them was even close to being ready to go. A political thriller involving a glamorous Jackie Kennedy type of First Lady.

"Ricky." Nat Ross, who hadn't heard anything Rick just said, went on to his own agenda. "I'm calling to tell you I know how you feel about Kate Sullivan, but I wish you wouldn't reject the idea out of hand of her playing the First Lady." There was silence so Nat Ross went on. "Listen, believe me, I hate her politics, too."

"Yeah?" Rick said. "So?"

"So, she's more right for the part than anyone else either of us know."

"Meryl Streep," Rick said.

"Unavailable," Nat answered.

"I haven't asked her yet," Rick told him.

"I have."

"Nat," Rick said, trying to keep his voice even, "when I made the deal with you, you promised me hands off. Don't let's change that policy or it won't work. Because I'll give you back all your nice money and go down the street if you try to tell me who to cast. And you know that."

"I'm suggesting, Richard. Only suggesting."

"Suggest elsewhere."

"I apologize."

"I forgive you."

Rick put the phone down, said the word "putz" out loud, certain that Nat Ross had just done the same thing on his end, and signaled to get off the freeway at Pass Avenue.

Kate Sullivan to play the First Lady. No way in hell. Everyone who knew him knew he hated that phony self-aggrandizing bimbo. Couldn't abide all of her grandstanding political horseshit. Half the time she didn't have any idea what she was talking about anyway. Was just a mouthpiece for her brother the senator. Besides,

Sullivan hated Rick too. Had for years. Since that fund-raiser for NOW or one of those feminist groups a million years ago, where she'd made some precious speech about the feminizing of the English language. And afterward, when she'd asked if anyone had any questions, Rick had raised his hand and asked her didn't she think it was a waste of everyone's time to focus on small issues like *herstory* versus *history* when there were so many crucial larger issues at stake for women, like day care and equal pay.

Even from where he'd sat that night in the far reaches of Norman Lear's garden, Rick could see Kate Sullivan's green eyes narrow angrily, and then she snapped something inappropriately personal back about how everyone knew "Mr. Reisman's position on women." Then she somehow managed to sidestep answering his question. Afterward one of the men a few rows up handed him a note that read *I guess the answer to your question will continue to remain a MStery*. No. He would not cast Kate Sullivan in this or any other picture of his.

In his office the spindle that held his telephone messages had fallen on its side from the weight of all the slips. "I'm afraid to look," Rick said, then righted the spindle and pulled all the messages off at once with an upward tug.

His secretary, Andrea, didn't hear him come in. She was facing the other way, typing and wearing the headphones from her Walkman, which was blasting music into her ears at such pumped-up volume Rick could hear the bass line from where he stood. When she looked up and saw him she jumped to her feet. "Oh my God." She ripped the earphones out of her tangled nest of blond hair and burst into tears.

Another boyfriend walked out on her, he thought.

"I'm sorry," she said, "I didn't want to be the one

to tell you. I mean I know how you feel about him and . . .'' She put her hands with the too-long red fingernails on his arms and squeezed.

Bobo, he thought, my God, he's gone.

''Charlie Fall is dead,'' Andrea said, her face streaked with tracks of runny eye makeup.

The unexpected shock struck Rick suddenly in a place deep inside his chest and spread into his limbs and his face. Charlie. Impossible.

''I'm sorry,'' Andrea said. ''Mr. Fall's secretary called a few minutes ago and said it was a heart attack.''

''No.''

''She said she tried you at home, but I told her you were probably on your way in. He was running very early this morning at the UCLA track. It was still dark and he was the only one there. By the time one of the other runners found him and they got him over to emergency he was gone. Mrs. Fall asked that you be called.''

Rick turned and walked into his own office, not bothering to close the door behind him, dazed with the terrible news. Charlie. Good God. Andrea, sniffling into a Kleenex, followed him in.

''Where is she? Where's Patty?''

''At home.''

''I'll go there,'' he said. ''Right now.'' But he was too paralyzed to move.

''The funeral's the day after tomorrow,'' Andrea told him, then tiptoed out and closed the door behind her.

Outside, from the reception area, Rick could hear the phones ringing again and again. He looked down at the telephone on his coffee table watching the lights on the various lines that would blink then stop as Andrea answered. Calls that were probably for him, which Andrea was holding so he could have some time to collect his thoughts.

Charlie. His best friend for almost forty years. Rick had been preparing himself to lose Bobo. In fact any time the phone awakened him at night he sat up and said the old uncle's name out loud. But not Charlie. Just two weeks ago in a screening room at Fox they sat together at Charlie's dailies, the viewing of which was always guarded carefully and secretly from everyone in the industry but Rick. But this time it had been obvious that Charlie was nervous having Rick there.

Even from the out-of-sequence pieces of raw work, Rick had seen the genius that Charlie's earlier films had only prophesied. It probably was envy, unadulterated envy, that brought the tears to Rick's eyes that afternoon when the lights went up and Charlie, stoked with elation, had looked him square in the eye and said, "Eat your heart out."

"Oh, I am," Rick said, unable to lie to Charlie, who knew him so well. "Believe me, I'm eating plenty here. It's fucking genius."

Charlie had sighed and smiled a big smile that showed the space between his two front teeth and said, "It's about time I heard you saying that to me, because it's how I feel every time I see *your* work."

"But this is better than all that. Better than anything either of us has done before now. It's extraordinary. I swear to you." The two men had embraced and walked out of the theater into the bright day. Charlie Fall was gone. A heart attack. And Patty. What in the hell would she do without him? Rick's eyes moved around his office at all of the photographs of Charlie he now realized he had scattered everywhere. He and Charlie together in black tie at the Oscars. The year Rick had won, and then another from the year Charlie won. That one with Charlie, shirtless and tan, wearing that big Charlie grin at the Santa Monica Pier, arms around each of his boys, who held fishing rods. The boys.

Rick's eyes ached. He could picture Charlie's boys now, sitting with Patty on the deck at the beach house, holding on to one another in their shared pain. He dialed the number at the Falls' Malibu house. The line had a too-fast busy signal, making it sound as if the phone on the other end was off the hook. He put the receiver down and walked over to his desk. It was a mess. Piled with papers. Memos from the executives upstairs, a letter from a film festival in the Midwest where they wanted to do a Richard Reisman retrospective. He remembered cringing when he opened it, thinking, *Retrospective*? The fucking word makes me feel like I'm dead. Dead.

There was a pile of script notes he wanted to look over one more time. An invitation to an AFI dinner, and a brochure that he hadn't had a chance to look at when it arrived. For a long time he sat in his desk chair and read every word of it, then he dialed the number printed on the bottom. When the woman at the other end answered, he couldn't say a word to her, because he was crying. A woeful cry of loss, the forgotten telephone receiver now lying on the desk.

"Hello?" the woman on the phone said. "Are you calling the Pritikin Health and Fitness Institute? Hello?"

Rick put the phone back in the cradle.

11

JUST THE WAY Charlie had requested it in his will, the Beverly Hills Unlisted Jazz Band sat on the stage of the chapel at Forest Lawn playing all of his favorite songs. They were swinging into the first few bars of "Blue Skies" when Rick drove up. Patty and the boys waved to him, smiling. Music and merriment, the way Charlie had asked for it to be. As the parade of mourners arrived they could hear the happy music through the outdoor speakers, and after their initial surprise, they understood, which was exactly what Charlie had hoped. Rick stood with Patty and the boys. Patty's hand held his tightly as people who knew how close he and Charlie had been spoke consoling words to him as well as to the family.

A man in his early twenties walked up to Rick and took his hand as if to shake it, then put his other hand around it.

"I'm a film student," he said to Rick, "and I just

wanted to tell you I was a big fan of Mr. Fall's and continue to be a big fan of yours. I think most of the young directors out there could take a few pointers from you old veterans."

Maybe it was the words "old veterans" (Charlie would have screamed with laughter over that one), or the fact that the band was playing "Fascinatin' Rhythm" and Rick was remembering one drunken night when he and Charlie walked down the beach sharing a champagne bottle as they rewrote the lyrics to that tune, calling it "San Diego Freeway." Whatever the reason, he couldn't control a huge bubble of inappropriate laughter that went right into the astonished film student's face.

Tonight he left the office late and drove over the hill to Westwood. He'd agreed last season to come in and speak to an evening class on directing at UCLA. In fact he and Charlie had been scheduled to do this one together. The classroom was so full of milling, chatting people that Rick had to edge his way toward the front, where Charles Champlin, who was going to be moderator, sat alone at a long table, glancing at some notes.

Rick liked Chuck Champlin. The critic was always kind to his films, even the ones every other critic destroyed. Champlin's sweet round face filled with concern when he looked up and saw Rick. The group of students were chattering so loudly he had to lean in toward Rick to be heard. "You know, after Charlie's death, I thought seriously about calling you and telling you we could easily have postponed this. I know how close you two were and . . ."

Rick tried a smile. "That's very sensitive of you, but I'm okay," he said.

"I screened *Quarter to Nine* for this group last week, and of course Charlie's *Sea Front*, and everyone is so eager to . . ."

Rick turned to look at the noisy laughing crowd, and when he did, his face got hot and he felt the panic of claustrophobia.

"Are you all right?" Champlin asked, noticing. "Because, Rick, honest to God, I'd sooner send these folks home than—"

"I'm fine, Chuck," Rick said, willing the panic to slide away. Once he was seated the students took that as a signal to stop talking to one another, and all of them sat so the class could begin. Champlin made opening remarks about Rick's history. He told them about Rick's father, the late Jacob Reisman, and his uncle, William "Bobo" Reisman, and how they had directed and produced dozens of films in the thirties and forties, and how Rick had grown up on studio back lots.

The shuffling around in chairs and the pages turning in notebooks all stopped when Champlin spoke about Charlie Fall and Rick's friendship. He said he'd been at the funeral, though Rick didn't remember seeing him there, and that Rick in his eulogy had said that he and Charlie always joked that "we were so close, if I ate Chinese food, an hour later, *Charlie* was hungry."

The class laughed, a kind of uncomfortable laugh, and remembering that he'd said something that inane in a eulogy made Rick cringe. Champlin went on to say more about *Quarter to Nine* and Rick looked out at the jumble of people whose faces blurred together, the color of their clothes blending each into the next, and he wanted to stand and say, "I can't do this," but now hands were up. Dozens of hands.

"Yes?" Rick asked, pointing to one of the people, and the evening was launched, while he sat there feeling flushed and hoping his mind would stay far enough ahead of his mouth to answer the questions. Not wander to Charlie, or to his own loneliness, or the frightening inability to sleep that had been infecting him for the last few days. But after a while, the knot in his abdomen melted away when he realized the questions were going to be the same ones he'd answered a million times before, and that he didn't need to worry, since the answers, the self-deprecating jokes and the put-downs of the industry he'd used for years, still worked in the same places, and after a while he was able to breathe easily. This was safe ground. Nothing too complicated or demanding. This he could deal with.

Before long, it was over, and Champlin was summarizing, and all Rick could think of was getting out of there and going home. Everything that had happened in his life these last few days played itself out against the fears and anxieties that sat lodged inextricably in his brain. Thank God, he thought, that my age-old system runs so smoothly that it's actually running without me. Because I'm not there. I'm lost someplace in my own fear. Heart-racing, nauseating fear. That I'll die. Or worse yet, that I won't die and that soon I'll be known as that decaying director who never had a life outside of his work.

In a flutter of notebooks closing and keys being searched for, the class stood and mixed and chattered, and finally all but one of them disappeared out the door. Champlin was talking to a tall bald man about Truffaut when a pretty blond woman who had left the classroom reentered and walked toward Rick. As she got closer, he noticed how beautiful her face was. Fresh. Young. And she had a great long, lean body.

"Excuse me," she said. "I'm Erik Blake's daughter Diane."

Erik Blake was the cinematographer on two of Rick's early films. "I told my father you were speaking tonight, and he sends you his regards."

Beautiful, he thought. Hands thrust into the pockets of her jeans. A blue work shirt, the color of her eyes.

"You were wonderful tonight," she said. "Even though I know you're probably not in the best of spirits."

He shrugged, not knowing how to answer. He wanted to say, True, so maybe you could cheer me up.

"I'm sure you're probably rushing home, and if you are, I'd understand, but how would you feel about going out for a cup of coffee?" she asked. Hah!

"Love it," he said at once. Great body. Maybe she'd like to make it with a depressed fat man.

"I'm parked in the lot next door, so why don't we meet over at Ships?" she said.

"Ships." He agreed and then watched her toss the blond hair as she headed for the door. Chuck Champlin's pat on the back and thank you made Rick turn and offer perfunctory apologies for being less than fascinating, after which he found his way across the UCLA campus to the parking lot. The girl was a knockout, but Ships, he thought. Why didn't I say, "How about my place?" Or some dimly lit bar instead of a big ugly coffee shop? But when he pushed the glass door of Ships open he was glad he hadn't said that because Erik Blake's daughter was not alone. Had never intended to meet him alone.

She was sitting in a back booth next to a man, and even from the door, Rick could see that the two of them wore matching wedding bands. For a long disappointed moment he considered turning to go, but she noticed him and stood and waved to let him know where they were seated.

"This is such a thrill," the husband said, standing to greet him. "I'm Harvey Feldman."

He was tall and athletic with an open boyish face, and Rick recognized him as a member of the sea of people at the lecture. He looked young. Not as young as the girl, but maybe thirty. Decaf, Rick said to himself. One decaf and you're out of here, asshole. You thought you were in hot pursuit of pussy, and here you are about to have a postmortem on your seminar with the husband of the pussy. When are you going to learn to stop listening to your cock?

"I know your uncle Bobo," the husband said, and gestured to a passing waitress. "My grandmother Essie Baylis was a Busby Berkeley girl. She lives down the hall from him in the lodge. She calls it the geriatric coed dorm."

Rick laughed.

"Diane and I go out to the home on Friday nights. We play cards with her and frequently Bobo is our fourth for bridge. He's a good counter. And at eighty-two, that's unbelievable."

"Eighty-five his next birthday. In a few weeks," Rick corrected him.

"Isn't that funny," Diane Blake Feldman said. "I could have sworn he told *me* he was eighty-two."

"Was he making a pass at you at the time?" Rick asked her. They all laughed.

"Well, isn't it a small world?" Rick said, using what Charlie used to refer to as his warm-nice-guy voice. "Bobo is a colorful guy," he said. The Feldmans were already drinking coffee, so when the waitress arrived she looked directly at Rick.

"One decaf," he told her, "shaken not stirred."

The Feldmans laughed at that.

"You know," Harvey Feldman said, "last time we played cards with Bobo, which was about two or three weeks ago, he said that he thought you and I ought to get together because I'm in a business that's filled with so many dramatic stories. He says there's a movie in nearly every one of my cases."

Great, Rick thought. My uncle Bobo is agenting for me, and I'm hoisted with my own prick. This *shmeckel* used his wife for bait and now he's going to try and sell me stories. Well sorry, pal. One decaf and out. Even if we're at the best part of the story when I'm finished. And even if you are nice enough to play cards with my uncle.

"And what is it you do that's fodder for such great stories?" Rick asked, hoping the kid would give him a nice three-or four-word answer.

"I specialize in open adoptions in which the birth parents and the adopting parents of a child get to meet and know one another."

"Now why would they want to do that?" Rick asked politely, hoping the answer wasn't complicated, but Harvey didn't get to answer.

"Ricky?" a voice asked, and Rick looked up. There were two girls. Both hot little numbers, both vaguely familiar, but no names came to mind.

"Blair Phillips and Sandy Kaye," one of them offered. Nothing. No bells. Christ Almighty. He didn't have a clue who they were.

"Of course, Blair," Rick said, grinning at one of them, hoping she was the one who was Blair. "Nice to see you. How's everything?"

"Great," she said. "We haven't seen you since the night we were all on Henry's boat," the other girl said. Bimbos. They were bimbos he'd partied with on someone's boat. Who was Henry?

"Well, thanks for stopping by, girls," he said.

"Yeah, a real pleasure to see you too, hon," one of them said, and they twitched off across the room to a table. The waitress put the decaf in front of Rick. He put cream in it from the little aluminum pitcher, then opened a Sweet 'N Low package and poured the powdery white sweetener into the cup and stirred. He felt embarrassed to look at the Feldmans after what had just happened with those girls, and not sure why. That kind of thing happened to him a lot. Maybe it felt so awkward now because these people knew Bobo.

"The reason people want to do that," Diane answered for her husband, continuing the conversation, "is because for every healthy baby, there are forty couples in Los Angeles who want to adopt it, and six or seven single people. So a birth mother immediately has forty-seven choices. By creating a situation that allows a young girl who gets pregnant and doesn't want to have an abortion to choose the parent or parents she thinks are best for that baby, you give people who the state wouldn't consider eligible an opportunity to be chosen. Older couples, gay couples, single people. In that way, it becomes a competition for people to convince the mother that choosing them is in the best interests of the baby."

"Stories," Harvey Feldman said to Rick. "I've got enough stories for *ten* movies. Because the adopting parents can and have been anyone and everyone. Not just the people who have the qualifications per the state agencies."

The hustle. The kid was putting the major hustle on him pretty good. And why not? Wasn't that, after all, what life was all about? Had things been otherwise, he himself would have been hustling the tall blond Diane into his bed. But the "my life is a movie" rap. That was the one he had to sidestep regularly. Everyone in the world who thought his or her life was screenworthy, which meant everyone, would corner him at some point and try to sell it to him.

Well, not tonight, kids, he thought. And then he slid out of the booth, quickly stood, and to avoid the possibility of their thinking they might convince him to stay for even another minute, announced, "I'm really sorry to do this, but I'm not much for socializing these days and . . ."

"We understand," Harvey Feldman said, and both he and his beautiful blond wife stood.

"Thanks for joining us" is what Rick thought he heard them say, when without even thanking them for inviting him to Ships, buying him a decaf, or offering to sell him what were surely profound stories about something he had already forgotten, he was in Ships' parking lot hurrying to his car.

12

ONE OF THE FEATURES that had been pointed out to Rick as a high-line perk was the wet bar in his office that the studio stocked with liquor and wine and soft drinks. No one who came there to meet with him during the workday ever asked for alcohol. So the liquor bottles which sat on the Lucite shelves were the same ones that had been delivered on the first day he moved in.

Today, as Andrea was washing the coffee cups in the sink, she noticed that the bottle of scotch was half empty. Rick had been drinking during the day. Poor baby, she thought. She had watched him these last few weeks walk out in the middle of a meeting, step into an empty office, close the door behind him, and, she was sure, stand in the unlit room crying. Crying it out, because he was still so filled with the pain of losing Charlie that the slightest reminder could set him off. And finally, once he'd composed himself, he would pass her desk again and with a last sniffle go back into his office and continue the meeting.

Tonight he was at a late story conference upstairs with Nat Ross and some writers, talking about a new project he wanted to develop. He told Andrea at five-forty-five, when he left, that if he wasn't back by seven, she could go home. It was nearly seven, and when she finished washing all the coffee cups, she wiped off the Formica counter and placed a square of paper towel on it. Then she turned each cup upside down on the towel to drip, dried her hands on her jeans, turned out the light in Rick's office, and left.

By the time Rick stopped back to get his jacket it was nine-thirty and a blue-black Los Angeles night had fallen, but he didn't bother to turn the light on in his office. He saw in the spilled light from the fluorescent ceiling bulbs in the reception area that his jacket was hanging on the back of his desk chair. When he picked the jacket up, his keys fell jangling from the pocket to the floor. As he stooped to pick them up, he realized there was someone else in the room. Sitting cross-legged on the sofa watching him.

"Don't get scared. It's me."

Kate Sullivan. Jesus Christ.

"I've got to play that part," she said. He saw the orange glow of the cigarette she was smoking. "You realize, of course, that I could just ask the studio to take that project away from you and give it to me and they would," she said.

"Then why don't you?" he asked. His tongue felt thick. Maybe he should pour himself a scotch. That would probably make this bizarre intrusion a little easier to handle.

"Because now that Charlie Fall is dead, you're the only person who can direct me in it."

He walked to the bar and poured some scotch into a glass. Without bothering to add any ice, he drank most of it.

"I was with Charlie a lot before he died," she said quietly. "He was helping me organize the fund-raisers for the battered-wives' shelters."

Rick emitted an involuntary grunt. Charlie. In the middle of the biggest project of his career he took time out to work for battered women. The guy was a fuckin' saint.

"After the meetings we would talk, sometimes for hours," Kate said. "He told me he was certain that no matter how hard he worked he'd never be able to zero in on the essence of behavior the way you did. It was why his last three pictures were on such a grand scale. Burton Holmes travelogues, he called them. India, Russia. Pieces where the characters were incidental to the grandeur."

The scotch fired Rick's mouth and throat, and he drained his glass and poured another. She was quite right. Her own box-office success was far superior to his and she could easily commandeer his project with just a nod.

"He talked about your pictures, in astonishing detail. The way Pacino put his fork down in one of them, or the look on Jack Nicholson's face in another, and the hysterical contagious laughter of a bad actress who looks not just good but brilliant after you've improvised with her and shot the scene while she was still in the palm of your hand."

In the half darkness he could see she was wearing jeans and knee-high boots and a turtleneck sweater, and he remembered reading the article in *Vanity Fair* about her a few months ago, and how while he did he'd thought that the picture that accompanied it must have been touched up. No woman her age could possibly look that young. But she did. And as if to prove it, she stood now and walked over to Rick's desk and switched on the desk lamp. After another sip, the second glass of scotch would be empty.

"So I screened them. Every last one. And he was right. Everything Charlie said about your work was right."

Rick felt weak and tired. "Kate, I'm glad to hear that Charlie loved me. But I already knew that. It's why losing him has made me feel destitute for the last many weeks. However, your coming here to tell me that isn't going to change my mind about you."

She was perched on his desk now, and as he poured himself another scotch, just a taste this time, he realized that Kate Sullivan was going to try to seduce him. She was prepared to flatter him, fuck him, whatever it took to get not just the part she wanted, because that would be easy, but him directing her in it as well. He finished the third scotch and poured himself just half a glass this time, which he finished in two gulps, then he sat on the sofa, holding the empty scotch bottle in one hand and the empty glass in the other. The dull buzz in his head was the only sound he heard for a long time.

"It's going to be tough for you without Charlie, isn't it?" she asked him. Her tone was familiar. It was the same one his mother had used when he was a little boy trying to be strong and she would ask, "What is it, my baby?" And all of his resolve to be a big boy would fall away, which was what happened now.

The tears rushed into his eyes, and he put the glass and the bottle down so he could hide his face with both hands, and then he really lost it, crying uncontrollably. Not just about Charlie, but about his own life, his whole meaningless, unrelated, narcissistic, valueless, lonely fucking life. Maybe it was because he feared that it was Charlie, a man whose life was so filled with meaning, so completely unselfish, who should have lived, and that *he* was the one who should have died. He was trying to contain his sadness and cope with a quantity of scotch he was unequipped to consume when he felt Kate Sullivan's arms around him. Smelled her perfume, felt her lips on his hands, then on his wet face, and her hands on his body.

"It's okay," Kate was saying, and her coolness felt welcome against the heat the scotch provoked inside him. Or maybe it wasn't the scotch that was making him blurry and confused and aching with feeling but her nearness and her scent of perfume and shampoo and cigarettes, and the undeniable truth, which was how much he wanted to fuck her. To pull that sweater over her head and feel her tits against his chest and then to fuck her eyes out.

Christ. A little voice in the back of his mind told him as she began unzipping him, undressing him, that this was worse than stupid. Not the way he wanted to behave with her. But she was taking her own clothes off now, and, God, he wanted her. Kate Sullivan, her lips and tongue on his stomach, moving down to put her wet mouth around his cock. And now when he looked down to see her there going at him, sucking him, licking him, he felt as numb and detached and alienated as if he were watching her through a camera. For an endless floating time she worked him, her hands caressing his thighs, her lips and tongue exploring his groin. And then she was on top of him, sliding him into her. Spongy and warm and slippery and fitting tightly around him. Moving again and again, riding him, taking him.

Kate Sullivan. Every young boy's masturbation fantasy. He was having her. No, you asshole, he thought. She's having you. Even in that high other world he entered just before his orgasm, the place in which there was never any presence of mind, this time he maintained enough consciousness to hate himself. For being so desperate to be held, to be warmed, so needy to hear someone, anyone, whispering reassurances that he would seek solace inside the nearest cunt, even though it belonged to the enemy.

"Oh, yes, yes." Her hands were in his hair now, nails digging into his scalp, and he could feel her strong thighs tense on either side of his hips as she forced her knees into the sofa to give her the leverage she needed to move her pelvis into him and away, and again and again, and now he would let go. God, he was an asshole. Now he would, oh God, oh God, let go. The rush went blasting through him, escaped, and as he lay there, eyes closed, before even the first tremor of aftershock, he felt her lift herself from the top of him abruptly.

By the time he moved up onto his elbows to look at her, not knowing what he would say, feeling weak and devastated, she had pulled on her clothes and was out of his office. A minute later he heard the door to the reception area close. He lay still for a moment, then pulled one of the loose pillows from the back of the sofa, covered his wet matted groin with it, and lay there.

What did it mean? Did she think it would be so good that afterward he wouldn't be able to live without her and he'd give her the part? Was she trying to say she could behave like a man and fuck without feeling? She had used him the way he had used so many women in his life, and this was probably how all of them had felt when he'd slipped silently out their doors. After a few minutes he was sleeping.

The clanging of the cleaning crew's buckets awakened him, and he managed to leap to his feet and throw his clothes on, and in the time it took them to get from the door of the reception area and into his office, he used his handkerchief to clean the sticky wetness from the sofa.

"Evening," he said, nodding to them and moving out into the darkened hallway, wondering for a split second if in the darkness he'd been able to get the sofa clean. The clock on the dashboard of his Mercedes said midnight. Mid-fuckin'-night. And he had an early meeting in the morning. Kate Sullivan. A wave of self-loathing rushed through him, and he could hardly wait until he got home to turn on the hot shower and scrub himself clean of her.

He had today's mail and the two scripts he was planning to read and he pushed the door to his house open, and the first thing he saw when he did was the chicken-in-a-pot, which had been served up on his good dishes, the two elaborate table settings, and next to each plate, a smaller plate containing a wilted salad. And in a bucket of what had once been ice but which was now water, there was a bottle of champagne.

He heard the snoring coming from the living room. Oh, Christ, he had forgotten all about Bobo. A week from Tuesday, his loving, gracious uncle had told him. Write the date into your book. And he had forgotten. My eighty-fifth birthday. I'll take a taxi to your house and when you get home from work we'll celebrate. I'll do all the cooking. And he had. Oh, shit. Bobo had arrived and made dinner, expected Rick, waited for him, and finally he had fallen asleep, and . . . Bobo looked angelic sleeping there.

On Bobo's birthday instead of rushing home and celebrating, as promised, he had been in a meeting and then getting drunk and fucking Kate Sullivan. The thought sickened him. Shit. He took a crocheted lap robe some girl, he couldn't remember who, had made him a few years ago that was hanging on the back of one of his living room chairs, covered Bobo, and headed for his bedroom.

"Ricky, honey, are you okay?" he heard Bobo's sleepy voice ask.

He turned. Bobo got slowly to his feet. "I was worried sick when you didn't show up."

"I'm sorry," Rick said, moving to him for an embrace. "I'm so sorry. I just forgot." Bobo patted him gently on the back.

"You look like hell," he said, with deep concern in his voice. "Go get some sleep. Before you go to the office, we can have breakfast together."

"Thanks, Uncle B.," Rick said and waited until Bobo was in the guest bedroom before he turned and walked toward the bathroom to shower. His clothes smelled of her, his body still retained the memory of her flesh against it. He stood rinsing the soap off until he had used all of the hot water, then fell naked into bed and was asleep in minutes. Until his dreams were interrupted by the loud blast of the doorbell.

He had to be imagining it, he thought, must have dreamed the doorbell rang, but then he sat up and listened and there were definitely voices out there. By the time he got a robe on and had opened his bedroom door, the voices were louder and a woman was laughing. When he got out to the living room, the picture he saw looked like something from a bad dream.

Bobo, in a pair of wrinkled cotton pajamas, had opened the door for, and was trying to play polite and gracious host to, Animal, a cocaine dealer with whom Rick had done some commerce in the past, and Gloria, a stringy-haired, hollow-eyed, too-skinny blonde who had spent the night in Rick's bed once. Maybe twice.

"Aaaah, Ricky," Gloria said, throwing spindly arms around his neck and kissing him on each cheek. "Can you believe it? Joseph and I met at a party and there we were, trying to figure out what he and I had in common, and then we realized it was that we both know and love *you*. So we decided then and there to come over and tell you that, before the moment had passed. Aren't you glad? You don't look very glad."

"Who's Joseph?" Rick asked her, uncomfortably

aware that Bobo was watching the whole scene. Gloria pointed to Animal, who for the moment looked almost as if he was blushing as he said, "That's my real name."

"Well, that's very nice, you two," Rick said. Lunatics like these could have guns with them, take offense if you didn't treat them gently. Especially because they were both as high as kites on something. "But I've got an early day tomorrow so I'm afraid I'll have to ask both of you to leave."

"Want *me* to stay?" Gloria asked. "I always got you to sleep real easily."

Rick felt shaky. Embarrassed. When Bobo had come to visit in the past, Rick had made it his business to produce the most socially acceptable friends he had to meet his uncle. These two were from the bottom of the barrel.

"He wants us to go, Glory," Animal said, looking now from Rick to Bobo and then back again. Rick's eyes couldn't meet Bobo's. Then, as if it were a peace offering, Animal extracted a vial from his inside coat pocket. "Want me to toot you up?" he asked Rick.

"No," Rick said.

"Not this time, huh?" Animal said, grinning a grin that showed his bad teeth. "How 'bout you, man?" he asked Bobo.

Bobo didn't say a word. His expression made the already nervous Animal look down at his feet and say, "Yeah, well, like maybe you'll gimme a call if you change your mind. C'mon there, Glory."

The girl looked hurt but she tried to make the best of a bad situation by patting Rick on the cheek and saying, "Call me, huh?" Then they were out the door. It was already a gray dawn outside and Rick's head was pounding. He looked at Bobo, who was looking long at him.

"Boychik," Bobo said, after their eyes had searched each other's for a long sad moment. "Tell me some-

thing. Isn't it time for you to take stock of what you're doing to yourself? To make a decision to be a man instead of a lowlife."

Those words, coming from the gentle Bobo, who could never deliberately hurt another human being, stung him. And they were mild compared to what he wanted to call himself.

"You're going on fifty, for Christ's sake," Bobo said, as if Rick didn't know that. "What in the hell are you going to do? Do you wanna die being known as a drug-taking womanizer who made a couple of movies? Love somebody, for God's sake, make a life for yourself, stop thinking with your dick before you're an old sick man and an old sick joke, because that's where you're heading. Charlie Fall is dead, but at least his charitable work lives on and his name lives on in his children and his memory lives on with Patty. You'll die and won't even leave anyone who will come and make sure your headstone didn't topple over with the last earthquake. Ricky, you've been my relative for nearly fifty years, and from way back, even before you got so heavy, when you looked good and you were dating Farrah Fawcett or screwing Jackie Bisset, I never stopped feeling sorry for you."

Bobo, who had taken a taxi all the way from Calabassas, then cooked an uneaten dinner, and been awakened twice in the same night, had dark circles under his eyes. The two men stood silently in the cold living room, the smell of the chicken that neither they nor the sleeping maid had cleaned up still in the air. "What are you going to do? And I mean right away, because I can't stand it."

Many answers tumbled around in Rick's mind, and the one that came out surprised him almost as much as it did Bobo.

"I'm going to adopt a baby," he said.

13

WHEN BARBARA SPOTTED A RARE DAY with a few open hours coming up on her calendar, she decided to get on the phone and schedule some personal appointments. Her psychiatrist, her hairdresser, and oh yes . . . thc postcard from Howie Kramer's office was beckoning. At least this time she'd gone as far as calling Marcy Frank and asking for the information on the woman gynecologist. But where did she put that number? The biggest problem with having three desks in three different locations was that the damn number could be anywhere. She shuffled through some papers, and was delighted to come upon the phone number of Dr. Gwen Phillips she'd scribbled down last week.

"My name is Barbara Singer. I was referred by Marcy Frank," she said. "I need to come in for a routine checkup."

"The doctor's out of town for three weeks," the

voice on the phone told her. "And when she gets back she's very backed up, but I can schedule you in, let's see . . . the earliest I have would be . . . in six weeks."

"Thanks anyway," Barbara said, hanging up, congratulating herself for at least making the effort, and relieved not to have to face the unfamiliar. So much for new doctors, she mused and laughed to herself when she thought about that character Billy Crystal used to play on "Saturday Night Live" who always said, "Remember, *looking* good is more important than feeling good," so she dialed her hairdresser.

"Well, Mrs. S., after December you won't have me to kick around anymore, so you'd better start thinking about which other operator you're gonna switch over to who can do your color."

Barbara looked up from the notes she'd been reading to pass the minutes until the timer rang to signal that the hair color had penetrated and she could get back to the office. Now she caught a glimpse of herself in the beauty-shop mirror, her face ringed with white cotton, her hair matted into bizarre bunches and coated with the gooey shoe-polish dye Delia applied to cover the ever encroaching gray. The pretty, skinny-as-an-arrow Delia was running a fat plastic comb through Barbara's ends, making sure the awful stuff covered every single surface of her hair.

"I'm going to get pregnant," Delia told her, "and all these chemicals aren't good for anybody who's pregnant, so by the end of this year, I'm quitting for a while."

"I'm glad for you, Delia, but sad for me. Maybe when you leave I'll just be au naturel for a while, and let my hair go gray."

"Oh my God, you're joking! That would be a disaster," Delia said, emitting an outraged laugh. Barbara wasn't joking. It was an idea she'd been considering for a while, but after that reaction she decided to reconsider. When her hair was colored and blown out she hurried to her car, thinking that after that affront from Delia, it was a good thing she was on her way to check in with her own therapist.

Morgan was more like a friendly old uncle to her after all these years and when she first settled into the peeling old leather chair, on which she had been responsible for some of the peeling, she felt relieved to be able to blurt out what was on her mind.

"I'm on overwhelm, Morgs," she told him. It had been nearly a year since she'd visited the old family friend who'd been her therapist off and on since the sixties. Today he peered at her over his smudged half-glasses, and his lived-in face registered genuine concern. "My kids aren't kids anymore. Heidi sometimes goes weeks without calling, and Jeff will be off to college in the fall to heaven knows where.

"I spend five half-days in the clinic with individual families and five at my private office with the same. I lead parenting groups all week and two on Saturdays for my working parents who can only come in on the weekends. And now I'm all fired up about a new group. It's for families whose babies are the result of the new technologies and arrangements, like open adoption, or insemination. I want to create a context, a language, a way for these children to talk about things. But I've got to tell you, I'm worried about it. What if it's a mistake and families like these want to be in the mainstream and not treated separately? What if I can't think of answers for them to give these children? I mean how can a couple tell the child of a gay father what the ugly names mean? What will those two little girls who have been born via a sperm donor think about men, and how will they relate to them when *they're* women?

"Last night I had a dream that I was sitting in my office and this creature walked in. It was somewhere between a stegosaurus and Dumbo. I mean, it was green and spiked but it had cute baby blue eyes and a trunk, and it said, 'I'm here to inquire about the new group!' " The thought of what a dream like that might mean sent her into a peal of laughter she knew by the look on Morgan's face was a little too hysterical. Then she stopped laughing and thought about what was going on in her life.

"I joined some fancy health club last month, paid the fee, and walked out after ten minutes because I couldn't handle the stress of destressing. I think after all is said and done, I'm a fraud. I keep saying I'm going to slowly cut back and take time to do nothing, but instead I keep piling it on myself. I just recited my life's schedule to you, Morgan, now you tell me, does that sound like the agenda of a woman who's looking for peace?"

Morgan took off the Benjamin Franklin glasses and wiped them with a handkerchief he pulled out of his pocket. "What does your mother think about the idea for the new group?"

"Are you kidding? It's so up her alley, I sometimes wonder if the real reason I'm organizing it is to please her. She thinks it's the first really important thing I've done in years."

Morgan raised his eyebrows and made a note. The walnut desk clock was ticking and she realized she'd been complaining for so long she was already halfway through the session. "Anyway, to hell with Gracie, let's get back to me. Am I taking on something so huge that I'll kick myself? The more I read about these questions the more complicated it all sounds, and I don't want to lead these people to think I have answers for them when I don't. I'll just be feeling my way *with* them. I know how to help families with developmental problems, but this feels so much bigger than that."

"I think if you make it clear . . . that you're there to find out the answers with them, then you're not leading anyone astray."

Barbara looked across the desk at Morgan's face and thought of all the times she'd left his office certain that his sage words of the preceding hour had just changed her life. Today the whole idea of spilling out her anxieties to him felt foolish, self-indulgent, and absurd.

"Do you know who Lucy Van Pelt is?" she asked him.

"No."

"Somehow I just flashed on her. She's a character from the cartoon 'Peanuts,' a little girl who runs a psychiatry booth as if it was a lemonade stand. She dispenses advice for five cents. And I guess all of a sudden psychiatry and psychology seem very silly to me. Like a cartoon."

"Now *that* sounds just like what your mother always says."

"Please. It's bad enough when I hear myself sounding like Gracie, but when *you* tell me I do, it only reminds me it was probably gross lack of judgment on my part to have a psychiatrist who knows her."

"Or a brilliant choice," he said. "Think of all the time and money you've saved over the years not having to tell me the things I already know about her."

"Good point," she said, but only because she was fond of Morgan and sorry if she'd hurt his feelings, which was probably why she didn't do what she wanted to now, which was to stand, say "I don't want to be here anymore," and leave, the way she had the health club.

"So you think Gracie thinks this group is destined to be your finest work?"

"Absolutely."

Morgan *tsk*ed at that. A significant *tsk*, and Barbara wanted to ask him what it meant, only somehow they went off on another tangent before she could. Heidi and her impossible boyfriend, Jeff's impending departure for school. And it was all such a jumble of so many thoughts, that by the time she pulled up at the drive-through at Carl's Junior to get a very late lunch, she had forgotten everything they'd decided she should do to cope. It had been a hundred-and-twenty-five-dollar visit down the tubes.

"Charbroiled chicken and a diet Coke," she said to an intercom.

"Anything else?"

"That's it."

"Three dollars and ninety-six cents," said a disembodied voice.

"Thank you."

"Have a nice day."

"Likewise," she said, thinking she had no idea whether she'd just spoken to a woman or a man. Faceless communication, like her answering machine, and her fax machine, and donor insemination. If she ever pulled that group together it would be demanding on her skills and a big responsibility, but there wouldn't be a dull moment.

"Aaggh."

"Sorry," Howie Kramer muttered. She had caved and called him. She couldn't wait six weeks to be examined, and when his receptionist said, "Name your time, Mrs. Singer," Barbara wondered how she would ever be able to give up a luxury like that. So now the light, the too-bright light, was bouncing from his head again, right into her eyes, and he was rattling on about one of his famous patients.

Barbara wasn't listening. She was worrying about Scottie Levine and how when she'd asked Ron Levine to come in alone so they could talk, he said on the phone, "That little kid is a mess. Don't you think I see it? Who wouldn't be, living with that shrew? And it breaks my heart because you know my son is my top priority."

"When can you come in?" Barbara asked him.

Silence. Then he said, "Let me look at my calendar." Silence. "You know what? I'm going to need to get back to you." Poor little Scottie. How could she help him?

"In a few years that kid will be in intensive therapy," Howie Kramer was saying as he scraped her inside with no grace at all. Barbara, startled at what seemed to be a mind-reading comment, wondered how he knew what she'd been thinking.

"What kid?" she asked as Howie removed the metal instrument from inside her. He was in the middle of rattling on with some story that she could tell by the look on his face he considered quite juicy. And though she hadn't been listening, now when she tuned in, it seemed it was, as always, about one of his famous patients. This time it was a woman who had a fear of getting pregnant.

"The baby's due next month. I mean she's one of those people who should just forget about motherhood. To begin with she didn't want to mess up her great body, which is why she figured out a way that she didn't have to. You know her. You've seen her on "Dallas," or maybe it was "Knots Landing." Anyway, she had her husband inseminate her sister. So now the baby's mother is her aunt and the baby's aunt is her mother. Kind of like that old song, 'I'm My Own Grandpa.' Remember that one?" Now Howie was inserting rubber-gloved fingers into Barbara, pressing down on her abdomen and at the same time laughing a red-faced wet-eyed laugh at his own joke.

"I'll tell you something, I could write a book, because I've seen it all," he said. Gracie was right, Barbara thought. In this town alone there were probably thousands of people having their babies in unusual ways.

"Well, everything seems okay," he said. He had finished the exam and was removing the gloves. "I'll call you if there's anything wrong with the lab report." Then he looked at her absently. "Did I do a breast check?" Of course going from examining room to examining room, body to body, he probably forgot whose what he had checked, and she was tempted to lie and say yes, but then she'd have to go home afraid there might have been something which had gone undiscovered because of her lie.

"No," she confessed and revealed her breasts, putting her arms behind her head so he could roll his hands around on them to examine her, a process that always made her nervous and one which she was certain required concentration, but not for Howard Kramer, who just continued to talk through it all.

"My wife knows her very well. They go to the same hairdresser. Sandy says she's had every kind of plastic surgery possible. There's a guy over in Santa Monica who specializes in breast augmentation, and he's the one who did her breasts and they are extraordinary. One night we ran into her at Jimmy's and she was wearing—"

"Howie!" Barbara said sharply. "What about mine?"

"Your what?"

"My breasts. Anything unusual?"

"No. They're fine. When was your last mammogram?" he asked, reaching for her chart.

"Nine months ago," she said, making as ladylike a slide from the table as she could, considering her top was wrapped in a paper gown, her bottom was sporting what felt like a paper tablecloth, and she was filled with K-Y Jelly.

"You're in great shape," Howie said. "You check out like a young woman."

"Thanks," Barbara said, as she disappeared behind the curtain of the tiny dressing area and winked a conspiratorial wink at her reflection in the small mirror on the wall, congratulating herself on the fast escape. Then she heard Howie say, "You know, I'm looking at your chart here, and I'm thinking that next time you come in, we should discuss a tubal ligation."

"Great," she replied. "Next time I come in, we'll discuss it in depth."

"Give my best to Stan," Howie said as he exited the examining room and closed the door.

"Only there ain't gonna be any next time," Barbara promised herself out loud.

"Oh here, Mrs. Singer," thc receptionist said as Barbara signed the MasterCard charge slip to pay the bill. "Before you go, if you address this card to yourself we'll mail it to you when it's time for your next checkup."

"Thanks very much," Barbara said, taking the card, finding a pen on the counter, and starting absently to fill it out. The doctor's phone rang and the receptionist answered it and spoke animatedly to the person on the other end of the line. Barbara took a moment to reconsider, put the pen back on the counter, slipped the blank card into her purse, waved a thank you to the distracted receptionist, and left Howie Kramer's office. Alone on the elevator she tore the card up, and as she exited into the parking lot, she threw it into the first trash can she saw.

The hospital corridor was bustling and she was hurrying to get to her office to get her phone calls out of the way before the staff meeting. She waved a hello to Louise Feiffer, who put up a hand to stop her.

"A woman left this in my office. I think she was interested in the new group. She said she saw the ad."

Barbara opened the envelope. In it was a piece of personalized stationery with the name Elaine De Nardo at the top.

> My name is Lainie De Nardo. I saw the ad about your group. I need to talk to you first though, alone if it's okay. If so, please call me, but don't say why you're calling unless you reach me personally. I'd appreciate your confidentiality. Thank you.

Barbara sat at her desk and called Lainie De Nardo, and as she listened to as much of her story as the woman could tell her on the phone, she knew that this was someone who needed the new group in a desperate way.

14

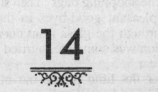

LAINIE COULDN'T BELIEVE that one of the customers actually came all the way from La Jolla every few weeks in a chauffeur-driven limo. And while the woman tried on dozens of outfits, the tall, black, uniformed driver leaned against the car reading a newspaper, where everyone in the store could see him through the big front window. After the woman was dressed again in her own clothes, fishing around in her wallet for her American Express card, she always said the same thing to Lainie: "I'll bet with what I spend here, I could put every one of your kids through college."

Lainie placed the woman's gold credit card on the imprint machine, slid the bar across and back over the card and the receipt, then wrote the word *merchandise* on the slip. Next to it she wrote the amount the woman had spent that day, usually in the neighborhood of six or seven thousand dollars. "Mitch and I don't have any kids," Lainie reminded her.

"Oh, what a terrible shame," the woman invariably said, looking at Lainie with sad eyes as though she'd never heard that information before. Lainie covered the woman's hanging merchandise with white garment bags splashed with the Panache logo, placed the sweaters and accessories in tissue paper, which she laid carefully into white Panache shopping bags. Then she and the woman exchanged pleasant good-byes as the chauffeur, who could see through the glass front door of the store that the transaction was complete, hurried to carry the packages to the car.

Long after the limo pulled out of the parking lot, Lainie would find herself still staring out the front window, remembering the look in that woman's eyes when she said how sorry she felt for Lainie and Mitch. She had seen that same look in the eyes of more people than she could count. "It's the way people probably look at lepers," she'd once said laughing to Mitch. But soon a customer would interrupt her thoughts to ask if Lainie could order the Donna Karan suit in pink, or if she had the white open-toed Bruno Magli shoe in a six, and she'd stop thinking about the leper look until the next time someone gave it to her.

Business was extraordinary. Women were driving to Encino from Santa Monica, Malibu, Brentwood, and Beverly Hills to shop at Panache. Studio designers were making appointments to come in and buy wardrobe for television shows. Sometimes they would bring well-known actresses along, whose glittering presence caused a big stir among the other customers.

Of course there were plenty of things going wrong all the time too. Little fires to put out, Mitch called them. A few weeks ago he'd caught one of the salesgirls stealing a large purse full of sweaters and had to fire her. And the other day a gorgeous transvestite came in, wearing a Valentino dress, and when the salesgirl who was helping him stepped into the dressing room and realized he was a man, she ran screaming out of the store. The salesgirl called from home later that day to say she'd never deal with anyone like that again, and Mitch said, "We'll miss you," because the transvestite had spent eight thousand dollars buying up a number of their size twelves.

Some customers tried to return clothes after they'd worn them. Usually it was a woman who could afford anything she wanted who had the gall to bring back a dress still reeking with the odor of her perfume, her deodorant, even her cigarettes. She would insist that she was bringing the dress back for a full refund because there was something wrong with it. When Mitch told her firmly, "Sorry, we can't take this back, you've obviously worn it out, and we don't take evening clothes back," the customer would go mad.

"Are you calling me a liar?" one dark-haired, very tan woman from Beverly Hills asked, her body tense with rage. Mitch knew she was the wife of a well-known movie producer. Behind her, through the large front window of the store, he could see her red Rolls-Royce with her personalized license plate MINDY.

He looked at her with the most benign look he could summon, no anger, no self-righteousness, no judgments, while she clenched her fists and contorted her face and said to him loud enough for everyone in the store to hear, "The goddamned dress is too small on me, and I only took it because your pushy salesgirl forced it on me, and if you don't give me every cent of my money right now, I'll tell every friend I have how badly you're treating me and I swear to you not one of them will ever set foot in this place!"

Lainie usually stood on the other side of the store by

the dressing room doors while one of those incidents took place, wanting to hide inside one of the rooms until the customer left. It made her sick to think that what the woman was saying might be true, that the anger of this one customer might have the power to destroy their business, and she was awed by Mitch's ability to not react.

At home they laughed about how he was the emotional Italian to Lainie's level-headed cool WASP, but in the store it was the opposite. She would get flustered, be churning inside while, for the sake of the business, Mitch always maintained his composure. Even when Mindy took the dress in question from the counter, balled up the sequined garment, which retailed at four thousand dollars, and with her eyes never leaving Mitch's, threw the dress onto the floor, then stomped out of the building, climbed into her Rolls, and drove away.

When she was gone, Mitch walked to the dress, picked it up, and called out to one of his salesgirls, "Put this in a box and send it to her house. She paid for it, she wore it, it's hers." And when Mindy came into the store a few weeks later, looking for something to wear to her friend's daughter's wedding, all of them—Mitch, Lainie, the salesgirls who had witnessed the scene, and Mindy herself—acted as if nothing had happened.

Lainie was five nine, with a long willowy body, ash blond hair, and pale blue eyes. She looked good in everything she wore, so she always wore the clothes they had in stock at Panache. When the customers saw her dressed in an outfit, Mitch knew they would want to try that outfit on themselves, and hopefully buy it. Sometimes, though, the plan backfired, because the customer would stand next to Lainie, who looked like an angel in a certain cropped jacket or short skirt in which the customer looked ridiculous. The result was sometimes a teary-eyed customer storming out frustrated and empty-handed.

But the new store had lighting and mirrors that could make nearly everyone look good. Mitch had spared no expense making sure of that. He had hired a film lighting director famous for working with beautiful demanding female stars, and insisted the designer pay attention to every corner of the eight-thousand-square-foot space. Even in the ladies' room, the customers' cheeks looked pinker than they were, and when they modeled for themselves in front of the full-length three-way mirrors, their bodies looked longer and slimmer.

In the first store there had been so little hanging space that Mitch kept some of the stock on a rack in his van, which was parked downstairs behind the building. When a customer asked, "Do you have this in a size ten?" he would have to excuse himself and run out the back door and down to the parking lot, sometimes in the rain, to check the merchandise. In the new store, there was plenty of hanging space for miles and miles of stock, a room for the back stock of shoes in all sizes, a steaming and pressing room, an alterations room, and an office for Mitch.

The first store was upstairs from a greasy-spoon restaurant on Ventura Boulevard in Woodland Hills and across the street from Valley BMW, where Lainie Dunn was working part-time as a cashier. The rest of the time she went to school studying English literature at Cal State, Northridge. Mitch and Lainie met at the restaurant downstairs when Lainie stopped in there for a quick lunch on her break. He spotted her beautiful face, put his cheeseburger and Coke on the little table across from her tuna-salad sandwich, sat down across from her, and said, "Now don't say I never take you to any fancy places."

He knew he was good-looking and funny. Women

always fell for him and he had confidence that this girl would like him too. He could see by the poor quality of her clothes that she didn't have money, but the way she tied the little scarf just so around her neck and turned up the collar of the jacket and pushed up the sleeves showed style. And it didn't hurt that she was break-your-heart pretty. Lainie smiled at the pickup line then glanced at his left hand to see if he was wearing a ring.

At Valley BMW she was the only female employee. Since her first day of work, every male in the place had come on to her. The fact that every one of them was married didn't seem to mar their persistence. Gino from the parts department, a guy with a wife and four kids, was so hot on Lainie's trail that once he actually ripped open the bathroom door while she was inside, probably hoping to catch her with her skirt up, which he did.

But he was stunned and turned off when he saw that her skirt was up because she was injecting her thigh with the insulin she had to have for her diabetes. Later Lainie laughed when she told her mother about the expression she'd seen on Gino's face. But the positive result was that seeing her with the needle stuck in her thigh had unnerved him and he'd stopped bothering her.

"Single," Mitch said that day, seeing her eyes looking at his hand. "And you?" Lainie nodded. Her face flushed when she looked at his dark long-lashed eyes, and that thick black hair nearly to his shoulders, and thought, Oh my God, is *he* gorgeous! And pretty soon she was telling him what she later admitted was "the fancy version" of her life.

That she was working at the BMW place because she liked the pretty cars and needed to pick up a few dollars because she was an English major in college. That her mother, with whom she lived, worked at Bradford, Freeman, a well-known law firm in Beverly Hills. She didn't say that she only took two courses every year in the English department because it was all the time she could afford to take away from work, or that her mother was the receptionist at the law firm.

Mitch nodded and heard very little of what she said because her face was so pretty he couldn't wait until she stood up so he could take a look at her body. But she still had most of her sandwich left, which she nibbled at between sentences, and didn't seem to be in a hurry.

Mitch told her that his father had just died and left some money to him and to each of his sisters. He'd been working as an accountant but was miserable doing that, so he decided to start a ladies' clothing store upstairs from where they were sitting. He also mentioned that he had a hard time keeping sales help because he was such a colossal pain in the ass to work for. But he said that part grinning broadly so she'd know he was kidding.

When she got up to leave, he offered to pay for her sandwich, which was already paid for, and when she told him so he said, "I owe you one." As he watched her walk away, he noted that the body was even hotter-looking than the face. After Lainie got back to Valley BMW and sat down at her desk, the phone rang and it was Mitch calling to say, "I think you should come and work for me, and one of these days I'll have you driving one of those fancy cars instead of drooling over them. Why don't you tell the boss you quit, and walk across the street?"

Lainie laughed, said, "Don't be silly," and hung up the phone. But after thinking about it for a minute, she stood, took her purse out of the top drawer of the desk where she always kept it, quit her job, and walked across the street.

Mitch was right about her sense of style, and it paid off. The way she pointed out to a customer that a particular pair of earrings brought out the color of her eyes, or that buying two different shirts to wear under a jacket offered more opportunities to get use out of the jacket, increased the store's take significantly at the end of every day.

When Mitch's mother died he was four, and his three older sisters, who were eight, nine, and eleven at the time, took on the task of raising him. Their father never remarried and the girls ran the household and "Mitchie's" life. They pampered him and treated him as if he were their living doll. They chose his clothes, and ordered the barber to cut his hair just so, helped him with his schoolwork, criticized his friends. It was like having three mothers. The up side of which was having three times the nurturing, the down side of which was having three times the nagging and interfering.

Fortunately, there was enough money from Joe De Nardo's plumbing business to provide them all with good clothes, cars at age sixteen, and an elaborate wedding for each of the sisters. Mitch was crazy about all three of his siblings. Betsy, whom he described as "very Valley," had a wild mane of hair, loved glitzy jewelry and sparkly clothes. Mary Catherine, with dark smokily made-up eyes and straight silky hair, was tall and leggy and always wore sexy suits with boxy jackets and very short skirts that looked sensational. She had been trying all her life without success to get into show business by auditioning for commercials. Kitty lived in Calabassas and loved to ride horses, which, after her husband and kids, was all she cared about. She looked like a Ralph Lauren ad, in her jeans and Shetland sweaters. It was undoubtedly from his pretty, clothes-conscious sisters that Mitch learned a sense of what was stylish and a knowledge about what appealed to women.

When the news got to the sisters that Mitch was in love with a new girl who was working in his little store, each of them came by to check her out. Mary Catherine and Kitty gave her their stamp of approval because she was pretty and friendly and seemed to be wild about their brother. But Betsy wasn't so bowled over.

"I took her out to lunch and believe me, I had plenty of questions for her. She eats like a bird so I asked her if she was watching her figure for Mitch. She told me no, she's careful for health reasons." The sisters were gathered at Betsy's house in Sherman Oaks one afternoon so their kids could swim in her pool. "Well, when I pressed her to see what that meant, she told me she's got high blood sugar, and she has to give herself shots before every meal. Mitchie knows about it and says so what!"

"He's right. Big deal, lots of people have diabetes. It's not like having cancer. You can control it," Kitty said.

"People like that have problems," Betsy said. "It's bad for your eyes, and also they pee a lot which is bad for the kidneys, and sometimes it's not good for them to get pregnant." Now the others were worried too. Mitch was the only one who could carry on the De Nardo name. All three of the sisters had assumed that any day he would fall in love, get married, and have a million kids.

"Maybe it's just a fling. Maybe he won't marry her."

But it was far from a fling. Lainie and Mitch meshed, united, clung to each other, and never had so much as a cross word between them. And the differences between their backgrounds and their personalities made them seem exotic and exciting to each other. She was intrigued with the fiery passionate man who laughed and cried and fought with his sisters on the phone with ferocity, then thought better of it all and called back to apologize with the sweetness of a puppy. "I'm a jerk. I take it back. I love you." It was the way people behaved in movies.

And Mitch had found a woman about whom he liked

to say, "She knows the rules of the road." Because Lainie knew how to be gracious and polite, somehow knew the proper way to behave in every situation. "She classes up my act," he admitted.

He proposed to her on bended knee in that sweet romantic way he had of doing everything. But before Lainie could say yes she knew she had to tell him what her doctor in Panorama City told her years earlier about the dangers of pregnancy for diabetics. It could be too much of a strain on the kidneys, and if there was a problem she could end up having to be on dialysis for the rest of her life. And worse than that, the baby of a diabetic might come out deformed or blind. Mitch looked a little pale as he listened, but finally he said what she'd prayed he would, "I don't care about any of that. I only care about being with you for the rest of my life."

When their bookkeeper told them they'd outgrown the store above the restaurant, they began working on the design of the new store, their dream store, which they supervised brick by brick, hanger by hanger. It would be two stories, with full bars on both floors, beautiful spacious dressing rooms, designer fashions with new California designers they hand-picked, both cocktail and casual clothes, and a complete line of shoes and accessories. They would do all the buying but they would need a large staff of salespeople, an expert in alterations, and a full-time cleaning crew.

A few weeks before the grand opening, Mitch took Lainie's hand, dragged her away from a conversation she was having about color chips with the painter, walked her outside to his car, and said, "Get in."

"Where are we going? We have a million things to do."

"Get in."

She did and he pulled his car out of the parking lot and drove west on Ventura Boulevard. "Baby, where are we going?"

Mitch reached over and patted her leg. "A surprise for my girl."

They drove for a few miles, and soon he stopped the car on Ventura Boulevard across from the old store.

"Why are we stopping here?"

"That's why," Mitch said, pointing at the window of the showroom of Valley BMW. The car in the front, the white 735I, had a big red bow on the top and a large sign next to it that said LAINIE, I TOLD YOU SO, I LOVE YOU SO, M.

It took Lainie a minute to understand. "Mitch, you're crazy. We can't afford the car."

"Yes we can. Thanks to all your hard work and the times you stayed in the store twelve hours straight. You're my partner and I want to give you this to let you know how I appreciate you. Let me have the pleasure of watching you drive that car out of the showroom. Please."

"You are absolutely—"

"The most adorable generous man on Earth?" Mitch asked, getting out of the driver's seat and coming around to open Lainie's door.

"Yes," she said, allowing herself to be led into the showroom to pick up her new car.

Two weeks later as the last of the cleaning crew wheeled the industrial vacuum cleaner out to his truck and hollered good night to them, Mitch turned out all of the lights in the new store and took Lainie in his arms. "This must be the way a Broadway producer feels just before opening night," he said. Lainie put her arms around his neck and plunged her fingers into his thick black hair. Mitch pulled her tight against him and looked into her pretty eyes. "I hope that guy with the big vacuum got this rug really clean," he said, his eyes dancing sexily.

"And why is that?" Lainie knew what his answer would be.

"Because the minute his truck pulls away, you and I are going to be rolling around on it." Even in his exhausted state, after weeks of attending carefully to every detail of the new store, he wanted to have her right there on the floor of the store. The big room was eerily lit by the streetlights and traffic lights from outside. Mitch was hard and kissing her with an urgency.

Lainie was turned on and buoyant with the good news she'd been saving to tell him. So cheered by it that any inhibitions about the windows all around fell away, as her blouse now did with Mitch's help. Then her bra, then he unbuttoned her skirt at the waist, letting it fall, and gently removed her panties, slid them down her thighs to her ankles, and in seconds she was naked in the wide expanse of room surrounded by the stark white faceless mannequins, some of them dressed in elegant evening clothes, the one next to her bare except for a very long string of pearls.

Mitch, still dressed, removed the pearls from the mannequin and placed them around Lainie's neck, and kissed her and teased her, wrapping the cold hard shiny beads around each nipple, then squeezing the circle of beads tightly around the nipple until it hurt, then letting the pearls fall their full length to the middle of Lainie's thighs. And as he teased her mouth with his tongue, he pushed his fingers and the pearls up into her, inside her vagina. The unusual sensation made her hotter as Mitch moved them against the tender walls inside her, then slowly pulled them out, and in again, fingers and pearls pushing into her, and out.

After a while he shoved the length of pearls as deeply inside her as he could, and gradually extracted them. Then he put Lainie's hands behind her back and tied her wrists together gently with the pearls as he fell to his knees. And while he reached up and his fingers manipulated her hard nipples, his tongue danced expertly against her aching swollen clitoris, and he moved his hands around to grab her buttocks and forcibly pull her closer to his face, now working her with his entire mouth, pushing it against her fiercely. And when the ache that filled her made her afraid that her knees would give, and when the heat inside her was so intense she was sure she was about to let go, to cry out, he stopped for an instant, slid out of his own clothes, pulled her down onto the floor. After he undid the pearls from around her wrists he said huskily, "Tomorrow, whoever buys these pays a thousand bucks extra."

"Mitch . . ." Lainie was too hot for conversation, and she slid to the floor with Mitch, who mounted her, and with a practiced move of his hips and thighs, his penis found the warm welcoming place inside her as she lifted her hips up, then dropped them with Mitch moving in her, and then again and again. She was loving him, loving the feeling of the way his moves controlled the heat of their union, and then she felt him harder and hotter as her own orgasm blasted through her just seconds before Mitch moaned, then writhed in the throes of his. And when the dreamlike heat of their passion fell away and they found themselves on the carpet of the new store, wet and trembling and out of breath, they laughed at themselves. Lainie decided it was time to tell him the good news.

"I went to a new doctor," she said, kissing his face gently. "I heard about him from a woman in my modern novel class. He's an endocrinologist who treats diabetics all the time, and he said if I keep tight control and monitor myself and do all the right testing, I can have a normal pregnancy and a normal baby."

Mitch sat up and took her face in his hands, looked long at her with full eyes. "Is that right? Lainie, that's amazing. Why didn't you tell me you were going?"

"I didn't want to unless I knew the answer would be what we wanted to hear. I saw the doctor a few weeks ago, one day when you were meeting with the contractor, but I wanted to wait to tell you when you weren't too preoccupied."

He held her pretty hand and kissed it again and again, then he asked, "So when do we . . ."

"Start?" Lainie smiled and he nodded.

"According to my calendar," she told him, "we just did."

15

BUT THE NIGHT OF SEX AND PEARLS didn't work. "It takes a long time and a lot of prayer for it to happen," Lainie told Mitch.

"Maybe I should have used rosary beads," he teased her. The new store opened to enthusiastic business, more than they'd imagined, and there was no time to take a sexy stress-free vacation, so the following month when Lainie was ovulating they borrowed a friend's boat in the marina, took a champagne picnic with them, and in the beautiful master cabin the boat rocked along with the rhythm of their ardent lovemaking. But two weeks later they discovered that hadn't worked either. Nor did the night at the Bel-Air Hotel, or the cottage they took for a night at the San Ysidro ranch in Santa Barbara.

For the next year and a half they tried all the fertility tricks Lainie heard about from friends and salesgirls in the store; and of course Mitch's sisters threw their two cents in. Lainie was doing all of it, drinking an herb tea from the health-food store called Female Blend, and standing on her head after they had sex to give the sperm an easier journey.

Most of her trips in the new BMW were to the doctor's office. She agreed to do everything he suggested, like having a test where he scraped the inside of her uterus to determine whether or not she'd been ovulating, and rushing to the doctor's office immediately post-intercourse so that he could check the motility of the sperm, while she felt gooey, uncomfortable, and embarrassed. The sperm were fine, the doctor reported.

She had five unsuccessful intrauterine inseminations, in case the vaginal mucus had been interfering with the chemical balance of the sperm. But no luck. She also tried everything she read about in various magazine articles, like having acupuncture on her lower abdomen to "open blocked chakras that might be preventing nature's positive flow."

One day at Panache Lainie was talking to one of the salesgirls from the shoe department, whose name was Karen, only she now spelled it Carin, since her astrologer told her that if she changed the spelling of her name it would change her life. Carin knew of a psychic who had helped two of her friends get pregnant. Lainie laughed.

"This I have to hear," she said. Lainie had listened to Carin's stories in the past about her various brushes with numerologists, tarot-card readers, channelers, and crystal healers. "Are we in Southern California or what?" she said laughing when Carin wrote the number of the psychic for her on the back of a Panache receipt.

The psychic's name was Katya, and she lived in a little white stucco house in the hills above the Sunset Strip. The tiny rooms that Lainie passed as she followed the babushka'd Katya were all painted in dark colors and reeked of the incense burning in holders Lainie recognized as the kind they used to sell at Pier One in the sixties. This is a joke, she thought, following Katya in to the farthest room in the house, and I hate that I'm so desperate. But she sat on a sofa across from the one where Katya sat. The thick odor of the incense was beginning to nauseate her.

"You have cash?" Katya asked her.

"Yes."

"Put it before me."

"How much?" God, I hope I have enough, she thought. Mitch would laugh really hard when she told him this part and then ask her, "You mean she wouldn't take American Express?"

"Fifty dollars."

She opened her wallet, and as she leaned over to place it on the table Katya spoke.

"You cannot have a baby."

The sound of those words unsettled her. When she called to make the appointment she hadn't mentioned a word about why she was coming in. Carin. Carin must have told her friend about Lainie's problem, and the friend told Katya so she could look magical when Lainie got there.

"That's right," Lainie said.

"There are many children in your family, some sisters have children, but none for you yet."

Lainie nodded. Clearly Carin had passed everything on. This is dumb. I'm paying fifty dollars for her to tell me what one of my employee's friends told her.

Katya had her eyes closed now. "You were afraid for so long because of your disease; now it may be too late. But we can try."

Lainie was surprised. She had kept the subject of her

diabetes quiet at the store and didn't think any of the girls knew about it. But maybe Carin knew, and told her friend who told the psychic.

"How do you know about my disease?"

Katya opened her eyes now and looked long at Lainie. "I'm a psychic, dear girl," she told her. This was impossible. There was no such thing.

"Do as I tell you and you will be pregnant."

Lainie listened.

"Just before you and your husband are together again to procreate, put a Bible under your bed. Next to it, in a box, put a dead fish."

"A fish?" It didn't matter how this crazy person knew about her diabetes. This was so silly she couldn't keep a straight face anymore. "What kind of a fish?"

"Any kind."

"And then?"

"And then you will conceive."

Lainie laughed out loud, all the way to her gynecologist's office. There was one more test he wanted to perform before he put her on Clomid next month, a fertility drug he said was guaranteed to work, and maybe even bring the blessing of a multiple birth. She didn't mention the Bible and the fish to him.

After he examined her, he looked worried.

"Mrs. De Nardo," he said, "let's hold off on the Clomid. I may want to put you in the hospital for a few days to do some exploratory surgery. There's not a horrible rush. I mean, we can wait until next month after you ovulate and see if you conceive this time, but if we don't start seeing results soon, I'd like to get a closer look."

Lainie never told Mitch anything about that conversation. A week later, on the day she was supposed to be ovulating, she went to a Christian bookstore and bought a Bible. Then she went to Phil's Fish and Poultry and bought a small salmon, which she brought home and put in the Stuart Weitzman box that had held her silver evening shoes, giggling to herself. "I can't believe I'm doing this."

That night when Mitch moved close to her, she said to herself, Somehow that woman knew about my diabetes, so maybe she knows about babies. Come on, fish! Do your stuff.

Even sex to make babies, which was supposed to be too calculated to be sexy, was steamy with Mitch. He spent hours nuzzling, nibbling, and licking at all the spots on her body he knew so well, and that night when they rose to fevered orgasm together, he said, "Come on, baby. Come on, my baby," before he collapsed in a final sigh on top of her and whispered, "You're my whole life, Laine," and fell into a deep sleep.

The next morning after Mitch left for work, Lainie, who would have forgotten if she hadn't dropped an earring that rolled to the floor and just under the bed, removed the Bible and put it in a drawer and took the fish out of the shoe box and put it down the garbage disposal.

She didn't have to be in the store until noon, so she ran a tub, and slid in. She always put the morning newspaper next to the tub on the floor, then leaned over the side to turn the pages. But now, before she started to read, she knew something was wrong. A searing cramp squeezed through her lower abdomen, and then another pain, and when she looked at the water it was bright red. She was hemorrhaging. All alone in the house, she was losing big gobs of blood. Slowly she lifted herself out of the tub, and as her own blood, diluted with bathwater, dripped down her legs, she managed to get herself into the bedroom to call Mitch. He was there in just the time it took for her to dry off, wrap herself in a robe, and prop up her feet.

"You're okay, baby, you're okay," he repeated to her over and over as he gently carried her to the car, then rushed her to the hospital.

Lainie's mother, Margaret Dunn, left work to come to the hospital to be near her daughter for the surgery. She was a bony, gray-haired woman who didn't talk much, and didn't expect anyone to do anything for her. Mitch included her in all the conversations with the doctors, took her to a silent lunch in the hospital cafeteria while they waited for Lainie to come out of surgery, and took turns with her tiptoeing into the recovery room to see if Lainie was awake yet. She had three ominous-looking intravenous tubes attached to her.

When she finally opened her eyes, it was Mitch's face she saw looking down at her, and she already knew by the expression he was wearing, the one that she teased him about by calling it "tough dago," what had happened.

"Mitchie," she asked, "I can't have a baby, can I?"

Mitch didn't speak, only shook his head sadly.

After they brought Lainie home, Margaret Dunn took two weeks from her job at the law office in Beverly Hills to sit by her daughter's bed every day. She walked Lainie to the bathroom, answered the telephone, straightened up the house, and served home-cooked meals on a tray. Friends from Panache came to visit with cards and gifts and cookies, and Sharon, a girl Lainie had befriended in an English class at Northridge, came with *Gift from the Sea* by Anne Morrow Lindbergh. All three sisters-in-law came at one time, filling the bedroom of Lainie and Mitch's condo with the overwhelming combination of their assorted perfumes, Joy, Tea Roses, and Opium.

The friends were understanding and kind. They offered sympathy for the loss of hope of ever having a baby. The sisters looked funereal, which was obviously the way they felt. Even the flowers they brought, white lilies, looked like the kind people brought when someone died. And they sat on the bed and spoke in solemn whispers.

When her strength came back, Lainie began a regimen of chemotherapy twice a week. Mitch would drive her to the hospital and wait, drive her home and sit outside the bathroom door while she was sick, then help her gently into bed where she would nap, while he went back to work at Panache. Her hair was falling out in large chunks, her skin was sallow, and she had no appetite at all. She still went to the store as often as she could. She had enough energy to do some work, but she felt sensitive about her appearance when she saw the pitying expressions on people's faces when they looked at her.

One day she stopped at Sherman Oaks Park, sat in her car in the parking lot near the playground, and watched the toddlers in the sandbox and the bigger children on the play equipment and wished she were dead. When the months of chemotherapy ended, the doctors scheduled a surgery during which they planned to take a tissue sample from each organ to determine if the cancer was gone.

"Mitch," Lainie said the night before the second surgery. She was naked against his naked back. "If they find any more cancer, I'm not going to go for chemo again. I'm going to elect to die."

The surgery found nothing. Mitch sent her a giant basket of flowers. He also sent a dozen helium balloons which floated to the ceiling in her hospital room, and he held her too tight, and she laughed when he climbed into the hospital bed next to her and said, "God couldn't take you away from me so soon. I'm too nice a guy."

The business was running like a top and Lainie's strength was returning, her hair was growing back, and her everyday life was normal again. Slowly and gently Mitch brought their sex life back to normal too. Loving her, it seemed, with a greater tenderness than ever.

On Mitch's thirty-fifth birthday, Lainie threw a party for him right in the store, with valet parking, a dance floor, a disc jockey, and a caterer. She invited Mitch's sisters and their husbands, all the employees of Panache and their spouses, a whole group of her friends from school, and the guys Mitch grew up with in the Valley. There was Dave Andrews, who owned a mattress company, and Frankie De Lio, who owned a chain of liquor stores, and Larry Weber, who was a successful lawyer.

When the disc jockey played Kenny Rogers singing "Lady," Mitch took Lainie onto the dance floor as if they were a couple of teenagers at a school dance, and some of the girls from the store let out a cheer when he pulled her close to him and they danced.

"You have come into my life and made me whole . . . ," Kenny Rogers sang.

"Larry Weber told me he has a client whose sixteen-year-old-daughter is very pregnant," she thought she heard him say into her hair, and she wondered why he was telling her that. "I mean as in so pregnant she's giving birth any minute."

Lainie looked into his face now to try to see where this was leading. "So?" she asked.

"So she's a kid and her parents didn't want her to have an abortion, and for a while the girl's mother was going to keep the baby and raise it as if it was hers, only now they decided that wouldn't be good for the girl, so they need to find a home for it fast."

"Look at that cute couple," Carin said as she and her boyfriend danced past Lainie and Mitch. For a few minutes Lainie didn't know what to say as they moved to the music, pressed tightly together, then she stopped dancing and stood in the middle of the dimly lit room and looked at him.

"You mean just like that. In a couple of days? Somebody drops off a baby?"

"I know. It sounds nuts, doesn't it? But maybe it's fate. Larry being here and asking me casually why we don't have kids, and me telling him all the stuff we've been through . . ."

Lainie looked away. A peal of laughter erupted from Mitch's sisters who were standing in a cluster with their husbands.

"I mean, maybe we're the ones who are destined to take the baby from this poor little girl."

Lainie had always thought Mitch was against adoption because an adopted baby wouldn't have the De Nardo genes. But here he was asking to take in some stranger's baby within hours. He was getting desperate.

"What do you think?"

"I don't know. I mean, it's so fast. We don't even have anything for it."

"What does it need? It could sleep in our bed. I can go to any drugstore and get diapers and formula now if I have to." He looked and sounded like a kid begging for a puppy. Next he would probably swear he'd be responsible for feeding it and changing it.

"I'll help with it. Hell, we can afford to get a full-time nurse."

"I'm so lost in your love . . . ," Kenny Rogers sang.

The next few days were about visits to the lawyer and signing papers in Larry Weber's Valley office, then running to the Juvenile shop to look at baby furniture. They bought a changing table, a crib, and a musical swing.

"Can't you just order them," Margaret Dunn asked, "and not have them delivered until after the baby is born?"

Mitch laughed at his mother-in-law's superstitions, and told the Juvenile shop to deliver everything that night. It would give him time to run home and get the third bedroom cleaned up and ready for the arrival of the baby.

The next morning Larry Weber called just as they unlocked the front door to open the store for the day to tell them that the girl was in labor.

"We're ready for her," Mitch said, smiling.

"It's a boy," Larry Weber said just before they went home for the day, and Mitch grabbed Lainie and twirled her around. "We're talking Joey De Nardo. We're going to have a boy." That night Lainie brought a picnic dinner into the baby's room, spread out a blanket, and they ate sitting on the floor, talking about how it would feel to have a little one in that very room any day now. They drank a lot of Santa Margharetta Pino Grigio with dinner, and when the phone rang at eleven o'clock they were in bed, both a little drunk, making love.

"We should have done it in the crib," Mitch said, "just to bless it," as the phone rang again.

Lainie turned over on her stomach and slithered to the phone to pick it up. It was Larry Weber.

"Hi, Larry," she said, feeling happy and playful and glad she'd gone along with this plan. In a few days they were going to go and pick up their baby, Joey De Nardo, and she would hold him and kiss him and raise him as if he were from her own body.

"The baby has something wrong with it," Larry Weber told her. "A heart defect. They don't think he's going to make it." Lainie closed her eyes. Mitch was nuzzling her back and moving his hands under her to her breasts. A baby. Forty-eight hours ago she was okay about never having one, then suddenly she was about to have one, and now she felt as if she'd been kicked in the teeth.

For some dumb reason the crib and changing table were all she could think about. Why did we ever get the crib and the changing table? That's why something bad happened and now we'll have to send back the crib and the changing table. She felt her whole body racked with a terrible wrenching misery. Stop, she thought. You can't fall apart over this. This was a baby you've never even seen. But she couldn't speak, so she handed the phone to Mitch.

"Hello?" he said into it. "Yeah? Yeah? Ahhh, that's too bad, Larry. Is the little girl okay? Uh-huh. Well at least she's okay. Yeah. Thanks." Mitch put the phone down and took Lainie in his arms. Naked against his nakedness, she could feel his chest heaving as he tried to hold in the sadness.

For months after that, Lainie's dreams were filled with babies. Babies that talked like grown-ups, faceless babies; one dream that recurred was about the sound of a crying baby. In the dream she would walk through some unidentifiable empty house, trying to find the baby, whose cries became more urgent as Lainie became more frantic. Maybe, she thought, I should go to a psychiatrist.

But how would she find the right psychiatric help? It was something she could never discuss with her mother, who didn't believe in talking about her feelings with people she knew, let alone some stranger. Yet she had to do something about these feelings of anguish and loss and fear. A fear that she would lose Mitch, a fear that her barrenness was making her ugly to Mitch. And that any day now he would leave her for somebody else, and the somebody else would become pregnant within weeks.

She would think about those things and work herself up into an anxious state, and then anything Mitch said felt like a dismissal to her. If he hung up the phone too quickly with her when she called him at the store, or if he was too critical of the way she handled a customer, she felt afraid that any minute he would turn to her and say, "That's it. I'm leaving you."

One night, after they were both warm with the satisfaction of their lovemaking, Mitch moved himself up on one elbow and looked at his wife's face.

"Lainie," he said, "I've got something serious I want to talk about. Do you think you can handle it?"

Lainie felt a flutter of fear. This was it, the moment she'd been dreading. What else, after all they'd been through, could he mean by something serious? He was going to tell her he was leaving her.

"Sure I can," she said, her brow furrowed.

"Laine, all these years when we thought we'd never have kids, I was okay about it. But when the adoption question came up, the reason I grabbed it was because I figured maybe it was God's way of telling us we needed a kid, and then when the poor little baby died, I didn't know what to think. Now something's in my head, and I want you to know that if what I'm going to tell you isn't okay with you, then I'll drop it. Forever. I swear. Because you're everything to me, you know that? Right?" Lainie touched his arm lightly and nodded, relieved at hearing all the affirmations of his love, and ashamed of herself for doubting him because of her own feelings of inadequacy.

"You have done so much for me, Laine. When I met you I was just some hotshot with a new business, floundering around with no personal life at all, but you, with your sweetness and the full-out way you love me so completely, gave my life meaning, and I'll never stop being grateful to you for that.

"A big reason our store is such a success is because of your devotion to it. I probably would have thrown the whole thing in the garbage fifty times, like after the flood when we didn't have insurance and all the clothes were ruined. You found that little cleaner downtown who specialized in suede, and stood over him till he made those jackets look like new, and then we sold them all. We made it because no matter what happened, you were always there with your patience saying, We'll work it out. I think you're a miracle. And that's why now I want it to be my turn. Now, *I* want to do something that I can do for us. I want to call a lawyer and have him help us hire a woman to have a baby for us."

Lainie's throat tightened as if someone were choking her.

"It will mean that instead of adopting a baby that was the product of two strangers, like we almost did, at least this way we'll know that half of this baby is a De Nardo. Part of us. I'm not asking this on a whim, Laine. Since your surgery I've been trying to figure out what I could do, and this seemed to me to be something that I can offer to us. Bring to the partnership. Because God knows, we've been good enough together all these years for you to believe what I believe. I mean that you and I are one. Remember we saw that old woman on television who said that marriage is two horses pulling in one yoke? Well, let this part, the part about making a biological child for us, be my part of the yoke."

"Mitch," she said, hoping she could get through this without crying, "it's a bad idea. You know what's happened historically in cases like this. This isn't as if we're putting part of me and part of you into some woman to carry for us. Whoever we hire is going to be having a baby that's yours and hers. And when the time comes for her to part with it, she's going to be giving up her own child. What if she changes her mind? Are you going to let her keep that baby? And never see it? Or share custody? Or are you just going to say, 'Oh well,' knowing that out there somewhere is your son or your daughter and you gave it up because the surrogate decided she couldn't handle it?"

She could tell by the look of surprise on Mitch's face this was not the response he'd anticipated. She was surprised herself at the power of her outburst. "Believe me, Mitch, I'm desperate to have a baby, but I won't do it that way."

"Lainie, don't decide now. This is a knee-jerk reaction and you ought to take time to think about it. What happened in the cases you're talking about was because those women weren't properly tested or adequately screened. We could sidestep that by making sure she took a battery of every kind of test, we could meet the kids she already has and see how healthy *they* are. Hell, we can afford to have ten different psychiatrists check her out. In fact, my sister Betsy knows about a place—"

"Betsy! I knew this had something to do with one of your meddling sisters: What did she do? See it on 'Oprah'? No, this sounds more like 'Geraldo.' 'Women Whose Husbands Impregnate Strangers.' " Lainie heard herself shout at her husband for the first time in their years together. Heard her voice shrieking and sounding like some shrew. Like Elizabeth Taylor in *Who's Afraid of Virginia Woolf?* But she wasn't sorry. She was pulsing with anger. "Betsy and those other two witches can mind their own business and get their noses out of my life."

"You're being a selfish little brat."

"*I'm* being selfish? If you want a baby so much and you're *not* being selfish, why can't we try to adopt again? We'll adopt a son and *he'll* carry on the precious De Nardo name. What in the hell do you think is so great about your genes that the world can't live without them?"

"Lainie, don't provoke me, goddammit. I'm getting

really angry at your attitude about this. This idea makes sense for us.'' She heard the hot anger rising in his voice, and she knew her temper was no match for his, but this was too much. She was not going to back down and give in to this insane request. ''I want to have my genetic child,'' Mitch said, fuming. ''And it *can* be done. People are still doing it all the time, and without problems. I've made calls to find out. I've talked to the best lawyers and the best psychologists, and they all assured me we can cover every possible loophole.''

Lainie was having a hard time breathing. ''Mitch, don't you ever accuse me of being selfish again. I had my insides taken out because they were riddled with cancer. There isn't a day that I don't drive by the park or see a woman pushing a stroller that I don't have to look away with tormented envy that I can't give you a baby!'' Those last words choked her and she had to turn away. ''If it sounds petty or selfish or small, then that's what I am! But I am telling you I could never look at another woman who had your baby inside her body.''

''But it would be *our* baby,'' he said. ''Yours and mine. Don't you want that?''

''More than anything,'' she said. ''But I can't do it the way you're describing. I'm sorry.''

''Change your mind.''

''No.''

''Grow up, Laine. If we adopted a baby it wouldn't come from your body. This way at least we know about *one* of its genetic parents. You say *I'm* narcissistic? Get your own ego out of it.''

''The subject is closed.''

''No it's not.''

''With me it is.''

They didn't speak for days. They slept in the same bed, but with their backs to each other. They worked at the store where they were cordial to the employees and the customers but when the two of them were alone in a room they said nothing to each other. Lainie's fears of abandonment were out of control. Lodged in her brain and in her heart, so that no matter how much makeup she put on, or how pretty an outfit, the woman she saw in the mirror looked like an ugly jealous hag.

She alternately thought about packing her bags, going away somewhere, anywhere, and never coming back, or begging Mitch's forgiveness and doing whatever he asked. The estrangement was unbearable. One night when everyone had gone and they were alone in the store about to lock up, she touched his arm.

"Mitchie."

"Yeah?" He didn't look at her.

"I'm not saying yes. But I'm willing to talk about it some more."

He moved close to her and held her silently. The scent of him so close after even a few days apart made her want to cry with relief. From the day they met, there had always been something irresistible to her about the way Mitch smelled. She loved to snuggle against him and bury her face in his warm neck, tasting and smelling him. This was the best man God ever made. A blessing in this world of too many divorces, and too much cheating, and all those stories about wife-beating she read about in magazines. This was a man who treated her like a queen, romanced her as if they were still courting, never failed to be there for her in ways that amazed their friends.

At his thirty-fifth birthday party so many people had stood to give toasts to Mitch's loyalty, big heart, and generosity that at one point Mitch had stood and said, "Wait a second, this is so good, I think I'd better check to make sure I haven't died."

Lainie remembered all that as she held her husband in her arms. How could she refuse him anything?

16

"YOUR HUSBAND was right, Mrs. De Nardo." The psychologist at the surrogacy center was an attractive gray-haired man in his late forties. Lainie and Mitch sat with him, and with Chuck Meyer, the surrogacy attorney. Mitch had dressed that morning in his best suit as if, Lainie thought with a stab, he were thinking the better he looked, the better his chance was of getting some surrogate to want to have his baby. "The press loves to blow things out of proportion. The cases that are worrying you are the sensationalized ones, and they're very rare. The truth is that ninety-nine percent of the surrogates don't change their minds. That's a much better statistic than you'd ever have with open adoption where the birth mother is usually a young unstable girl who suddenly finds herself pregnant and is frequently ambivalent about having the baby in the first place.

"The women with whom we work are grown-ups.

They're educated, middle-class women who want to do this for their own reasons. And the reasons aren't financial. In fact, the most recent research proves that the women who are surrogates aren't doing this for the money. As far as the psychological issues are concerned, aside from the tests, which are numerous and demanding, we're here to ask them the tough questions. And believe me we do.

"I don't hesitate to ask if they're willing to give up sexual relations with their husbands from the time they sign the contract. Or what they're going to tell their own parents who will feel that this baby is their grandchild. We give them months to think it over. And during that time we talk to the other people in their families who are going to go through the experience with them. We see their spouses, their children, to find out if there will be anyone who might make it difficult for them, or create a problem.

"We reject eighty-five percent of the women who apply. We tell them we simply cannot have them in our program if there's the least indication that a problem might surface. And still we never lack for applicants. I understand your reluctance, and I'll be glad to ask some of the very happy families who have worked with us to contact you and share their experience. Or to have you meet the surrogates, get to know them, and feel free to come to me at any time and say, 'This isn't for us.' "

Lainie could feel Mitch looking at her. You don't have to decide now, but the sooner you do, the sooner we can have a baby was what his look was saying.

They chose the third surrogate they met. Her name was Jackie. She was blond and blue-eyed, and kind of chunky in a cute round way. Lainie liked her better than the others because she was warm and easy to talk to. When Lainie and Mitch walked in on the day of their meeting, Jackie stood and hugged her. It was startling, but a very sweet gesture, and an embarrassed Lainie was overwhelmed by the cloud of Jackie's perfume, which she recognized as Shalimar.

The minute they sat down Jackie pulled out pictures to show both Lainie and Mitch of her teenage son from a youthful failed marriage. The son was a tall, handsome, confident-looking young man.

"I'm on Weight Watchers," Jackie assured them when the meeting was winding down. "And I always get a little blubbery before my period, which is now. So I hate to sound like I'm doing a commercial for myself, but if you pick me, we can start right off in two weeks and two days. I run as regular as a clock."

There was nothing threatening about her. The first candidate had been a pretty, redheaded former actress, who said she wanted "to live this and then put it into my work." The second candidate, busty and dark-haired, seemed inappropriately taken with Mitch. Jackie was Irish, funny, looked kind of like a heavy-set version of Lainie, and she said everything she was thinking. Or as Mitch said, "She has no filter between the brain and the mouth."

Their plan was that Lainie would meet Jackie at each doctor's appointment. She would bring them the sperm she'd lovingly coaxed from Mitch less than an hour before. On the morning of the first insemination, at home Lainie realized she'd forgotten to get a specimen jar from the doctor, so in the dishwasher she sterilized a small jar that had once held Cara Mia marinated artichoke hearts.

Mitch laughed so much when she handed him the funny little jar, he was afraid he wouldn't be able to perform. When he finally ejaculated, he grinned, and then in his off-key imitation of Mario Lanza, sang,

"Cara mia, mine. Say those words divine. I'll be your love till the end of time." Lainie was still chuckling about it in the car all the way to the doctor's office.

"Tell me all about Mitch," Jackie asked her while they were waiting for her to be called in by the nurse. Lainie didn't know where to begin, what to tell her.

"Well, he's from an Italian family, his mother died young and he was raised by his sisters—"

"And now he's real close to them. Right? Italian men and their families. They get all hooked in. Italians are like the Irish, you know. They cry at commercials for the telephone company. Right? A few bars of that song about touching someone and they're bawling like idiots. Right? *I'm* like that too. A total sob sister."

The door from the doctor's office opened.

"O'Malley?" the nurse asked.

"Me," Jackie said, standing, then turned to Lainie.

"Hold a fertile thought," Jackie said and followed the nurse.

The doctor's office was in Century City on the eighth floor of the medical building. Lainie looked down from the waiting room window at the bright blue swimming pool across the street at the Century Tower apartments, where a lone swimmer swam laps. Dear God, I'm waiting here for a woman I met two weeks ago to be impregnated with my husband's baby. A baby I'll take from her and raise as if it were his baby with me.

Jackie had passed every test, had health statistics that were enviable to Lainie with her own history of diabetes. Jackie's IQ was high and her scores on the psychological testing had been as high as possible. There was, of course, no way to know what the hormones of pregnancy could do to anyone's mental state, or how she'd react to the sight of the biological baby she'd promised to give away.

"You have to be prepared, Mitch," the psychologist

had said, "in the worst-case scenario to give up the baby. Do you think you can do that?" Lainie had looked over at Mitch. It was during one of the many sessions they'd spent with this man who probed and pushed at difficult issues in a way Lainie was glad to know he used with the surrogates, but uncomfortable with when they were used on her and Mitch.

"First you tell me she's the picture of mental health, then you tell me she could change her mind," Mitch said defensively.

"We all need to be clear that anything can happen, and you have to be prepared for what you plan to do in every eventuality," the psychologist said, turning to Lainie, who noticed that Mitch had never answered the question he'd been asked. "And will you be able to deal with seeing another woman heavy with your husband's child? I don't want to scare you away, and you don't have to answer me right now. But answer that for yourself."

After nearly an hour, Jackie emerged from the gynecologist's office. "He made me lie there with my feet up for a long time to give everything a chance to do its work. And this will kill you: after he inseminated me, I asked him, 'Was it good for *you*?' It cracked him up." Then she squeezed Lainie's arm. "Say a prayer, girl," she said.

Later at a table outside of Michel Richard on Robertson Boulevard, Jackie pulled out an envelope full of some new pictures of her son.

"Isn't he a hunk?" she asked proudly. "Sometimes when we're together, people think he's my boyfriend."

"He's darling," Lainie said.

"*This* baby will be too," Jackie told her, taking a big swig of her iced tea and putting the glass down. With the cold wet hand that had just held the glass, she took Lainie's hand across the table.

"Don't get nuts about this. It's going to be great for all of us. Meanwhile you and I get to spend some time getting acquainted, which isn't so terrible. *Capiche*? That means—"

"I know what it means." Lainie smiled.

"My second husband was Italian," Jackie said.

Lainie didn't remember any mention of a second husband in the lawyer's office. Jackie saw the surprise on her face.

"It was a short one. Lasted less than a year. I don't even use his name. My Tommy was real little then and this guy had two teenage sons who used to knock my kid around. I didn't like it. We fought about it, and I just figured I'd be better off saying adios. You know?"

Lainie nodded, but now she wondered what else Jackie hadn't told them about herself.

"So you and Mitch have a great marriage, huh?"

Lainie smiled. "We love each other and are very happy."

"Boy," Jackie told her, gesturing to a waiter for coffee, "I envy that. And I'm going to have it someday. Down the road. I tell you, I'm going to have it."

Two weeks later, Jackie got her period.

"Hey, listen, we have all the time in the world," Mitch said when Lainie called him at the shop with the news just after Jackie called her. "These things take months, sometimes they even take years, but let's keep hanging in there, sweetheart. We'll have a baby in our arms before you know it. I love you, Mrs. D.," he added, "and when I get home, I'll show you just how much."

"Me too," Lainie answered, and she *did* love him. More than ever.

It was the morning of the ninth insemination when Margaret Dunn's boss called to tell Lainie that her mother had fallen in the ladies' room at work for no apparent reason, and had been taken to Century City Hospital.

"I'm on my way," Lainie said, then remembered she had to be at the doctor's office in a few hours with Jackie or risk missing an entire month until the next ovulation. When she went downstairs to tell Mitch about her mother, he was dressed for work, reading the morning paper.

"You know what?" Mitch said. "You go take care of your mother. Me and the Cara Mia jar can handle it, if you get my meaning. We're very intimate. I can just drive into town myself to the doctor's office and drop off the jar. What time does the womb usually get there?"

"Mitchie!" Lainie gave him a little slap on the arm. "She gets there at noon." She hated it when he made jokes about Jackie. The events of the last many months had created a bond between the two women. Lainie always looked forward to their time together. Not just because each doctor's visit could be the one when Jackie might finally conceive, but because their post-insemination lunches had become filled with the intimate chatter of two close girlfriends. The conception would bring an end to those meetings, and the baby's birth an end to the relationship.

It had been agreed from the first that Jackie would never know the De Nardos' last name. And the phone they had installed at their house for her calls would be removed once the baby was in their care. That was the way Mitch told the lawyer it had to be. "I don't want her changing her mind one day and knocking on my door."

"With the success of the store, you realize that you and Lainie have a pretty high profile," the lawyer warned him.

That made Mitch nervous. "Don't even let her glance at the credit card receipt," he told Lainie. "Always pay for everything with cash.'' It was odd and uncomfortable for her, this secrecy coupled with intimacy, but soon, God willing, they'd have the desired result.

''Call me from the hospital if you need me, and I'll get over there right after I drop off the baby juice,'' Mitch said with a last kiss. Lainie was off to see her poor mother, who had been complaining about headaches for weeks. Lainie hoped the fall was unrelated and didn't mean she had some kind of neurological problem. She hadn't told her mother a word about the surrogate. Maybe once Margaret got through whatever this problem was, Lainie would explain it all to her, and she would be happy to learn that soon she would be a grandmother.

Mitch pulled the car into the parking lot of the medical building but kept the engine running so he could hear the end of the news. After he turned the car off, he felt in his shirt pocket for the little slip of paper containing the doctor's suite number, and when he found it he took the paper bag and got out of the car.

''Shit,'' a woman's voice echoed through the cavernous parking lot. ''I'm leaking all over the place, goddammit.''

Mitch looked over at where the woman stood next to an old beat-up convertible with the hood open and a red-vested parking-lot attendant, who stared dumbly at the steaming engine. He was about to turn and head for the elevator when he realized the woman was Jackie. When he walked back to where she was standing and Jackie caught sight of him, she shouted a greeting.

''Hey, Mitch, long time no see! I got a busted hose, which is a complaint I sincerely hope *you* don't have, honey!'' she said, laughing, then stopped herself. ''Listen, no offense. I'm a little punchy here. How's your mother-in-law? Lainie called me this morning to say she couldn't be here today, and that you were making the drop-off. I hope everything there's all right."

"They're going to run tests on her all afternoon so Lainie's going to stay at the hospital and hold her hand. Thanks for asking." The steam rose in a cloud out of the open-hooded car. "You going to be okay here?"

"Yeah, sure," Jackie said. "I called the auto club. They're on their way. So if you go on up and give that to the doc," she said, nodding toward the paper bag, "I'll be up in a few minutes to collect it."

She smiled. Mitch smiled too.

"I hope it happens," she said.

"Me too. It means a lot to me."

"To me also," she said, putting a hand on his arm.

Lainie had reported to Mitch after each of the previous inseminations how much she liked this pudgy, soft-faced woman, and what an essentially good person she was. When Mitch looked at Jackie now, he believed it. After evaluating her psychological makeup, the lawyer had pointed out to them repeatedly how high she rated when it came to altruism.

This wasn't a moment Mitch had ever expected to have with the surrogate. Except for the initial meeting, which now seemed very far in the past, they'd never spoken. Lainie was in charge of every step of this: making the final decision about which woman they chose, scheduling the doctor's appointments, going along to ensure that everything went well. But now, as he stood in the cavernous underground parking lot of the medical building, looking into Jackie's eyes, knowing who she was about to be to him for the rest of their lives if everything went as planned, Mitch felt overwhelmed. His sisters had encouraged him to do this, to get himself a blood child of his own. But surely they must feel the way he did that there was something about it that interfered with the sanctity of marriage.

"Why are you doing this?" he heard himself asking, then felt surprised that he'd actually asked her that.

"Because it gives some meaning to my life," she answered. "Because I believe it's one of the few things I have to offer. No one's manipulating me, Mitch. I want to have a baby for a couple very much, and if I don't do it for you, I'll do it for someone else. You may not respect me, because you probably have some set idea about how women are supposed to conduct themselves and this isn't it. But make no mistake, you aren't using some lower-class cow's body against her will or because she needs the ten-grand fee. Though the ten grand won't hurt me."

"I never thought—"

"Let me finish. I'm sure you didn't, but just in case it crosses your mind, I want you to know I'm every bit as excited about this as you are."

"I'm glad to hear that," Mitch said, realizing suddenly that she was still holding on to his arm.

"Of course, I'd be lying to you if I said that *this* part was any fun. I mean, the doctor's kind of a horse's ass, like most doctors are, and the inseminations are uncomfortable, but what gets me through it is knowing that I'm going to be pregnant, Mitch. Pregnant. Do you have any idea how glorious that is? Of course you couldn't. But I do, because I remember how I felt when I was carrying my Tommy, and the earth-moving importance of it. I was making another human being deep inside my body. Just knowing I was doing that made every minute of my day, even taking a walk or a nap, feel productive and creative and necessary."

Her hand was holding his arm a little too tightly now, and her pretty blue eyes, eyes that were the same color as Lainie's, were welling with tears.

A white auto club truck came tearing around the parking-lot ramp, and the driver pulled up next to Jackie's car. Jackie let go of Mitch's arm, found her auto club card in her purse, and handed it to the young man as he got out of the truck.

"Why don't you go on ahead," she said over her shoulder to Mitch. "You can tell the nurse that as soon as I'm finished down here, I'll be up."

"That's okay," Mitch told her coolly, leaning against a nearby green Jaguar. "I've got a couple of minutes. Why don't I just wait for you?"

Two weeks later the lawyer called the store to tell them Jackie was pregnant. Mitch took the call, and when Lainie overheard him say, "Aaaaalriiight! I'm having a kid!" she rushed back to his office. He put an arm around her, nodding the good news as he continued to talk to the lawyer, who was reminding him of the details of their contract with Jackie. The next big medical bill would be for the amniocentesis, which would be performed between week fifteen and week seventeen of the pregnancy.

Lainie could feel Mitch's body trembling with excitement. When he asked, "Is Jackie feeling all right? Should I call her? Is she having any morning sickness? Does she need anything?" she smiled up at him. But at that moment she felt a sick feeling that was envy combined with anger. It crawled up the back of her neck and seemed to hang there and spread to her shoulders like a clammy shawl.

Mitch's concern for Jackie made perfect logical sense. Then why did it feel painful and wrong? She hated the look of ecstasy on his face when he reported to her what the lawyer had just told him, "Her breasts are already two sizes bigger than usual," and then laughed. Jackie's breasts, she thought. I'm listening to my husband and another man talk about some woman's breasts.

She was queasy. Why had she agreed to this? How was she going to survive nine months of this? She gave Mitch a little tap on the arm and mouthed the words *I'm going home* to him when he looked at her. She was hoping that would get him to hang up the phone and say, "No, no, let's celebrate. Let's go have a champagne dinner together somewhere." But instead he nodded and waved to say good-bye and turned his interest back to the lawyer on the phone.

Lainie walked out to the new BMW and got in, not sure what to do or how to get herself to stop feeling this sick anxiety over news that was supposed to be happy. Instead of going home she drove to Santa Monica, parked her car, and sat on the sand at Will Rogers State Beach, watching the waves come in. When she got home it was nearly six o'clock and a vase of two dozen roses was waiting outside the door of the condominium. She took them in and opened the card, which read *Thank you for being my wonderful wife. I love you, baby. M.*

A nausea, worse than the ones she'd faced during her chemotherapy, stayed with her. She was still feeling that way a week later at a family dinner with Mitch's sisters and their families when Betsy raised her glass and said, "To the baby and the health of the woman who's carrying it." It seemed to Lainie as if everyone's eyes were on her. She wished she could get up and walk out on the smug sisters with three kids each, their cocky husbands punching Mitch on the arm with their macho, you-son-of-a-bitch punches that men give one another as congratulations for sexual prowess.

But worse was the way she felt about her envious self. I'll be okay, she thought. It's only nine months. After that, Jackie will be out of our lives forever. For Mitch to have a baby of his own blood, I can survive that. She had no way of knowing that her pain had just begun.

17

WHEN HARVEY FELDMAN stood to greet Rick Reisman, he could tell by the red face of the secretary who showed the well-known director in that Rick had been flirting with her. Jesus, the man was looking more and more like Orson Welles, Feldman thought.

"So what brings you here?" he asked as Rick sat in the leather chair across from his desk.

"I want to talk about open adoption," Rick said.

"Which aspect of it?"

"The prerequisites."

"Do you mean for the birth mother or the adopting parents?"

"Parents."

"The prerequisites are whatever qualities the birth mother wants for the parents of her baby."

"Meaning?"

"Meaning I've placed babies with single parents,

gay couples, a few couples who otherwise would be considered too old to adopt."

"Which is how old?"

"Forties. You want to hear the stories? I've got scrapbooks filled with them."

"I'm nearly fifty."

"So?"

"Is that impossible?"

"I don't follow."

"Well, what's too old?" Rick asked, leaning forward.

The dawn broke on Harvey Feldman's face. "Are you telling me that you're here to talk to me about you, yourself, wanting to adopt a baby?" There was a mixture of amusement and disappointment in his voice. Rick realized that the young lawyer with show-business fantasies had thought he'd come here to talk about stories that could be made into movies.

"I am," Rick said.

"What brought *this* on?"

"My approaching fiftieth birthday. The relative certainty, however heartbreaking, that 'the right woman' who will love me forever isn't out there somewhere waiting for an overweight, overworked, anxiety-ridden movie director to take advantage of her fertile body. I also have a desperate desire to have some kind of family. I lost my parents in an airplane crash in the fifties. Bobo is my only living relative."

"It'll be difficult," Feldman said after a while. "Ever married?" Rick shook his head no. "They'll ask me that . . . the birth mothers. They'll wonder if you're gay."

"I'll bring them affidavits from women I've plundered."

"Do you have a preference about the gender?"

"I'd probably do better with a boy, but . . ." He

shrugged, and he had the sudden urge to stand, apologize for what was clearly a momentary lapse of sanity, and run back downstairs to the parking lot and his car. But there was something about the fact that the guy wasn't laughing at him or trying to talk him out of it yet that kept him in the chair.

"Here's the bottom line if you're serious," Feldman told him. "I already told you that there are forty-seven possible choices for every birth mother. The only way you can beat the odds is to convince one of them that you're unequivocally the best person to love and raise the baby she's carrying. Do you think you can do that? Win out over couples who have picket fences and puppies, and in some cases other children? More important, do you think you *are* that? When you adopt a baby, you adopt at least twenty years' worth of responsibility for another human being."

"Well," Rick said, and for the first time he looked around the office. On a bookshelf behind him was a picture of Harvey Feldman and his pretty wife, and on their laps, two little girls.

"My family," he heard Feldman say.

"I see that," Rick responded, but when he looked back at Feldman, he realized the young man was gesturing at all the pictures on every wall. Babies. Gurgling, grinning, posing bare assed, in bathtubs, through crib bars, wearing too-big hats and toothless grins. Sometimes alone, frequently held by beaming adults with a kind of light in their eyes Rick knew his own eyes had never had.

He stood to go. This had truly been a lunatic idea. One of those grasping-for-straws moments that sound great in the wee hours of the morning when you're desperate. Now, with the cold gray light of the smoggy L.A. day staring at him, it was nothing more than a lonely fat man's way of admitting the truth, which was that he'd let his life pass him by. He offered Harvey his hand, but Harvey had turned away and was pulling some files out of a drawer.

"Listen," the lawyer said, "it's a long shot. I doubt if anyone will choose you, but so what? I'll throw you into the mix and see if anyone's interested. Fill out an information form for me and I'll see."

Rick sat down again. Harvey handed him a form.

"Tell me the down side," Rick said as he wrote his vital statistics onto the slots on the form. "The dangers. The part I should worry about. I mean, surely it can't be as easy as one day they pick you and then somebody brings you a little bundle and says, 'He's yours.' "

"Nowhere near as easy as that. The bad news is that the birth mother, who you support for the last few months of her pregnancy, has the right to ask for her baby back until she signs a consent that's been accepted by the department of adoptions, or approved by the L.A. superior court, or the L.A. County department of children's services. It's supposed to take six months, but sometimes it can take closer to a year. So you could possibly support a birth mother, pay all of her hospital bills and doctors' fees, fall in love with a baby, and have that baby snatched away from you and all your money lost. If you want a baby badly enough, you have to be prepared to let this little pregnant girl stomp on your heart."

"How often has that happened?"

"In my practice, once in fifteen years. That's not too bad. The birth mother asked for the baby back after two days. The adopting parents were devastated, but they wanted a baby so much they found another birth mother a few months later, and started again. Now they have a son."

Rick sighed and walked around the room, looking closely at each baby picture.

"So, my chance to be chosen, unlike myself, is very slim. Suppose I try to increase my odds by doing something dazzling, like buying the birth mother a car or a fur coat?"

"That would be trafficking in babies, and that's illegal. Every cent that goes toward supporting the birth mother is accountable to the court. Submitted in a financial statement under penalty of perjury. I've had a couple list an ice-cream cone they bought when they took the birth mother to the beach."

"So my only chance is to be Mr. Nice Guy. So nice that I beat out the picket fences and the dogs."

"But, Rick, don't even bother filling out the card unless you understand that the whole point of these relationships, yours with the girl, is to make her feel okay about her pregnancy in a world that makes her feel like dirt because of it. To let her know that she's okay, and that by giving you the baby she's doing the right thing.

"Let me tell you a little bit more about these girls. Most of them are sent to me by their church groups and their right-to-life groups. Most of the time they haven't been out seducing boys; more likely they've been raped by some friend of the family or date-raped by some hotshot at the high school, and are too mortified to talk about it. When they come into this office, or send their sometimes barely readable letter, they've not yet spoken the words 'I'm pregnant' to anyone else.

"Some of them haven't been to a doctor yet. They broke open a piggy bank and bought an early pregnancy test that they did at home, locked in a bathroom they share with the rest of the family. Or they've just missed two periods and they're trying to hide morning sickness at the family breakfast table and they're scared to death. I try to create a cocoon for them. A time during which it's okay for them to be pregnant. I mean, hell, they already *are* pregnant. They don't want abortions, so why not make them feel as if all is well, and not only are they going to emerge from all of this just fine, but that some nice couple is going to be able to love this baby that they're bringing into the world.

"Wait until you meet some of these girls, Rick, and I hope you do. You thought I was just some pushy hustler when I told you there were some very moving stories in these girls. Well after you get to meet and know some of them . . . you tell me."

It looked to Rick as if Feldman was holding back tears, and he wondered if this was the lawyer's standard speech. Nevertheless, he looked down at the desk at the form he'd now completely filled out about himself, and he signed it.

When he got back to the office, Andrea looked nervous.

"Nat Ross's office called. They want you up there right away."

The door was open, and he could see there was a group of four or five people waiting for him. Nat Ross, Ian Kleier, who was Ross's second in command, plus a few underlings, and . . . shit, Kate Sullivan and a few of her entourage.

"Ricky!" Nat Ross said with such glee, it was as if he were a kid on a hot day and Rick was the ice-cream man. Rick felt numb the way one does in the face of certain disaster.

"Sit, my friend, and we can get you coffee or a Coke or a glass of wine, maybe even a coffee cake," Ross added and Rick wondered for an instant if the son of a bitch was making fun of his weight. "What's your pleasure?"

"Nothing, thanks," Rick said. His desire to bolt was

so strong that sitting was an effort, so his compromise was to perch on the edge of his chair, his two hands holding firmly onto the rim, readying himself to stand and run.

"I'm here to tell you," Nat Ross said, "that Kate is insane about the White House story. She has now called me, how many times, Katie, eight times? Nine times?"

Rick didn't look at her, but out of the corner of his eye he saw Kate Sullivan turn in her chair and answer demurely, "Maybe even more."

"Now to me, the idea of the two of you together would make such a full-out blockbuster picture that it brings tears to my eyes. So I wanted to do this honestly and aboveboard and cut through all the crap, and say that to you both, and tell you if we can be big kids and drop all the personality stuff, we can make a picture that this studio will back a thousand percent. So let me get your input on this. Okay?"

There was what seemed like an endless silence. Rick's mind raced. This was unconscionable, to be put in this position. The point was clear. The picture was now Sullivan's. If he said no, next week it would be Sydney Pollack or Garry Marshall called in to direct a picture Rick had been developing passionately for how long?

"I pass," he said, standing and walking out the door, straight to the stairs, not bothering to wait for the elevator. His head rang as he pounded all the way down, took a deep breath, opened the door to the third floor, and made his way along the deeply carpeted hallway to his office.

"Pack my things," he said to Andrea, who tore the headset off and said, "Huh?"

"I said pack my things. I don't work here anymore." The phone rang.

It was Nat Ross, Andrea came to the door of his inner office to tell him. Rick was putting photographs into a box he'd pulled from the closet.

"I'm out."

"He knows you're here."

"There's no more to say," he told her. "You finish this, please, I'm leaving."

He was in the parking lot about to get into his car when Nat Ross approached him. It was odd to see Ross in the parking lot, since no one ever did. The joke was that if you arrived on the lot at six A.M. and felt the hood of Nat Ross's car, it was already cold. And he was rumored to leave at midnight.

"Ricky, don't be dumb." He was walking toward the car. "I gave you an overall deal here and a lot of money after your last two pictures did no business at all. You're not exactly a hot property. In fact, the reality is, you're a fucking Popsicle. And I'm the guy who got the money for you because I bet my board here that you have at least one more picture left in you, and we might as well be the ones who get it."

Rick started the car. Who would fault him if he ran this cocksucker over now?

"This is a real chance for you to come back. With the biggest star in this town. Don't be dumb," Nat yelled after Rick's car as it squealed out of the parking lot.

"So what do you want? You think it's all a bowl of cherries?" Bobo asked. This morning his teeth had been bothering him. Now while he and Rick sat on the bed playing gin, the yellow dentures smiled at them from a glass on the chest of drawers across the room. "Your father and I struggled plenty. I told you how we fought with that bastard Harry Cohn till we were blue in the *gederim*. You're a spoiled no-goodnik. A few things fall apart, a couple of flops, and you're having a career crisis. What do you want, for Chris' sake?''

"I guess I like my career like I like my pastrami," Rick answered. "Hot and on a roll, and at the moment it isn't either of those. The writer on *Time Flies* dropped dead in a Pizza Hut, the second draft of *Count on Me* came back and it's a serious disappointment, I lost the rights to the novel of *Bloody Wonderful*, and then there's Kate Sullivan. Kate Sullivan is doing *Always a Lady*, and I'm not. It was my project for two years, and they gave it to her, Uncle B., so I walked. Packed up my office and walked."

"Gin," Bobo said, laying his matching suits on the card table.

"Et tu, Brute?" Rick laughed. "Christ, how did you do that so fast? I've got nothing here." Rick fanned his cards out on the table.

"You're a lousy shuffler and you owe me sixty-three cents," Bobo said.

"I took my phone off the hook and I've been all alone for days, trying to decide what to do."

Bobo looked at him, frowning. "What are you worrying? You got the world by the balls. There's a million stories out there. In your life alone there's a million. Make a movie about me and your dad. Two young guys in the early days in Hollywood. Make a movie about what it was like to be a kid on the back lot in those days, from the kid's point of view. You want to tell a good story? Tell the one about your parents dying in that plane crash. The biggest loss this business ever knew."

Bobo shuffled the cards as he spoke and Rick grinned as he watched the old cardshark whip them back and forth between his hands, fanning them, cascading them, making them rise and fall at one point as if they were defying gravity.

"No," Rick said. "I won't tell that one."

Bobo shrugged and dealt the cards with a spin.

"Ingeleh, listen to me. Go make a deal with another studio. Don't sit around at the old folks' home with all the *alter kockers* who are waiting to die. *I* feel too young to be here. So what in the hell do *you* get out of a place like this?" Rick hadn't even picked up his cards. Bobo's were already sorted.

"I'm learning about what it's like to be retired," Rick said, "because that may be what I do next."

After he'd lost seven dollars and seventeen cents to his uncle, Rick said good-bye to the old man and hugged him. When he did, he could smell the English Leather cologne Bobo still splashed on every morning.

"Don't do anything stupid. You're one in a million, kid. Those *shmeck-drecks* who took away your project should all kiss your ass and thank you for the privilege."

"I'll tell them," Rick said.

"Meanwhile, just so their target ain't so big, you should take off a couple of pounds," the old man added, giving Rick a kind of sharp rap on the arm that he remembered his father giving him when he was a little boy that meant, Do what I'm telling you or you'll regret it. Rick said, "Yeah, yeah, yeah," and headed for the exit.

He'd been doing nothing for nearly three weeks. Stuffing his face with junk food, watching game shows and soap operas on TV, inviting an occasional lady to come over to cook dinner and "roll around on top of me naked," which was how he'd once described a sexual evening to Charlie. "They call me, I say bring dinner. They feed me, we do it, I fall asleep. With any luck, they're gone before breakfast." It was a schedule he kept in between the six-month-long "steady girls."

That morning at the beginning of the fourth week, as he lay in bed at ten o'clock in the morning counting the knotholes in the vaulted ceiling over his bed and telling himself that fifty was the perfect age at which it was excusable for him to have a mid-life crisis, the phone rang. Harvey Feldman didn't announce himself. Just started talking the minute he heard Rick's voice.

"If it's safe to assume you're still interested, one of my clients is a fifteen-year-old pregnant girl named Lisa," he said. "She's from Akron, Ohio. She's in town with her sister and she's already met a few families. I told her about you. She didn't seem to mind that you were single, and seemed curious to meet you. It's a very long shot. But if you like I can ask her to come over."

Rick couldn't believe his own reaction. Panic. More anxiety than he could remember feeling in years. Stage fright. "Listen, I need a little while to straighten up and shave and shower and . . . how pregnant? So the baby's due when? Christ, I don't even know if I should waste this girl's time, Harvey." He'd been struggling so much about how to handle his split from the studio that he'd pretty much put the baby thing out of his mind. It was a crazy spur-of-the-moment idea he'd had in the middle of the night, designed to try to save himself. And then in a panic he'd run to Feldman and afterward felt so dumb. How could he sit now and be interviewed, as if he were up for a part, by some little pregnant girl? This was lunacy.

"Rick," the lawyer said, "if you've changed your mind, if it isn't right, if it isn't something you're dying to do, hang up the phone. I've already told you how committed you have to be to something like this to make it right. And only *you* know the answer to that."

Rick lay silently, still looking at the ceiling. Finally he spoke.

"What time?"

"How's four this afternoon?"

"I'll be here."

* * *

Lisa was six months' pregnant and told Rick she had been referred to Mr. Feldman by her right-to-life group. She was blond and green-eyed and pink-skinned and wore what was probably a hand-me-down polyester maternity top over some faded jeans. Her older sister was waiting in the car in Rick's driveway, despite Rick's attempts to have Lisa go out and get her.

"She doesn't want to interfere," Lisa told him.

Each time Lisa asked him a question and he answered it, she made a check mark with a plastic Bic pen on a little tablet from which she'd read the question. "And would you continue to go to your job after you adopted my baby?" She read the question without looking at him.

"I would," Rick said, "but I would have someone very qualified here to care for the baby while I was gone."

Lisa made some kind of a note.

"How many hours a day do you work?" she read.

"That depends. If I'm in the development stage of a project I can sometimes be home by six. If I'm shooting, sometimes I can be gone all day and night." It occurred to him that the words *development* and *shooting* meant nothing to her. He was about to explain when she frowned and looked him in the eye.

"Mr. Reisman," she said, "I'm scared that you wouldn't see the baby enough. And that you don't have enough extended family to care for it. Only that old uncle of yours that you mentioned, and I doubt that he's really interested. The honest-to-God's truth is I'm really worried about how fat you are at your age. I mean, you could die when the baby's only a year old, and then what'll happen to it? You don't have a wife, and from what I can figure, it doesn't look much like you're planning on having one either, as busy as you are and all. And that sounds a little weird to me too. So the way I see it, there's not much point to our going on and me asking you questions about my baby's education and all. Is there? 'Cause there's not a shot that I'm gonna pick you, and I hope you'll understand."

It was so blunt that Rick almost laughed, but there was something about the little girl's serious face that stopped him.

"I understand," he said, rising. She stood too, her pumpkin of a belly protruding in a kind of point from under the maternity blouse. Then she moved her notebook and her Bic pen into her left hand, thrust her right hand out for Rick to shake, and when he had, she walked briskly to the front door and was gone.

Rick looked down at the lavish spread of food he'd had his housekeeper put out on the coffee table in order to impress the girl, who hadn't touched one bite: an elaborate cheese tray, a caviar mousse, homemade brownies, and fruit. And after he heard Lisa's sister's rented car pull away, he sat down and ate most of the food himself.

18

WITHIN A FEW WEEKS he was relieved to find that despite Nat Ross's opinion, there were still some studios who were interested in him as a director, and soon his lawyer was negotiating to make a fine deal for him at Universal.

"And who told you so?" Bobo asked. The old man had been moved from the lodge to the hospital a few days before, when he complained of leg pains. Seeing him lying in a bed hooked up to an IV made Rick feel panicky. "Now you'll get some projects going and maybe forget all this nonsense about babies, you lunatic. Yes?"

Three more birth mothers had rejected Rick in the last two months, and each time he'd told Harvey Feldman to throw away his application. "It was a mistake. I can't handle it. Please, don't call me anymore."

But Feldman persisted. After the last one, a pretty twenty-year-old, walked into his house, took one look at

Rick, and said, "No way, José," and left, he'd actually started a new and serious diet.

"Ingeleh," Bobo said, "I think I'm supposed to have a pain pill and the nurse isn't answering my buzzer. Do me a favor and check the nurses' station for me."

"Sure, Uncle B.," Rick said, and as he walked to the door he bumped into Bobo's nurse.

"Here I am, Mr. Reisman," she said to Bobo and then added quietly to Rick, "Why don't you step out for a while while I bathe him too?"

As he walked down the carpeted hospital hallway, Rick saw someone wave at him. It was Harvey Feldman.

"Essie's in for surgery," the young lawyer told Rick as he walked closer. "How's Bobo?"

"Okay, I think."

"Listen," Feldman began.

"Never mind," Rick said, putting up a hand to stop him.

"I have an idea for you. There's a little girl named Doreen, from Kansas, who's very far gone in her pregnancy and getting very worried so—"

"No."

"Wait. She was supposed to give her baby to my clients who flew her out here a few weeks ago to meet her. The couple, I'm sorry to say, are what you'd call 'Beautiful People,' so when she stepped off the airplane—did I mention it was *their* airplane, which they sent to fetch her—anyway, after they saw her, she's short, bucktoothed, and wore glasses, they sent her back."

"Nice folks," Rick said.

"Needless to say, Doreen is heartbroken," Harvey said, "and she probably wouldn't come back here. On the other hand . . ."

"Not for me. Honest to God, Harvey. I'm sorry I

ever took your time in the first place. I can barely hold my own life together let alone be responsible for a—"

"Mr. Feldman." A nurse stepped out of a room down the hall where Harvey Feldman's aunt Essie was.

"Call me," Feldman said over his shoulder to Rick, "if you change your mind."

Kate Sullivan's picture was on the cover of two magazines in the airport newsstand. There was no question she was an exquisite-looking broad. Rick bought some chewing gum and the *Wall Street Journal*, picked up a pack of his favorite, Peanut M&Ms, and was going to have the cashier add them to his tab when he decided to be a good boy and put the candy back. He folded the paper under his arm and walked down the airport corridor, watching the people pass him on both sides, his eye as always framing much of what he saw as shots in a film: a picturesque moment of two women who were clearly a mother and daughter reuniting in a tearful hug, a Sikh walking hurriedly along at the same pace and side by side an old Hasidic Jew.

I'm losing my mind, Rick thought. I've been moving rapidly in this direction for years, but now I've arrived. In exactly four minutes, according to the schedule on the television screen above my head, an airplane will land and in it, courtesy of tickets purchased on my Visa card, will be Doreen Cobb, a fourteen-year-old pregnant girl from Kansas, and her mother, Bea. If all goes well in our conversation, which the mother insists has to take place in the airport, Bea will leave Doreen here, so I can move her into my secretary's apartment to have a baby for me.

If things don't go well, Doreen will fly on to Nevada with her mother, who's leaving tonight to see her eldest son and his wife. Harvey Feldman had explained that Rick was going to be Doreen's final try at open adoption and if there was no match to be made, the girl agreed to give the baby up to a home in Nevada.

I shouldn't be doing this, he thought with a pang of guilt mixed with fear. There's much too much potential for pain for everyone concerned. The little pregnant girl, her mother, me, but especially the innocent unborn baby. I shouldn't be doing this. Then why am I so swept up in the forward motion of this plan? The girl has already been hurt by some phonies, or should I say some other phonies, who thought she was too ugly to ever bring forth the brand of baby they thought they should have. Wouldn't another rejection be too much for her adolescent ego? Isn't it exquisitely selfish of me to drag her through that possibility one more time?

No, he thought, arriving at the gate and watching through the window as the big carrier was being motioned in toward the gate. Because I won't reject her. If she'll have me as the adopting parent of this baby, I'll grab the chance and commit myself to making the experience good for the girl and for the baby.

He needed love in his life so desperately. To give it, to get it, to exchange it, to hang on to it because he was finally starting to know it was all there really was in this world that mattered. And not having it was making him shrivel into nothingness. Bobo and Charlie and Patty and the kids had been the greatest source of his pleasure, his strength, his good feelings about himself for most of his life. Now Charlie was gone and Bobo was hanging on by a thread. Somehow he had to find a repository for all the love he knew he could give, and maybe a little baby was the answer. Babies required so much attention. Perhaps giving that attention would make him stop thinking only about himself.

So that's why I'm here, he thought, joining the group at the gate waiting for the passengers to emerge from the flight. As the stream of people began to flow, he looked closely at the faces of every passenger, until he saw the unmistakable mother and daughter step arm in arm through the door. Within an instant the tiny gray-haired woman spotted him, looked piercingly into his eyes, tapped her wide-eyed daughter on the arm, and the girl, seeing him now too, flushed red. Then they all moved together to meet face to face.

Rick extended his hand but Bea Cobb ignored it. She was all business. "Where can we go?" she asked.

"We can go to one of the conference rooms at the Red Carpet Club, where I'm a member," Rick offered, but Bea waved that idea away with a gesture, then pointed to a nearby cocktail lounge. "What's wrong with that place over there?" she asked.

For the first time in his always-running-the-show life Rick thought to himself, I will not make waves. I'll do whatever she says. "That'll be just fine with me," he said.

The two women walked hand in hand and Rick looked at the face of the girl, who snuck a peek back at him, and when their eyes met it was with the mutually awkward shy and wary smile that probably characterized the meeting of a mail-order couple. With each of them thinking, If this works out, this stranger will soon be related to me in a lifelong way.

She was as described, wearing glasses, with an upper lip that protruded in that way it does with people who have an obvious overbite. She looked very much like her mother, who was a few inches taller and also shaped like a little fireplug, except that Doreen's hair was wispy and fine and blond and the mother's hair was gray and cropped close.

The cocktail lounge had the malty stink of stale alcohol, and Bea Cobb, squinting to adjust her eyes to the low light, spotted a table in the corner, tugged her daughter in that direction, and when they got there sat.

There were no waiters, only a bartender, so Rick took their orders. After a few minutes he brought two diet Cokes and a light beer for himself.

"Well now," Bea said, looking at him while Doreen looked everywhere else but. "I guess the first thing I want to know is how come you're not married?"

"I can't explain it," he said. "I *wish* I hadn't let all this time go by without having one woman to feel close to and love, but I guess I was afraid."

"Afraid of what?" she asked him. "Why would you be afraid? Being married and having a family are the best things anyone can do in this world. You think making movies is more important?"

Rick held tightly to the cold beer glass and tried to decide what to tell her. He thought back over the last few months, and how he'd wanted to impress the young pregnant girls he'd met in his living room and in Harvey Feldman's office, and that the harder he seemed to try, the easier it was for them to see through the ruse. Maybe, you asshole, he thought, you ought to take a deep breath and tell the truth.

"When I was a little boy my parents were looked on as royalty in Hollywood. He was a brilliant producer and director and she was one of the most beautiful and gifted actresses alive. When their private plane went down with my dad flying, it was an enormous tragedy. I was their only child. They doted on me. My father had been an astute businessman who invested his money wisely. So after their death, as a heartbroken, emotionally needy adolescent boy, I found myself with millions of dollars. The news hit the papers, and when the numbers got out, I became very popular. In fact, it didn't take too long, after I moved in with Uncle Bobo and Aunt Sadie, for women to start finding me. Dozens of them, every size and shape and age, some of them nearly my mother's age.

"It was every boy's dream, but too much, too soon, and I knew instinctively that I couldn't trust any of them. Because it wasn't my beautiful eyes they were after, or all the other things they claimed made me so attractive. I was a little boy, and I missed my mother, so I went out with these women and that wasn't the answer. And pretty soon, I started to eat. Because food was something I could trust. Food didn't have an ulterior motive for making me feel good.

"I never really got obese; pudgy enough to make sure that certain women keep their distance, but most of the time the combination of the money and the burgeoning success of my career made up for the fat, and made a lot of them hang in there and put up with my neurosis. Eventually, when it came down to it, by the time I was really at an age where getting serious with someone was what I should be doing, I found myself so cynical, so burnt out, that I never could close a deal with any woman." What a lousy story that is, he thought, but sadly it's the truth.

Doreen's mother clucked her tongue, and the sound broke Rick's reverie. "How long ago was the accident?" she asked.

"Thirty-two years. I was eighteen."

"You're fifty?"

He nodded. "Will be this year."

"Same as me." She laughed, outraged at that idea. Rick was surprised. None of the women he knew in Los Angeles who were fifty would ever let their hair get gray, or for that matter admit they were fifty.

"I'm a grandmother seven times already, and you're wanting to adopt a baby?" She laughed again. "I think you're crazy."

He smiled. She was looking at him now in a friendly way, as if their mutual age made them comrades.

"What'll my daughter do here for the next few months?" she asked him.

"There's a young woman who's been my secretary for several years. She has a large apartment in a nice neighborhood. I'll pay Doreen's share of the rent while she lives there as the girl's roommate, and provide all of Doreen's other expenses, find her the best medical care, and if she wants to, I'll help her enroll in some continuing-education classes at a nearby college."

She was nodding a little nod that Rick hoped was a nod of approval.

"My other seven kids all had a meeting this week. They told me I was crazy if I let Doreen go off with some sharpie who's trying to buy her baby. They think she ought to have it at a home somewhere, and then forget about it for the rest of her life."

"And why don't you?"

"Because," she said, looking over at her daughter, who looked back at her wistfully as if she knew what her mother was about to tell him, "I didn't have eight kids, I had nine. My first one was born when I was Doreen's age. But in those days they didn't have any such thing as open adoption. So my child, my oldest son, who is thirty-six years of age this year, is out there somewhere, and I don't know where. I don't know anything about him, except his birthday, which is March third. And on that day I always think about him. I light a candle for him every year."

"That's very sad," Rick said.

Her eyes held his for a while and then a smile broke out on her face and she said, "Fifty years old! You and I were teenagers at the same time. Did you like Elvis?"

"To me he was the King," Rick answered, grinning.

"To me too," Bea Cobb said.

"I had the good fortune to meet him," Rick told her.

"No! Spare me," she said. "How did you meet the King?"

"In the seventies I had a secretary who used to be a dancer. She danced in some of his movies, and they became great friends. So she invited me on the set of a television special he was shooting, and I actually shook his hand."

"With *this* hand?" she asked, taking Rick's right hand in her two small ones.

He nodded.

"Ooooh," she said, doing a little mock shiver. "I touched the hand that touched the King."

Bea Cobb and Rick Reisman laughed together, and then she said, "I want to tell you something, okay? And you might as well say okay, 'cause I'm going to tell you what I think even if you don't. You don't know what in the hell you're getting into. You think having a baby is something that'll do the same thing for you as buying a new car. Lift your spirits, make you feel sexier.

"Well, take it from me, that's not anywhere near what it's about. And when I leave here, you're probably going to say to yourself, That hick doesn't know a goddamned thing. But that's okay because I don't give a damn what you think. I'm telling you from a life of a whole lot of experience that raising a baby turns a person around in ways they didn't even know there were. Teaches you patience, humility, and the real meaning of pain. On top of that, a child makes you tell the truth, because they don't buy into any lies. And anyone can see in your scared and sad eyes, you've probably told a lot of those in your many long years."

This whole day felt surreal to Rick. And this was the strangest part of all. Being dressed down by this odd little woman who had his number in spades. He was sad and scared and wanting to adopt a baby for all the wrong reasons. But they were reasons which had been compelling enough to get him all the way to this part of the process.

"So now," she said, "I'd like to have one more Coca-Cola, and after that, it'll be time to go check in at the gate."

Well, Rick thought, that dismissal is loud and clear. He tried to hide his disappointment. You knew your chances were low, he told himself, and it was an insane idea anyway so . . .

"What about you, Doreen? You want another cold drink too?" Bea asked.

"Yeah, okay," Doreen answered, and it was the first time Rick heard her voice. He sighed and stood to go and get another round for all of them. And while his back was turned, there must have been some moment that passed between mother and daughter during which the decision was made, because then the young girl said with a laugh in her voice, "But if I were you, I'd forget the beer and make it a diet drink. 'Cause you're going to have to shape up if you're planning to be a father."

19

ONCE EVERY FOUR OR FIVE DAYS, Andrea would drive into the city from the Valley and when she did she would stop at Rick's house and drop off "the girl," which is how Bobo referred to Doreen. But despite the old man's *tsk*ing and shaking his head, and protesting at the "*misbegoss* of this crazy new world," Rick had already seen the grudging look of respect in the old man's eyes when Doreen beat him at gin rummy. Rick loved to observe the way Bobo got caught up in conversation with her when she asked him about his early film career. One at a time she had rented and watched each of the films Bobo and Rick's father, Jake, produced.

"The kid's a sponge," Andrea reported to Rick one day at the office. "She signed up for a literature course at Valley College, because my place is five blocks from there. I couldn't get past the syllabus for the class, and she's already halfway through the books. Not to mention that she's reading to the baby."

"How do you mean?"

"She read somewhere that if you talk to the fetus and sing to it, that makes it feel good, reassures it with the sound of your voice. Well, she said she's a lousy singer, so she went and got all these children's books out of the library, and every night she lies in bed, reading stories to her own stomach."

Rick liked the idea of Doreen's genes having reading and learning and especially cardsharking in them. There was something about counting down the months until the baby's arrival that forced life into him, enriched every choice he made, now that he knew he was making it not only for himself but for the baby as well. His baby. He was still eating more than he should, but not as frantically or as often. And more than a few times he would turn down a date in order to take Doreen to dinner, or say no to a visit from a woman to get the rest everyone told him he would need when the baby came.

"Harvey Feldman said I shouldn't ask you this," he said to Doreen at dinner one night at the Hamburger Hamlet. He had ordered a broiled chicken breast; Doreen had ordered the onion soup, a salad, a bacon cheeseburger, and a strawberry shake. She stopped in the middle of the sip of the strawberry shake and a little of the pink still bubbled in a line above her upper lip as she put her hand up and said, "Don't. Because I won't tell you anything about the father of this baby. And if you have to know, I'll go right back to Kansas and forget our deal. He was in good physical health and he was tall. That's all you get." She was serious, so he dropped it.

He had come to love his time together with her. She was confrontational and outspoken, a bright spot in his world, which was filled with the backstabbing politics and outsize egos of show business. A few times he took her with him to an invitation-only screening. On those nights he would notice she would wear a little blusher on her already pink cheeks, and a tiny bit of mascara on her otherwise invisible blond eyelashes. And always, because of her years of watching television night and day, she recognized more of the faces in the audience than he did.

"Michael Keaton was there and Jack Nicholson," he heard her telling her mother on the phone one night. And then she let out a shriek of excitement.

The man who lived two doors down from Bobo in the lodge was Arnold Viner. Viner had been a studio publicist who had represented Rick's father and Bobo for years.

"It's right out of Sartre," Bobo said. "If anyone had asked me in nineteen thirty-nine to describe hell, I would have said living near Arnold Viner and being too old to run away every time he walked by." Bobo and Viner had had a fight in the early forties about an item that appeared in the paper, and they were still arguing about it ten minutes before they took Viner over to the adjacent hospital with a massive stroke. Bobo insisted on staying in the intensive care unit by his side.

It was a day on which Rick was visiting, so he stayed too. He sat in the waiting room, reading some scripts he had in his briefcase and making notes on them until a few hours had passed. When the machines stopped bleeping and the doctors came in to confirm that Viner had died, a red-eyed Bobo came out to the waiting room, and took Rick's hand.

"I sat in there because I knew his time was up," he said, "so I figured eventually the angel of death would come, and I could beg him to throw me into the deal and take me too. My luck, right? I fell asleep in the chair and missed the whole transaction." Rick put an arm around Bobo and walked him back to the lodge.

They hadn't reached the room yet when he heard his name being paged on the loudspeaker.

"Richard Reisman, telephone."

He took the call in Bobo's room. It was Andrea's voice.

"Doreen's bleeding. A lot. She called me at the office so I came right over. We tried to reach you all morning, but you weren't in Bobo's room. So I took her to the doctor. He said it's placenta previa. She has to stay in bed for the rest of the pregnancy. All the time, including her meals in bed too. She can get out briefly to go to the bathroom or shower. That's all. Listen, she's a doll, but I'm not exactly the nursy type, and I have to come to the office every day. What do I do?"

"Pack her up and move her to my house. The housekeeper's always there. Doreen can stay in the guest room and be tended to during the day. If that's not enough I'll get her a full-time nurse."

"We'll be at your place by the time you get home," Andrea promised.

Bleeding. Harvey Feldman, the lawyer, had forgotten to mention miscarriage, never discussed premature births or still-borns or any of the ways in which a pregnancy could end. And for some reason, losing the baby during the pregnancy was one of the possibilities that had never occurred to Rick. During all of this he had carried the vague feeling that somewhere in this seemingly unnatural set of circumstances was the potential for disaster, and maybe this was it. He stopped briefly at his office at Universal to pick up some scripts he needed to read, then hurried home.

He was relieved to see Doreen already settled in the bed and very chipper when he walked into the freshly painted yellow guest room. She had an apologetic expression on her face as she lay on the bed with her little feet propped up on a pile of pillows.

"My mom's gonna be real unhappy about this," she said.

"The bleeding?" he asked.

"No, my staying at your house. She doesn't think we should live together till after we're married." Then she made a face at him and laughed.

"Very funny," he said. "Did you call the school and tell them you were dropping out?"

"Yeah," she said sadly. "I'm going to do all the reading anyway. The trouble is there's not that much left, and I'm going to be stuck like this for a month."

He had walked directly from the garage into her room, so he was still carrying the pile of scripts he'd brought home to read. He dropped them on her bed with a thunk.

"Here," he said. "Read these for me. I have to start them over the weekend. You can tell me which ones are good and which are stinkers."

"Really?" she asked. "Are you kidding? You really want *me* to read the scripts that you might want to make into a movie? Me?"

"Sure," he said, sitting at the foot of the bed. "Would you do that for me?"

"For you, yes," she said, her little round pink face very serious, her blond lashes batting hard behind the glasses. "But keep in mind," she said, "if I'm critical, it's because I *am* a student of the classics."

"I'll certainly factor your literary background into my assessment of the critiques."

"Oh, thanks ever so," she said, assuming the haughtiest voice. Then she opened the blue cover of the top script and looked at the title page. "Well here's one that's bound to do wonders for your career. It's called *The Hand of Doom*. I think I'll start with this and work my way up."

He started toward the door. "*You,*" he said, "are a piece of work."

"What's for dinner?" she asked.

"I'll ask Nellie," he said.

"Nellie went home early, her mother's sick," she told him.

The point was clear. Dinner was up to him.

"What do you like on your pizza?" he asked.

"You'd feed pizza to the woman whose body is nutritionally responsible for your child?"

"I'll make a salad," he mumbled grudgingly.

"Be sure to throw in some protein," she shouted after him.

Standing in the kitchen alone he chuckled, trying to imagine what the personality would be of the baby that came out of that girl. A feisty little pink-faced girl? A tough, smart-mouthed boy? Four more weeks and, God willing, he would be holding the little creature in his arms.

A few evenings later, Doreen, who had fallen asleep over one of Rick's scripts, was awakened by the sound of the doorbell. The doctor had told her she could go as far as the bathroom, and the front door wasn't much farther than that, so she figured it would be all right if she answered it. Whoever was at the door was making a big racket, loud, with the brass door knocker. Doreen couldn't find her own robe, but an old one of Rick's was hanging on the inside of the door, so she threw that one over her nightgown and hurried to see what was so urgent.

The woman who stood in the doorway was so gorgeous to look at, at least to Doreen, that she was certain this must be a movie star. It wasn't Candice Bergen, but she looked a lot like her.

"Is Mr. Reisman at home?"

"No he isn't," Doreen said.

"Do you expect him soon?"

Doreen nodded.

The woman moved forward, backing Doreen into the living room.

"I'll just wait here," she said, plopped down in a chair, picked up a magazine, and began leafing through it. "Tell you what," she said to Doreen without even looking up at her. "I'll have a scotch and water."

"Great," Doreen said, and was about to head back into her room to get back into bed when the blond woman said, "Make it for me, okay?"

Doreen looked at her and said, "Honey, I wouldn't know scotch if you cooked me in it. Make it yourself," and went back into her room. After a few minutes she could hear the woman talking loudly to someone, and she realized it must be into a telephone because there were no other voices out there. Uh-oh, she thought, what if she's making long-distance calls? What if Rick doesn't even know her and *I* let her into the house? I better keep an eye on her.

So she put the robe on again and walked back into the living room. When she got there, the woman was drinking some kind of alcohol in a glass she'd found in one of the cabinets and smoking a cigarette. The butt of a previous cigarette had already been put out on what Doreen recognized was one of Rick's good china plates, which this lady had obviously pulled out of the cabinet when she couldn't find an ashtray.

"I figured if I waited long enough, this asshole would come to his senses and call me, and then not one fucking word. I mean, it's such bullshit. So after a few weeks went by I called his office three times, and he never called me back. And that bitch secretary of his, that Andrea, kept saying, 'Sorry, Mona, he's so busy,' you know? Then I read in *Variety* that the studio dumped him.

"Well, you know what a softie I am. Right? I felt sorry for him, so I sent him a really sweet note that he never answered, and I called his house and left message after message on the fucking machine, and he still didn't call me back, and then I read in the *Hollywood Reporter* that he made a deal at Universal, so I sent him some flowers over there, and you think he calls me one time? Zippo. Not even a thank-you note from the rude little asshole. And Katy Biggard said she saw him on the beach in Malibu last week, and that he must be dying or something because he lost all this weight, and you know what a pig he's always been. You'd get sick if you saw him naked. Anyway, I got really worried about him and came running over here and this troll who works for him answers the door, and she wouldn't even make me a drink. I'll tell you, I'm just sick and tired of it. So listen—''

Doreen had heard enough. ''This isn't an ashtray,'' she said, grabbing the plate away from Mona, who had been tamping out another cigarette and now dropped hot ashes onto her own hand and screamed. Doreen grabbed the phone away from Mona. ''He is not an asshole or a pig,'' and slammed it into the phone cradle. ''And Andrea is not a bitch.'' Then she grabbed the five-foot-nine Mona by the arm and steered her toward the door. ''*I* am not a troll, and *you*,'' she said, opening the front door and shoving Mona out through it, ''are not welcome here!''

Before she could shut the door in the stunned Mona's hang-jawed face, Mona bellowed, ''Who the fuck *are* you? I'm going to tell Rick about this and he's going to fire your fat ugly little ass for treating me like this. So I just want you to tell me right now who you are!''

''I,'' Doreen said, realizing that she was wearing Rick's robe, untied it and let it fall dramatically to the floor as she told the flabbergasted Mona, ''am the mother of Rick Reisman's baby.'' And then she closed the door in Mona's stunned face.

Doreen remembered what her mother once told her about how to deal with a man: Wait until his stomach is full before you break any bad news to him. So she waited until she and Rick finished the dinner Nellie had left for them that night and were about to watch the news on television. Then she told him about Mona's visit. He didn't react visibly until the end of the story, when to Doreen's delight he let out a big laugh. There was enormous relief in it, and he obviously loved imagining little Doreen pushing big Mona out the door. "I'm sorry," he said, hoping Doreen wasn't insulted by his laughter, but the feeling was too rich to hold inside.

Things were coming together for him at Universal the way they never had before. All of his new projects were exciting, and within six months one of them was sure to move onto the floor, and he would be back in the world where he operated best. Interacting with the actors, taking close-up pictures of human behavior. That was when he felt most comfortable, creating those moments of truth.

There was one script that had its hooks deeper into him than the others. The leading character was a brilliant scientist who discovers a possible cure for cancer, and the story is about the battles he fights when he enters a nightmarish world of people who don't want that cure to be found just yet.

"Robert Redford," Doreen said the minute she finished reading the script, "and nobody else. Maybe with you directing, Clint Eastwood could pull it off."

Sometimes Rick had to stifle a laugh when she talked that way. Since she'd started doing some of his reading she was beginning to sound like a salty, too hip, William Morris agent.

"Redford is perfect," Doreen went on, "because this character has to have that kind of gorgeousness, since every woman in the whole movie falls in love with him."

"I'll send it to his agent," Rick said.

"Smart move," Doreen told him and moved on to the next script in the pile. She had two weeks to go until the baby was born, and these days she just kind of slid from room to room, from chair to chair. The big event of her day was, without fail, turning on the television and watching "Jeopardy!"

"What is Soledad prison?" he heard her say out loud, answering the question with a question like the "Jeopardy!" contestants. "Who was Geppetto?" And when she got the answer wrong she would say to herself, "*Doreeeen*, you are so stupid!"

"Last year in school we had a discussion about our ideal man," she said one night when Rick got home just as the "Jeopardy!" closing credits were rolling by. "Guess who I picked."

"Who?"

"Alex Trebek. He is truly brainy, which to me is the most important quality anyone can have."

"I have a bachelor's degree and two master's," Rick said, realizing he was feeling jealous of the game-show host.

"I know," she said. "When I found out I was going to meet you, I went to the library in Kansas City and read about you in that big book about directors that came out a few years back. It tells all the details of your life. It had everything in it about you and your parents and Uncle Bobo, with pictures of them when they were young."

"Kansas City was a long way for you to go to check up on someone," he said.

"Not someone," she said abruptly. "Maybe the father of the only baby I might ever have. Those other people from Los Angeles, the first ones Mr. Feldman introduced me to, they didn't seem as if they had a lot going for them upstairs, and that's why I didn't pick them."

A lie. She thought she had to tell Rick a lie to cover, and it made him want to reach over, touch her hair gently, and tell her that he knew the truth about what had happened with that couple, and it didn't matter to him. But there was something about the way her jaw was set that told him to allow her to rewrite the uncomfortable story about that rejection with any ending she wanted.

"It's also why I went to the library to check up on you."

"How did I stack up?" he asked her gently.

"Not bad," she answered.

Sid Sheinberg called that night to tell Rick that Robert Redford not only loved the project but wanted to meet on the fifteenth about doing it, less than a week away, and Rick excitedly told Doreen. She nodded.

"There you go," she said.

At Doreen's most recent doctor's appointment, the doctor set Rick up with a beeper system.

"In case," the doctor explained, "you're not in your office when she goes into labor, and we need you right away." Every morning before Rick left for work, he attached the beeper to his belt and gave it a little pat.

"No false alarms," Doreen promised him. "I know you're busy, so I won't call unless I'm as sure as I can be that I'm ready to burst."

"I'll be there for you," he promised in return.

There was something indescribable about being in a room with Robert Redford. Even to Rick, who had known and worked closely with many famous stars. Maybe it was seeing with one's own eyes that the actor's look, the exquisite face, the stance, the bright-eyed boyishness, had nothing to do with the camera, but was very real.

"He'll only be in town for these eight hours. At five-thirty he gets on an airplane and will be out of the country for six months. He loves the script. He loves the character, he loves your work. There are a few creative points he'd like to change."

That was the part of what the agent said that stuck in Rick's stomach. What could those points be? The character of the scientist was certainly not perfect. He was neurotic, a drinker, maybe Redford didn't like that. But changing that would take all the bite out of the work.

"I'm sure you know if he says yes, it's a go project, and my sense of it is that if you iron out those three points, he'll be ready to shoot it the minute he gets back."

Redford. The image of Doreen's little face the day she suggested Rick try to get him came rushing back to Rick as he began telling Robert Redford about the genesis of the project and what had made him interested in it in the first place. Redford nodded and smiled, and Rick could tell by the comments he interjected that they agreed completely on the tone of the piece. *Thank God.*

Doreen. Last night when he walked by her room, he heard her reading passages of *Alice in Wonderland* out loud. Any day now she would be going into labor, and his baby would be born. A baby. A fifty-year-old man adopting a baby. Somehow in the conversation with Redford, the subject of children came up. Probably because Phillips, the character in the script, had children, and Redford asked Rick if he had any. "Well . . . almost," Rick said, and he found himself rattling out the entire story of Doreen and the impending birth and adoption.

"Now *that's* a story for a movie," Redford told him. Everyone in the meeting, all the executives and agents laughed at that comment. And now they were coming to the down side. The part of the meeting where Robert Redford would tell Rick what changes he thought the material required. Rick knew he would have to determine then and there if he thought the changes would work for or destroy the material as he saw it. He was about to steer the conversation in that inevitable direction when the unmistakable sound of the beeper he was wearing on his belt filled the entire room. Everyone turned and looked at Rick.

"Must have been something I ate for lunch," Rick joked as he jumped to his feet. Doreen, the baby, his baby, was about to be born. To come into the world and be his heir, his family. Now, it was happening now, right in the middle of this coveted meeting with Robert Redford. A meeting that couldn't be changed or rescheduled for at least six months, after which the chance for the project to happen, the intense interest that could get Robert Redford to commit and the movie to be a certainty, would surely be gone.

"Gentlemen," Rick said, with a slight bow of his head, "the scientist with the cure for cancer will just have to wait, because as of this moment, I'm about to be a father." And on very light feet, he left Robert Redford's meeting and went to take Doreen Cobb to the hospital.

20

ONE DAY AT PANACHE, Carin told Lainie she had heard about a way that adopting mothers could actually breast-feed their babies. The adopting mother taped to her nipple a tiny tube that was attached to a container of formula. The baby sucked on the tube and the mother's nipple at the same time, and eventually the adopting mother's hormones took over and her own breast milk came in. Lainie didn't tell the well-meaning Carin that her body would be unable to produce those hormones. Just thanked her for the information.

Lainie and Jackie had agreed that probably it was best that their next meeting would not be until the amniocentesis, which was fourteen weeks away. Time went by quickly, and no news from Jackie was good news, because it meant that the pregnancy was holding. When the Jackie phone rang in her house and Lainie heard Jackie's by-now-familiar voice saying, "I'm a tank.

You'll faint when you see me," she meant it when she answered, "I can't wait."

As she opened the door to the neonatal doctor's reception area and saw Jackie, something about looking at her there made Lainie reel in disbelief. This wasn't just an idea anymore. There was exquisitely apparent evidence, round and swollen evidence, that Mitch's baby was inside this woman.

"What do you think?" Jackie asked, stretching her legs out, then pulling herself up to her feet to come and give Lainie a Shalimar-scented hug.

"I think you look great," Lainie said.

Jackie stepped back and looked down at her own large middle. "*There's* our little honey," she said. "And today we're going to see it."

A young dark-haired pregnant girl across the waiting room put down her magazine, looked over at the two of them, and smiled. "We're having a baby together," Jackie told her. The girl raised her eyebrows, not sure what to say, and seemed relieved when the nurse opened the door and called for Jackie and Lainie to come into the examining room.

Now, from where she sat on the folding chair that the doctor had pushed into the back corner of the room for her, Lainie could see just the top of Jackie's round belly, which was shiny with oil. The neonatal doctor, handsome with gray hair which looked odd with his very young-looking face, had gently spread the oil on it, the way one lover spreads suntan lotion on the other. The oil made the instrument he held in his hand move more easily on Jackie's abdomen.

The room was dimly lit so that Jackie, Lainie, the nurse, and the doctor could better see the speckled, writhing figure projected on the tiny TV monitor that was mounted close to the ceiling in the far corner of the room. It looked to Lainie like bad reception on a broken television, but this was the long-awaited picture. The doctor was using it to determine the location of the amniotic fluid, some of which he was going to extract. With the help of his nurse, who held a pointer against the screen, he very carefully showed Lainie and Jackie that the baby had all of its fingers and toes, a perfect spine, and a healthy heartbeat.

"Jesus, when my Tommy was born, they sure didn't have *this* kind of thing," Jackie said from her supine position on the table. "In those days, you just crossed your fingers and hoped for the best. Can you tell what it *is* yet, Doc?"

"Yes. It's definitely a baby," the doctor joked.

Jackie emitted a yelp of a laugh, and the grainy figure on the sonogram seemed to jump.

"I mean the sex," Jackie said.

"Not from this, but in a few weeks we'll know. Do you want us to tell you when we do, Mrs. O'Malley?"

"Hell yeah," Jackie answered. "Don't we, Lainie?"

Lainie had never even thought about knowing the baby's sex before it was born, and whether she wanted to or not. She had asked Jackie to have the amniocentesis to be certain the baby had no genetic defects. She had no idea how Mitch would feel about knowing the sex before the birth.

"Absolutely," Jackie told the doctor. "That way they'll know if they want to name the baby Jackie for a girl or Jack for a boy," and then she laughed again. "That's a joke, Doc. *My* name is Jackie, and it's *their* baby." The doctor nodded with a slight smile.

"Look," Jackie said, pointing suddenly. "Every time I laugh, it bobbles all around. Isn't that adorable?"

Lainie tried to focus hard on the screen, but couldn't tell which part of the baby was which, or where the baby stopped and the rest of the picture started. This wasn't what she'd imagined at all. She'd thought that what she would see would look like the photos in the books she'd rushed out to buy the day she heard Jackie was pregnant, *A Child Is Born* and *The Secret Life of the Unborn Child.* Now she squinted when the nurse turned on the bright fluorescent overhead lights.

"Mrs. O'Malley, I'm going to give you a light local anesthetic on the spot from which I'll extract the amniotic fluid. You'll feel a slight ping and that's all," the doctor told Jackie.

"What about when you put the big needle in?" Jackie asked, her voice sounding almost childlike.

"That shouldn't hurt," the doctor told her.

"Easy for *you* to say." Jackie laughed nervously.

The doctor didn't react.

"Laine?" Jackie said, picking up her head to look back at the spot where Lainie sat.

"Yeah?"

"Could you move a little closer and like . . . hold my hand?"

"Sure," Lainie said, looking at the doctor to ask if that was all right with him. And when he nodded, she moved close to the table and gently took Jackie's hand in hers. While the doctor extracted the amniotic fluid and Jackie squeezed Lainie's hand, the two women looked into each other's eyes and talked about maternity clothes, and which store they would go to when the amniocentesis was over.

An hour later, they were in Lady Madonna in Encino. For so long, Lainie had averted her eyes in the mall every time she passed a maternity store. Now she stood right in the middle of one, turning a rounder that held tops and slacks as she tried choosing some clothes for Jackie.

"In gray I look like the Goodyear blimp," Jackie shouted from the dressing room. "In pink, more like Petunia Pig."

"Black is supposed to be slimming," Lainie called back, picking a large black T-shirt and some black pants with an elastic panel front and bringing them over to the curtained dressing room. When the slightly parted curtain revealed a naked Jackie with enormous breasts that sat on top of her huge abdomen, Lainie started to back away, but Jackie opened the curtain wider and puffed herself out proudly.

"Is this a shocker?" she asked. "And this is only at seventeen weeks. We could be having an elephant, Mother."

The ten-thousand-dollar surrogacy fee didn't include a budget for maternity clothes, so Mitch agreed to give Jackie "a few hundred dollars extra" to cover that cost. He thought it was fine that Lainie went along to shop with her.

"I love your taste," Jackie had said, "please come and help me, so I don't get stuff that makes me look dumb."

The black two-piece outfit was perfect, and so were a white sailor top with red pants, a sundress and a few T-shirts and some maternity jeans, four new bras, and half a dozen pairs of underpants. Everything was so expensive. Jackie said she didn't need nighties because she slept in some extra-large men's T-shirts. "Unfortunately without benefit of the extra-large men," she added laughing.

When Lainie pulled the cash out of her wallet to pay for everything the saleswoman seemed surprised.

"We get so few people paying cash," she said, almost suspiciously.

"That's because she isn't allowed to leave any traces," Jackie said, grinning, giving Lainie a friendly little poke in the side. Lainie hated this part. The secrecy. Being unable to tell Jackie about certain aspects of her life. While the saleswoman was putting the new clothing in bags, Lainie looked around at all of the display outfits, which had been stuffed with padding to create the effect of pregnant bodies, and tried to imagine how she would have looked in them if this had been her own pregnancy.

"Looks like you're buying her a whole wardrobe," the saleswoman said, making small talk. "Is she your sister?"

Lainie shook her head no.

"Cousin?"

Lainie shook her head no again.

"No relation?"

"No."

"Amazing. The resemblance is so strong. Except for the fact that she's . . ."

"Pregnant," Lainie said.

"Fat," Jackie said, and the three women all laughed. The saleswoman handed the package to Lainie who handed it to Jackie, and the two women went off to lunch.

When Jackie was in her sixth month, Lainie decided it was time to tell her mother what was going on. So she drove to Beverly Hills and met her for lunch in the Bedford Café, a tiny little corner restaurant she knew her mother loved. It was near the law office where she worked, and most days she would go there alone and read the newspaper while she ate the meat loaf, which was a specialty of the place.

"I know it's strange, and I can appreciate your having some doubts about it, but believe me, everything has been handled very carefully, and if we can have a healthy baby that comes from Mitch, I'll be a happy woman."

"Mmm-hmmm, ' Margaret Dunn said, her face tense with disapproval.

"Mother, you and I both know I could have died, but I didn't. And now I feel that I'm blessed for every day I live on this earth. Imagine how lucky I am to be able to have a baby too. Please be happy for me."

"Dear, I'm happy you're getting what you want. But I'm afraid it will never work out properly. This way of having babies is a way to please men," she said in a strained voice, and her gaze was over Lainie's shoulder. It was where she always looked during those rare times when she had any meaningful conversations with her daughter.

"What does that mean?" Lainie asked.

"It means there is no way on God's earth that either of the two women will ever be able to feel one hundred percent good about it."

Lainie looked at her mother, then at the waitress walking toward them carrying a meat loaf plate for her mother and a turkey sandwich for her. "It will be okay, Mother," Lainie said. But what she was thinking was, You're right, Mother, you're absolutely right, but it's too late now.

By the time Jackie was at the end of her seventh month, most of Mitch and Lainie's friends knew about the surrogacy. Some gasped when they heard, and several of the women said, "I could never do that. You're so brave." Some of the salesgirls at the store insisted that on a Sunday afternoon in May they wanted to give her a baby shower at Carin's house in Laurel Canyon.

"Who else should I invite?" asked Carin.

"Well, there's my mother, and my three sisters-in-law, and a few girls from school."

The day of the shower was uncharacteristically clear, and Lainie thrilled at the sight of the cake shaped like a bassinet that sat on a white-clothed table. Next to the table stood a real white wicker bassinet, which was one of Betsy's many gifts for the baby, and piled high inside it were the ribboned and frilly packages from the other sisters. The three of them sat together and chatted among themselves, and at one point Lainie thought she overheard Betsy ask Carin, "Is the surrogate coming?"

"Oh, no!" Carin said in a tone that sounded as if she was shushing Betsy.

Sharon, who was an old friend of Lainie's from Northridge, was pregnant herself.

"I've been layette shopping for me, so I just got one of each for you."

"Oh, thank you." Lainie was delighted with every T-shirt and diaper pin.

Sharon, puffy-faced and swollen around the ankles, had to sit. "I am so tired of carrying this baby. If you want my opinion, *you're* the one who's doing this the right way."

Lainie was grateful to her mother, who chatted amiably with everyone and put on a social face Lainie had seen her use at the law office or on special occasions. The sweet small talk and supportive faces of the girls from the store made Lainie feel warm and expectant. As she opened each gift, the squeals that rose from the group and the tiny delicate baby things in her hands moved her. According to the amniocentesis, the baby was going to be a girl. Rose Margaret De Nardo. After Mitch's late mother, Rose, and of course Margaret Dunn, whose friendly attitude at the shower may have been the result of hearing the news of a namesake.

Carin, who was a sometime artist, had bought the baby a tiny chair in unfinished wood, which she painted pale pink. On the back of it in darker pink flowery letters she had painted ROSE MARGARET DE NARDO. Faith, the seamstress at Panache, had made a needlepoint pillow with a looped ribbon at the top so that it could hang from the doorknob of the nursery. The words on the pillow were *Shhh*! *Rose Margaret De Nardo is asleep.*

Lainie held each gift up for the others to see, then held it close to her chest. There were tiny smocked dresses and baby-size ballet slippers. White baby socks trimmed with satin ribbons and the smallest pearls she'd ever seen. After the gifts and the cake, all three of Mitch's sisters gave reasons they had to leave, said their good-byes, and were gone. The closer friends who knew all Lainie had been through to get to this point in her life moved around her, and each of them hugged her. Lainie wept for joy and some of them cried along with her.

Her mother helped her carry the gifts to the BMW. And before she got into her own old Chevrolet, she said to Lainie, "It was a nice party, a good start. Let's pray it all goes well."

It took three trips back to her car to get all of the gifts inside the condo. Just as Lainie closed the door to the garage for the last time, the telephone rang. It must be Mitch calling from the store, where he was doing some paperwork, to find out how the shower went. No, it was Jackie's line. Jackie. Lainie grabbed it.

"Hi!"

"Hi. I've been trying to get you all afternoon," Jackie said, sounding a little annoyed. "I wanted you to meet me today, because my son's in town, back from his dad's, and I told him about you, so I thought maybe we could get together."

"Oh, Jackie, I'm sorry. I'd love to meet him," Lainie said.

"Well, maybe another time," Jackie said. It was clear she was feeling hurt. "Where *were* you?"

Lainie was about to burst out with the happy answer, but something made her take a deep breath first so that she would sound calm when she said, "At a baby shower."

"For *our* baby?" Jackie asked.

Lainie bit her lip. "Yes."

"Wow," Jackie said, sounding excited now. "How was it? Who gave it? What presents did you get?"

"My friend Carin gave it at her house. And everything looked so beautiful and pink, and the food was great, and I couldn't believe the things they bought and made. I had no idea there were such cute clothes in the world!"

"Oh yeah," Jackie said wistfully. "Girls' clothes are a million times cuter than the ones they make for boys. Tell me about everything."

Lainie looked over at the dining room table where she had piled the gifts. As she looked at each package, she remembered what was in it and described it in detail to Jackie, who reacted with giggles on the other end of the phone.

"And the chair," Lainie said, high on reliving her perfect afternoon. "The smallest chair you ever saw, painted pink, and in darker pink letters it says across the back Rose Margaret De Nardo. Can you picture that? Her name on the back of a—" Lainie stopped cold. The last name she'd kept secret for so long was now out in the open. She'd blurted it out in a dumb attempt at bragging. Mitch would be furious. Dumb, dumb. How could she be so damned dumb?

"It's okay," Jackie said after a while. "I've known your last name for a long time. Even before I was pregnant. Way back in the beginning of all this, I snooped around in the doctor's office when the nurse went to the can. I even know about your store. In fact, the funny thing is, I realized then that I once applied for a job at the old store in the Valley, upstairs from a restaurant. Mitch interviewed me, only he didn't hire me. I thought I recognized him the day we all met. Pretty funny, huh?"

Lainie felt flushed with embarrassment and discomfort and didn't speak.

"Don't worry, Lainie. The reason I never told you I knew was because it was so important to you two to keep it a secret, and if I told you I knew, you would worry. But you don't have to be afraid, because I'm going to live up to this bargain, believe me."

"I do believe you," Lainie said. But this news pulled away her safety net and made her afraid. "I believe you."

"Good," Jackie said. "That's real good."

21

BY FOUR O'CLOCK Rick was in Doreen's hospital room holding his son, David, in his arms. Somewhere far back in his mind, he knew he'd lost Robert Redford for his film, but it just didn't matter. In fact, to keep Doreen occupied while they readied her for the delivery, he told her the story of his exit from the meeting, and as he did it sounded like something that had happened to someone else, or in a dream. Certainly not earlier that same day, to David Reisman's father. And David was surely the best-looking baby ever born. He had a lot of red hair, and big green eyes, and a cleft chin, and a little dimple just above the left side of his mouth.

Doreen, uncomfortable after the delivery, couldn't stop smiling from where she sat on the bed watching Rick, who was wearing a sterile blue gown, sit on a nearby chair and make gurgling sounds at the baby, lost in the awe he felt for this sleepy infant.

"Is that nurse you hired gonna work out?"

"I hope so. She seemed nice. Annie's her name."

"She looks like Nell Carter."

Rick smiled. "She's been a baby nurse for nearly thirty years, so I guess she knows her Pablum, or whatever they eat."

"They don't eat anything at first. They *drink* formula." She looked out the window when she said, "They gave me a shot that would keep my milk from coming in."

A nurse breezed into the room.

"How are you doing?" she asked Doreen.

"Good as I can be," Doreen answered.

"I need to take the baby just for a few minutes, Mr. Reisman," the nurse said. "Dr. Weil is going to be making rounds, and wants to see the little guy in the nursery. If either of you cares to talk to Dr. Weil, I'll send him over here."

"I do," Rick said, carefully handing the nurse the baby. "In fact, I'll walk down to the nursery."

The nurse placed David in the Plexiglas crib, which she wheeled out the door.

"Would you like to meet the pediatrician?" Rick asked Doreen.

"What's the point? After this week *I'll* never see him again. He doesn't need to get to know me." It was said in a sensible tone, without anger.

"What *are* you going to do?" Rick asked, walking toward the bed. Doreen wouldn't look at him.

"Get a job somewhere in the Valley till I'm feeling like I'm ready to go home."

"You know I'll keep supporting you until you do."

"I know," she said. "Even though you're not supposed to. It'll just be a few months. I promise."

"Take as long as you need. You can make it six months or eight months."

"I don't want to go back looking fat and tired."

"That's how *I* always look," he kidded.

"I'd like to get a tan and a little sun bleach in my hair and tell all the kids at home I was on a long vacation."

"Good idea," he said, and patted the blanket over where her foot was sticking up. "I'll be back in a few minutes."

When he got to the door, she called him.

"Rick!"

He turned.

"I've got to tell you something. I've been thinking a lot about this and I'm worried about leaving the baby with you." He tried not to show his concern.

"Why is that?" he asked.

"For the simple reason that you walked out on Robert Redford. Which proves to me that you are truly and sincerely dumb." Then she laughed that hearty open-mouthed laugh that he had come to love.

Two days later, he arrived at the hospital with the baby nurse to take David home. The law stated that in order to prove abandonment, Doreen couldn't leave the hospital and go to the same place as the baby, so Andrea came to the hospital that morning to take Doreen back to the apartment in the Valley where they'd lived together before the hemorrhaging.

In the parking circle at Cedars, before Annie placed the baby in the infant seat, a pale Doreen kissed the little pink boy, and Rick could see the tension in her face. But when Rick hugged her doughy little body, she lost all control and shook with sadness as the sobs took over.

"I don't know if," she began, then sobbed another sob, "I don't know if I'll miss my baby more . . . or if . . . I'll miss you most of all." She sniffled and he held her very tightly, this little round cherub of a girl.

"Promise me one very important thing," she said, looking up at him.

"Name it."

"That you'll read to him. He's used to it now, because he's heard lots of stories. I left all the children's books at your house. They're in the nursery in the closet."

"I'll do it," he said.

"He's all set, Mr. Reisman," Annie said quietly.

Rick, Doreen, Annie, and Andrea all peeked into the backseat at sweet little sleeping David, dressed in a pale yellow going-home suit that Bea Cobb had crocheted for him and mailed from Kansas two weeks before.

"Well, then, I guess we shouldn't keep him waiting," Rick said. He gave Doreen a last hug and helped her into the passenger seat of Andrea's car, and stood next to Annie, the nurse, waving as Andrea drove off into the hot California day.

For weeks he awakened with the first sounds of the stirring baby, then followed Annie from room to room, watching her techniques. He insisted that she, in turn, watch him critically when he fed or burped or bathed or changed David, to make certain he was well versed in every aspect of his son's needs.

And to keep the promise he'd made to Doreen, he held the tiny little bundle of boy on his lap and read from the books Doreen had left for him. *The Runaway Bunny* and *Little Bear*, *Make Way for Ducklings* and *The Little Red Hen*. Sometimes both he and the baby would lie on their backs while Rick held the book above them and the baby looked up at the colorful pictures, kicking his feet and waving his arms wildly.

There were a few other actors interested in the part for which he had lost Robert Redford. There were other projects that were looking promising, and soon his schedule was filled with back-to-back meetings. But he always made sure to return early in the evening to be there in time for David's dinner. Annie would put the little guy in his infant seat on the kitchen table, and Rick would spoon some of the newly permitted rice cereal in, then watch most of it dribble out. When David smiled, Rick would laugh out loud. Many times Rick would be feeding the baby and on the phone at the same time, in order to justify rushing home so early in the day. That way he could do business and tend to the baby simultaneously.

And of course there were his visits to Bobo.

"Look who's a father, I can't believe it," Bobo said. Two of the old man's women friends were with him, gathered around Rick and the little baby in the dining room of the lodge at the Motion Picture Home. Rick held the bottle expertly and watched his son chug down ounce after ounce of Similac.

"I fed you a bottle just like that," Bobo said to Rick, "only you weren't *that* cute." The old man laughed and jabbed Essie Baylis, Harvey Feldman's aunt.

"My Harvey got you that baby?" the old woman asked. Every time Rick looked at Harvey Feldman's old aunt, he couldn't get it out of his head that she'd once been a Busby Berkeley girl. He would try to sort out the features of her face that must have been pretty then, and to imagine her as young, wearing one of those silly costumes.

"That's right," Rick told her.

"He's a genius." The old woman smiled.

"How come you're not married?" Stella Green, Essie's friend, a tiny woman who walked with the help of an aluminum walker, asked Rick. Stella had worked as a secretary to Jack Warner for years.

"Don't get him started," Bobo told her. "He's not married because he's a schmuck."

Stella Green nodded as if she understood. Rick laughed.

"Uncle B., I've got a son now, why do I need a wife?"

"I'll have the soup," Bobo said to a passing waitress, then pulled out a chair and sat. "Essie darling, you want maybe a cup of soup? How about you, Stella?" The two women demurred and said their good-byes to Rick and the baby, who smiled a little at them around his bottle, which made both of the women happy.

"Who do you have at home taking care of the little *pisher*?" Bobo asked Rick, peering closely at David. "Every week he gains five pounds. Look at the size of that guy. Hiya, bruiser. Say, Hiya, Uncle Bobo. You can call me Grandpa, you know. I wouldn't charge you extra if you call me Grandpa." Rick loved to watch Bobo with the baby.

"What do you hear from the little girl?" Bobo asked Rick, suddenly serious-faced.

"Not a word. It was part of our agreement. When she's ready to go back to Kansas, she'll call me and I'll send her off. She doesn't want to see David though. Maybe never."

"Who can blame her, the poor kid?" Bobo *tsk*ed. "If I was a younger man, believe me, I'd go and find the son of a bitch who made her that way and go and kill him. Oy, is she a good kid. A tough cookie."

David had drained the entire bottle.

"Give him here," Bobo said. "I'll get a burp out of him. Won't I, slugger?"

Tenderly Bobo placed the baby's stomach against his own shoulder and patted, patted, patted the tiny back with his arthritic hand.

"He might need a little Dr. Brown's celery tonic, which always does it for me."

"And me." Rick laughed.

David didn't need it. His burp filled the room, and the waitress, who had just put the soup bowl down in front of Bobo, applauded the wonderful accomplishment.

"I got a way with kids," Bobo told her. "Not like this guy here. He has a way with broads. But me, kids love me. When this baby gets a little bigger, I'll teach him how to play Go Fish and Spit in the Ocean." David was asleep on Bobo's shoulder. Rick used the camera he always had with him these days to take a picture of the two of them.

On the morning David turned six months old, Andrea called. "I wanted to say happy birthday to David, and to tell you that Doreen is ready to go back to Kansas. She's lost all the weight, a miracle since she's been working at Mrs. Field's Cookies for the last few months. She says she feels good, and would like to leave on Monday. Do you want me to arrange a flight for her?"

Rick and Doreen hadn't spoken since they parted at the hospital. Keeping the silence was their tacit agreement that there were no recriminations for either of them.

"I'll do it. If it's all right with her though, I'd like her to leave on Monday night. There's somewhere I'd like to take her on Monday afternoon."

"I'll tell her. And just in case you were curious, she hasn't said a thing about the baby. Even in the wee hours when we sit around in our pajamas and talk about our deepest feelings. Mostly she's been telling me about her mother and how much she misses her, and how worried she gets about her older married sister, Trish, and her kids. Apparently the brother-in-law Don is kind of a bad guy. Anyway, Doreen's got her strength back and she talks to her mom nearly every day. Sometimes they even pray together on the phone.''

''I miss her,'' Rick said. ''And I'll miss her even more knowing she's so far away.''

''Me too. She was a breath of fresh air around the strangling bullshit of this town.''

Rick got off the freeway at the Vine Street exit and drove south, and when Doreen, who had been silent for nearly the entire ride, saw the marquee of the Merv Griffin Theater, she let out a hoot.

''Oh my God. 'Jeopardy!' Look, there, that's where they do 'Jeopardy!' My 'Jeopardy!' The Alex Trebek 'Jeopardy!' ''

Rick made a right turn into the parking lot.

Doreen opened the window of the Mercedes and stuck her face out. ''We're stopping. We're parking! Are we going to . . . are the other people in those cars going to see 'Jeopardy!'? I can't believe it.'' Rick's smiling face had the answer.

''We are. Oh, we are. Oh thank you. Thank you.''

She was literally bouncing up and down in her seat, and the second they were parked, she threw the car door open and ran ahead of him to the front of the theater. There was a very long line of people waiting, and she ran back to Rick, seized his arm with her tiny hand, and said, ''C'mon, let's get in line.''

''It's okay,'' he said, ''don't worry,'' and moved her instead toward the front door where a blue-blazered page was waiting.

''I'm Richard Reisman,'' he said to the page, feeling Doreen's excitement by the way her hand, which was now holding his, couldn't remain still. ''We're guests of Mr. Griffin.''

The page pulled a folded sheet of paper out of his

inside jacket pocket, opened it, read something from it, and gestured for Rick and Doreen to follow. They walked through the cool building and then the page pushed open a heavy studio door. Doreen gasped when there in real life was the familiar set she'd seen on television for so long. There were two seats closed off by masking-tape ribbons right in the center of the first row. As the page led Doreen and Rick toward them, Rick could hear Doreen making tiny sounds of joy in her throat.

The page removed the masking tape so they could be seated and said, "We'll be shooting two shows while you're here, and then three more later this afternoon."

"Two shows!" Doreen said excitedly, then elbowed Rick. "We get to see two." As the page turned to go she said, "Um, sir," and he turned back to look at her.

"Is Mr. Trebek here?"

"Oh sure."

Doreen gave out with a little yelp of pleasure. Within seconds of the page's departure, the studio doors opened and hordes of people flooded in to be seated. The studio became a buzzing hive of activity and excitement, all of it reflected in Doreen's eyes. The camera crew assembled, and an announcer named Johnny Gilbert did the warm-up, but it wasn't until the entrance of Alex Trebek when Doreen moved to the edge of her seat, never taking her eyes from him, her face lit with excitement.

When Trebek moved toward the audience, she pounded Rick's arm. "A sheet of paper. Ohh, why didn't I bring a sheet of—" Rick pulled a piece of blank white *From the desk of Rick Reisman* notepaper from one of his pockets and a pen from another and handed it to Doreen, who had already leapt to her feet and was thrusting the paper into the face of the handsome Alex Trebek, who smiled at her.

"Please," she said. "Can you make it out to 'Bea Cobb, who is the best mother in the world'?"

"If I say that, *my* mom will get jealous," Trebek joked.

"Ahh, she won't find out," Doreen said, and then gave him a smile with just a little hint of flirtatiousness.

"You're right," he said, handed her back the signed paper, and was on to the next fan, as Doreen clutched the paper to her heart and choked out a thank you.

"My mom's gonna freak out," she said, sitting back down in her seat, alternately looking at the message then clutching it against her chest. She held it that way during the entire taping and in the car on the way back to Andrea's. When it was time to say good-bye, it amazed him that she hadn't said one word about the baby.

"Call me collect if you ever need anything," he said.

"Maybe just a picture of David. For Christmas?" she said and asked at the same time.

"You've got it," he promised.

22

LAINIE felt herself being awakened by the sensation of Mitch fondling her, waking her with his hands all over her body, his tongue moving slowly down her body. She must have fallen asleep while they were watching television in bed, and Mitch had stayed awake. Maybe something on television had made him feel sexy. No, Mitch always felt sexy. Mitch, delicious Mitch, wanting her.

"Mmm, baby," he said. "I love you. How I love you, my baby—"

And the phone rang.

"The machine . . ." Mitch said. "The machine will get it." He was inside her now and very hot. "The machine'll pick up," he managed.

The phone rang again, and again. Maybe it was . . .

"Jackie's phone," Mitch said, finishing Lainie's thought.

But then the ringing stopped. Mitch sighed with relief

and then he was kissing her and pressing his hard chest into her breasts and then he was up on his knees, pulling her legs up on either side of him, spreading her legs high around him, pushing deeper into her so she could feel him all the way at the small of her back. "Oh, God, Mitch, Oh, God . . ." But the phone rang again and broke the moment, and a frustrated Mitch collapsed on her and reached out for the receiver.

"Oh, God, Mitch," Lainie heard a voice on the phone cry. "Oh, God."

"Jackie."

"I'm in labor, and I hurt so much. Oh, God."

"Did you call the doctor?" Mitch asked, climbing off Lainie and sitting at the edge of the bed to talk to Jackie. Lainie could see how nervous he was.

"Yeah, yeah, and Chuck Meyer too. They're both meeting me at the hospital."

"What about the car and driver?" Mitch was holding the phone loosely to his ear, and Lainie, whose pelvis was still ringing from the abruptness of his wrenching himself out of her, could hear every word Jackie said.

"Did you call for the car?"

"It's on the way, but Mitch, please, I know I said I wouldn't do this, only I forgot how much this hurts and how scary it is to do it alone, and I don't have anybody else to call. I know we decided you shouldn't be there, but I'm begging you. You've got to do this, please say you'll meet me at the hospital. I mean, Jesus Christ, it's *your* baby too. I can't do this with some lawyer I hardly know and a limo driver I never saw before. I need you there."

"I'll be there," Mitch said. "Stay calm, Jackie. Will you? Promise me you will?" he asked her in a very gentle voice.

Then he was throwing on his clothes. Lainie watched him numbly. Waiting for him to say, "C'mon, let's go." But a minute later, he had his car keys in his hand and was shoving his wallet into his pants pocket.

"Mitch . . ." Why hadn't Jackie asked for *her*? Maybe she thought that Lainie would be able to say no to her, but at this stage Mitch would do whatever she asked. "Mitch!" Mitch stopped and looked at his wife, then put his hand to his face as if to say, What in God's name am I doing? It hadn't even occurred to him that she should be coming along. He looked embarrassed and more flustered than before.

"Oh, baby," Mitch said. "I'm sorry. I'm out of my mind with worry here. I know this wasn't in the plan we made, but I think I should drive out there. She sounds panicked. I probably won't get there until it's over, but what if it's a long labor? What if decisions have to be made about the baby?"

"What would you like *me* to do?" she asked.

"What do you *want* to do?" he asked. He was standing nervously at the bedroom door, looking as if he wished she'd say, "Call me when it's over," so he could leave, but she didn't. She jumped out of bed and opened her closet.

"Start the car," she said. "I'm coming with you." She heard him run down the stairs and out to the garage as she pulled out various choices in her closet, hating this situation. What to wear? Who cares, she thought, pulling on a pair of jeans and a big cotton sweater. Jackie was the one everyone would be looking at. Not her.

By the time she had her clothes on, she heard Mitch honking the horn. There wasn't time for makeup, or even to brush her teeth. She rushed out into the chilly night and got into the car. They drove wordlessly down Ventura Boulevard toward the freeway. A digital clock above a bank told her that the time was 1:10. There was very little traffic. Lainie felt stung, pushed around, angry that Jackie hadn't kept their bargain. The friendship during the pregnancy had been a good thing, but she had specifically told Mitch she couldn't bear to watch him helping Jackie through the delivery.

They had put it into a contract they'd worked out with Chuck Meyer, the lawyer. They would come to the hospital after the baby was safely in the hospital nursery. But if Mitch continued to drive as fast as he was now and the labor was long, they would be there to watch the delivery. She looked out the window and reminded herself that Jackie had very little in her life, and that was why she had broken her word about calling them. Jackie knew that after the baby was born there would be no more relationship with Mitch and Lainie, so for one more night she needed them there. One more night, and maybe a day or two in the hospital. Then they would have their baby, and that's what mattered.

Sliding doors opened. Lainie followed far behind as Mitch raced through them and down the hall through the hospital. Around corners, and through doors and down ramps, past brightly lit nurses' stations and open doors to patients' rooms, through which Lainie caught glimpses of people connected to IVs.

By the time she got to the labor room, Mitch, and the limo driver, and a nurse, and Chuck Meyer, the lawyer, surrounded Jackie, who lay on the bed connected to an IV, holding court. Lainie stood quietly in the doorway. It wasn't until the limo driver had said good-bye and wished her well and Chuck Meyer stepped out to call his wife that Jackie looked past Mitch, who was brushing a curl out of her face, and noticed Lainie standing quietly in the corner.

"Hey! Lainie!" she said. "Isn't this great? We're having a baby."

"Great," Lainie said. Good God, it was true, she

thought. It was like that commercial she remembered from years ago, for oven cleaner that you sprayed on and then left to do the work. A woman in the commercial was playing tennis, and when she hit a winning point over the net, she looked at the camera and said, "I'm cleaning my oven!" Lainie was standing in a labor room in her jeans, thinking, I'm having a baby.

Within minutes Jackie was in hard labor. Mitch and a nurse stood on either side of the bed while Lainie remained quietly in the corner. She could tell by the way the back of his La Coste shirt stuck to him that Mitch was sweating. Soon, with an entrance worthy of a star, the doctor swept into the room, made some comment about having to get out of his girlfriend's nice warm bed, and examined Jackie's pelvis. The anesthesiologist was a woman, and a moment later she came in, turned Jackie on her side, and gave her an epidural. After that, everything went fast. Somebody handed out sterile masks and gowns and boots and caps; the gurney was rushed into the delivery room. And again, Lainie, who was now dressed from head to toe in blue cotton like the others, stood alone in the corner of the tiled room.

She watched the group of people gathered around the table where Jackie lay, chattering nervously about something, and all she could see was their eyes. It took her a few minutes to sort them out now, and when she did, she realized it was Mitch who stood by the head of the table, holding Jackie's hand.

I'm not ready for this, Lainie thought. Her whole body was pulsing with panic. She didn't want to look, was afraid to see the blood, and now all she could think about was her own surgery. That day when they wheeled her into the operating room. She remembered that as she was falling into the drugged sleep, she already knew what the outcome would be. That her uterus would be removed, that her ovaries would be removed, and that she would never, never . . .

The sudden cry of the baby as it burst forth from Jackie and into the doctor's hands brought Lainie back. "Here comes your girl . . . girl . . . a little girl," she heard voices say. And she watched as the tiny bloody baby was gently handed to Mitch, who Lainie could see was crying as he looked tenderly down at the tiny thing. She felt the nurse's arms strong around her back, moving her toward the center of the room so she could watch as Mitch handed the baby to Jackie. It was a tiny, pink little girl who looked like Jackie.

Jackie looked long at the baby, pursed her lips hard and closed her eyes as she handed the squealing baby to Lainie. The squeals were like sounds from a puppy. While Lainie stared at the baby's tiny face, the doctor put a small bulb in the nostrils and extracted some mucus or blood with a sucking noise. Lainie felt Mitch next to her and the doctor sliding the baby out of her hands to care for it.

"Thank you, oh thank you," Lainie said, half laughing, half crying, leaning over to hug the exhausted Jackie. "Dear God, how can I ever thank you? What could I ever do for you or give you that could possibly mean as much as that precious little life you gave to me and Mitch? Oh, thank you," she said again, and while she held Jackie in her embrace she could smell the very distinct odor of Shalimar, and feel Jackie's sweaty face against her own cool one.

"S'cuse me, please," someone said, brushing Lainie out of the way. With a tug of the gurney they wheeled Jackie off to the recovery room.

Mitch put his arms around her. She turned and held him tightly, and they both cried. Neither of them was able to speak through the emotions. Through her tears, Lainie saw nurses, who were probably used to seeing people behave like this in the maternity ward, smile knowingly as they passed. Eventually, silently, Lainie and Mitch walked, arms around each other, out of the hospital to the parking lot.

The morning light found them in their own bed, locked in each other's arms. When Lainie opened her eyes, she saw that Mitch's were already open, looking at her happily.

"We have a baby," he said.

She grinned. "Yes, we do." They kissed and held each other.

"Let's go see her," Mitch said.

"You got it."

They showered and dressed quickly, all the while chatting about the details of the night before.

"I was a basket case, wasn't I?" Mitch asked.

"You were perfect."

"And it wasn't so bad for you. Was it?" he asked her earnestly. "I mean, that it happened that way. I mean, that we ended up at the hospital last night, instead of just showing up the next day at visiting hours?"

"Honey," Lainie said, "we have our baby. That's what counts. Did the doctor say when she can come home?"

"We'll find out today," Mitch told her.

Jackie's hospital room was filled with the scent of flowers from the huge bouquet that displayed a card from the lawyer's offices. She was in the bathroom when they arrived. Mitch thought they should stop into the hospital room and invite Jackie to walk down to the nursery with them, "just as a final nice gesture."

Lainie looked at the bedside table where some of Jackie's cosmetics sat. Lipstick, blusher, and the big round bottle of Shalimar. When the bathroom door opened and Jackie came out, Lainie was surprised at how well she looked. Jackie let out a little yelp when she saw them.

"That baby is so beautiful. Have you seen her today?" she asked.

"No, we'll go together," Mitch told her. Linking arms, the three of them walked down the hall, Jackie scuffling in her slide-on slippers.

"There," she said, pointing to a crib in the back that bore a sign saying O'MALLEY: GIRL. The baby, that beautiful baby, was surely the most beautiful in the nursery.

"Jesus," Mitch said, "she's something special. None of those funny little marks they usually have. God in heaven. This is truly a miracle."

Lainie's heart felt full of hope. It had worked. Mitch's plan had worked. Despite her fears and pain and doubt, at last she would be taking home a baby. She was lost in her own thoughts about the baby's homecoming when she heard Jackie say, "Well, we did it, kiddo. We goddamned went and did it."

"That's the truth," Mitch said with a triumphant voice. "We sure as hell did." When Lainie turned and saw the look that passed between them, Jackie's so fulfilled and Mitch's so potent, it felt as if someone had kicked her in the chest. The three of them were celebrating the birth of their baby. The father; the mother; and the surrogate, the substitute. But, Lainie thought, there's no doubt that the substitute mother is me.

23

CLINT EASTWOOD was now interested in the part for which Rick had lost Robert Redford, and Rick was flying to Carmel to meet with him several times a week. But he always tried to get back in time to be with David, even if it was for just a short while every evening. The beautiful fair-skinned little boy brought a lightness to Rick's world that shifted the way he looked at every other aspect of his life. He was sitting at the kitchen table eating a late supper one night and making some notes on a script at the same time when Annie, the baby nurse, came in.

"Mr. Reisman, he's asleep. It's ten o'clock and I just talked on the phone to my sister. She's feeling kind of poorly, and I was wondering if I could drive over to her place down by Western Avenue and take care of her? I'll come back here real early in the morning. Little David just finished a full bottle and he'll probably stay down until I get back in the morning. But if he doesn't,

I left you some sterilized nipples, in case he wakes up and is hungry; all you've got to do is unscrew the top of one of the Similac bottles, put the nipple on, and give it to him. You know how to do that."

"You bet I do, Annie. You go to your sister's. David and his old man will be just fine."

"Oh, and his passy. He's chewing on his little pacifier now. He loves that thing, only sometimes he loses it and starts in to cry. All you have to do usually is put it right back in his mouth and he goes right back to sleep. If he's really crying hard, sometimes it takes two or three tries before he takes it back in . . . so be patient now. Okay?"

"Okay," Rick said. He was proud of himself for finding this terrific woman to take care of his son. He heard her bustling around, getting ready to go and spend the night with her sister, and before she left she asked, "You want me to leave my sister's telephone number?"

"Not necessary," Rick told her and waved a little good-bye just before she closed the front door behind her.

At eleven-thirty he had just turned on "Nightline" when the front doorbell rang. Jesus, it might wake the baby. He hurried out to see who it could be. A vision. The young secretary from the production office next to his at Universal. Long dark hair down to her waist, huge eyes, off-the-shoulder black dress.

"I was at a dinner party in the neighborhood," she told him before he could say a word. "And I got your address from this copy of *Vanity Fair* I borrowed from your office one day. It has this address on it. So when I realized this was where you lived, I figured I'd come by and hope you were alone."

"I'm alone," he said.

"So . . . can I come in?"

He opened the door all the way. Just because he had

a kid now didn't mean he was going to give up getting laid.

"Boy, this place is gorgeous," she said, handing him his copy of *Vanity Fair* and circling the living room.

"So are you," Rick said.

She giggled. "You are so cute," she told him, and then stopped to look at him. "And I've seen every one of your movies."

"And which one was your favorite?" he asked, moving closer. Very close. In a moment she was against him, wiggling out of the top of her dress, and then her hands were on his belt, and then they moved to undo his trousers, and just as her dress hit the floor, David let out a shriek.

"What was that?" the astonished girl asked.

"My son."

"You have a son? A baby? Do you have a wife? Oh, geez, I thought you were single."

"I am," Rick said, and he flew into the baby's room, zipping the zipper the girl had—Christ, he didn't even know her name, but the girl had unzipped his pants. Now he grabbed the fallen pacifier from next to David's little squealing face and gently placed it into the baby's mouth, hoping the touch of it next to the little tiny tongue would quiet him. But David wouldn't take the pacifier in, and continued to scream.

"Take the passy, baby. Here's your nice passy, Davey, Daddy's giving you your wonderful pacifier and . . ."

"Nyaahhhhh." David spit it out again.

"Maybe you should dip it in some honey," he heard the girl say. She was standing naked, naked and perfect in the doorway of the baby's room. "That's what my parents used to do for me," she told him. "Why don't I go and see if I can find some for you?"

You know you're about to make it with a very young girl when she still remembers what her parents put on her pacifier, Rick thought as he stood by the crib patting the wailing baby's back. She returned in a minute with the honey jar. Rick opened it, dipped the pacifier into the honey, then leaned over the crib and placed the pacifier in the baby's mouth.

"Mmmmm-mmmm-mmm," David said, sucking away. "Mmmm," and within minutes he was asleep.

The naked girl was against Rick now. "Let's dip this in some honey too," she said, and slowly moved down onto the floor of the baby's room, taking Rick along with her.

"I'm worried about his little BMs," Annie told Rick one morning at breakfast.

"His what?" He was gulping down some coffee, rushing to catch an early flight to Monterey to meet with Clint in Carmel.

"Little David. He's not having any."

"Not having any what, Annie?"

"Bowel movements."

"Not any?"

"Nope."

"Since when?"

"A few days."

"The pediatrician. Let's call Dr. Weil right now," he said, looking at his watch. It was seven-thirty in the morning. No doctors were in at seven-thirty in the morning, but surely the answering service would track the doctor down, call him at home.

"He's out of town," the answering-service operator said, "but Dr. Solway's on call."

"Then get *him* on the line for me," Rick ordered.

"I'll have to call you back, sir," the operator told

him. He gave her the number. David, who usually waved his arms and made gurgling noises, lay listless in Annie's arms.

"The first couple of days, I figured he was just constipated like we all get sometimes, only now, he's not right in himself, and I started to think there's more to it than that." She looked worried.

"Ever seen this kind of thing before?" Rick asked her.

"Not that I can remember right off," Annie answered. "Constipation, yes. But not this bad." The phone rang.

"Mr. Reisman." Must be the woman from the answering service.

"Don't tell me you can't reach the doctor," he snapped.

"This *is* the doctor, Mr. Reisman," the woman's voice said. "I'm Dr. Solway, Dr. Weil's associate. How can I help you?"

A woman. "My son, he's nine months old. He's been constipated for . . . how long?" he asked Annie.

"At least five days," she said.

"Five days," he told the doctor. "And he seems to have no energy. Very quiet. Weak."

"Bring him right in," the doctor said. "I'll meet you at our offices as soon as you can get there."

Good-bye, eight-fifteen flight. Good-bye, Clint Eastwood.

"We're on our way," Rick told her.

Annie sat in the backseat, holding David's tiny hand in hers. From the car phone Rick called Andrea at home and told her to call Clint Eastwood and cancel the meeting.

"You'll be okay, little honey. You'll be all right," Annie crooned to the silent baby.

In the elevator in the doctor's building, Rick looked at the limp baby dozing on Annie's shoulder, and panic filled him. What *was* this? What if it was serious, crippling, a terrible disease that would last forever? A lifetime of taking him to doctors and specialists, and him not being okay? No. It was nothing.

The tall, black-haired, blue-eyed woman, Lee Solway, took the baby in her arms and carefully undressed him. She had quickly sized up Rick and Annie, and knew right away it was Annie she should ask all the questions about the baby's habits and schedule and food intake. Annie answered the questions carefully and thoughtfully. Rick sat nervously, watching the doctor examine and probe the baby, who now lay passively and all too quietly.

"Have you noticed any decrease in the strength with which he's been sucking on the bottle?"

"Come to think of it, I have," Annie said. "But I just put it down to his not being hungry."

"Are you giving him solids?"

"Yes. Dr. Weil started him on rice cereal last month."

"Does he have the rice cereal plain?"

"I mix in some formula."

"Do you only introduce the foods Dr. Weil tells you he's permitted to eat?"

"That's all I give him. And Cora, too. She's the woman who takes over on the day and a half when I take off."

"So there would have been no reason for you to have ever given this baby honey?" The doctor held on to David's tiny body with her right hand, and turned to look at Annie.

"No, ma'am."

Rick stood. He'd been only half listening to the questions because he knew he didn't know the answers to them, but the word *honey* caught him by surprise, and he froze.

"What's wrong with honey? *I* gave him honey last week. A little on the pacifier to get him to take it."

The doctor looked at Rick. "Well, I'm afraid that what's going on with him now may have to do with the honey. I want to put him right into Children's Hospital this morning to be certain, and hope that he's not so constipated that I can't get some stool samples. I think he has infant botulism. The constipation and the decreased muscle strength all make it look like that to me."

"From honey?"

"The *Clostridium botulinum* organism has been isolated in honey specimens that have been fed to infants and make them sick. Babies under a year are susceptible. I don't want to scare you, but there are theories now that undetected cases of infant botulism may be behind sudden infant death syndrome. His breathing is very shallow too. I'm going to call an ambulance."

Rick had a ringing in his ears. This couldn't be happening. The doctor went into her office while Annie dressed David, who cried a faint bleating cry, and Rick could hear the doctor making arrangements for an ambulance to come to the medical building.

"We're off," she said when she emerged, and brushed past them. "They'll meet us downstairs in the parking lot."

Honey. The crushing reason Rick had given the baby honey suddenly slammed him in the face. To get fucked. To shut my son up so I could do it on the floor of his room with that girl who showed up at my door and dropped her dress. Christ, God is killing my son to punish me for being the lowest, most despicable human on the face of the earth. Please don't make this baby suffer for my vanity and excess and weakness.

Blindly, guilt-ridden, aching with the horror that tore at him, he got into the ambulance with Annie and the baby and the doctor, and as it lurched out into the street, he put his face in his hands and felt deep shame and despair.

24

FOR A WHILE Lainie's negative feelings slipped away. Just waking up and knowing there was a new baby in the next room gave every morning the excitement of Christmas. The sweet powdery smell that filled the nursery, the silky feel of baby Rose's fine hair, the luxurious softness of little crevices under that teeny chin elated Lainie. She would lift the warm little cherub out of her bassinet and place her tenderly in the middle of the big bed next to Mitch, who in his sleep would reach over and fondle the baby's foot. And Lainie would overflow with happiness.

Her family. At last. She wouldn't let her insecurities mar her joy. Not even the first several months of walking the floor all night with her scrunch-faced colicky daughter. And when Mitch held the tiny girl in his arms, he was transformed. All the pressures of the business day, the constant worried look he had in his eyes when he was in the store disappeared at home. He became so relaxed and unwound when he held the baby that more than once when he sat in the rocker to feed her, after she fell asleep he did too.

The joy, the bliss of watching each new developmental step occur seemed to bring Lainie and Mitch even closer every day. Lainie called the store every afternoon to report in about the success of every feeding, every ounce of weight gain, and Mitch listened with rapt attention.

"Hold on, baby," Mitch said to her one afternoon. She heard him click off. He was probably going to pick up the phone in the back office so he could talk to her more freely than he could from the front counter.

"Listen," he said when he picked up again. "I invited my sisters and their families over for dinner next week."

Lainie was silent. She knew there was an estrangement between Mitch and his sisters. That once she came into his life they stopped being as close as they were when he was single. Sometimes she felt as if the reason the breach existed was that she and Mitch didn't have children.

"Maybe now that we have a kid too, things will get better with all of us," Mitch said, expressing Lainie's thoughts out loud.

"Maybe."

"Hey, you know what my mother used to say when I fought with one of them?"

"You told me," Lainie answered. "She always said, 'Blood is thicker than water.' "

"They're dumb sometimes, and so are their husbands, but the truth is that besides you and my little honeybunch of a girl, they're all I've got. I need to make the effort. So I want to make sure you don't mind if they all come for dinner with their kids this Saturday."

"Sure, honey. You know I'm crazy about the kids. And they'll get such a kick out of seeing their new cousin."

"I love you, Lainie," Mitch said. "There'll never be anybody like you." And he hung up.

Lainie put the phone down in its cradle and was reaching for a pencil and paper to start making a grocery list for next Saturday when something made her feel oddly chilled. Maybe it was the sentiment Mitch had just expressed. The way he'd said it sounded awkward, as if someone had walked into the office as he was saying it. His voice sounded strained and forced.

Crazy. Her exhaustion because of the baby's sleeping problems was affecting her moods and making her too sensitive. Just the other day she had snapped at Carin. Dear Carin, who was so gentle that when she came upon a spider in the ladies' room at Panache, she ushered it into a paper cup and set it free outside rather than kill it.

"I'm sure happy you haven't heard from that woman again," she said to Lainie, "because I always had this fear she'd show up one day and want the baby back."

Lainie glared at her. "That was never an issue or a question for Mitch or me, so worry about your own problems, will you?" Carin had apologized repeatedly for the rest of that day.

Lainie would try hard to get herself together for Saturday's dinner and do her best to be good with Mitch's family. She would have to. Aside from her mother, the three De Nardo sisters and their husbands and children were baby Rose's only family. And like Lainie, Rose would be an only child, so whatever the price of giving her a relationship with her cousins, it was worth it.

Mitch loved wearing his Bar-B-Q apron and standing over the hamburgers, turning them gently again and again until they were perfect. The children chased one another around the tiny garden outside the sliding doors, and Lainie thought about how nice it would be when she and Mitch found a house in the Valley with a big yard. Then the children could play running games outside, and by then Rose Margaret would join them.

"You know what?" Betsy's husband, Hank, asked, looking closely at his new niece. "The weird thing is, she doesn't look one bit like Mitch, and she *does* look like Lainie. Isn't that funny? That's really funny."

Except for the times when they had to get up in order to separate fighting kids, Kitty and Mary Catherine stayed close together, each of them nursing a glass of white wine Lainie had served them. They didn't include her in their conversation until finally she moved over to where they sat, holding baby Rose over her shoulder.

"Is she sleeping any better? Mitch mentioned that she was having some problems," Kitty said.

Infant small talk. Lainie realized that that's what it was, but appreciated that at least something was being addressed to her.

"Not yet," she answered. "She still wakes up once or twice a night. How old were yours before they really were on a schedule?" She hoped that by asking advice from them, she could bridge the gap and warm them up a little bit.

"About nine years," Mary Catherine said, obviously joking.

"I swear, my Chrissy still wakes up at three or four A.M., but some babies start sleeping through by six months," she added. "It'll go by real fast."

"Who wants cheese on their burgers?" Mitch called out.

"Me!" some of the kids hollered.

"Not me," Lainie said, patting baby Rose's tiny bottom, trying to be true to a diet. The irregular schedule of the baby's life and feedings and the catch-as-catch-can meals she was stuffing in when she had time had put twelve pounds on her in two months. Mitch said he loved it because it gave him "more to grab."

"Don't tell me *you're* on a diet," Betsy said.

"Just being careful," Lainie answered.

"Oh right, you have to because of your sugar problem. Right?"

"Burgers coming up," Mitch hollered. "Lainie, where's the plates?"

"Why don't I hold her while you help Mitch?" Kitty offered.

Lainie's first instinct was to say no, but the whole purpose of the get-together was to be good to one another, so she handed the baby over to her sister-in-law and went to get the table organized. Crazy. Maybe her frustration with the added weight was making everything everyone said sound so awful to her. She would have to be more tolerant.

At the dinner table everyone dug into the food and Rose fell asleep on Mitch's shoulder, and soon everyone was laughing at stories about Grandma Rose and Grandpa Mario De Nardo. Lainie felt glad that she had agreed to have the family come to dinner. For the most part they were harmless, just not too smart. And as long as she didn't let them get to her, Mitch could have what he needed with them.

By dessert, all the adults had consumed a little too much red wine. Except Lainie, who found herself in the position of being the only sober adult at the party, and she noticed that the others were starting to get even more tipsy. She was carrying a platter of cookies to the table when Mitch stood, tapped on his wineglass with a spoon, and still holding the baby, raised the wineglass and said, "I'm going to make a toast now. With all my gratitude, to the woman I love dearly and passionately. My sweetheart and Rose's mommy."

There was a moment when there was no sound but the crickets of summer, until Hank blurted out, "Yeah, well, now you better make a toast to Lainie."

The shock of the joke made everyone freeze, except for Lainie, who was so stunned by it that her first impulse was to laugh, and when she laughed, all of the others did too. The laughter woke the baby, who cried, and Lainie was relieved to have an excuse to walk away. She put the cookies she'd been carrying down on the table, and hurried into the kitchen to get a bottle of formula.

She stood in front of the open refrigerator, staring in, forgetting for a moment why she was there. When she remembered and pulled out a bottle, she dropped it, grabbed a dishtowel, and stooped to wipe up the broken glass and spilled formula. She could hear the baby outside crying, so she grabbed another bottle, which she took out and handed to Mitch.

By now, the others had forgotten the bad joke and were back to exchanging stories about the De Nardo parents. The evening ended with promises of "next time at our house" and "the kids loved seeing you," and the sisters and their husbands were finally gone.

"Thank you, baby," Mitch said, hugging Lainie, with little Rose between them.

When Rose was a little over a year old, Lainie started back to school, three nights a week. Mitch was thrilled to come home early on those nights to feed and care for the baby, letting the saleswomen in the store take over some of his responsibilities. Many nights he would take Rose to Sherman Oaks Park.

Lainie loved school. She would do most of her studying late at night after Mitch and the baby had fallen asleep, but some days she would sit outside on her back patio while the baby played in the playpen or slept in the pram. Today she was particularly exhausted after a long night of walking the floor with a fretting baby, and her weight was high, and when she caught sight of herself in the mirror, she found herself thinking how much she looked like Jackie. But as the year had gone along and she became increasingly involved in her schoolwork, getting her studying done was far more important than wasting time in beauty parlors, or at health clubs and all the other places she would have to go to work on looking good.

The baby was asleep in the pram that morning and it was gloriously sunny and clear that day, so Lainie decided to put a few of her textbooks in the bottom of the big blue carriage and sit outside. While her daughter napped in the fresh air, she would read a few chapters. She was just out the door when she saw Mrs. Lancer, the older woman who lived next door, in her yard.

"Oh, is that the little baby?" the woman asked, hurrying over to the fence to look in the pram. "Isn't she darling? And you. You are so wonderful. The way you manage to take such good care of her, and you go to school, don't you? I mean forgive me, it's none of my business, but a few times I've seen you with all your books on your way out the door. And I just assumed . . ."

"I'm at Northridge in the English department," Lainie said, loving the sound of it.

"And yet you still have time to look so gorgeous," the woman said. Gorgeous. Lainie hadn't felt gorgeous in a long time. "Now and then when my husband and I go walking around the track at Sherman Oaks Park, I see you there with your husband and the baby. You always look so stunning, all dressed up to kill. I say to my husband, How does she do it? I guess at your age you can do everything."

The woman continued to talk, but Lainie wasn't listening. Sherman Oaks Park, she was thinking. She hadn't been there in more than a year. Mitch went there with the baby all the time, but Lainie was never with them. Her neighbor must have seen some other couple there and thought it was the two of them. All dressed up to kill. So gorgeous, she had said. Well that made Lainie certain the woman wasn't talking about *her*. She felt like an overweight mess.

After a while the woman said good-bye, and Lainie wheeled the pram over to the little patio area, took out her books, and sat for a long time. Finally she realized she hadn't read a word. She was staring at the page thinking again about Sherman Oaks Park. Maybe while the baby was still asleep she would use the quiet time to do the laundry. She wasn't getting any studying done anyway. So she put the books back at the bottom of the pram, on top of the shiny pink comforter, and wheeled the pram back into the house.

"Right back," she whispered to the sleeping little girl, then hurried upstairs to her bathroom hamper to get her dirty clothes and Mitch's so she could take them down to the laundry room. Through the open bathroom window she could see the beautiful sunny day outside, and she smiled. Mitch, my Mitch, she thought. After all we've been through, at last our world is in place.

Maybe next year instead of just taking random classes, I'll start trying for a degree. And if business at Panache keeps up the way it's been going, pretty soon we can hire a nanny. Then I'll be like those women I always read about in magazines who have it all. Husbands and babies and careers, and . . . She had been hugging Mitch's shirt to her chest through all of those thoughts, but now when she held it up to her face, her euphoria was drained in a wave of shock. The smell on the shirt, all over her husband's shirt, was very familiar to her. It was the smell of Shalimar.

In Barbara Singer's office she sat forlornly across from the pretty dark-haired psychologist, and couldn't believe she was saying the words, "I think my husband is cheating on me with the surrogate." It sounded so absurd that after she said it, she let out a little laugh, then stopped to catch her breath so she wouldn't cry. "Oh, God," she said, and then told Barbara everything.

After she'd heard it all Barbara asked, "Lainie, let's talk about what you're afraid will happen if you confront Mitch."

"That maybe he's not seeing Jackie and he'll laugh at me. We own a very chic women's store. Every day women come in and give him a big hello hug, and one of them could have been wearing Shalimar."

"And what about what the lady from next door said?"

"She's kind of scatterbrained. She could have seen anybody in the park and mistaken them for Mitch and me. I mean, I'd feel like a fool if I accused him and I was wrong."

"And how would you feel if you were right?" Barbara asked, looking into her eyes.

Lainie looked away, then answered, "I couldn't survive the pain."

"Lainie," Barbara said. "You're a very strong woman. You stood up to cancer, and won. Can this possibly be as bad as that?"

"Worse," Lainie said. "I love this man. He's my whole life. I only said yes to this whole thing because I was afraid that Mitch wanted his genetic child so badly that if I said no . . ." The rest of the words were too difficult to get out.

"That he would leave you?" Barbara asked.

Lainie was crying and could only nod. "People are passing AIDS around. I don't know what Jackie's life is like now. Or what it was *ever* like, for that matter, regarding men. But if my husband really is cheating on me, he could be killing me." Barbara didn't comment. "I saw your ad about the group in *L.A. Parent*. I was so excited because it looked like something for us. I was going to ask Mitch to come to it with me so we could discuss what we were going to tell Rose about her birth when she got older. Now I'm here to tell you that I need help about something more urgent than that. I'm so afraid."

"Bring Mitch to the group," Barbara said. "Maybe the group will give you the courage to confront him, because you can't go on much longer harboring these fears."

"I can't," Lainie wept. "You're right. I can't."

25

THE PEDIATRIC INTENSIVE CARE unit is a place you never want to be. Many of the patients who are being cared for there come directly from the rooms in which they were born, and when they finally leave in many cases it will be because they're dead. The parents who sit the vigil beside the cribs share a silent terror that they may be the next to go home. Without their baby.

When Rick, Annie, the by now barely conscious David, and the stern-faced Dr. Solway arrived at the hospital, they went directly to pediatric ICU. There were four other cribs besides the one in which they now placed the limp and silent David. Rick turned away while a nurse inserted an IV tube into the baby's arm, and when he turned back he saw the doctor placing a tiny mask over the baby's expressionless face. The mask, Dr. Solway told Rick and Annie, who hugged herself as if she was chilled, measured the level of David's breathing to determine whether or not he had to be put on a respirator. He did.

For now, the IV would be used to give him drugs, in order to make tolerable the process they would have to do immediately, which was called intubating. Intubating, Dr. Solway explained carefully, as if she were teaching a class, meant that the doctors would insert a tube into David's nostril which would pass down into his lungs. The tube would be connected to a respirator, which would breathe for him. Rick and Annie were asked to leave the room during the intubation.

While they stood in the hall, Rick, trying not to picture what the doctors were doing, looked at the big black woman who still hugged herself with her chubby arms, over one of which hung the little blue sweater in which she had dressed David a few hours earlier. What was she thinking, he wondered. The truth? That because Rick was such a venal whoremonger, he had made his own son severely ill? Maybe even killed him? Annie must know *exactly* what had happened.

She had come back early that morning, the morning after Rick gave the baby the honey on the pacifier. Come back early, as promised, from her sister's. The young secretary's car was probably parked in the driveway, where Annie usually parked. So Annie probably patiently found another parking place on the street, walked in the front door, and began to straighten up the living room, finding the girl's black dress still lying there in a heap.

And in the baby's room, which is where she undoubtedly went next . . . Rick's clothes. Everywhere. She must have taken those to the dirty-clothes hamper and then, with the baby on her hip, gone into the kitchen to do Rick's dinner dishes from the night before, to get the baby's breakfast. Maybe she was feeding David when the girl walked nude from Rick's room, where she and

Rick had spent what was left of the night and themselves, leaving Rick in an unconscious sleep. The girl could have even greeted Annie and made a fuss over the baby after she slid back into her dress, picked up her shoes, and left.

Twenty silent minutes went by until the doctor called Rick and Annie back. David was asleep now. Dr. Solway stood next to his crib. Annie let out a low moan when she saw what had been done to the baby, and Rick held on to the back of a chair for support.

"The nasotracheal tube is connected to the respirator, which you can hear is now breathing for him. Those are cardiac monitor leads, and of course that's the intravenous line. We'll continue to ventilate him mechanically and feed him this way for the next several days. After that, hopefully, he'll begin to come around. At least to be able to be fed eventually through a nasogastric feeding tube."

Rick was aware of a woman standing near the crib farthest from them. She was crying quietly as she looked at what had to be her own very ill baby.

"What medication will you give him?" Rick asked the doctor.

"We won't. In adults we can use an antitoxin, in infants the only treatment is to support them until they get better on their own. I'm sorry to tell you that there is nothing else to do now but literally sit this out. If you like, I can arrange a room for you to live in down the hall, so that you can be with him, or you can commute from home. I suggest one or both of you do the former. Because even though David is too weak to open his eyelids, there will be many times when he's awake, so he can feel and he can think, and at those times the sound and the touch of someone to whom he's bonded will be extremely important to his well-being."

Bonded. Part of the parenting lingo. The new father

was a total man who spent time caring for his infant. Trying to create the kind of deep connection which babies in the past usually only had with their mothers. This baby didn't have a mother, or a father who spent all the time caring for him. Annie. To David, hers was the most familiar voice, the most welcome and soothing touch, Rick thought. He was surprised at how envious he felt toward the large black woman, who couldn't take her eyes from the now unconscious child in the crib. David looked as if he were dead.

"Poor baby," Annie said softly. "Poor little baby."

"You can touch him," Dr. Solway said. The young doctor's jaw was set firmly and her eyes were emotionless. Rick wondered how much time she'd spent in this room, and how many babies she'd seen in such serious condition.

Annie put her large dark hand on the little pink arm of the baby that didn't have an intravenous tube connected to it.

"We're here, darlin'. Me and your daddy are gonna be here every minute." Then she looked at Rick. "I can sit by him all day, if you want to take the nighttimes. Or just the opposite. Whatever you say, Mr. Reisman."

"Annie," he said. "You can spell me. How would that be?"

"What does 'spell you' mean?" she asked him.

"It means you can be in and out, talk to him, touch him as much as you want. And if please, dear God, he ever gets off the respirator alive, even hold him. But except for getting a few hours of sleep, I'm going to stay in this room day and night."

Annie patted him softly on the arm.

"I'll go in to the nurses' station and check about getting you a room," Dr. Solway told Rick. She left Annie and Rick looking anxiously at what seemed to be a shell of baby David, listening to the constant repetition of the sound of the respirator as it fed him the breath of life.

Dr. Weil was back from his vacation and he called in a specialist from the San Francisco area to confirm Dr. Solway's diagnosis. The specialist was able to extract a stool sample, which was sent to a laboratory in northern California. During the visits of various doctors to the baby's bed, Rick would move out of the way so that they could have better access to David.

Twice a day Annie would come, and for some of the time while she was there Rick would move to a nearby waiting room and eat the meal she had brought for him from home while Annie sat with the baby, patting him and talking to him. But aside from those meal breaks, and approximately three hours a night when he went to the tiny Spartan hospital room to sleep, he never left the side of the crib where David lay motionless.

Now and then he would doze in the chair, waking suddenly at the piercing sound of a baby's cry, wishing it were David's. But, sadly for him, it was the cry of a baby across the room. Occasionally he would pick up bits and pieces of the other parents' conversations. The diagnosis of cancer in one case. The raised hopes as a baby began to show progress in another.

He watched the very California-looking couple who always wore sweatclothes and whose baby was not on a respirator so they were able to take turns holding her. He wondered about the sickly looking woman who was always dressed in a bathrobe. She was obviously coming from a wing in the hospital in which she herself was a patient. Then there was the oriental couple who were always holding hands as they stood wordlessly over their baby, who frequently cried, an inconsolable rasping cry.

Once the thought floated through his numb brain that he should call Patty Fall and tell her what was going on, but he couldn't bring himself to get on a phone and talk to anyone, and somewhere in the back of his mind, he seemed to remember her telling him she was taking the boys to Europe for a month or two. All day every day he would read aloud quietly to David from the familiar children's books he had read to him so often in the rocking chair at home. *The Cat in the Hat*, *Babar*, *Curious George*. Silly, funny, wonderful stories, just to be certain the sound of his voice was there in case the baby, his son, could really hear him.

" 'The dolls and toys were ready to cry. But the little clown called out, "Here's another engine coming. A little blue engine, a very little one. Maybe she will help us." The very little blue engine came chugging merrily along. When she saw the toy clown's flag, she stopped. "What's the matter, my friends?" she asked kindly. The little blue engine listened to the cries of the dolls and toys. "I am very little," she said, "but I think I can, I think I can." And she hitched herself to the little train. She tugged and pulled and pulled and tugged, and slowly they started off. Puff, puff, chug, chug, went the little blue engine. "I think I can, I think I can." ' "

Rick put his thumb and forefinger under his reading glasses to wipe his tired eyes, and when he glanced up, standing in the doorway was his uncle Bobo.

"Two weeks in a row you jilt a guy and don't even tell him why? What in the hell's the matter with you?"

It was true. For the two weeks Rick had been in this room, he hadn't thought about anything or anyone but the baby. Bobo was leaning on a cane, frowning at Rick.

"Uncle B.! How did you get here?"

"I called your house twenty times. Finally I get the baby nurse, and she tells me where you are. So I hired a kid to drive me over here. One of the volunteers at the home. He's waiting for me downstairs."

"I'm sorry," Rick said. "I should have called you."

"What's that you got there?" Bobo asked.

"A storybook. The doctor said he can hear me. So I talk to him, and I read to him."

"What am *I*? Chopped liver? *I* can't talk to him?" Slowly, with the help of his cane, Bobo walked to the crib where the baby lay silently. "Davidel," the old man said, "it's your favorite relative." Bobo's own hearing problem always made him talk too loud and Rick was afraid this intrusion on the other families would be upsetting. "I'm gonna tell you a story about your daddy when he was just a baby. Not as young as you are now. Maybe two or three years old."

The oriental couple was looking over now. Bobo turned to Rick and said as an aside, albeit in the same loud voice, "Jesus Christ, he looks like hell." Then he turned back to the baby. "Your daddy was always a smart little guy. And his mommy and daddy, God rest their souls, they were *crazy* about him."

"Uncle Bobo—" Rick started to interrupt him, but Uncle Bobo lifted his cane and waved it at Rick with a gesture to remain silent.

"Well, your grandpa Jake, my brother, he was Jewish, but your grandma Janie, she was gentile. So in their home, they celebrated all the holidays. Easter and Passover, Christmas and Hanukkah."

Now Rick noticed that the sickly looking woman in the bathrobe was listening, and the round-faced red-headed day nurse had walked in carrying a chart but was now stopped in the door from the nurses' station, listening to Bobo.

"Now you probably remember that the dish I cook the best, after my famous chicken-in-a-pot, is potato latkes. Right? And as soon as you get outta this place, I swear to God I'm gonna make some for you. So every Hanukkah it was a tradition that I would come to your grandma and grandpa's house and cook up a batch for all of us to eat."

Rick sat back in his chair now. There was no stopping Bobo from telling this story, and even the California couple, the wife holding the baby, were facing him, listening to what he was saying to the inert David.

"Anyway, this particular year, Hanukkah and Christmas came close together, so the Christmas tree was up and the menorah was lit, and your grandmother, a stunner, a gorgeous and wonderful girl, asks your dad, 'Ricky sweetheart, can you guess who's coming to our house tomorrow to make potato latkes?' And your dad looks at her with big wide eyes and asks, 'Santa Claus?' "

All the adults in the room laughed. Especially Rick. And when he looked over at the door of the room which led to the nurses' station, there were now three nurses there who had stopped to listen to the story. They were all laughing big hearty laughs that cut through the tension in that room for a much-needed respite.

Bobo. God bless him for coming here. Rick stood now to hug the old man, and when they both turned to look at David, for the first time in weeks the baby moved his free arm toward his chest.

"He moved," Rick said.

"What do you think?" the old uncle said. "I *always* keep them rolling in the aisles."

"He moved," Rick said to the nurse.

"So," Bobo said to Rick, "you'll call me tomorrow and tell me how he's doing?"

"I will," Rick said and they embraced again. Then Bobo, with a wave of the cane to his fans, went to find the driver to take him back to the home.

After that, David's progression began to be visible. Within days he was able to move his arms and legs on his own. Weakly, but Rick hung on to every shred of hope. Rick had lost thirty pounds during the endless days of not even thinking about food, and only eating to refuel himself for more hours near his son. To be around to hear the statistics about blood oxygen, and the oxygenation of the baby's skin, and the numbers on the heart monitor, and which of the baby's veins would best hold a change in the IV tube.

The day a nurse was able to come in and briefly disconnect the baby from the respirator, Rick held him in his arms and rocked him, singing, crooning, begging him to get well. And Annie held him and told him how she missed him at home, and when they reconnected him and Annie sat down in the chair, Rick walked as far as the hospital cafeteria for dinner, realizing it was the first time in over a month that he'd left the hospital floor.

With agonizingly slow progress, David Reisman became more and more animated. There were a few days of testing the baby on what the doctors called "sprints," which were short periods of turning off the respirator, while he breathed on his own. One day they asked Rick and Annie to leave the ward while they removed the tube so the baby could begin to breathe on his own permanently.

For the next few days Rick held him close. His suck reflex was coming back, and he was able to take food from the bottle Rick fed him tenderly. Every burst of bubbles that rose in the bottle gave Rick a sense of triumph, because it meant that David was now getting sustenance from his formula.

"We're going to go home in a few days I think," he said to the tiny face. "And I'm real glad. I'm glad because it means you aren't sick anymore, and that makes me very happy . . . because I love you, little guy. I love you a lot."

The baby's little eyes blinked, and then a flicker of a smile crossed his little face, around his bottle. It made his father smile too as Dr. Weil and Dr. Solway walked into the ward to tell him that tomorrow morning they were releasing David to go home.

"There's something I'd like to suggest you look in to," the serious-faced Dr. Solway said to Rick the next morning, as he was packing the few toiletries and clothes he had kept in the hospital room. She had knocked on the door and said she wanted to come in to say good-bye. He thanked her again and again for her swift diagnosis which had saved David's life. Always her response was a slight nod and a wave of the hand to dismiss him.

"Whatever you suggest is good by me," Rick said today.

"I know about a group that's starting," she said. "A support group for families who have come by their babies in unusual ways. I think it's safe to say that you and David fall into that category."

Rick smiled. "There's an understatement."

"A very gifted child psychologist I know is organizing it, and I think you and David would benefit from it. I'd like to call her and ask her to include you."

"Doctor," Rick said, "I haven't been to my office in nearly two months. My career is on a roller coaster that's frequently on the downhill slope. I have been consumed with worry and guilt and anguish and thought about nothing and nobody but this baby for so long that earlier while I was waiting to pay the exorbitant bill I owe this hospital, I discovered that I was standing there rocking back and forth, because I'm so used to doing that with the baby that now I even rock when he's not with me. And *you're* telling me you think I should take even more time away from my work to sit in a room with some shrink and a group of other people who got their babies in strange ways and shoot the bull about problems?''

"Yes'' was all the pediatrician answered.

"I'll be there with bells on,'' he said.

26

ALL OF THE PARENTS in the new group were invited to sit outside and watch as their little ones dug in the sand or pushed themselves around on the rolling toys or splashed at the water table. The activities were set up in the yard adjacent to the large playroom where the adults would meet. Barbara's intern Dana was the child-care assistant.

"Looks as if your son is going to be a pulling guard," Shelly said to the familiar-looking man. He knew he'd met him before, and he was pretty sure it was at some event having to do with the business. Goddammit, he thought, why did I come here? I'm not going to sit around and participate in some kind of a true-confessions therapy group and tell everyone my problems. He wasn't ready to tell a group of strangers he was HIV-positive and watch them recoil. He would let the people who needed to have the information have it, but for now that was all.

"I'm Rick Reisman," the man said, extending a hand for Shelly to shake.

Oh, God, that's who he was. Rick Reisman, of course. Shelly had seen him earlier in the parking lot across from the building, struggling with the Aprica stroller, a moment Shelly knew only too well himself, but he hadn't been able to figure out why he looked so familiar. Now he realized they'd met at a fund-raiser at Barbra Streisand's house in Malibu.

"Shelly Milton," he said. "We've met."

"Of course, Shelly," Rick said, recognition filling his eyes. "I met you at that party. You were with your writing partner . . ."

"Me!" Ruthie said, walking over. "Ruth Zimmerman," she added, putting her hand out and shaking Rick's.

"So you adopted a baby?" Rick said, his eyes moving from Shelly to Ruthie.

"No," Shelly said. "Sid is our biological child."

Rick tried not to react. Zimmerman and Milton were a well-known comedy-writing team. But Shelly Milton was gay. Rick remembered when Davis Bergman, a married man, a law partner at a big-time entertainment firm, came out of the closet to have a long love affair with him. It was gossip all over town.

"Artificial insemination," Shelly said, knowing what Rick was thinking, and longing to grab Ruthie by the sleeve and drag her out of there. The group hadn't even started and already he was feeling defensive. No, this wasn't going to work.

"*We* did that," the pretty blond woman said. She was dressed in a chic cream-colored pantsuit and was kneeling on the ground where she diapered her baby daughter on a plastic pad. Ruthie couldn't believe that anybody who had a waist that small had ever given birth. "Only we used a surrogate." Aha! Ruthie thought. I knew it. The blond woman's darkly handsome husband was inside the playroom looking at the children's art push-pinned on all the walls.

"Now *that's* something I want to hear more about," Ruthie announced, "because if I ever have another baby, this time I want someone else to be in labor and then tell me about it. In fact, I'd prefer that they *didn't* tell me about it."

The blond woman was unsmiling and tense. She gathered the dirty diaper and the soiled wipes, put them efficiently into a Ziploc bag and tossed the bag into a nearby trash bin, then carried her daughter over to be with the other little ones.

David dropped shovels full of sand into a yellow bucket, and Sid pushed a Tonka truck along with one hand and held his Mickey Mouse bottle in his mouth with the other. Barbara Singer came outside and sat on the side of the sandbox, watching and encouraging the play. As she saw Lainie put Rose down in the sandbox, she noticed Mitch come out to look on lovingly as Rose joined in the play.

"My daughter's a party animal," Mitch said.

Lainie felt a heaviness fill her chest. Yes, she thought. Just like her mother. Jackie.

"That little baby Rose looks like a clone of *you*," Ruthie said to Lainie, who tried to force a smile. "And not one drop like her father. What does the surrogate look like?"

Lainie waited for Mitch to answer that.

"Beautiful," he said. "Like my wife."

Lainie worked hard to keep the smile on her face. "We're Mitch and Lainie De Nardo."

"Hi there" came a loud shout from inside. "Sorry I'm late!" It was Judith Shea. Her pretty auburn hair was flying. Her alert round-faced baby girl was in a papoose carrier on her back, and in her arms she carried her toddler daughter, whose chubby little legs were wrapped around her waist. "Say hi to everyone, girls," Judith urged.

For Barbara the explosive warmth was a welcome contrast to the nervous expressions of the others. "Two more little honeys for your group," Judith said, putting her daughter down, freeing her hands. "Judith Shea . . . inseminatee," she said with a laugh as she walked around to the others introducing herself.

Rick looked her over. Sexy as hell, a little thick around the middle, but then she'd just had two babies. Pretty little Jillian joined the group in the sandbox, and now that everyone had arrived, Barbara walked over and spoke to the toddlers.

"While all of you play with Dana, I'm going to go right inside that door with your mommies and daddies and Jillian's baby sister, and we're going to have some coffee and get to know one another better. So if you get lonely and want to come and say hello, you can just walk right in that door, and that's where we'll be until it's time for snack."

None of them even looked at her, but what she said seemed to register on their faces. The parents walked inside, where each of them sat on one of the toddler-size chairs she'd placed in a circle near a small table containing the electric percolator, which was now exuding the rich dark odor of freshly brewed coffee.

"I'd like to open by requesting that we get some larger furniture," Rick said, "since these chairs were obviously made for munchkins." The others laughed.

"I'll try to find bigger chairs by next time," Barbara said, looking around. Four families. Five little ones. It was a good start, she thought. Enough people to get some good talk going, and small enough to be intimate. "I want to welcome all of you. This is a very unique group, specifically designed for families with children whose birth circumstances were unusual. I believe in the necessity for this group, because modern technology is creating, and our society is embracing, extraordinary and wonderful ways to bring babies into the world. No one knows that better than all of you. But because these babies are so special, they and their parents bring with them a special set of needs and problems for which there is no precedent.

"These needs create situations never faced before, and require answers which, if we find them in our group, will not only help these special children through their lives but maybe can serve as pathfinding information we can pass on to other families." Every now and then she could hear her voice sounding exactly like Gracie's. And for a minute she had the odd feeling that somewhere in the room, just outside her peripheral vision, Gracie was perched, smoking a cigarette and saying, "Well said, dear girl."

"Each of you has taken a risk to have a child in an unorthodox way. Now those children are growing and developing, and soon they'll be out in the world with other children, and they'll have questions about their origins. We're here to deal with your responsibilities to your children, and how much you're prepared to tell them about themselves. How you'll present the information, and how you'll talk about their specialness at different stages in their lives. We'll also work on the way your particular baby or babies came into the world and how that continues to affect you and your spouse, or significant other, and other members of your extended families, parents, siblings, et cetera.

"So when Sid and Rose Margaret and David and Jillian and even little baby Jody are asking, 'Where do I come from?,' we'll have prepared loving responses. Responses we'll figure out together. And I mean that literally, because I certainly don't know what they are yet myself. But I think the important thing is to treat them and their questions in a way that helps these children to grow up feeling loved, loving, and confident."

"How can there be any answer to 'Where do I come from' besides the truth?" Rick asked.

Judith's baby was whimpering. Judith took her out of the carrier and rocked her against her shoulder. "I guess," she offered, "it depends on how comfortable you are with the truth. I don't particularly want to tell my daughters, 'Your dad was a number on a vial of sperm.' I'd like to make it sound better than that."

"Truthfulness for young children doesn't have to mean you tell them the whole story all at once. There are certain ways to give information that are more age appropriate than other ways, and you give them the information in stages. Broad strokes that are honest instead of details that they might not be able to handle," Barbara said. "And, Judith, I think wanting to let your daughters know that there was a living, breathing person who donated that sperm is a great idea. Because once they understand that they're a part of him, they'll want to think of him as someone special."

That made Lainie think about Jackie. About Mitch and Jackie, and she nearly jumped with surprise when she felt Mitch take her hand and hold it gently. Why is he holding my hand? Trying to make everyone think we're happy. Trying to make *me* think that.

"The method I used to get a baby was open adoption," Rick said. "David's birth mother actually lived in my house for the last few months of her pregnancy."

"Does she still see the baby?" Lainie asked.

"She hasn't seen him since we left the hospital."

"Where is she?" Shelly asked.

"In Kansas."

"Nice and far away," Judith said.

"I have no problem with her being around David. I

think of her as his mother. He has her feisty ways, and her pink skin, and her blood flowing through his veins. And she's a terrific, bright human being. When he can understand, I want him to know she's his mother."

"You think that because you're single," Ruthie said. "If you had a wife who wanted to mother him, I'll bet things would be different."

"Maybe," Rick said.

"These are the kinds of complicated things we'll get into in this group," Barbara said. "I suspect that involvement with a birth parent can probably get touchy down the line. Particularly, Rick, if you chose to get married someday."

"No chance of that," Rick said.

"Are you gay?" Judith asked Rick.

"Not that I know of," Rick answered. "Want to step into the other room and find out?"

"Are you homophobic?" Ruthie asked Judith.

"Hell no," Judith said. "I was just wondering why an attractive single man is so adamant that he won't marry."

Ruthie changed the subject. "Do the two of you have any continuing relationship with the surrogate?" she asked, looking at Lainie and Mitch. Lainie's heart beat faster. Out of the corner of her eye she saw Barbara stiffen.

"No," Mitch said now in answer to Ruthie's question. "We have no communication with the surrogate. None."

Barbara's and Lainie's eyes met for a second, but Barbara's moved back to Rick. "How will you handle the fact that you have a little baby with the women you date?" Barbara asked him.

"I'll have them stop by at midnight and leave at six A.M.," he said in a teasing voice. "That way David will never know they're there."

"I knew I didn't like you the minute I laid eyes on you," Judith said to Rick, but it was in a kidding voice.

"Oh yes you did," Rick kidded back. "I'm still living on the fact that less than a minute ago you called me attractive." Judith laughed. "Listen, I'm not serious. I don't know what I'll do. I've temporarily sworn off dating, and maybe someday I will find the woman for me. Though it becomes more farfetched all the time. I usually find myself dating women I wouldn't want to involve with my child."

"Now there's a comment on your taste," Judith said.

"You're going to be trouble," Rick said, grinning at her.

The others laughed.

"Do you know the birth father of the baby too?" Mitch asked Rick.

"No, I have no idea who he is. The young girl who's David's mother won't tell me. Maybe she doesn't even know. But I think it's pretty safe to assume it was some high-school kid who threw her over," he said.

"And the two of you?" Barbara asked, looking closely at Shelly. He showed no apparent sign of being in less than perfect health. His arm was casually draped around the back of Ruthie's little chair. "Have you given any thought to what you'll tell Sid when the time comes for him to start asking?"

"I'll tell him to mind his own business," Shelly joked. The others laughed.

"That's funny and glib," Barbara said, "but it's not answering the question. I know you're a writer and comedy is your specialty, but I also know you had this baby for serious reasons. And I really wonder what you'll tell him."

"Well," Ruthie said, looking at Shelly, "we can certainly tell him how much we love each other, and that that's why we had him." Then to the others she explained, "We're best friends. Shelly is gay, and Sid was a turkey-baster baby."

"And what if he asks you *how* you had him?" Judith asked.

"It'll be easier to describe than sex," Ruthie said.

Another laugh from the others.

"We don't know," Shelly said, "which I guess is why we're here."

"He's so smart it's extraordinary," Ruthie said, sitting tall in her chair, her happy thoughts of her son dancing across her face. "So verbal. With an amazing sense of humor. He's already talking like a much older child. I mean, I think he is, because people are always amazed at the things he says."

"Like the other day," Shelly said.

"I didn't mean that," Ruthie said, anger crossing her face.

"I know, but it's important. It's one of the reasons we're here."

Ruthie explained what Shelly meant in a way that made Barbara sense she was carefully holding her rage inside. "Sid was at some other little kid's house for a play date. Some little boy in the neighborhood. And he came home using a new word he'd learned there. The word was 'faggot.' " Ruthie and Shelly held each other's hands tightly. "We realize it's the beginning of a lifetime of explaining, and we want to explain it the best way we can."

"We don't want him to think we have separate bedrooms because I snore," Shelly said. "I want him to know that I'm gay, and that that's okay no matter what people outside our family and our home may tell him. That it doesn't make me any less his father, or our relationship less loving."

"He'll know you love each other and love him," Barbara said, "because he'll feel it, and I'll help you work on the words you can say to him so you can express it to him verbally too." She was glad to see Ruthie and Shelly exchange a look of relief, and she said a secret prayer that she'd be able to do what she was promising.

"You see," Shelly said, musing, "I think if he doesn't know that right away, he'll never have any idea of who I was."

"Was? You sound as if you're not planning to be around for him to get to know you," Judith said.

Barbara heard Shelly's deep intake of breath and saw Ruthie look out the window at Sid. "None of us knows how long we'll be around," Barbara said gently. "But I think what we're hearing today is that our yardsticks for behavior are out the window when we try to use them against the new life-styles."

After a quiet moment the discussion moved into the group's mutual everyday parenting problems—pacifiers, temper tantrums—until they were interrupted by the cry of "Mommeeee" from the play yard. Ruthie, Lainie, and Judith all jumped to their feet and ran to the door. The cry had come from Sid, who had poured sand all over his own head. Ruthie picked him up and brushed him off tenderly.

"They're all getting hungry," Dana announced.

"Let's bring them in for clean diapers and snacks," Barbara said, and Lainie and Rick and Judith walked over to the sandbox to clean the sand from their little ones, too. As Barbara watched the parents interact with their babies, she felt shaky. Dear God, she thought. I hope I haven't bitten off more than I can chew. These are tough, complicated situations, being lived by smart people, and their problems aren't just about the future. They're about how to function day to day.

Rick Reisman may have finally bonded with his little boy during the illness, but he still feels incapable of having a relationship with a woman. And Shelly Milton faces the possibility of AIDS every day of his life. He might look fine now, as he marches around the room with Sid on his shoulders, but there is the specter of the HIV virus always looming large in the lives of that family.

And the De Nardos. Does Mitch really still have some connection to the surrogate? That secret will have to come out soon too. Barbara looked at Mitch standing next to his wife, touching her back while she held little Rose on her lap and tied the baby's tiny shoes. If what Lainie suspected had any validity, there was plenty of pain ahead, not just for her and Mitch but most of all for little Rose.

"I don't want to be didactic about how the group will progress," Barbara said as she and Dana poured apple juice into dinosaur paper cups, "because in my experience I find the sessions usually take on a life of their own, and people talk about whatever's going on with them at the time. But I have some ideas for jumping-off points and directions we might want to take. For example, we might want to talk about how much we want to tell the children and when. How to create a support system, how to handle the unrealistic expectations of holidays. How to help them feel continuity with their birth families by stories and letters. Rick, you might want to make a photo album for David with pictures in it of his birth family and his adopted family, going back to grandparents. So David can be familiar with his origins."

There was more talk among them all, light and guarded, along with a snack of crackers, raisins, and cheese, then they all sang "Two Little Blackbirds Sitting on a Hill," "The Wheels on the Bus," "The Itsy-Bitsy Spider," and Barbara read to the children from *Spot Goes to the Farm*.

When everyone was gone, Barbara and Dana piled the little chairs into a tower and pushed them into the corner. After Dana left, Barbara, who always prided herself on her ability to view these groups in a clinical way, sat on one of the small blue plastic chairs, and after she thought about everything that was said today, for some inexplicable reason she had a good cry.

27

ARTIE WILSON, one of the network executives in comedy programming, told Shelly in passing that he was looking thin, and Shelly obsessed about it for hours. "Shel, he meant it as a compliment," Ruthie swore to him. "He knows we hate him because he made us take the clam joke out of the script last season because he thought it was suggestive. He was trying to be a charming network executive."

"Now there's an oxymoron if I've ever heard one."

"Don't you know by now that when someone in Hollywood says you're looking thin it's the ultimate flattery?"

The ten staff writers were like ten mental patients, each one with a different neurosis, each one with a unique style. Just before Ruthie and Shelly walked into the meeting with them Shelly would say, "Bring me the whip and the chair, it's time to tame the animals." It was said with love and recognition of the fact that he and Ruthie were cut from the same cloth as those lunatics, but as producers it was their job to control the output, which meant keeping the writers and the writing focused.

They also felt that part of their job was to protect the writers, to keep them in good spirits and make the atmosphere at work as much fun as possible. Sometimes Ruthie even lovingly made and brought in muffins for their early-morning meetings. Unfortunately there was no way to protect the staff from Zev Ryder, the executive producer, who was always on everyone's case. He was the person with whom Ruthie assiduously avoided contact on those days when Shelly didn't make it in to work. If he somehow managed to find her, he was certain to harass her.

"Where's your funny half?" Ryder would ask her. Ruthie knew that behind their backs he called Ruthie and Shelly "the Dolly Sisters," and referred to some of their material as "sissy humor." He despised all of the writers and they all returned the sentiment. Nevertheless, in spite of him and thanks to Ruthie and Shelly's talent, the writing on the show was top-notch, but sometimes it was impossible to save the day from Zev Ryder's bad vibrations.

Like the morning that Jack Goldstein, a skinny wild-eyed Einstein-haired writer whose bizarre and hilarious ideas always read as if they were drug inspired, burst into Ryder's office. Ryder had pulled one of Goldstein's sketches from the script that morning, and the reason he gave for doing so was "not funny." Ryder was on the phone when Goldstein pulled the telephone out of his hand and hung it up, then leapt across the desk, grabbed Ryder tightly by the collar of his Ralph Lauren shirt, and breathed into his face.

"Say something funny! You're the executive producer of a comedy show. I defy you to say one funny thing. One funny word and I won't kill you. A joke, a stolen joke, a quote from somebody else to show me you know what's funny." He was holding both sides of the collar in his big clenched fist, pulling Ryder's fat little neck together in a wad in his hand. Ryder's eyes were huge with shock. "You see, you can't do it, not even to save your worthless life. Because there's not a funny bone in your entire family, you bastard. Go on, goddamn you! Say something funny!"

Ryder's mouth was open and he was emitting strange little choking sounds and by now all of the other writers who had heard Goldstein screaming had gathered in the doorway of Zev Ryder's office to watch. Ryder was blue in the face. His eyes were starting to pop out and finally, seeing them all there, in a desperate plea he managed to say, "I'm dying. Please. I'm dying." At which point Goldstein threw him back in his chair, said, "All right. You got me. *That's* funny," and walked out of Ryder's office and, of course, off the show.

It had been more than a year, and Zev Ryder saw to it that though there was no doubt that Jack Goldstein was a comedy genius, he coudn't get a job anywhere in the business. And any time after that when Zev Ryder didn't like the script, he'd make some comment like "Look out, you pigs, because it's possible that Jack Goldstein needs someone to talk to while he stands in line at unemployment."

Today the group of writers had turned the conference room into a miniature golf course; Styrofoam cups with the bottoms ripped out were the holes, the golf balls were wadded-up tinfoil from the morning bagel delivery, and their pencils and pens were the clubs. When Ruthie and Shelly walked into the room to start the meeting, two of the guys were standing on the conference table arguing over a shot.

"People, let's get to work," Shelly said.

Ruthie pulled out a chair and sat and waited while everything from the grumbling about the ratio of onion bagels to pumpernickel bagels, to the condition of one of the guys' pancreas, to the jokes about somebody's pregnant wife finally stopped. She was just about to start talking about the show when Jerry Brenner, a forty-year-old fat little man who was once a stand-up comic, started telling a joke to his partner, Arnie Fishmann. But when he noticed the room was silent, he raised his voice to share it with all of them.

"A woman says to her friend, 'I don't know what to do. My husband just came home from a doctor's appointment. He told me the doctor said he either has AIDS or Alzheimer's, but he's not sure which one it is. I'm so worried. What should I do?' " There was a groan from someone and a chuckle of anticipation from someone else, and then somebody, Ruthie didn't look up so she didn't know who it was, uttered, "Good old Mr. Good-Taste Brenner."

"So the friend says, 'Here's what you do. You send him out to the supermarket. If he finds his way home, don't fuck him!' "

The roomful of writers offered the only kind of approval they allowed, which was never laughter, just a few snickers and a couple of grudging "That's funny"s, while Ruthie, who couldn't look at Shelly, felt decimated, and Shelly doodled on a yellow legal pad, hoping his discomfort didn't show.

It took a while for Shelly to reach Davis to tell him the news, but there was no answer at his home, not even an answering machine, and when he called Davis's law office, Davis's secretary told him, "Mr. Bergman is out of the office for a while. But he will be checking in. May I tell him who called?"

"Sheldon Milton," Shelly said.

"May I tell him what this is regarding?" she said.

"It's a personal call," Shelly said, glad he wasn't talking to Elise, the secretary who had worked for Davis when the two of them were together. After almost three weeks passed, Davis returned the call. He was cool and uncomfortable on the phone, and after Shelly said he needed to talk to him, they agreed to meet that day at lunchtime outside the L.A. County art museum, which was halfway between their offices.

"Isn't it odd," Shelly said to Ruthie later, "how you can worry and fear the way something's going to go, sure that it will be one way, and then it turns out to happen in a way you'd never even imagined?" In his fantasy he had been sure that he would tell Davis the news and Davis would become anxious and afraid for himself and his wife, Marsha. Maybe he would be accusatory or snide. But when Shelly walked up the steps to the stark grounds around the museum where the blazing hot Los Angeles day made the cement look glaringly white and he moved to the bench where Davis was sitting and Davis turned and looked into his eyes, it was clear to him that Davis had AIDS. And that he had been trying to figure out how he was going to tell Shelly.

"What about Ruthie and your son?" Davis asked after each of them had told the other their news.

"They've both been tested and they're fine."

A teacher led a group of children who walked in double file past the bench, and after some instructions from the teacher the giggling, fidgeting group disappeared through the front doors of the museum.

"Why didn't you call me, Davis?"

"Because I've only known for a few very numb days, and I wanted to pull myself together so I could tell you without falling apart. I haven't left the house since I heard. I haven't talked to anyone. Marsha was tested too and she's fine, but she's completely blown away.

You remember that she's been seeing a psychiatrist three days a week for years? Well, now she talks to him on the phone on the other four."

There was something funny about that statement that made them both laugh out loud. But then Davis turned serious. "She's afraid I'll lose my job at the firm if anyone finds out. That none of the clients will want to meet with me if they know. She was the one who dragged me in to be tested, after weeks of my having night sweats and high fevers. She'd been reading all about AIDS and obsessing about it and driving herself and me crazy. Just the type of person you like to have around when you're feeling too weak to lift your head," he said with that ironic half smile of his Shelly remembered. "So finally I went with her, and we both got tested."

Suddenly there was the sound of screeching brakes, and then the sound of crunching metal and shattering glass as one car rammed into another on Wilshire Boulevard. And from their distance, on the bench near the front entrance to the museum, both men turned and watched as the traffic piled up and the angry drivers emerged from a gray BMW and a red Jeep Cherokee to shout blame at each other. It sounded as if a woman from inside of one of the cars was yelling out to a man on the sidewalk to call an ambulance.

"What can I do for you, Davis?" Shelly asked, turning away from the accident. "Is there anything I can do?"

The brightness was gone from Davis's face, but inside the pained expression and the pallor of illness, Shelly still saw the pensive, intense bright man he had lived with and loved. So much that losing him had once seemed to be a reason for giving up his own life.

"Forgive me for the way I left you," Davis said.

"I did that a long time ago."

"It's funny," Davis said, "I had taken to thinking about the time that you and I were together as the best I'd spent in my life so far. Now I may have to think of it as the best time in my life."

"You've got lots of life left," Shelly said.

"It would be easier for Marsha if I didn't."

"I never thought I'd hear myself say this," Shelly said, "but fuck Marsha!"

They smiled at each other.

"I'll always love you," Davis said.

"I'll always love you too."

The screaming cry of an ambulance filled the air on Wilshire Boulevard, and Shelly turned to watch. Within seconds the ambulance had wedged itself into the street as near to the collision as it could get, and the two paramedics emerged, opened the passenger door of the BMW, and removed an injured bloody passenger. The driver of the car gestured angrily for the gawking people who had gathered to get out of the way. The paramedics moved the injured woman onto the gurney, which they slowly inserted into the ambulance, then they closed the double doors, scrambled inside, and pulled away. Their shrill siren pierced the day again and the traffic moved to the right to let the ambulance pass. When Shelly turned back to finish their conversation, Davis was gone.

A few nights later, baby Sid woke crying. His diaper was filled with a gray liquid stool that had seeped out all over the crib. After Ruthie changed him and the bed and scrubbed down the changing table, she rehydrated him with a bottle of water and got him back down to sleep. But just after she slid into her own bed, he wailed again and emitted another dark loose bowel movement.

Shelly, groggy with sleep, stood in the door of the

nursery where Ruthie removed Sid again from the crib, again to repeat the cleaning-up process. "What's wrong?" he asked.

"I know the doctors say he's fine and not to worry," she said, "but I always do anyway."

After she told him, they looked long at each other. They were both tired from their work schedules, feeling guilty for not spending more time with the baby. They stood next to the changing table where Sid, too ill to cry, lay watching as his mother and father hugged each other closely.

"He has a stomach bug. That's all," Shelly told her, rubbing her head tenderly. "And don't forget what Freud said."

"What did Freud say?" Ruthie asked, glad that she was still his straight man after all these years.

"Sometimes a poop is just a poop."

The stomach flu was gone the next day.

28

EVERYONE WHO ATTENDED David Reisman's adoption ceremony melted when they saw the boy at the courthouse dressed in a pale blue seersucker suit and tennis shoes. The bright red hair Rick didn't have the heart to let any barber cut tumbled in curls all around David's handsome face. Downtown at the cold marble-halled courthouse Patty Fall, who had purchased the suit and dressed David in it that morning, shared the moment happily and brought both of her sons along to share it too. The judge, a man younger than Rick by a few years seemed bemused by the whole process. Sadly, Uncle Bobo was feeling too ill that day to come all the way downtown, so Mayer Fall, a USC film student who was planning to make a video of the event anyway, dedicated it to Bobo.

Everyone who appeared on camera was instructed by Mayer to say, "Hi, Uncle Bobo." Strangers in the courthouse were waving to Bobo via Mayer's camera.

Mayer got the uniformed guard to wave and say, "Hi there, Uncle Bobo," and of course so did Harvey Feldman, the lawyer, and in the middle of the proceedings even the court reporter and the judge raised a hand and waved to Uncle Bobo. David, as instructed, looked into the lens and said, "Unca Bobobobobo."

Afterward everyone went to the Falls' beach house for a late lunch, and as the perfect day was coming to an end, Rick and Patty, alone on the deck, looked out at the waves breaking and watched Mayer Fall, a grown man of twenty-one, playing in the sand with David.

"It's great to have a relationship with a baby, impossible to have one with a woman. Babies give you unconditional adoration. Babies don't expect you to buy them an engagement ring to prove that you care about them, and babies don't pout if you smile at another baby. To babies," Rick said, holding up his wineglass, and Patty Fall filled the glass with more wine as she shook her head knowingly.

"Boy, are you in for a rude awakening," she said, pouring some into her own glass too. "Babies grow up and walk all over you. And if they're yours, as you already know they have the ability to break your heart worse than any woman ever could. I can absolutely guarantee you that within a matter of years, that kid will be on the take from you worse than any gold-digging woman you've ever imagined, and you know what? You'll give it all to him gladly. Charlie always did with our kids," she said with love but without any sentimentality. "He was a pushover beyond description."

"Look at those two," Rick said, grinning at the game Mayer was playing with David, making piles of sand that the baby kicked down, after which Mayer moaned in mock dismay, which made the baby erupt with laughter. Patty watched Rick watching them.

"Mayer and his girlfriend are very serious," she said. "It's hard to believe that soon I could be a grandmother and you're the daddy of a little baby."

Rick smiled. "I remember Doreen's mother saying something like that to me when I met her. She's my age and she has seven grandchildren and couldn't figure out why I'd want to do this. To start being a parent at this ripe old age."

"Oh, I understand why. It's already changed you immeasurably."

"Nah. I'm still a fat old lech."

"But a mellower old lech. And not so fat anymore. In fact, you're starting to look pretty damned sexy."

"Yeah, yeah, yeah," Rick said, smiling and looking at his best friend's widow across the table, then taking her hand. Her tan face was lined from the years of too much sun at the beach. But her green eyes were still as bright as when she was the young secretary in a producer's office at Columbia Pictures where a dashing Charlie Fall came to have a meeting with her boss. And while he waited for the producer to get off a phone call, in the ultimate flirtatious move Charlie proposed to her.

"So how's by you these days?" Rick asked her gently. "Are you surviving okay without him?"

"Oh sure," she said. "I'm okay. My kids hang around a lot, my mother flies in from Seattle every few months." And then she opened her eyes wide and tried to hold back a funny grin that was forming around the corners of her mouth when she said, "I'm even being courted by various swains these days."

For some inexplicable reason, though he couldn't think of why, the idea of Patty's dating made him feel affronted, and Rick blurted out his first thought, "But the problem is, who could ever live up to Charlie Fall, right?"

The green eyes flashed, and Patty took her hand out

from under his. "Nobody has to, Ricky," she said quietly. "That's not the criterion. Not that I have to explain this, but I loved Charlie completely for twenty-seven years, and somebody else will be somebody else. I'm not so stuck with some concept of how my relationship with a man has to be, I'm not hanging on to some unrealistic archetype that no human being can ever live up to."

"You mean like certain other people you could mention and that's why they've never married?"

"If the shoe fits, honey . . ." she said, smiling. "Listen, you know as well as I do that Charlie Fall had his faults, believe me, and so will my next husband."

"Husband? You're already that serious about somebody?"

"No, but I want to be. Unlike you, I'm crazy about intimacy. I love having the same person in bed next to me every night and every morning. Having somebody boss me around who gets pissed at me for bossing him around. I like a guy who does the *New York Times* crossword puzzle over my shoulder, and gets the references to sports and geography but leaves the song titles and names of playwrights to me."

"Sounds awful."

"Go to hell."

"I'm sure I will, because I still like a high-volume turnover of pieces of ass I've barely spoken to mainly because they can barely speak. I long for naked lust with exotic strangers in dubious locations, and particularly love waking to find black lace underwear and bondage equipment hanging from my chandelier *and* my appendages." Patty's outraged laughter made him go on. "I like to start my day uncertain if during the foreplay of the night before, I played the part of the shepherd who buggered the sheep or the sheep itself. That said . . . want to marry me?"

Patty let out a sound that was somewhere between a scream and a giggle. "I think we're a match made in heaven," she said. The sun was big and orange and very low in the sky and the two of them watched as Mayer put David on his shoulders and ran into the surf, then pranced through the waves to the beach, kicking water everywhere, making the baby scream with delight.

"Patty," Rick said to her though he continued to look down at the boys on the beach, "I know I idealized my late mother enough to make Oedipus look aloof. But I'm sure you know that in the more recent years, you've always been the standard against which I've measured every woman in my life. You're smart and funny. You made a family for Charlie and those boys that I've always envied and admired and coveted. You're going to find somebody one day soon, and he's going to be the luckiest man that ever lived. And I'm here to tell you that if he doesn't worship the ground where you walk every day, you call me and I'll kill him. Promise?"

Patty reached over and took his hand back. "I promise."

The phone rang and Patty reached for the portable receiver on the wicker table next to her.

"Hello? Yes, Andrea, he's here. I'll put him on." Patty gave Rick the handset.

"Secretarial assistant to moi?" Rick said into it.

"Mister R., listen. I've got Doreen Cobb on the other line."

"Doreen? How great! My God, it'll be great to talk to her. Can you patch her through?"

"She sounds kind of depressed," Andrea said. "She knows that today was the adoption."

"Put her through," Rick said. There were a few clicks and then Rick heard Doreen's sad little voice on the other end of the line say "Hello?"

"Hello, Doreen," Rick said, wishing he knew how to make the day of David's adoption easier for her.

"I'm sorry to bother you, I mean, I know I'm not supposed to but . . . it's just that I . . ."

"You're not bothering me. I'm really glad to hear your voice. How's Bea?"

"Bea's okay," she said, and he could hear muffled sounds on the other end of the line that he knew were her pained sobs.

"Doreen, can I do anything?" he asked gently.

"Oh, no," she said. "I knew today was David's special day . . . and I just wanted to hear about how it went."

Rick listened to more sniffling and sobs, and tried to think of something he could say. "It went great and he's a tiger. He's walking, he's talking up a storm. In fact I can see him right now from where I'm sitting. He's right at the place where the sand meets the surf, mushing his fat little feet into the wet sand and screeching at the top of his lungs every time the waves come."

"Oh good!" Doreen said, sounding sincerely cheered by the report.

"Oh and by the way, I've become part of a parenting group." He knew she would think that was funny. "All of us are parents who got their babies in unusual ways."

"Ahh, that's so sweet," she said. "I'll bet it's fun for you."

"And one of the ideas the group leader had was for me to make a scrapbook for David, photos of his families, extended families and birth families. So I've been thinking about calling you, to ask if you'd send me some pictures of you."

"Oh, God," she said laughing. "There's never been a good one yet."

"And some of Bea, and of your sisters and brothers and their kids so David can see his cousins."

"Oh fun!" she said. The news that she was still included in David's life seemed to lift her spirits. "I'll start putting them together today. I know Bea has one of the whole family at a picnic table and . . . what? I'm on long distance!" Someone had come into the room on her end of the line.

"I have to go now," Doreen said abruptly, and without a good-bye, she hung up. Rick continued to hold the receiver as if he thought she might come back on the line, but then there was a dial tone. Disappointed, he put the phone back on the table.

"Not that it's any of my business," Patty said, "but this is where the system falls apart a little for me. I mean, how do you separate out your responsibility to this girl from your gratitude? Please don't think I'm being cold about all of this. I know how much the baby means to your life, Ricky, but I don't get it. She chooses you to be the one to take her baby. To me that part is good, I guess, because she feels as if she has some control over it all. Knows that the flesh of her flesh is with someone she deems okay. But isn't the theory that, barring Christmas cards and an occasional photograph, you make a clean break after the baby's handed off?"

"That's the theory," Rick said. "But it only works on paper. Something happens. It happened to me, anyway. Maybe because she lived in my house, maybe because she's so unique, but I care and will always care about her well-being. And now, at least when she's falling apart from the pain of the rest of her life, she can call me and still get some joy from knowing her baby is thriving. Not that I'm some great expert, but I don't understand how the other ways of doing this can work. A woman pretending she never had a baby? A mother not looking at the calendar on the day she gave birth and wondering where the baby is?"

"You realize if she'd put David with another family, they might have been less sympathetic about her needs. A family with a mother who felt threatened by the intrusion."

"Yes I do. But she picked me, and her mother let her pick me. And maybe that was why. Because they both knew instinctively that I would never deny them a relationship with this baby. Or with me, even if the day ever comes, and you and I both know it won't, when I marry."

"Do you have any idea who the father is?" she asked. Mayer was walking up the beach with David toddling along next to him babbling away.

"As far as I know," Rick said, "when it comes to paternal influences, this kid is stuck with just little old me."

"God save us all," Patty said, flashing a smile as David climbed onto Rick's lap, salty and sandy. Rick stood him on his feet and peeled the soggy bathing suit off. "I'll take him inside and wash him," he said. And just as the bathing suit got past his thighs, David peed all over Rick.

"Well that's *his* comment on the situation," Rick said.

"Maybe your daddy better go in and take a shower *with* you," Patty suggested to David, who clapped his hands with glee at the idea.

A few days later the photographs from Doreen came in the mail. David's only interest in them was throwing them all around the room or biting on them, but Rick shuffled through them all. He smiled as he looked at the one of Doreen and her mother, remembering the life-changing day he met them at the airport.

He always viewed everything with his director's eye,

even these photos of Doreen and her sisters. Cheryl, the prettiest one, who unlike Doreen seemed to have confidence in her appearance. Susan smiled with her mouth but her weary eyes and body English were a giveaway of an unhappy young woman.

There were a million stories in the photo of the whole family, children and spouses included, at what appeared to be a picnic in a pretty-looking park. The poses people took, where they placed themselves in the shot, the expressions on their faces were all so telling. One more time he went through the whole pile of photos, and stopped for a long time at the one of the assembled family at the picnic, because now he saw something in it that made him afraid. Could it be? But then he dismissed the thought as his overactive imagination and put the pictures away.

29

SOMETIMES after work Judith would pick up her two little girls who had been at home with the housekeeper all day and take them to the park. While she went through the ordeal of lifting the wiggling baby out of the infant car seat and gentling her fat little resisting body into the Snugli, then putting the stroller together while an impatient Jillian whined, she wondered if maybe her position on men and relationships was too tough.

"Every couple has their deal," her friend Jerralyn told her one day at lunch, "usually unspoken, and as long as each of them keeps the deal they're in good shape. He provides clothes and trips, she sticks around, he cheats, she ignores it. She flirts, he thinks it's cute. The partner you end up with is the one who offers a deal you can live with and vice versa."

Judith didn't ask Jerralyn what the deal was she had with her husband, Tom, just said, "I guess I haven't met a man yet with a deal I like." But the idea of making a deal, unspoken or otherwise, was abhorrent to her. This evening she held baby Jody on her shoulder and pushed Jillian in the swing when a little toddler boy lurched into the play-equipment area, screaming, "Daddeeee! Daddeeee!" Jillian moved back and forth, little fists holding tight to the chains of the enclosed baby swing, and watched the little boy with fascination. Then, liking the sound of his chant, she took it up as her own.

"Daddeeee! Daddeeee!" she cried, her elfin voice echoing through the park. Each time she called out, the sound went right through Judith, who felt anguished that there might never be anyone to answer the cry. There must be a good man out there somewhere, she thought as a gray dusk fell around her. A sudden chill in the air made her wrap both girls in her own sweater and hold them close to her chest as she headed for the car. I'll find him, she decided. I'll tell Jerralyn, who's always trying to fix me up with one of Tom's friends or some guy she met on a ski trip, to go for it. To say that despite all of my refusals in the past, I've had a change of heart and I'm ready to take a shot.

The first man on Jerralyn's list was in the computer business, so wonderful looking he could be on the cover of *GQ*. This was the fellow Jerralyn and Tom had met on the ski trip. He talked a lot about his physical condition and eating habits, and when they got down to the details of Judith's life he seemed fascinated with the story of how she came to have her daughters.

"That is so great," he said over coffee. "You are a real original." But she knew it was all over with him when she finished the story and he said, "Well . . . it sounds to me like an extrapolation of masturbation."

"Pardon me?"

"I mean that it's something you can do on your own

if you have to, but so much better if you do it with a partner." He laughed at his own wit. "I mean, isn't that a great analogy?"

The second one was a banker, very well dressed and in his mid-forties, who took her to the Bistro for dinner. When he asked about her life she told him about her donor babies and as she did she saw a look of terrible distaste on his face. But she went on to finish the story, about the anonymity factor and the list from the cryobank containing the limited information, and just as the waiter put her dinner in front of her the banker asked, "How do you know the donor wasn't some serial killer like that guy in the Midwest who killed all the people and ate them?"

She didn't have an answer for him. Nor did she have one bite of the very expensive dinner.

"Sorry I wasted your time," she told Jerralyn.

"One more, give me one more chance. This one is different, and just to be on the safe side, I already told him about you and the girls. After my batting average on the first two, I figured if this one couldn't handle it right from the giddy-up, I better not even send him around."

"And?"

"It intrigued him. He's never been married or had kids, so it's all kind of foreign and fun to him. He's one of my husband's oldest friends. Cute, bearded, balding but sexy. Frank's very sexy. A real-estate developer. Likes to scuba dive, surf—"

"Jerra, you're starting to sound like the rundown sheet from the sperm bank," Judith said, and both women laughed, a kind of hopeful this-might-be-a-good-one laugh.

Jerralyn was right about the sexy part and Frank was very flirtatious. He held her hand across the dinner table and looked into her eyes with a knowing amusement that was very appealing. Judith felt herself drinking a little too much wine. Her policy about going on these dates was to meet the men at the restaurant because she didn't want to expose her children to them and vice versa. But tonight, halfway through dinner, she was feeling heady from the alcohol and wishing that she'd let this one pick her up at home. She knew she shouldn't be driving in this condition. How was she going to get home? She ordered coffee with dessert and drank several cups of it black, and was relieved when she started feeling closer to earth.

He never mentioned her children and neither did she. He talked about the real-estate market, and about a boat he had in the Caribbean and about various trips he'd taken on it. She talked about her job at the advertising agency and the clients she worked for. After they'd run out of food and superficial things to talk about, he paid the check and they walked outside.

"Thanks for dinner," she said, extending her hand. "It was nice to meet you." He held her hand lightly.

"Where did you park?" he asked.

"Around the back."

"Come on, I'll walk you."

"It's the station wagon with the two car seats in it," she said, wondering if that was a good opening to talk about her kids. Jerra told her he knew about them.

"Ahh, yes," he said, "the donor babies." She had parked in the back because when she'd arrived, the parking lot in front had been full. There was so much crime in these neighborhoods at night, she'd rushed from her car to the restaurant, afraid as she often was these days that someone was just waiting to grab her. And when someone did she gasped.

It was Frank. At her car, in the now empty parking lot, he turned her to face him, pressed her against the side of her car, then forced his mouth on hers. She could smell the garlic from the pasta on his beard and she didn't like his mushy wet kiss. She tried turning her face away, but he took her chin in his hand and moved her face back to his.

"Don't turn away," he said. His body was pinning hers hard now, and she was uncomfortable and a little afraid.

"I've got to get home," she said.

"To your kids?" he asked, smiling, but it wasn't a friendly smile.

"Yes," she said and tried to slide away from him, but now she realized that what she'd thought was a little heat from this guy was overpowering force. She felt a panicky quickening in her chest. Now he moved his hands to her buttocks and pulled her pelvis against his very excited one.

"No," she said, moving to get away.

"What's the matter?" he asked. "*I've* got sperm. Don't you want some of *my* sperm?"

She felt sick to her stomach, and when he placed his fuzzy garlicky face against her again, she stuck the high heel of her shoe into the arch of his loafer. He let out a grunt of pain, but wouldn't let go. Now he was talking in a weird little soft voice he must have thought was seductive. "I want to please you, baby. Won't you let me?"

"I will let you, and here's how," she said, trying to contain her rage. "It would please me inordinately if you would just fuck off."

"Cunt," he said, pushed her against the car hard, and walked away.

"You want to know why women use anonymous donors? Look in the mirror, you pig!" she shouted after him. In the car, she screamed out loud for a few minutes and cursed the fact that she'd been stupid enough to let herself be fixed up. When she flipped on the radio dial, the audiocassette she'd been playing for the children earlier that day came on, and Snow White in her trilling little voice was singing, "Someday my prince will come."

When she talked about it in the group she was surprised at how comforted she felt. There was something about blurting out the horror of it all that was therapeutic and healing. Ruthie and Shelly cracked jokes, but they lovingly offered suggestions, even tried to think of some good single men for her. And Rick Reisman turned to her and said, "Even *I*, with my long record of insensitivity, have to say those guys you went out with were monsters."

"I think we should go around the room and talk about dumb things people say to us and all the times we've wanted to tell them to shove it up their nose."

"Well put, Ruthless," Shelly said. "I think what she means is, let's figure out how we're going to respond to stupid questions with a little bit of grace."

"Yeah. Grace," Ruthie said. "How do you respond gracefully to this one, which I am so sick of I could kill, 'You mean Shelly's Sid's *real* father? How did *that* happen?' I always want to say, 'Come over for Thanksgiving dinner and taste my moist turkey, sweetheart!' " Everyone howled at that one.

"I've got one that people say to me all the time that all of you will love," Rick said. " 'Well, won't it be nice that by the time the baby's in his twenties, he'll be able to wheel you around the old folks' home just like you do your uncle.' " That got a hoot from Ruthie and a big laugh from all the others.

Now Shelly piped up with one he'd kept even from Ruthie. "How about this one? I've now had two different people on two different occasions ask me, 'Aren't you worried that when Sid grows up he'll be gay?' "

"No!" Ruthie said, then thought, and added, "I

don't know why I'm surprised, I've actually had someone ask me, 'Did you and Shelly ever do it just to see if it would work?' " An outraged moan rose from the group.

"How about, 'Didn't it feel bad to know you couldn't have Mitch's baby and another woman could?' " Lainie offered, and the laughter stopped abruptly as everyone looked at her serious face. Barbara was surprised to hear Lainie volunteer that, since, though she and Mitch had attended all of the meetings so far, she'd been very quiet at every one of them.

Mitch looked at his wife with surprise. "You're joking!" he said. "What insensitive clod came out with *that*?"

"Your sister Betsy," Lainie said, and it must have been her own delivery that tickled her because she laughed along with the others, though Mitch was embarrassed and serious.

"Well, it sounds as if the biggest thing that separates your children from others is the way they happened to join their families. Because developmentally they all appear to be right on track," Barbara said.

"It's true," Rick said. "I was thinking today as I was driving here about what each of us has gone through to have these babies, to seduce the stork to visit our lives. And it cracked me up because I decided that we ought to call ourselves the Stork Club."

Everyone loved that, and Ruthie promised to have sweatshirts made for all of them, and the babies too, with that name printed on them.

"It sounds to me as if today's discussion should be about the language of unusual birth situations. So let's see if by discussing it we can find a way to handle them."

"People seem to be titillated by my story," Rick

said. "I've had men leer when they hear it, as if I'd been sexually involved with David's mother."

"*Seem* to be titillated?" Judith said. "You just heard about the guy who tried to nail me in the parking lot."

"It sounds as if it brings up people's own fears about the two things in the nineties that are the most frightening. High technology and sex," Barbara said.

"Not necessarily in that order," Shelly added.

"And when people are afraid, they're frequently hostile. The important thing to remember is that the quality of your relationships with your children has nothing to do with the way they came into the world. And if others have problems with it, those are just their problems.

"Many of the issues can be taken care of by semantics. When people say 'real mother' or 'real father,' you can correct them with 'birth mother' or 'birth father,' or 'biological parent,' which I've heard you use, Ruth," Barbara said. "But I think the first thing to do is expect people to ask dumb questions, anticipate them, and get comfortable with your answers so when they ask them in front of the children, which they undoubtedly will, you'll be loose and confident about it all."

"Well, what *are* the answers?" Judith asked, and Barbara thought about it for a while.

"Probably the best answers that will work well when the children overhear them, and even when they don't, will be the ones that have to do with how happy you are to have these children in your lives, and that really is the bottom line. So in answer to the question about the surrogate, Lainie might say something like, 'Mitch and I are so happy to have our wonderful daughter, Rose, in the family, and that's what really matters to us.' "

"I guess it would be pretty hard to argue with that," Judith said.

"Not for Betsy," Lainie said. "And the irony is *she*

was the one who suggested we try the surrogate in the first place.''

''So the rules are,'' Judith said, ''expect people to be dumb.''

There was silence as Barbara nodded, but Ruthie Zimmerman, never one to leave well enough alone, had to have the last word. ''And then,'' she said, ''tell them to shove it up their nose,'' and everyone fell apart laughing.

30

GRACIE HAD THE FLU, and she told Barbara she could manage to get from her bedroom to the bathroom, but she insisted that the kitchen, though it was approximately the same distance, was too far. She categorically refused the idea of "some stranger nosing around my house," which was her description of any help Barbara might hire for her. So every morning on her way to work, Barbara stopped and picked up a bran muffin, then used her key to get into the old apartment just off Fairfax, made a pot of herb tea, and brought her mother breakfast in bed.

Gracie joked when she bought the duplex in a neighborhood populated mostly by old people that she was moving in as an anthropologist, to study the life-styles of senior citizens. Now she had a multitude of friends, and the women in her circle took turns bringing her lunch every day, and tending to her. She seemed to be relishing the attention, but the flu bug had taken its toll and she was weak and uncomfortable.

Her choice for dinner was soup from Canter's Deli, where Barbara stopped every evening. Then in Gracie's tiny kitchen she would pour the steaming chicken noodle or matzoh ball or kasha soup from its cardboard carton into a bowl, put some bread on the side, and serve it to Gracie along with tales of her day at work. Sometimes Jeff would meet her at Gracie's, and Barbara could tell by the way he tried too hard to be okay about it that it was devastating to him to see his mighty and forceful grandmother in this diminished state. The once booming voice that was usually so big it could shake the house was now little more than a whisper.

One night when they got home he asked, "Is Grammy going to die, Mom?"

"Yes, honey. One of these days. I mean, she'll probably recover from this flu any minute and soon she'll be racing me down San Vicente Boulevard again, but eventually we'll lose Grammy. And you know what? We'll miss her terribly and be grateful for all the years we've had her, and all the funny, crazy things we learned by having her in our lives."

He had nodded at her words, but a few minutes later when she was on the phone talking to Stan she saw Jeff slip away into the powder room, and then from where she sat at her kitchen desk she could hear his sobs from behind the closed door. Both of her children were attached in some powerful, heartful way to their grandmother, who was better by far at grandmothering than she'd ever been at mothering. When she got word that her grandmother was down with the flu, Heidi called all the time to see how she was feeling, and Barbara had to admit to a wave of jealousy for the amount of attention her daughter gave her mother.

After the anniversary party Heidi had gone back to

San Francisco, and in a few weeks she informed Barbara that she had quit her job in the offices of the American Conservatory Theater, a move necessitated by the fact that the no-good mother-loving boyfriend worked there too, and they were through forever. She was very serious about moving back to Los Angeles. It was an idea Barbara loved, until Heidi added that she was hoping to move back into her old bedroom, "just for maybe like six months or a year or so, until I'm squared away and have some money saved up."

Barbara's reply was a startled "Really?"

"Don't sound so thrilled, Mother," Heidi said, and Barbara heard that same bitchy edge in her daughter's voice that she sometimes regrettably used with her own mother. After they hung up the phone, she wondered if it had escaped Heidi's memory that her former bedroom was now more of an office than it was a bedroom. Barbara had filled the room with books and files.

If she had to change it back to a bedroom it would mean renting storage space for the contents. But turning the office back into a bedroom would be the least of it. Heidi hadn't lived at home for anything but school vacations in six years. Even a few of the summers during her four college years were spent away from home. One year she waitressed in Santa Barbara where she took a summer course, and another year she attended a work-study program at UC Davis. It had been a long time since she and Barbara had had extended day-to-day contact, and Barbara was worried about how that would work out.

I'll make it good, she thought. It won't be the way it was when she was a teenager, because she'll have a job to go to every morning so I won't see her until the end of the day. Most of the time not even then, because she'll be dating. Dating. What would it be like for Heidi to be living at home and going out with some man and not coming home for a day or two? Now she was dating thirty-five-year-old men. One of the group leaders at the hospital was Barbara's age and she was *married* to a thirty-five-year-old man. Not a good idea, Heidi's living at home. Though she had to admit it had cozy overtones. If she did decide to move to Los Angeles, Barbara and Stan would have to encourage her to find her own place without making her feel as if they didn't want her in the house.

Mothers and daughters. Why was it so complicated? Tonight while she was helping Gracie, practically lifting her from the chair to the bed so she could change the bedclothes on which her mother had spilled some of her dinner, she wondered if Heidi would someday have to do this for her. And suddenly the idea of being the aging mother seemed appealing and she had an urge to crawl into the newly made bed and ask Gracie to please feed her some soup.

"My new group is really working out well," she said. "They've really connected with one another. They have a great sense of humor about themselves. And probably because they went through so much to get these babies, they don't let anything get in the way of their happiness. It's a real lesson, watching them."

"Well I'm delighted to hear it's going well, I knew it would, but I don't know how the hell you're going to do all that you do and ever have time to make a wedding too."

"Make a what?"

"I talked to my granddaughter today," Gracie said, smiling, then pushing her spoon hard into a matzoh ball and breaking it into bite-size pieces. "And she told me we're going to have a wedding."

"What?" Barbara asked, stunned.

"Ooops, did I spill the proverbial beans?" Gracie asked with a guilty look. "Didn't she tell you yet that the errant boyfriend showed up and said he's decided he can't live without her?"

"Mother, you're not serious."

"I'm sure she'll call you tonight and tell you herself," Gracie said and tucked her napkin into the high collar of her flannel nightgown. "For whatever it's worth, she sounded deliriously happy."

Bad news, Barbara thought. Probably a ploy from the guy to get Heidi back into bed, but it would never last until a wedding. "I won't chop the liver or devil any eggs yet, Mother," she said.

"You had two kids when you were her age."

"I also had Stan. This guy Ryan is a flake. She told me so herself. Not exactly a gentleman of strong character, shall we say?"

"Well, Mother dear," Gracie said to her with irony, "as you always used to say to me . . . you don't get to pick." Then she laughed a big hearty laugh, which should have cheered Barbara since it was an indication that Gracie was on the mend, but Barbara didn't notice.

Ronald Levine was waiting outside the door of her Wilshire Boulevard office when she arrived in the morning. His face was ashen and his eyes were filled with rage. He didn't have an appointment but he'd come to tell her that his estranged wife had left a message on his answering machine saying she and their son, Scottie, were off to Hawaii. She didn't tell him where in Hawaii or for how long. He was seething, and when Barbara opened the back door to her office he strode in behind her.

She was early because she'd planned to make some phone calls before her first appointment, but Ronald Levine's pain filled the room. His broken posture looked wrong for the smart Armani suit he wore as he paced in front of her desk, cursing Joan and blaming Barbara.

Barbara listened without saying a word, letting him get it all out. Finally he collapsed in the chair across from her desk and wept, his face on his arm on her desk, his body heaving with agonized sobs.

"Look what we do to one another in the name of love," he choked out between his sobs, and after a while he raised his face to her and asked, "Have you ever been divorced?"

"No," Barbara said.

"Can you imagine what it feels like to have to share your child with someone you hate? Who's acting despicable, trying to turn the child, the only creature on this earth you can love and relate to unconditionally, against you? No, you can't." He spoke in a small voice.

"It must feel awful."

His eyes were angry as he stood. "Don't give me the sympathetic-psychiatrist talk, you supercilious bitch," he screamed. "It feels *worse* than awful. I want a life with my son, and I don't even know where he is. Why did I come here in the first place? To pay you to say inane shit to me like 'It must feel awful.' " For an instant Barbara thought he was going to leap across the desk and grab her. "You have to help me get full custody. You have to tell the court, the judge, the powers that be that I'm the sane one. That his crazy mother spends every waking minute trying to drive him crazy. Will you say that?"

"I'll say whatever I think is best for Scottie," Barbara answered as evenly as she could. Ron Levine stormed out of the office and the phone rang. Barbara answered it numbly. "This is Barbara Singer."

"Hi, Mom."

It was Heidi, calling to break the news Barbara already knew. She was engaged. Ryan had presented her with a ring, she told Barbara, with a glow in her voice when she said his name as if he was and always had been a great guy. They were looking at apartments big enough to contain at-home offices for each of them. One of which, Heidi confided to her mother, could "maybe become the um . . . you know." And Barbara felt a stab to the chest because she *did* know that the "you know" meant a nursery.

The words "you don't get to pick" scurried again and again through her brain the way the messages of lights moved letter by letter across the Goodyear blimp, and she tried to let it go.

"I think we may want to ask you and Dad to consider the Bel-Air Hotel," Heidi told her.

Barbara had never priced the making of a wedding before, but she knew the Bel-Air Hotel, with its lush gardens and swan-filled lagoons, would be top of the line. She wondered if the future son-in-law had been someone she respected, someone who treated her daughter well and made her happy, if she would have relished the idea of making a wedding at the Bel-Air Hotel, of doing whatever the kids wanted, instead of feeling defensive and worried and annoyed by this news.

Why is it, she thought, the one area we're certain about with every ounce of our intuition, our intellect, and our years of wisdom happens to be, ironically, the one area in which we are completely powerless. "Insight doesn't mean a thing, and criticism is the kiss of death," Gracie had warned her.

"We'll come down in a few weeks so you can meet one another, and then we can talk more about the date and the place and all. Love you, Mom," Heidi said, signing off.

Barbara sighed as she hung up the phone, closed the back door through which Ron Levine had made his thunderous exit, and opened the front door for her first family of the morning.

31

DAVID REISMAN had a demanding personality, and though he put up with being taken care of by the nurse during the day, he was only completely happy when his daddy was home. He loved the nights when they roughhoused on the bed, then as Rick after a long day's work snored away, David used him as a pillow while he watched a "Sesame Street" video.

Of course they both loved playing in the pool with Rick holding David on the surface of the water, urging him to kick, kick, kick his chubby little feet. Patty was right, Rick thought when he held his son in his arms and the scent of the Desitin he had spread on his little bottom wafted up through the baseball pajamas. This baby owns me. I'd throw myself in front of a truck to save him, and every time he grins one of those little impish grins, I could weep.

Tonight David climbed into his lap. After they read a few of his favorite books, Rick picked up the scrapbook he'd been working to complete any time he had a spare minute. He had searched his drawers and filing cabinets and come up with a treasure trove of photos of his own family to include, so that David would know about his adopted family's history too. Pictures of the Cobbs, pictures of the Reismans. Rick mixed them on the pages, using his gift for the visual to juxtapose and combine them, and the album became David's favorite before-bed picture book.

Rick loved it too. Each image of his family brought memories tumbling into his head of his Hollywood boyhood in the big home in Bel-Air, of his father and his uncle, two handsome, dashing young Hollywood rakes, of his incomparable parents whose perfection might have tarnished had he known them when he was more than an adolescent. But he hadn't, and he was finally realizing at age fifty that the memory of their relationship, probably vastly rewritten to be perfect, contributed to making each relationship in his own life pale by comparison.

"If the shoe fits, honey," was what Patty had said to him when they talked about people who couldn't find love because they had some unshakable idea in their heads about how it should be.

"Uncle Bobo, Grandpa Jake," David recited, pointing at all his favorite photos. "Ooooh, Grandmama Jane, Grandpa Jake."

Rick looked at the picture, which was David's favorite. It was an old studio publicity shot of Jane Grant and Jake Reisman, so beautiful and elegant. And the way they looked at each other made it easy to see they were completely in love. Tonight, looking at the photo filled him with regret about his own wasted years, and he said a silent prayer to the two of them.

Help me, he thought, looking at their image, still missing them as much as he did thirty years ago. Help me so I can change, really change, and make a connection with a woman in this lifetime. Being a father has taught me I know how to love and feel and hurt, and put someone else's needs before my own. This little heavenly creature has raised my consciousness almost too high, so that some days the sky is almost bluer than I can stand it, the music sweeter than I've ever heard it before, and I know now that I want to share that with a woman.

David was squealing over every photo, reciting the names of each person, remembering who they were. "Birfmuvver" was how he said birth mother, "Birfmuvver Doreen, Grandma Bea, Auntie Trish and lots of carrot tops," he shouted, pointing at Trish's children and her husband, Don. Rick looked closely, very closely at the photo now, and felt a surge of sickness pour into his stomach.

The next morning Patty stopped at Rick's office toting a Saks Fifth Avenue shopping bag. When Rick peeked out of a meeting to ask Andrea a question he saw the back of a blonde with a great ass and was surprised when the blonde turned and it was Patty. She looked like a kid dressed in her faded jeans and funky sweatshirt.

"Hi," she said, her pretty smile brightening the room. "There was a sale in the boys' department, and since you always dress David in outfits that look like polyester leisure suits, I thought I'd take the liberty of my status as his unofficial aunt and buy him a few little items."

Rick walked over for a Hollywood kiss, a kind of touching of the sides of faces, and for an instant he wasn't sure if it was Patty's scent, somewhere between suntan lotion and Sea Breeze, that made him want to take her in his arms, or if the reason was his protracted absence from sex. "What's wrong with leisure suits?" he asked, backing up. Andrea was reaching into the bag pulling out the various shorts, T-shirts, and pants Patty had bought for David.

"Nothing if you're dressing Uncle Bobo," Andrea said. "And by the way, shouldn't you be on your way there now?"

Rick looked at his watch.

"I should. I'm going to close this meeting in my office, and then go get David and head out there."

Patty looked disappointed. "Ohh, too bad," she said, "I was going to ask you to come have a quick lunch with me and help me figure out some questions I have about Charlie's estate."

"Why don't I give you a call," he asked, "and we'll do it over the weekend?"

"Great," Patty said.

On his way to Calabassas, Rick thought maybe he should have invited Patty to join them for lunch out at the Motion Picture Home. Bobo was crazy for her. "A woman and a half," he said about Patty. "If I was a little younger I'd sweep her off her feet." Bobo no longer waited outside the entrance of the home the way he used to, because the journey from his room to the front was now too long and too arduous. He had a walker, which he refused to use at all except when Rick and the baby came to visit. And only every now and then would he agree to be helped out of bed to his feet and work his way down the corridor, just so he could show off Rick and David, whom he called "my boys." His enfeebled body used everything he had to move along beside Rick and behind David, who found the long carpeted corridor the perfect place to toddle.

But though Bobo's body was failing, his mind was still on full throttle. One day last week he shook his head watching the baby, and said, "My life has been full of surprises. If anyone would have told me, a man who has seen as many years in this century as I have, that I would approve of such a thing as you and that baby—no, I take back 'approve,' and change it to 'give my blessing'—I would have said 'completely *meshugge*,' but you know what? It's a hell of a good thing."

Today as Rick walked with David on his shoulders through the hospital corridor past the nurses' station on the way to Bobo's room, the nurse who was sitting there looked up at the two of them and said, "These visits with that baby are keeping him alive."

"Hi, lady," David said.

"Hi, baby," the nurse said, waving.

"My boys," Bobo said as they walked into his room. He was propped up on the bed.

"Uncabobobobo," David said, and he climbed onto his great-uncle's bed, sat next to the old man, and put his two fat little hands on Bobo's old face. "Hiya, Uncabobo."

"Yeah, sure. Don't try to charm me, you little stinkpot," Bobo said, smiling a smile minus his teeth, which were in a glass on the table across the room. Rick spread a blanket on the floor of Bobo's room, sat David on it and put a few toys on it, and the baby fell on them gleefully. Then Rick took his uncle's hand.

"Uncle B., I need your advice," he said to Bobo, and he told him his worries about Doreen.

"Ricky," he said when the story was told. "There's a reason why these ways of operating didn't exist in my day, or if they did it was so far underground, nobody knew or talked about it. Because somewhere along the way the idea breaks down, and is too full of whaddyacallit . . . complications. Never cut and dried, and that's true no matter what that fancy lawyer tried to tell you. And here's why. Can you walk away and say good-bye forever to that little girl? She gave you the most precious thing in life.

"Sure, if you have no heart maybe you say, 'It's not

my problem.' But even with the crazy life you lead, you're a guy who turns the world upside-down for somebody you love. Do I know it? How many other old *kockers* in this place have a regular visitor like you? Only me!" Rick wanted to put his face down on the blanket and cry. How he loved this old man. This sweetheart of a human being who saw through to the good in him. And how unbearably sad that David would grow up and never know or remember him.

"I trust your heart. You'll figure out a way to help that kid. Meantime, who's the woman?"

"What woman?"

"In the past few weeks, either my eyes are worse than I thought, or you're actually looking svelte."

"Svelte?"

"Okay, svelte is pushing it. But cute would be accurate," the old man said, now opening both eyes and laughing. "Some dame is finally getting to you, please God?"

"Absolutely not."

"Don't lie to a dying man. On second thought, lie to me, so I can go to my grave with a grin."

"You're delirious, Uncle B."

The old man laughed again. "No, I'm not" was all he said before he fell asleep. What is he talking about, Rick thought while he packed up the baby's things, and with David back on his shoulders he headed down the corridors that were lined with the black-and-white photos of Hollywood stars on his way to the parking lot. But when he got to the freeway entrance to go east, back to the studio, he passed it, took the one going west instead, and drove out to Malibu to be with Patty.

Andrea was just about to turn on the answering machine and leave for the commissary. She already had her purse in her hand, and Candy, the new girl who worked across the hall, was waiting outside for her so they could have lunch together when the phone rang. Shit, Andrea thought. Maybe I'll just ignore it. Rick had called her a few minutes ago from the car to say he was making a stop before he came in, and that he probably wouldn't be back until three. So it wasn't him calling.

"Andrea," Candy called from the hall. "Should I start over there and get us a table?"

"No, I'll just be a second. Richard Reisman's office."

"Uhhh . . . hello. Uhhh, is Mr. Reisman there?"

"No, he's not." It was a funny voice and she could tell by the sound it was long distance. "He should be back in a few hours. Can I say who's calling?"

"Are you Andrea?"

"Yeah." Come on already, she thought. I'm like starving here.

"I'm Bea Cobb. Doreen's mother. This is an emergency and I need to talk to him right away."

She sounded panicky. "Why don't I try and find him for you, Mrs. Cobb?" Andrea said. "I'll have him call you as soon as I do."

Andrea put the phone down and went to the door. "Candy, I can't go to lunch. Something important is happening and I need to try and find Rick."

He wasn't at home, he wasn't in the car. She even called the Hamburger Hamlet in Beverly Hills where he sometimes liked to take David for a late lunch, but he wasn't there either. If he missed this call he'd be devastated, but she couldn't imagine where he might be.

"Well, isn't this a nice surprise?" Patty Fall said, opening the front door. "I was just hosing off the deck and planning to sit out there and do some paperwork. Come on in, you two."

David toddled through the living room and followed Rick and Patty into the kitchen.

"Shouldn't you be at work?" she asked Rick.

"I'm playing hooky. I just left Bobo and he's so obviously not long for this world that sometimes I'm afraid to leave him. Afraid I'll never see him alive again. It's so hard for me to think I'm really losing him that I guess going back to my office to work on a production schedule felt mundane."

"Well, I'm glad you decided to come here," she said. In a practiced way she gathered several plastic kitchen utensils and containers, scooped David up, and led Rick outside, past the deck and down to the beach. While David poured sand from one container to the next, Rick and Patty sat close to each other.

"Death is a part of life, Ricky. Bobo will die and you'll go on. You've had an unparalleled relationship with him. And he was a great influence on you."

"Sometimes I think he doesn't want to live anymore. That he's just hanging on until he nags me into getting married."

Patty laughed. "Who does he have in mind as the bride?"

"Beats the hell out of me. Today he accused me of holding out on him. Said I looked too good, so there must be a woman in my life." David had pulled off one of his shoes and was now filling it with sand.

"He's right," Patty said, smiling. Rick looked at her. When their eyes met they held each other's gaze and he saw her eyes searching his. "Is there a woman?" she asked.

Rick wasn't prepared for the surge of feeling, a combination of gratitude for her friendship and longing for her. A need to hold her and kiss her and cry with her over the loss of Charlie and Bobo. And to thrill with her over David. The ringing of the telephone on the deck broke the moment.

"Be right back," Patty said, and scrambled up to the deck. "Yes. Hello?" Rick heard her voice drifting down to the beach. Then she gestured for him to come, so he picked up David and ran to the deck to get the phone.

"Mr. Reisman, I just had an emergency call from Doreen Cobb's mother, Bea. I can call her back and patch her in to you at Mrs. Fall's if that's okay," Andrea said on the phone.

"It's okay," Rick said as Patty took David and gently wiped the sand from his little feet.

"Hello?"

"Bea."

"I'll get right to the point. Have you talked to my daughter lately?"

"Not for a few weeks. Why?"

"I thought maybe she'd show up out there. To see you or the baby, because a few days ago she ran away."

"No," Rick said. Ran away. Now he knew he had to be right about the son-of-a-bitch brother-in-law. Goddammit. Why hadn't he said more to her when she called on the day of the adoption? Why hadn't he said, Doreen, this is a formality, not about the real connection you'll always have with this boy. You'll always be David's family. We love you. "Bea, have you called the police?"

"Well, I was going to, but my son-in-law Don told me to just leave it alone. He says it's a teenage thing she has to work out for herself, and that in cases like this the police can't do much, and that she'll come back."

The son-in-law probably hoped they'd find her dead somewhere. Rick felt hamstrung. He was lost in his own mental picture of Doreen's anguish. From far away he heard Bea say, "Don's been my adviser since my husband died eight years ago. He practically raised Doreen. Trish's husband. In those pictures we sent, he's the one with the red hair."

"Listen, Bea," Rick said, his head ringing with fear. "I'd call the police if I were you."

"Yeah, maybe," she said in a voice that made him know she wouldn't.

"And if I hear from her—" he began.

"You tell her to come home," said her mother, "because everyone in this family loves her and wants the best for her." But Rick knew the truth and feared for Doreen's life.

32

LAINIE DECIDED that the only sign of Mitch's deception was his patent avoidance of her. In the store while customers were around he was always the Mitch of Lainie and Mitch, the beautiful couple, with an arm around her, or a tender pat on her cheek. But at home, his eyes avoided hers. When she went off to bed, he stayed up late, saying he had work to do. Most mornings he was out of bed and in the shower even before the baby woke.

In contrast to his treatment of her, the way he focused on little Rosie, held her, kissed her, gave Lainie more evidence that his coolness to her wasn't simply due to his preoccupation with some problem at the store.

Why don't I tell him I know what he's doing? Lainie would wonder at three in the morning as she sat awake in their bed. And memories of looking out the bedroom window in her childhood room at dawn came back.

Memories of watching her father return from God knows where, sometimes so drunk he'd forget to turn off the headlights on the car. She would hear him tiptoe up the stairs. And when she figured he was asleep, little Lainie would hurry down in her pajamas and turn out the car lights, then hurry back to her bed where she would feel that same kind of helpless feeling she now had about Mitch.

Is that what I should do, Lainie thought, wait until things blow over? Sit it out, the way my mother did until he died, so she could collect the insurance? Not me, Lainie thought, I'm not going to live a lie. But instead of saying a word, she went on about her life, her day, caring for the baby, stopping by the store, going to her classes, unable to shake the taunting question that was stuck in her chest and her brain.

That cuckold lives in bliss
Who, certain of his fate, loves not his wronger
But, O, what damned minutes tells he o'er
Who dotes, yet doubts, suspects, yet soundly loves!

A group of students from an acting class were doing a reading of *Othello* for Lainie's Shakespeare class. I don't need an Iago to torment me, she thought, listening to the dialogue. I'm my own Iago. Driving myself crazy the way he does Othello. There is no way that Mitch De Nardo, my husband, is screwing the surrogate, she thought, trying to be rational. But the Iago part of her asked, Really? If that's true, then walk out of this classroom, right now, and drive past Sherman Oaks Park. Didn't Mitch say he was going to take Rosie there to play tonight? Didn't he think you'd be safely in school so he could take Jackie's daughter to visit with her? Why else would he be so eager to do that if he didn't have something going on with Jackie.

No, Iago; I'll see before I doubt, when I doubt,
prove;
And on the proof, there is no more but this,
Away at once with love or jealousy.

The actor reading the part of Othello had a giant voice that belied his slight build. It was hard to believe the emotion he could call up, reading from a script and sitting on a folding chair, but everyone in the room seemed to be leaning in toward him, feeling Othello's grief and pain. When it was time for the break, as the rest of the class headed for the Coke machines Lainie walked to her car.

There were two teenage boys shooting baskets, a family sitting at a picnic table eating, and a jogger making his way around the track. The playground was empty. A strong wind blew some sand out of the sandbox and made the swings sway back and forth, as though ghostly riders were pumping them into the sky. "I do not think but Desdemona's honest." Sitting in her car, Lainie felt stupid to have let her insanity make her walk out on the last half of her Shakespeare class to rush over here to see if Mitch was with Jackie. If she went home now he would notice she was early and wonder why. But that would be okay. She could tell him she missed the baby and wanted to see her before she went to sleep.

Mitch's car was in the garage and the condominium was still as Lainie made her way quietly up the stairs. When she opened the door to the nursery, what she saw filled her with relief and joy and embarrassment for her own doubts about her beloved Mitch. There he was in the rocking chair, asleep, with the sleeping baby snuggled against him. Sick, I am so sick, so insecure that because of the smell of some perfume anyone might wear and some neighbor's remark, I might have been crazy enough to lash out at my husband with a ridiculous accusation.

Mitch De Nardo, the sweetest, best man in the world, had simply been distracted by problems at work. She would wake him now, and after they put Rosie in a night diaper and down to sleep in her crib, Lainie would somehow get Mitch to come to bed early, where she would make sweet love to him. It had been too long, and their loving would make them close again.

"Mitchie," she said, touching him tenderly.

"Huh?" Mitch looked up at her, realized he'd been put to sleep by his own lullaby, then looked down at the sleeping baby. "Little angelface wore me out tonight."

"What did you two do together?" Lainie asked, taking Rose from him and gently placing her on the changing table.

"Oh, it was great. We took a long ride."

In the evening? During rush hour, they took a ride? "Where?"

"The beach," Mitch said, yawning, standing, and stretching. "Want me to put her night diaper on her?" he asked.

"I can do it," Lainie said.

"Great," he said, not looking at her. "Now that you're here, I'm going to go back to the store. I've got a stack of invoices that I have to look over. The bookkeeper's coming tomorrow, and I'm not ready for her. I want her to do all the store bills and all of our personal stuff too." He patted his pants pocket and found his car keys. "Don't wait up" were his last words, and he was gone.

The next day Lainie took Rose to the zoo with her friend Sharon and Sharon's baby. Rose pointed her tiny finger at the elephant and said, "Elatin." "Yes!" Lainie said, thrilling to the sound of her daughter learning to talk.

"Mine still hasn't said a word," Sharon said.

Lainie pushed the stroller from cage to cage, next to Sharon and her stroller, and she still couldn't shake the heavyhearted feeling she had about whatever it was that was going on with Mitch. She didn't feel close enough to Sharon to tell her what she was going through. In fact, she didn't feel close enough to anybody. Oddly, the only woman with whom she'd ever felt any real intimacy was Jackie. For obvious reasons—the months of insemination attempts, the startling fact which never grew less startling that she was carrying Mitch's baby—but also because Jackie was someone who demanded intimacy, barreled into your life and opened up hers in a warm, unafraid way. She paid attention to your feelings and told you about hers.

Not like the rigid way Lainie had been taught to behave with everyone. If those qualities were hereditary she hoped that Rose would inherit them. Jackie was a good person, Lainie thought, and then she felt foolish about the fears and fantasies she'd been having about Jackie and Mitch.

"I've been going to a gym," Sharon said as they stopped at a food center to get sandwiches for themselves and to give the little girls some finger foods they'd each brought along. "Because I've been feeling as if I'm never going to get back in shape, and Jerry hasn't touched me in months. But you know, it's funny, when I was pregnant, we had sex all the time, so I don't think it's my being fat that's bothering him."

Lainie put some pieces of banana on the little tray attached to the front of Rosie's stroller. This was more than Sharon had ever revealed about her personal life in the past. Usually when they got together they talked about what they were reading in English class, or how having babies at home was getting in the way of their studying.

"My sister said it happened with her husband too. As soon as there was a kid, his whole attitude changed. As if he was saying, 'Now that you're a mother, I can't get hot with you anymore.' " Lainie nodded sympathetically. The thought cheered her. Maybe that was why Mitch wasn't sexy with her these days. And if that's all it was, she could fix that in no time. Get him away for a weekend. Bring some slinky lingerie, drive him wild the way she always used to.

On the way home from the zoo, she and Rosie would stop off at Panache to see Daddy. Lainie would take him aside and tell him they should plan a trip together. Her mother could take Rosie for the two days. The store would survive for forty-eight hours without Mitch, and they would find a hotel somewhere on the ocean and just be sexy for hours and days.

All of the girls who worked in the store oohed and ahhed over Rosie when Lainie walked in carrying her. In her little hand she held the string of a helium balloon from the L.A. zoo.

"She's so big," Carin said. "Can I hold her?" Rosie grinned and went to Carin easily. "Mitch said he had to go to the bank," Carin told Lainie. "He'll be back any minute." Then she took Rosie over to the three-way mirrors to play "see the baby." Lainie told Carin she'd be in the office in the back of the store, and she went in to call her mother at work so that when Mitch got back she'd be armed with baby-sitting dates that were good for her mother's schedule.

The office was pristine. The bookkeeper had obviously finished her work, and in one high pile were the store's current bills, checks attached and ready to stuff and mail, and in another Lainie and Mitch's personal bills with checks attached. Lainie dialed the phone, then shuffled through the mail absently while the phone at Bradford, Freeman rang in her ear.

"Law offices of Bradford, Freeman. How may I direct your call?"

"Mother?"

"Oh, hi, dear. Hold on. I've got three lines ringing all at once. Don't go away."

Gas bill, very high, water bill too, Lainie noticed. Gelson's Market, she had a charge account there. It was an extravagance, but Lainie loved their perfect produce, their great deli, and their sweet-smelling bakery, though this month the bill was exorbitant. Pacific Bell. A long itemized bill of every toll call. Pages of calls. While she waited, she lifted the check and looked down at the list of calls.

West Los Angeles, Santa Monica, Studio City, her mother's phone number. Another West Los Angeles. Long Beach. Long Beach. Who did they know in Long Beach besides . . . she looked across the page at a phone number that was definitely Jackie's. She looked at the date, then at the calendar. A school night, the call was made from their house at six-forty, just after Lainie walked out the door to go to her class. Her hand moved down the page. Two weeks later, Long Beach. Time, six-forty-one. She would leave and Mitch would call Jackie, to tell her that he and Rosie were on their way to see her, and Rosie, who couldn't talk yet, couldn't tell the secret to Lainie. And that's why Mitch wasn't making love to Lainie. Dear God, it was true.

"Hi, baby!" She turned with a gasp as if she were the one who had been caught, when all she'd been doing was looking at her own telephone bill. Something she'd never bothered to do in the past because Mitch always took care of those things with the bookkeeper. And he knew under normal circumstances she would never look at, let alone scrutinize, a phone bill. She put the phone back in the cradle.

"Mitch," she said, feeling her face shaking and not

sure if she was going to be able to ask the next question. If the answer was yes it could pull out the underpinnings of her entire life. She remembered the serious way Barbara Singer told her, "You fought cancer, you can handle this," and it gave her the strength to ask, "Have you been seeing Jackie?" Please God, let him say no, she thought. Let the phone calls he made to her just have been about some legal problem or other, or some unpaid medical bill.

Mitch looked down at the floor and didn't answer.

"You have," Lainie said, wishing she had died, wishing that the cancer had killed her instead of letting her live to stand in this room feeling like an empty, miserable shrew demanding an answer. "And you've taken Rosie with you too, haven't you?" When he finally answered, it was by way of a slight nod.

"Why? How? What could possibly make you do that after all you and I went through to make this work? Mitch, I felt so inadequate for so many years that I agreed to let you have a baby with another woman. But there wasn't one step of the way during all of it when I didn't have to stop myself from begging you to call it off because of how much it hurt. Don't you understand that one of the reasons this awful world is able to go on is because a woman desperately wants to feel the baby of the man she loves inside her body? Not to watch some other woman glory in the feeling of that life. I might as well have watched you make love to her. Did you do that, Mitch? Did you make love to Jackie? You can tell me everything now that it's all out. Her perfume was on your shirt, your telephone calls to her are in black and white on our phone bill. Was it sexier with her because she still has her insides?"

She was screaming at him, her voice rising up to the ceiling, reverberating, she was sure, throughout the whole store so the salesgirls and the customers could hear every word. Finally she was letting out the pain, the rage, the hurt she had felt about all of this for so long. And Mitch didn't try to silence her, just stood in that spot, in the doorway of the office, looking down at his black leather loafers.

"Mama," she heard Rosie's voice call out from somewhere in the store, then she heard Carin's voice say, "Mama's busy now. Why don't we go and try on hats? I'll bet Rosie looks cute in hats. Come on. That's a good girl."

"I didn't touch her," Mitch said. "I mean, maybe a little hug once before we parted, that must be how the perfume got on me, but I took Rosie to see her because she came here one night to the store, just before I was closing up. The girls didn't know who she was, and I nearly fell over when I saw her.

"I thought she didn't know anything about us. I thought it was why we had that special phone and paid for everything in cash. She told me she'd known our last name for years. That she once applied for a job at the old store and met me there. That when we first walked into the lawyer's office that day to meet her, she remembered me, even though I didn't remember her. She also told me that during the pregnancy you dropped our last name once by mistake.

"She sat right down over there and said to me, 'Mitch, this isn't blackmail, it isn't a threat, it's just a truth. That baby came from my body, from my egg, from me, and I need to see her. Need to know her, need to be with her.' She said it wasn't blackmail or anything like that, but that she had to be in Rose's life. Tell Lainie it's okay, she said. She begged me. She said, 'I won't hurt their relationship.'

"I told her she was nuts. Completely crazy to think I would ever go for what she was saying, or that *you* would. I didn't believe it wasn't blackmail, so I offered her money, lots of money to go away forever, I wasn't even sure where I would get that kind of money, but she didn't want it. She wasn't holding out for more than I was offering. She didn't want money. And all of a sudden I realized while I was sitting there that she wasn't crazy at all about wanting to be with the baby. What was crazy was any of the three of us agreeing to bring a baby into the world under those circumstances. And I take the blame. Because of my colossal ego, I ended up making you go through the tortures of the damned, and then Jackie too, and created a situation that just can't ever work the way we thought it would."

"And without telling me, or asking me, you took Rose to see her."

"I thought if I asked you it would kill you," he said defensively, making Lainie wild with rage that he could think that position was defensible.

"So you lied. Made the baby a party to your lie."

"I knew once Rosie could really talk I couldn't do it anymore. And I had hopes that maybe if Jackie saw her once or twice, maybe she'd understand how tough it was on all of us to do it, and change her mind. Or that somehow I'd be able to tell you and we could work it out. Lainie, I did a bad thing by sneaking around you. But the real bad thing was a few years ago when I didn't say to you, 'Let's keep trying to adopt, instead of giving up because we had one bad experience.' And I should have said to my sister, 'Mind your own damned business, I don't care if the baby's a De Nardo. I want Lainie to be okay about it.' But now it's done. I made a baby with that woman, and I can't pretend it didn't happen, and neither can she and neither can you."

Lainie looked at his face and hated him. "Mitch, I'm going home. I'm taking Rosie with me. Tonight, on my way to school, I'll drop her at my mother's. While I'm gone I want you to go to our place and get everything out of there that you need, because I won't live with you, can't stand what you've put me through, and don't want to be anywhere near you. We can discuss the arrangements of our divorce through lawyers, and also what will happen to Rose."

"Lainie, please—"

"No, Mitch," she said. "The last time you said 'please' to me, I agreed to do what you were asking, and it did damage to a lot of people's lives."

33

BARBARA TOOK A SIP of coffee, looked at the clock, and realized it was time to begin. "I think what we've been seeing here is that many times we find ourselves talking about thc same problems all the parents in my groups talk about, separation anxieties, setting limits, sleeping."

"Sleeping? Never heard of it," Judith said. "By the time Jillian was sleeping through the night, I had Jody. I think the last complete night I slept was the night before Jillian was born."

There were a few amens to that as the others settled into their chairs. Every week the members of this group seemed genuinely glad to see one another, to have found a unique level of trust among themselves, and a sense of pride in their differences from the rest of the world. It was a chemistry Barbara always hoped the people in her groups would have, but it didn't always happen.

When the groups clicked, the members continued

their relationships long after the year of meetings was over. When they didn't, there was no way she could interest the members in engaging one another. In those cases the entire year could be spent with the parents barely looking at one another, and leaving with relief after the last session.

"The best solution for me and my little ones about sleep has been to take them into my bed at night. I read that book *The Family Bed*, and figured, why should a little person have to be cold and alone when we can all cuddle together and I can make them feel secure?" Judith said.

"Would you consider taking in a chilly big person?" Rick asked her.

"I should have known *you'd* turn that into a joke," Judith said, laughing and throwing the cloth diaper she'd been wearing on her shoulder as a drooling pad for the baby at Rick. "And believe me, I can use the laugh. You all know what I've been through with men, and on top of that, I can't seem to find a housekeeper I like. Some days I feel like I'm on complete baby burn-out."

"Want to talk about any of it?" Barbara asked.

"Which is the bigger problem? The men or the housekeeper?" Ruthie asked.

"Good question," Barbara said to Ruthie, then turned to Judith. "Which *is* the bigger problem. The men or the housekeeper?"

Judith thought for an instant and grinned. "Well, you know how hard it is to get good help." Everyone laughed. The discussion turned to their mutual guilt about working and parenting, and how hard it was to part with the babies every day. All of them except Lainie worked, and she spent several nights a week in school and many of her days studying.

Mitch hadn't been to the last few group sessions and there had always been an excuse from her about his having to be at the store. Today when there was a rare quiet moment in the discussion, she spoke up. "Mitch and I are separated. I asked him to leave after I found out that without discussing it with me, he'd been secretly taking the baby to see the surrogate."

"Oh, my God," Ruthie said.

"What would make him do that?" Shelly asked.

"She came to him and begged him to let her see the baby. He was afraid to tell me, but he believed it was the right thing for her to be with the baby . . . so he agreed."

"I guess there's no denying that she is the baby's mother," Rick said matter-of-factly, and Lainie looked as if someone had kicked her.

"Explain why you said that, Rick," Barbara said, noting that the light feeling among them was gone.

"I don't mean to sound like all the dumb people in the world, and I didn't say 'real mother,' but that woman has a biological connection to that baby. And from what you're saying, an emotional one too. I'd worry like hell if it was my baby about disconnecting from her. Her genes and her history are very much who Rose is, and who she is going to grow up to be. Listen, I don't really know Mitch at all," Rick said. "In fact, from the little I've come to know him in here, I didn't particularly like him. But I'll bet there's something in him that says the genetic mother should have a relationship with the baby. And he may have handled it poorly, but I think his instincts are right. Please don't in any way take this personally, Lainie, but I think the concept of surrogacy is a disaster. I believe that just as adoption is a way of solving two problems, surrogacy creates not just problems but potential tragedies."

"That's what I think," Lainie said, trying to stay collected. "I mean, that's what I think now. But when it was happening, I didn't know what to think. I felt as if I had to do something and do it fast, because so much time had gone by with me trying to have babies and then being sick, and Mitch wanted it so much. I felt that if I couldn't give him a baby I was worthless. But now I know I never should have said yes to any of it."

"I understand the confusion," Judith said, "because I don't know how anyone could not want to relate to their own genetic offspring. To know that somewhere out there was a product of you, and not feel related to it, not needing to know it, just doesn't make sense. Don't get me wrong, I think Mitch is a bum for doing anything behind your back."

"What about your sperm donors?" Rick asked Judith. "You want them in your life?"

"Believe me," she shot back defensively, "I wish they were available for baby-sitting. No, seriously, I only wish I had an important relationship in my life. But I don't. So I started without that elusive him."

"I think Lainie's problem right now has more to do with the idea that there was a deception after such a carefully thought-out plan about how to conduct the surrogacy. Mitch seems to have changed the rules on her without telling her what the new rules are, and breached their trust."

"The shit," Judith said.

"Can't you fix it? Talk about it?" Ruthie asked.

"I'm still too raw," Lainie answered. "I'm still beating myself up for agreeing to do it in the first place, and jealous and sick with shock that he could lie to me. I'm trying to find a way to understand his behavior. Right now it feels to me as if we had a good life together, but somehow we've managed to turn it into something that can never be right."

"So change your definition of what's right," Judith said. "That's what *I* did. Don't get bogged down in the idea that there's only one version of family. If family to me was only for husbands, wives, and babies, I'd still be waiting for the phone to ring. There's got to be a way to make it okay. To work something out about the surrogate that you and Mitch and the surrogate can live with."

Lainie thought about it. "I don't know if I'm capable of being as big about all of this as all of you are in your lives. In fact I know I'm not. I had some boundaries inside me I set up for the way behavior was supposed to be, and Mitch crossed them. So something tells me this is as far as I can go with him." Her pretty face looked long and pale and pleated with the furrows of pain. "Please let's let it go, please let's talk about somebody else's problems."

Barbara looked around to see who wanted to speak next.

"I got a call from a part of my son's extended family and need to talk about that in here," Rick said. He was planning to tell them about his conversation with Bea Cobb, but in order to make the impact more clear he backed up and told them more about how he and Doreen came together. He was surprised at the way his voice shook when he talked about the day he met Doreen and Bea Cobb at the airport, and now how worried he was about what sounded like Doreen's fragile mental state, and where she might have gone. It had been days since Bea's call and he hadn't had one more word.

"You're dealing with some very complicated emotions," Barbara said. "Doreen is probably and will always be grieving for the loss of David. Adolescence can be pretty traumatic under the best of circumstances, and a classic time for running away, but she's had to deal with the added upheaval of an unwanted pregnancy and a separation from the baby. And of course we don't have any idea what she's been through with school and friends and boys, not to mention the other members of her family. Clearly she has a lot to overcome.

"It sounds to me from this very distant vantage point as if she's got some difficult times to get through. This running away is a cry for help. It sounds as if you and this girl forged a very powerful attachment. But for the long term, I believe you're going to have to have faith in that inner strength you told me she has to get her through this. Has the family called the police?"

"No," Rick said, holding himself in check for fear that by facing this he would fall apart right there. "And it worries me. The padrone of the family is the husband of the eldest sister, and I don't trust this guy. I don't know, maybe I'm crazy but I have a terrible feeling he . . ." Ruthie moved to one side of Rick and Lainie to another and they each put an arm around him. "If anything happens to that little girl . . ." he began, but he was too choked with emotion to finish the sentence.

"We're going to need to focus on what both Lainie's and Rick's dilemmas bring up," Barbara said, "which is what your obligations and agreements are to the extended families of these children, and when and if you let these needs affect your lives. It's a topic that's affecting all of you."

"Not us," Ruthie said.

"Well, I don't know," Barbara said. "Suppose the time came that one of you found a romance, a mate?"

Neither Ruthie nor Shelly knew what to say to that. A long uncomfortable time passed during which there was only the squeaking of chairs and a sigh or two.

"Good God," Judith said. "It's all so painful."

"But worth it," Ruthie said, looking out the window at the children playing. "Being a parent is definitely worth it." The others sat in quiet agreement.

* * *

He *is* handsome, Barbara thought, looking at Ryan Adler across the dining room table, and I can sure see why Heidi is so attracted to him. He's also very good at charming. Big smile, polite, deferential to Stan, to me. And my poor child is falling all over him. Her voice is shrill and she's trying too painfully hard. She jumps with terror every time he gestures in her direction and when dinner is over they're leaving here and going to a hotel to spend the night. I can't stand it.

"Get ahold of yourself, honey," Stan said to her when he carried the last of the dinner plates through the swinging doors to the kitchen.

"Why?"

"Because," Stan said, "you look as if you're ready to cry out there. This is supposed to be a joyous occasion, remember?"

"I hate him," Barbara whispered. "I've forgotten everything I ever learned about psychology. I want to pour hot coffee in his lap and push his face into the ice cream."

"Would anybody have been good enough for her? And remember, mothers know nothing. Gracie hated me."

"Present tense, honey. Hates, hates."

"There you are, and I'm a goddamned prince on horseback. So maybe it's time for you to let it go."

"You're right," she said, hoping the classical music coming out of the speakers in the dining room was preventing Heidi and Ryan from hearing her. "I should let it go, I'm going to let it go. But can I poison him first?"

Stan laughed and picked up the coffee tray and went back through the swinging doors into the dining room. Barbara said a quick prayer for strength and followed.

"Should we start talking about dates?" Stan asked, putting a cup in front of Ryan. "I mean, I have a pretty full calendar for the rest of the year so I thought we should go over some possibilities. What are we talking about in terms of time?"

Heidi and Ryan answered at the same time. She said December and he said next summer, and then they each looked at the other with disdain.

"That's too soon, sweetheart," he said. Barbara's stomach tightened.

"What are we waiting for? Neither one of us is in school," she whined.

"Honey, what's our hurry?" Ryan asked her as if he were talking to a child. And he is, Barbara thought. "This way your folks will have more time to get it all planned." He patted her hand, but she pulled it away. Barbara knew her so well that before a pout was even on her daughter's lips she could tell that Heidi was furious.

"I don't want to wait until the summer," Heidi said, getting edgy in a way Barbara recognized, and though she would never admit it, she liked the direction the conversation was taking. It escalated from there. Heidi got whinier and Ryan got more supercilious. Barbara tried to remember later what the exact moment was, maybe when he used the word *childish*, or just after she said snidely they'd have to make the plans fit in with Ryan's mother's schedule, but Heidi jumped up from her chair and ran upstairs in tears. When she was gone, Ryan looked at Barbara and Stan with a shrug grown-ups frequently use with one another that meant, Kids. Who can understand them?

Barbara wanted to go upstairs and put a bureau against the door so Heidi wouldn't come back down again.

"She's not easy," Ryan said. "As I'm sure you already know, but I adore her."

Both Barbara and Stan were silent.

"Dinner was lovely," Ryan said, standing, "and I think what I should probably do now is make my way back to the hotel, and hope she's feeling a little bit better about all of this when the dawn breaks."

Barbara's back teeth were tightly clenched as she and Stan both stood. They all walked to the front door, passing the wall of family pictures, and Barbara caught sight of a picture of Heidi at three years old in which she had the same expression on her face as she had had a moment ago when she'd rushed upstairs.

When Ryan was gone, Stan took Barbara in his arms and asked, "How do we tell her it's not going to happen?"

"Unfortunately, we don't," she answered. "We just wait for her to figure that out on her own."

34

WITHOUT MITCH IN HER LIFE, Lainie lived each day by rote. She took care of the baby's needs, and in the evenings when she had school, she dropped Rosie off with her grandmother Margaret and went off to class. Mitch called and left apologetic messages on the answering machine, messages in which he begged her to call him back and talk to him, see him, promising her he could make her understand.

She would lean against the wall, still holding her books from school, listening to the long speeches he made to the answering machine, alternately hating him and longing for him. Sometimes she would rewind the machine and play the messages again just to hear the parts where he swore his love to her. Rosie, sitting on the kitchen floor, would hear his voice, look up, and gleefully shout, "Daddy!"

Within a week, Mitch's messages went from pleading

to annoyance, and then from annoyance to anger, and from anger to rage. "Pick the fucking phone up, Laine, and call me back, or you'll hear from my lawyer." She'd never heard that tone of voice from him, and there was a part of her that was glad to hear him so overwrought.

"Yes, Mitch," she said on the night he said that, picking up the phone and turning off the answering machine, relieved that the baby, who had now taken to repeating every word everyone said, was asleep.

"You've got a lot of balls, Lainie. I have every right in the world to our home and to my daughter." It wasn't her imagination that he emphasized the word *my*. "What can you possibly think you're doing by ignoring my phone calls? I've been too nice to come over there and break the door down, but believe me I will if I have to. I'll come over there and take the baby the hell out of there."

"No, you won't, Mitch. Because you love her and you know you're doing the best thing for her by letting her stay with me. Not you and not Jackie."

"Hey, I told you I've got nothing going with Jackie."

"Not anymore since I broke up the party."

"Lainie, I can't change any of it back to the way it was. I wish I could. But now is now and I want to see my daughter and you'd better stop trying to get in the way. So come up with a time that's good, and I'll pick her up and bring her back later. Then we can start talking about the issues around her custody."

"You work all day every day, sometimes until late at night. I'm at home and have been her primary caretaker since the day she was born. I may not be her biological parent," she said, still not believing that she was having this conversation, "but with the possible options, my availability and dependability and history with her make me the best candidate for solid parenting, genes or no genes."

"We'll see," Mitch said. "When will she be ready?"

"At ten in the morning." Lainie's own rage was bubbling in her chest. She knew that was Mitch's busiest hour at the store, but Mitch rose to it.

"I'm there," he said, and hung up.

Seeing her husband sitting nervously in their living room was unquestionably odd. They had chosen every piece of furniture, every picture on the wall in that room together, and now he was an outsider. She missed him so much that if he'd said, "I love you. This is dumb," she probably would have said, "You're right. Go get your things and move back in while I fix lunch." But he didn't ask to come home. Instead he sat with his hands folded, as if he were a prom date being looked over by the parents of the teenage girl.

The baby had been up at five A.M., and was still down for her morning nap. Mitch was quiet for a long time. When he finally spoke, it was in a voice so constricted by pain it was almost unrecognizable. "I want to see her every day. If she so much as coughs, I want to know about it. I'm not happy about her living anywhere but with me, but right now I'm knocking myself out to keep the business going and I've got to be in the store so much that what you said last night was right. It wouldn't be any kind of a life for her." It was like a speech he'd rehearsed, as if fearing that once he tried to be spontaneous, he'd lose control. And when he turned to Lainie she saw the passion behind the exterior, and more anger than she'd ever seen him express with anyone.

"But I'm warning you, Lainie. One misstep and I'll be all over you. I'll close the goddamned store down, and we'll forget about the life-style, because I'll take over raising her and you can go get your old job back at Valley BMW."

The bastard, the rotten lousy bastard. "Mitch, what

do you want from me?'' The curious mixture of feelings that made her at once want to pummel him and fall into his arms, begging him to fix all of this, bewildered her.

''All I want is for my daughter to be okay,'' he said. ''Everything else is incidental. So if right now she's okay living with you, then that's what I want. I'm through begging you to understand all of this, because I don't understand it myself. And I can reassure you I'm not stepping away from her life. In fact, I'm going to come back to those group sessions too, because I don't want to miss out on anything that has to do with her. Understand that and—''

A whimper floated down from upstairs and then a ''Mamaaaa . . . ,'' and Lainie turned and hurried up to the baby's room. When she walked in, Rose was standing, holding on to the side of the crib, and seeing Lainie made her little face brighten. ''Up, Mama. Up.'' Her baby, her sweet baby girl. The worst thing Lainie could do was fall apart. She had to prove to Mitch that she was the most stable force for Rosie right now.

''Daddy's here, sweetheart,'' she said, trying to smile.

There was pure joy in Rosie's face. ''Daddeeee,'' she squealed again and again while Lainie put her on the changing table. And just as she was placing the dry diaper under the sweet little bottom, she felt Mitch standing close behind her. So close that for an instant she thought he was there to put his arms around her and say, Let's be a family again. But instead he spoke directly to Rose. ''Hello, Daddy's angel. We're going to go play today,'' and he moved away. When the clean diaper was on and a pink playsuit over it, Mitch hoisted the diaper bag strap onto his shoulder. ''See you at five,'' he said and took the baby out of her arms.

''Bye-bye, Mama,'' Rosie said, opening and closing her little fist in a wave that was aimed at her own face.

Lainie waved a little wave back to her and said, "Bye-bye, my sweet girl."

After that Mitch came back to the weekly sessions of the group. He would bustle in as if it were a business meeting. Sometimes he'd even take notes. He never said much, certainly never talked about what he and Lainie were going through. And Barbara left it alone, waiting for one of them to talk about it, but neither of them did. Lainie would watch him hug and kiss Rose good-bye after the session and then leave. Always she wanted to go after him, grab his sleeve, and say, What about me? I know you want to hug me too. Please, Mitch, come home.

The loneliness of life without him created an enormous void. She tried to fill it with school. She even joined the gym For Women Only in Studio City where Sharon belonged. Sometimes she would go to classes there in the morning when Mitch took the baby, but she preferred the early-evening aerobics class. She would drop Rosie off with the ever-stoic Margaret Dunn, who had actually gone out and bought a box full of baby toys, which sat waiting for Rose in her living room.

One night after Lainie left school, she picked the baby up at her mother's and headed home on the freeway. In the garage she pulled on her backpack of books, came around to the passenger side of the car, opened the door, and gently lifted the sleeping Rosie out of the baby car seat. Then she closed and locked the car and started out of the garage, stopping in terror when she saw someone stepping out of the shadows. It was Jackie.

Lainie's adrenaline raced and she put one of her hands around the back of the baby's head, as if to hide her, and rushed past.

"Lainie," Jackie said, "stop! I'm not the enemy. Let me come in and talk to you for five minutes. That's all I want."

"Get out of here, Jackie. You made a deal with me and Mitch. You told me that after the baby was born you were going to get out of our lives. But you lied." She was trying to find her house key as she moved along the stone path through the foliage leading to the door of her condo. Jackie stayed close behind her.

"I know what I said, but, Lainie, I need you to listen."

Lainie opened the door and looked at her. "I don't care what you need. Go away. You've done enough." The sharpness in Lainie's voice awakened Rosie, who opened her eyes. And then, though she was just getting to an age where she was afraid of strangers, she smiled, showing all her new teeth, and put her arms out to Jackie. It was clear this was no stranger.

"Hello, darling girl," Jackie said, her own blue eyes filling. The baby bounced up and down with glee to see her. "I made the deal because I was stupid," she said to Lainie. "I thought the pregnancy experience could be separated out of the experience of creating an ongoing life. But it can't. I need to be with her. Listen, Lainie, you and I and Mitch could fight about it like those people in New Jersey did, and all those other ugly cases, and maybe I'd lose, but you know what? I'm her mother. She has my genes, and she grew inside me and she'll grow up and, yes, she'll have lots of De Nardo in her, but one day you'll hear her laugh my big dumb laugh, or hear her voice on the telephone and for a second you'll think it's me. Or you'll see her putting on weight in the same spots I do, and just like you see your own mother in you, we all do, you'll see me in her.

"Lainie, I made a mistake, a big one. And so did you and so did Mitch. You were probably afraid he'd love you less or leave you if you said no to the whole idea, and I had some big need to feel important and special the way I did once before in my life, and that was when I was pregnant and gave birth to my son. So for each of our own reasons we went for it, and pretty soon, before we knew it, my baby with your husband was growing inside me. Well, all I can say is that even though I've only seen her these few times since she was born . . . I love her.

"Let's continue the good relationship we had when I was pregnant and let me be with her. Look at me, Lainie, and talk to me from the womanness inside you. Not the place that's afraid maybe someday Rose will decide she likes me better than she likes you, and not the part where you're afraid your mother or Mitch's sisters will tell you you're crazy for letting me be around her, but from the feeling, caring person who knows what it is to hurt and suffer and be taken advantage of, because I know in that part of you, you have to believe nobody can have too many people loving them, too many mothers looking out for them.

"I don't want Mitch. Believe me, I never have, or you would have known it instinctively and never picked me as a surrogate. And Mitch doesn't want me. But what he understood when I came to him, in some primitive instinctive way, was something that shook him to the core and made him bring the baby to me—he understood that no legal papers in the world are going to make me not her mother.

"And by doing that was he cheating on you? Fuckin' A, he was cheating on you, worse than if he had been screwing me six ways till Sunday every time we met. Because his was a lie of the spirit, and it was bad for Rose to be a party to it. Mitch should have been able to speak up and say to you, 'Lainie, I did bad. This whole thing was wrong. I should have kept on trying to adopt, because as long as Jackie needs to be near this baby, we have to work something out.' Only he was afraid. He had fallen into his own macho trap. And then he saw how much you loved the baby. How connected you were to her from day one, and how transformed you were by having her. He was afraid if he even mentioned my name you would hate him or leave him or both.

"Lainie, what do we do? Don't keep that baby from me. Let me see her sometimes, I beg you."

My God, Lainie thought, what can I do? Their eyes were locked as Lainie rolled back and forth from her heels to her toes in a way she had learned that the baby found soothing. Rose had her tiny head against her chest now, and was making that keening noise she made just before she fell off to sleep.

"This is a nightmare," Lainie said, and she heard her own voice sound almost unrecognizable and filled with pain. "And what makes it so difficult is that I look at you and I think, This woman is right. If I had given birth to Rosie, no matter what I'd signed or how much anyone had given me they'd have to kill me first before they could take her away. Dear God, why did I ever agree to this? Dear God, forgive me for being a party to this, Jackie, I'm so sorry," she said, and wept, and the two women embraced and wept holding on to each other with the baby, their baby, asleep in the middle of their tearful embrace. And when Jackie left, after Lainie promised to try to figure out what to do about all of it, the scent of Shalimar was still in the foyer.

35

THE MEMORIAL SERVICE for Davis Bergman was held at the big rambling house in Brentwood that Shelly and Davis had completely remodeled when they were together. As Ruthie and Shelly entered the backyard where the rented white folding chairs, the ones with the padded seats which cost a little more per chair, were lined up in rows facing a rented podium, Ruthie watched Shelly trying to maintain his equilibrium. But as they turned the corner and he looked at the rose garden he'd created and tended, and saw it now in full bloom, the profusion of open peach and fuchsia and crimson flowers made him stop and emit a pained sound. As if someone had kicked him in the stomach. For a long moment he was immobilized.

Marsha Bergman, Davis's widow, was surrounded by a group of her friends. Shelly and Ruthie walked to the area where she was standing in order to wait to express their condolences. But long before it was their turn, someone gestured to Marsha from across the glaring turquoise of the pool, and to their relief, since neither of them knew what they would say to her, she turned and walked in that direction. Shelly said he recognized some of the people from Davis's law practice, but Ruthie didn't see one familiar face.

In the newspaper that morning, the cause of Davis's death was listed as pneumonia. Ruthie suddenly wondered why she'd come to the memorial service of a man she had once hated. She had a strong desire to turn around and leave, but she knew Shelly needed to be there, needed her to get him through this, so she stayed, holding his hand and feeling his anxious presence next to her. Soon most of the white chairs were filled, and she took Shelly's arm and led him to the end seats in the back row.

The service was a kind of free forum with friends of Davis getting up and talking about their memories of him. Sometimes two people would start for the podium at once, and one would defer to the other and sit down. Essentially all the people said what a wonderful guy Davis was and what a happy couple he and Marsha were, and how much they would miss him. Ruthie looked at Shelly to see how he was bearing up, and noticed for the first time that he was holding a small pile of note cards in his hand. When he saw her looking at them, he handed them to her and whispered, "Quick. Punch these up!"

The cards contained notes in Shelly's funny little handwriting that he had prepared so that he could get up and speak about Davis. About his relationship with Davis. *(A) Hilarious sense of humor about our situation. (B) Every day I spent with him was a gift*. Ruthie looked up from the note cards and into Shelly's eyes, and shook her head. "Shel," she said, "I love you. But this material won't play to this crowd." She knew that was the last thing he wanted to hear, and how much he wanted someone to listen to how hard it was on him that Davis was gone.

At first she saw resentment on his face that she would try to deprive him of this moment, and she was sure he was going to jump to his feet the minute the next speaker was through and storm the podium. But then she saw the resignation, and he took the cards back from her and looked down at them. These were Marsha's friends, at Marsha's house, and they didn't want to hear what Shelly had to say about his love for Davis. Throughout the rest of the speeches, as he listened he took each of the note cards and slowly tore it into small pieces and stuffed the pieces into the pocket of his shirt.

The Hollywood show-business community is small and it didn't take long for Zev Ryder to learn that Davis Bergman, who everyone knew was a former lover of Shelly Milton's, had died, and how. "Oh, fuck! You mean to tell me I'm peeing in the same men's room as this guy? I don't know about the rest of you, but I'm gonna start using the can downstairs. What if it comes off on doorknobs? Oh, Christ. Sometimes at meetings I've picked up half a doughnut out of the box. What if *he's* the one who ate the other half?"

Zev didn't say those things in front of Ruthie and Shelly, just everybody else. And nobody had the nerve to tell him to shut up. Ruthie first got wind of the remarks when Ryder's secretary, a tall, severe, black-haired, white-skinned woman everyone in the office called Morticia, tried to apologize.

"Isn't he just being the bastard of all time?" she asked Ruthie one morning when they both emerged from cubicles in the ladies' room.

Ruthie rinsed her hands and avoided looking at what she knew was her own exhausted face in the mirror. "If you're talking about Zev, yes, he's always the bastard of all time, also the rat, the pig, the schmuck, and the shitheel. So what else is new?'' She pulled a paper towel down from the metal container on the wall, and watched Morticia apply the dark purple lipstick that made her white skin look even whiter.

''But all the stuff he's been saying about Shelly is really over the top,'' Morticia said, rubbing her purple lips together to get some effect that Ruthie, who seldom wore makeup, couldn't understand. ''I mean, he's got the writers afraid to eat the muffins you make. Haven't you noticed how many are left at the end of the day?''

''Meaning?''

It was clear that Morticia, whose real name was Alice, was reluctant to tear herself away from the mirror, but now she did, and she looked squarely at Ruthie. ''Listen, Ruth, I'm telling you right now, you can't quote me. I've got a daughter to support, and you know if Zev suspected I'd said a word he'd throw me out of here . . . but I happen to know he's looking for a way to screw up Shelly's contract. I've heard him on the phone with the Writers' Guild, looking for loopholes, ways to dump him and not have to pay him full salary. Not telling them who he is when he calls, but asking the contracts department at the Writers' Guild what kind of breach of contract, like not showing up, has to take place before you can fire somebody without a payout.''

Ruthie gripped the cold porcelain sink hard, and felt her whole body trembling with anger. ''What did you mean about the muffins?''

''Well, after he heard that Davis Bergman died, and everyone knows that Davis and Shelly used to be . . .'' Then she gestured with a kind of hands-apart shrug, meaning she didn't know what word to use for what Davis and Shelly were to each other.

''Lovers. They were lovers . . . go on,'' Ruthie said.

''Well, it totally freaked him out. Because he knows

you and Shelly live in the same house, and you make those muffins all the time, and you *know* how health-conscious Zev is, so . . ."

"So now he's campaigning to dump us?"

"Not you. Shelly."

"There's no such thing as that. We're a team, and he can't fuckin' do this. It's discrimination. I'm calling a lawyer."

"Oh, shit," Morticia said. "You bring a lawyer into this and I'll be dead meat. He'll know it was me. I have too much information."

The white face got even whiter as Ruthie took her hands and looked into her eyes. "Alice," she said. "Shelly and I have a child to raise, too. I can't let that vicious, bigoted little man destroy our family the way I've seen him do to other people. I won't hurt you in any way. I promise. But I guaranfuckin'tee you, I'm not going to sit by and let Zev Ryder pull down our lives."

There was a rehearsal at two o'clock. When Ruthie got downstairs, her assistant handed her a pile of phone messages. One of them was from Shelly. It said he wouldn't be at the rehearsal. He had to leave abruptly to go to a doctor's appointment. In the studio she slid into the back row of seats, and when Zev Ryder saw her sitting alone she felt him looking over at her while she sat making notes on the script in an effort to avoid him. And that night when she got home and Shelly was sick with a flu which the doctor informed him would probably keep him at home for a week, she knew Ryder would use the absence as a reason to get rid of them without pay.

She kicked her shoes off wearily and brought Shelly some soup, fed and played with Sid and bathed him, and heard Shelly calling to her from his room.

"Let me see the new pages," he said.

"Don't worry about the pages, I've got that covered."

"The doctor says I'm going to be stuck in bed for a while, but there's no reason why I can't write my stuff from here." Ruthie gave him this week's script. It was true he could write from bed, and the changes Shelly made that night before he fell asleep were better than any of the other writers could do in a week's worth of meetings. But the flu was one that left him bedridden for two weeks, at the end of which, on a Friday, he got a call from Morticia saying, "Mr. Ryder wishes me to tell you that because of your protracted absences, you're no longer on the staff of the show."

"The filthy little turkey didn't even have the balls to do it himself," Ruthie said.

"I've been out of the office a lot, Ru. He can prove it. But you can't quit. He'll destroy you if you do. You have to hang in for the baby's medical insurance and the weekly paycheck. Promise me you'll keep going in until we figure out what to do."

Bright red rage made her want to scream. There's no fucking way I'll keep working for that monster! But she looked at Sid, now climbing all over his daddy, and she said, "Yeah, okay. I promise."

On Monday the nanny didn't show up and Shelly was too weak to get out of bed, so Ruthie packed up Sid and took him with her to work. The baby had been to the studio often enough for her to know that if she put him in the portable playpen in a corner with just the right toys, he would amuse himself with the pound-a-peg or the "Sesame Street" pop-up, and except for an occasional loud squeal would be less disruptive of the meetings than most of the writers themselves.

Today Ruthie sat at the head of the table near the playpen, and she could tell by how shockingly quiet it was that everybody knew everything, or more accurately, everybody knew something. She was going to have to clear up the story now, before any of the rumors went any further.

"Guys," she said, "Shelly doesn't have AIDS."

"Oooops," Arnie Fishmann said as he knocked over his Styrofoam coffee cup and the tan liquid made a large puddle on his yellow lined legal pad and then seeped off it onto the conference room table. Three of the other writers stood and gathered napkins from the coffee cart and mopped up the spillage. Ruthie waited until all the wet napkins were in the wastebasket before she went on. "He's HIV-positive, but he doesn't have AIDS. He's very vulnerable, but please God, he'll go on for a long time."

This group of clowns has a gag line for everything, she thought, but for some reason, they're acting like humans for a change. "You can't catch it by working for him, by laughing with him, or by peeing in the same urinal. I don't have it, Sid doesn't have it, and as you all know he is Shelly's biological child, and we both drink from his glasses and use his towels and hug him and kiss him all day and night.

"But the point is Zev Ryder fired him. He says he fired him because he's been out and doesn't do the work. You all know what I know and what Zev knows, which is that Shelly can phone it in funnier than all of us in the room can make it even when we work until midnight. This is homophobia. This is discrimination. I intend to get a lawyer and sue that son of a bitch and bring him down for hurting the career of my partner and my best friend and my son's father. And I can't do it unless you fellows are prepared to stand up and talk not just about Shelly's contribution to the show but about Zev's dangerous and damning condemnation of him. Of us. And his horrible treatment in general of every one of us—the women on the staff who get sexually harassed by him, the writers who are spiritually annihilated on a regular basis. Because you have to know that an attack like this on one of us is really an attack on all of us and that next week it could be you, Fishie, or you, Jerry, for whatever reason he can think of. So please say you'll stand behind us and help us fight this man, and kick his ass the way he's been kicking all of ours for so long."

No one looked at her or spoke. Even Sid was quiet in the playpen. The only sound in the room was the sound of Arnie Fishmann lifting and dropping and lifting and dropping a pencil, which plunked repeatedly on the conference room table. Somebody sighed, one of them cleared his throat, and after a few minutes Ruthie got the message. They were all too chickenshit, too threatened to put their asses on the line for a friend.

"Okay, fellahs," Ruthie said, wishing she had the strength to throw the table over on them. "Let's write something funny."

36

"TODAY I THINK we need to talk a little bit more about support systems," Barbara said to the parents, all of whom were now wearing the Stork Club sweatshirts brought in by Ruthie and Shelly.

"Why does that expression, 'support system,' always make me think of an underwire bra?" Rick asked.

"Because, as usual, your mind is in your groin," Judith said, laughing.

"There are people in your lives who are going to enhance your children's worlds, families with other children their age, Mommy and Me groups you can attend regularly at schools or temples and churches in your neighborhoods. Try to branch out and find people who are dealing with the same developmental issues you are, and whose children will love having play dates with yours.

"I also recommend that you stay in touch with and visit your families, and have them visit you. The more people there are for these children to love, the better. Ruthie and Shelly, you're lucky you have all your parents still alive and well. Get them out here to visit Sid, and take him back to be with them."

"You haven't met our parents or you couldn't have used the word 'lucky' in reference to any of them," Shelly joked.

"Oh, I don't know. They did raise the two of you, so they must have some good qualities," Barbara said.

"You're right," Shelly said, serious now. "Our families would love to be with Sid."

"What about you, Judith?"

"I have friends from work, and particularly my friends Jerra and Tom, who don't have any kids. They love it when I bring the girls by. It makes their own family feel bigger when they include us in their celebrations."

Barbara looked at Lainie. "Our situation is pretty screwed up right now because we're still living apart, but my mother and Rose have a very nice relationship. She takes care of her some evenings when I go to class or to the gym, and I like knowing they're together. I always feel when I pick Rose up at her house that the two of them arc better for having spent the time together. I also have my friends Sharon from school and Carin from work, and they're a lot closer to Rose than my sisters-in-law. Her so-called real family."

"My sisters have been pretty busy lately," Mitch said defensively, "but sometimes Rose gets to be with her cousins, and I think family is real important." Without looking at her, Barbara could feel Lainie's tension from across the room.

"Well, we've learned by virtue of this group that we have a new definition of that word," Barbara said. "A family is what and who you make it. And that's why I think it's healthy to widen the circle of people who love the children, so they feel they have many ways to turn for affection and warmth."

"You know, I was always so proud of the fact that Shelly and I are so self-sufficient, didn't need anybody, but now I think you're right. It's important for the kids that we expand their worlds," Ruthie said.

Barbara looked at Rick. "What about you, Rick?"

"My uncle Bobo has been everything to me, and the other person who's been an incredible support to me is the widow of my best friend. She's completely unlike anyone I've ever known. A great mother to her own kids and a kind of wise aunt to David, so that's been very worthwhile, and her sons are like nephews to me.

"Anyway," he said, his thoughts slipping away to all the sweet things Patty had done for him and for David, "she's been a fine friend to me and I really respect the way she takes the time to—" That was the moment when he looked around the room and saw that all of the others were smiling knowingly at him, and he stopped short. "What's so funny?" No one answered, they just continued to grin. "Why is every person in this room wearing a dopey grin?"

"You're in love with her," Judith said, and when Rick flushed purple the others erupted like schoolchildren. "It's completely obvious to every one of us."

"Oh, please," he said. "I think very highly of her. Very highly, and I've known her since she was a kid. I mean, my best friend was her . . ." Rick stopped then to think about it, and he was obviously rattled. "Let's go on to somebody else," he said to Barbara, who picked up the ball by looking around at the others.

"The point is to try to find people the children can count on to be positive forces in their lives." There was a big silence in the room, punctuated only by the happy sounds from the play yard, until Rick spoke, this time to himself, but out loud.

"Maybe I am," he said, and a titter of laughter filled the room. "I mean, I'll be goddamned. Maybe I'm in love with Patty."

After the group he walked with David to the car, thinking he should call Patty and tell her. But he was sure she would laugh and hang up, or say, "If this is your way of trying to get me into bed, dream on." Or maybe she'd say that she wanted him too.

On the second day of shooting his new film he crouched next to the big double bed on the set, having a quiet conversation with his two stars, while the crew waited patiently behind the scenes. Over and over he talked to the two formidable talents facing each other, their heads on the satin-covered pillows, and told them the back story of what their characters had been through to get to this moment.

Shooting scenes out-of-sequence was a necessary evil, but he was going to make it work by talking them into the heat of the moment. For a long hushed time he waxed poetic about how hungry the characters must be for each other, how they were finally to be consummating their love of so many years. It was the kind of moment he was famous for capturing better than any other director in the business. And it was the close personal work he did with the actors just before the cameras rolled that was the key.

He'd been lulling them into the mood for nearly an hour, telling his erotic story, but timing was everything and he could tell by the way they were looking at each other now that they were ready to go at it. He knew that it was time for him to stand ever so slowly and steal away out of the shot, behind the camera, and softly say, "Action."

It worked. The passion between them during the shooting of the scene was powerful. Rick felt elated when he called, "Cut and print it!" Now, right now, he should shoot the close-ups, get them set up while the mood was thick and sultry. But just as he was about to do that, he looked around and saw Andrea enter through the heavy studio door. He knew when he saw her there that something was wrong. He always cautioned her not to come down and disturb him unless there was an emergency with David. Only his son had the power to call everything in his life to a halt. "What's wrong?" he asked.

"Doreen Cobb," she said, coming closer and handing him a yellow Post-it with a phone number written on it. "She called from a phone booth. She sounds awful. I told her I'd do my best to get you to call her as soon as possible. She was pretty shook up so I'm not sure, but it sounded like she said she was at Port Authority in New York."

The thought of that child in a den of horror like the bus station in New York City sickened him. If she'd run away as far as New York, she had to be leaving something pretty bad. As bad as he feared. He motioned for his first AD to come over and said, "Call a break. Ten minutes. Fifteen tops. I have to make an emergency phone call."

The young man looked at Rick as if to say, How can you sacrifice the momentum of the shoot to go and make a phone call? But Rick was already out the door, heading to his trailer. The minute he was inside he dialed the New York City area code and the number Andrea gave him. It only rang once.

"I'm sorry," Doreen's very shaky voice said instead of hello.

"Doreen, just tell me you're all right."

"I am, I mean, I think I am. I'm scared of all the weirdos here, but I'm all right."

"Dear girl," he said, trying not to imagine how small

and afraid and alone she must be in the vast Port Authority, "can you tell me why you ran away?"

"Um . . . well I, I ran away because I couldn't . . . I couldn't . . . um . . . ," she sobbed. "I couldn't stay there anymore."

"Doreen, does this have anything to do with David's birth father?" he asked. "Doreen, who is David's birth father?"

More sobs and finally she managed to ask, "Do you know?"

"I *do* know. I think I know. Did he rape you?"

"I hate him."

"Is he still abusing you?"

"I can't go back there."

"Doreen, you have to go back and report him. Turn him in. For your sake. For the sake of the rest of the family. Does Bea know?"

"Oh, no. It would kill her. She thinks they're happy together. It would kill my sister too. Ruin her life and the kids' lives too. And I love those kids—"

"What about *your* life? I care about your life. Go home and tell Bea. She'll give you the strength to do this."

"I can't."

There was a knock at the trailer door. Damn. Rick opened it and gestured with a please-wait hand up to the assistant director who stood outside pointing at his watch, mouthing the words, What about the dinner break? A dinner break. If he let those two actors out of that bed, he would totally destroy the mood for close-ups. What was he thinking? He'd *already* destroyed the mood by walking out. Fuck the mood, he thought. I'll get it back. I'll figure it out later. There's a life at stake here.

"Give them the dinner break now," he said out loud.

"What?" Doreen asked on the phone.

"I was talking to my assistant director," he said. The AD nodded and closed the door. "Forgive me. Doreen, please listen to me and go home now, work this out. You can do it." He knew he shouldn't, mustn't, wasn't supposed to say the next, but all the rules were broken anyway so he decided he would bribe her. "I'll tell you what. Go home now . . . do you have money and a ticket?"

"Yeah."

"And if you do, if you go right now . . . I'll send you a ticket to come and be with me and David at Christmas. Would you like that?"

The voice on the other end of the phone now was the voice of a very young girl. "Oh, wow! Really? Yeah! That would be the best! To see the baby? I'm going home!"

"Doreen. You must put a stop to this man. No one can do that for you."

"I know," she said. "I will." But Rick was unconvinced.

"David and I both love you," he said, and the line went dead.

"Mr. R.?" Andrea opened the door of the trailer. "Is Doreen all right?" He nodded an absent nod. "The cast and crew are on dinner," Andrea told him.

The cast and crew? Yes. He'd better get back to his own problems. He was in the middle of shooting a forty-million-dollar film, the success or failure of which could make or break his career.

"Fine," he said. "Just bring me a sandwich." Now, where am I, he thought. Yes. The love scene.

37

SO WHAT DO I DO? What's the etiquette when you think the teenage birth mother of your son has probably been raped by her sister's husband, which makes him the birth father of your child? Do you try and hire someone to kill the bastard, or just sit and wait for the phone to ring?" Then he added wryly, "And I *used* to think my relationships were complicated."

"Rick, from all you've told us, Doreen is very strong," Barbara said. "She convinced Bea to let her come here and give you the baby instead of having him at a home and giving him away in an anonymous adoption. She lived in your house and you got to know her strength intimately. Up until recently she was able to keep what both of you felt was a healthy distance from the situation. It seems to me that you may just have to wait and trust that she'll work it out."

"I disagree," Lainie said. "I think he owes her a lot, and that he needs to actively figure out a way to do something for her. She gave him an incredible gift, the way Jackie did me and Mitch, and in taking the baby he took on a lifelong relationship with her."

Everyone turned to look at Lainie. She was even more pale and beautiful today, though her big blue eyes were ringed with red. "Jackie came to see me, came to my home one night and told me what she's been going through, and I'm beginning to have some understanding about how she feels. I still haven't forgiven Mitch, but at least I know now that there's some part of me that's starting to think maybe I can do what Judith talked about in one of these sessions. To learn how to change my definition of the way things are supposed to be." Her emotions stopped her from saying more.

Barbara turned to Mitch. "Do you want to talk about this?" She hoped there wasn't any judgment in her voice, because for weeks what she'd felt like doing was grabbing him by the collar of his shirt and saying, Talk to this woman and work it out. Maybe now their moment was here.

"I wish I knew what to say," Mitch said, and all of them watched as his tough front fell slowly away. "I come here and sit in these groups, and sometimes I'm feeling as if I want to run out there and grab Rose and leave with her. And other times I'm wishing like hell I knew how to break down and beg all of you to help me, because all I really want is for my daughter to have a good life."

"And what do you want for your wife?" Barbara asked.

"For her to understand I meant to do something loving and made a mess. That I love her and miss her and want her back, want my family back. But that I still believe we must somehow include Jackie in Rose's world."

Barbara only nodded, and then she looked around at

all of their concerned faces looking at Lainie. There was no doubt that the people in this group cared about one another. At the end of each session, before they went home to face their respective problems, they all hugged one another and wished one another well. And she was warmed by the way their interest in one another's lives seemed genuine.

"Make it work, Lainie," Ruthie urged. "Remember what we're learning in here about new rules."

Lainie couldn't look at any of them.

"Life is too short to waste time withholding your love, Lainie," Shelly said. "We know that very well," he added so softly it was as if he was talking to himself. "Particularly in our family." Everyone looked at him, and he wondered how they would react to what he was about to tell them. "Because I've been diagnosed as being HIV-positive."

Barbara glanced at Lainie, Mitch, Judith, and Rick for their reactions, and then at Ruthie, who had had no idea Shelly was going to tell them today. Her eyes shone brightly with her love for him.

"I haven't wanted to talk about this in here," he said. "It's been hard on our lives, particularly for Ruthie, and though I'm feeling pretty damn good most of the time, I've been fired from my job in an acute case of prejudice. I worry about my family and how they'll be treated when more and more people find out. I want to keep writing, maybe even write about what I'm going through, but I've never written anything but comedy, and this ain't particularly funny."

Barbara could tell that no one knew how to respond. She was surprised and glad when Rick spoke.

"Shelly, you're an extraordinarily good writer," he said. "You have a completely unique point of view. I've watched your show at least a dozen times, and I always know which material comes from you and Ruthie, because the script always has your insight and style. You could write a hell of a screenplay about anything. And I for one would be very interested in it.''

''You're being kind,'' Shelly said.

''No, I'm not. I'm being my usual selfish self. I think working with you would be profitable in every sense of the word. If you deprive the world of your talent because some homophobic jerk fired you, you're making a giant mistake.''

Ruthie looked at Shelly and wondered what he was thinking. Rick Reisman may have had some bad luck in the past, but some of his films were classics. He was shooting one now that already had the buzz of success all over town.

''You don't have to write an AIDS story. I'll sit and pitch any idea you like with you. Don't stop working, Shelly. You're too damned good,'' Rick said.

''I appreciate what you're saying,'' Shelly said, looking at Rick, ''and I'll certainly think about it.'' Ruthie crossed her fingers. If Shelly sold a treatment of a story to a studio, or better yet a screenplay, his spirits would soar. And thinking practically, his medical insurance would continue to be covered by the Writers' Guild.

The children were toddling in to find their parents. Dana gestured to Barbara that it was break time, but Barbara asked her to entertain the children for a few minutes longer so that she could bring up one more issue.

''Before the children get here, as I'm sure you're all aware, the Christmas holidays are fast approaching, and I wanted to talk about the stress that sometimes accompanies them. The stress for the parents is from the obvious. The traffic and the crowds, the financial pressures. Those adults who have had joyous family experiences at holidays frequently try to recreate those experiences, and that's potentially frustrating.

''Those parents who *haven't* had good holiday experiences sometimes try to better the experience for their own children, which doesn't always work out the way they'd hoped either. So what I strongly urge you to do is to keep your plans simple. Ask yourself how much of the plans really are about the needs of the people in your life now, versus your needs from the past.

"As for the children, even the best toddler has a hard time with holidays for a lot of reasons. His or her schedule is frequently changed around. Nap times, mealtimes are all topsy-turvy. The departure from their routine can make them grumpy or cranky and upset. Holiday situations may force them to be confronted by a lot of strangers who could seem frightening. So my suggestion is that you stay aware of your child's needs to keep as much of his or her life-style as intact as possible. Let them eat at home at mealtime and *then* take them to the party. Plan outings after a nap, don't insist that they be chummy with strangers at parties, because they won't want to be.

"I'm bringing this up now so you can avoid the trap of inflated holiday expectations. I'm personally feeling sad about spending Christmas without my children, because my daughter is spending the holiday with her fiancé and his mother, and my son is going on a ski trip with a friend. My mother is going back east to be with my sister, so maybe I'm projecting my own trepidations, but I thought I'd mention it."

"I've invited Doreen to come and be with me and my uncle and Patty and the boys."

"Wow!" Judith said. "That ought to be emotional."

"I'm hoping to get her out of her environment in Kansas and maybe find out what's really going on with her."

"We're just going to a few parties," Ruthie said.

"I don't feel too much like celebrating," Shelly added.

"Well, it's going to be just me and the girls and some friends," Judith said.

Lainie didn't say a word.

The children were at the snack table now and the parents rose to join them. They had a snack, sang "Five Little Monkeys Jumpin' on the Bed" and "We're Goin' to the Zoo." Then Dana read to them from *Goodnight Moon*.

Barbara watched the families share hugs and holiday wishes with one another. Mitch parted uncomfortably with Rose, getting only a nod from Lainie. Ruthie and Shelly walked out with their arms around each other, and Rick helped Judith with her double stroller. After Barbara and Dana put away the toys, Barbara made notes on all that had happened and wondered if what she had told them about the holidays would help them, or herself.

38

IT WAS A FRIDAY a few days before Christmas when Barbara stopped on South Robertson Boulevard at a Christmas tree lot run by the Boy Scouts of America and bought a large Douglas fir. Then she helped two Boy Scouts tie it to the top of her car and she drove home. When she stopped the car outside her house, she thought about just leaving the tree outside all night and waiting until Stan came home from his business trip tomorrow morning so that he could help her carry it in and set it up.

Of course in this city nothing was sacred, so she knew there was every chance she could come out tomorrow and someone would have stolen the tree. That was reason enough to pull the car closer to the front door and bring the big unwieldy thing in alone. The other reason was that doing all the chores to set up the tree would be a good test of her competence.

Sometimes when she worried about what her life

would be like if there were no Stan, she would silently challenge herself to face some task alone for which under ordinary circumstances she would have asked Stan's help. "If I can fix this fallen shutter without asking Stan to do it for me, I'll know that if the time comes when he dies first, I'll be okay." Once she told her friend Marcy Frank about the way she played that mental game with herself. It was during one of those reveal-your-inner-fears lunches that close friends have, and when she'd finished, hoping for some corroboration from someone else who had been married to one man for as long as she had, Marcy laughed, then raised her eyes heavenward and said, "And *this* woman is a psychologist?"

When the lights were strung, she plugged them into the wall socket next to the tree to make sure all of the bulbs had survived another year, and they had. By then it was ten o'clock and she still hadn't had any dinner, but instead of taking a break she went out into the garage and found the three boxes marked ORNAMENTS, piled them on top of one another, and brought them into the living room. In the silence of the empty house, she pulled each familiar figure and ball out of the protective paper in which she'd wrapped it so carefully last year.

Every one had a memory that came with it. The tiny glass angel she and Stan and the kids bought on that weekend in Williamsburg, and the adobe house they'd bought when they visited Santa Fe, and the ceramic Minnie Mouse Heidi had begged for at Disneyland. But unlike Christmas tree decorating sessions in the past, tonight there was nobody for whom she could hold one up and say, "Oh, look. Remember when we got this one?" Get used to it, she told herself. Until there are grandchildren, you'd better get used to it.

At eleven she felt tired but on some kind of tear to

finish the task. She was remembering all those Christmas mornings when Heidi and Jeff would push open her bedroom door and leap on her and Stan when it was still dark outside, while both parents longed for just a little more sleep. The lonely way she felt tonight made her think she would give up sleeping forever to have them around for another Christmas.

At midnight, still only half finished, she decided she had passed her own survive-without-Stan test, and leaving the lights on the tree aglow she went upstairs to bed. The next day by the time Stan arrived, she had finished the job and was sitting on the sofa, staring blankly at the lit-up tree, feeling depressed.

"Let me guess," he said, sitting next to her and sliding his arm around her waist. "I'll bet you're sitting here remembering every Christmas before this one as idyllic, aren't you?"

"You mean they weren't?"

"Which one shall I call up for you? The one where your mother brought seven homeless people over here for dinner and one of them threw up all over our bathroom, and one of them stole my wallet? Or how about the year where Heidi knocked the tree over and started a fire in the living room? I liked the one when your sister, Roz, came in from back east and brought some fish with her on the plane, which we all ate and got food poisoning."

Barbara laughed. "You're so right. I'm doing exactly what I cautioned all of my patients against, about having some Currier and Ives fantasy around their past holidays."

"Listen, my love," Stan said, holding her close. "These are going to be the best years of our lives. Once we get Jeff squared away, we'll do all the real traveling we've been talking about for years. Maybe we'll even find a spot we really love up north, and buy a second home. Think of it. With no kids around, I'll be able to run after you naked all through the house."

"Sweetheart, at the speed I'm running these days, it won't be too tough to catch me."

"Precisely! But that's okay because at my age I forget what I'm supposed to do when I catch you."

Their jokes about aging had become a favorite way to make them both laugh, which they now did, and then Stan took her face in his hand, turned it toward his, and said, "Honey." She knew his smile so well. "That's something we both know I'll never forget."

"You promise?" she said grinning.

"You can take it to the bank."

His sweet gentle kisses by the glowing tree warmed her, and when he tugged at her sweater, she helped him remove it, and soon they were making love on the floor.

"Maybe it's not so bad with the kids out of the house," she said as Stan caressed her.

"I say to hell with the little brats," Stan answered, touching her, loving her, making her sadness of the last many hours disappear.

When they lay spent, Stan asleep beside her on the floor, the phone rang. Barbara ran through the house naked to answer it. It was Heidi, and in just "Hi, Mom," Barbara knew there was something seriously wrong. First there was a lot of crying. Then there was a jumble of words Barbara couldn't understand. While she listened patiently, trying to sort it out, Stan brought her a bathrobe, which she slid on. Finally she understood what it was Heidi was trying so hysterically to tell her. Ryan Adler, her fiancé, had married someone else. The someone else was a woman named Bonnie West, who was a local San Francisco radio personality.

"We had this fight, and we weren't speaking, but like I just figured it would blow over and he'd be coming back. You know? I mean that's what always happened before and um, she's his old girlfriend from a really long time ago, and so during the time I was waiting for him to call me, he was . . . marrying her. I am so lame. I can't believe I had to hear this from someone who saw it in the paper. Can you believe I ever trusted this man?''

Barbara bit her tongue.

''So now, I mean you are really not going to believe this part, I mean this is so totally deranged, it's sick. He calls here the other night, and he's um, whispering, and I heard his voice and I'm going, Don't crack, Heidi, don't say anything. Just let him talk, and you're going to die when I tell you, Mom.'' Stan brought Barbara some coffee and she gestured to him that Heidi was going through a trauma as she listened to the rest of the story.

''He said, 'Oh, God, Heidi, why did I do this? Why did I marry her? I mean it's so clear to me now that you're the one I really love.' So I said, 'You're crazy, Ryan. That's why.' And then he said something about how his mother thought Bonnie was more right for him than I was, and I said, 'Thanks a lot, that makes me feel really great!' Anyway, the worst part is he said, 'Can I come over?' I mean, can you believe this? This man wanted to come over and have sex with me and still be married to *her*! How could he think I'd say yes to that?''

''What *did* you say?'' Barbara asked, surprised by this burst of intimacy from Heidi, whose answer to the question ''What's new?'' was, notoriously, ''New York, New Jersey, and New Hampshire.''

''I'll tell you something, Mom. I was feeling so bummed out and so completely lonely at that moment that it was real hard to say no. Because all I wanted was one more hour of him saying he loved me.''

Poor child, Barbara thought. My poor child. ''But?'' she asked, knowing she shouldn't.

"Don't worry, Mother," Heidi said with disdain for the question. "I didn't do it. I hung up and took the phone off the hook. But, um, now I'm really sad and you have to help me, because they've moved into his place which is right near here, and I've got to get out of here. Fast. I don't think I can survive bumping into either one or the two of them."

"Let me see what I can do," Barbara told her.

There wasn't a moving company available on such short notice, so Barbara called Hertz Rent-A-Truck in San Francisco, and she and Stan flew up. They spent Christmas Eve day packing up Heidi's apartment, all of the kitchen supplies, clothes, and finally the furniture, and moving everything down the two flights of stairs, loading all of it onto the truck. Stan drove the truck as Barbara and Heidi followed behind him in Heidi's car. Barbara drove and Heidi cried all the way home. When they arrived in Los Angeles, they went straight to a storage rental space Barbara had called before they left. With the help of some of the night-shift employees, they unloaded it all and finally went home.

Heidi spent Christmas morning sitting on the sofa, staring at the blazing fire in the living room fireplace with damaged eyes and a lovelorn expression over an affair that Barbara knew she believed she would never get over.

"It takes time, honey," Barbara said, sitting on the sofa next to her. "And you have plenty of time."

"Yeah" was all Heidi said. Barbara tried to maintain some holiday spirit. Though it had been a while since she'd done it, she remembered her old recipe and made a huge stack of what turned out to be delicious pancakes. Then she turned on a tape of the Mormon Tabernacle Choir singing Christmas carols, but she had to turn down the volume so she could take a call from Jeff, who was skiing in Snow Mass. She was glad for him that he was far away from the Singer household blues that morning, and changed the subject when he asked, ‘‘How come the goonball is there? I thought she was gonna be with her dorky fiancé.’’

At about eleven A.M. the doorbell rang. When Barbara opened the door she was surprised to see Marcy and Ed Frank, their son-in-law, Freddy, who looked like Ed, and their daughter, Pammy, Heidi's childhood friend, who was very pregnant.

‘‘Uh-oh, I can tell by the look on your face that we should have called first,’’ Marcy Frank said apologetically, probably because Barbara, still in her bathrobe, looked bedraggled from the ordeal of the last thirty-six hours. ‘‘But we were right up the street at my sister-in-law's house and we thought you two would be lonely without your kids around, and we wanted you to see Pammy's enormous tummy.’’

‘‘Uh . . .’’ Barbara wasn't sure what to do. What she wanted to do was say, ‘‘Go away’’ and close the door, and she was considering doing that when Heidi, curious to know who was there, got to her feet, walked to the door, and when she looked out at the four people, who were surprised to see her, and then saw Pammy's stomach, she moaned, began to cry, and left the room to go upstairs.

‘‘Maybe we should go,’’ Ed Frank said.

Barbara sighed. ‘‘Oh, come on in,’’ she said. ‘‘Stan, honey, make these people an eggnog while I go take care of Heidi.’’ She was relieved when just as she stepped into Heidi's old room where Heidi lay in a fetal position on the unmade bed, the phone rang. Before Barbara could get to it, Heidi uncurled herself and reached for it.

‘‘Hello?’’ she said in a stuffed-nosed voice. ‘‘Oh, Merry Christmas to you too, Grammy, only this is Heidi, not Barbara.’’ Barbara sat down on the bed. ‘‘I'm home because, um, my boyfriend married someone else, so I didn't want to stay up there anymore, because I was, um, too hurt. So my mom and dad came up with this humongous truck and they spent all day moving me here, and I'm going to live with them for a while till I figure out my life."

As soon as she got all of that out, her mouth opened wide in a cry that couldn't come out. She was shaking with inward sobs, and Barbara moved closer to where she was sitting on the bed and held her hand. Heidi listened to whatever sage advice Gracie was dispensing on the other end of the phone. Advice to which Heidi kept nodding until she got her bearings, then finally she said, "I know. You're right. I agree. No, I know. You're right and I will, I promise. Okay. Here's my mom."

"Hello, Mother," Barbara said.

"You have to have her moved into her own place before the first of the year," Gracie said instead of hello.

"Well, Merry Christmas to you too," Barbara replied.

"You with all your psychiatric training know better than anyone that after all her hard-won independence, moving in with you now is the worst thing that could happen to her. That girl has to get back on the horse. Stand on her own two feet as soon as possible," Gracie said in her I-mean-business voice.

"Mother, she's fine. A few weeks in her old room might be healthy for her, a little return to the womb, with Stan and me pampering her. How bad could that be?"

"Don't do what's right for you, Barbara. Do what's right for her," Gracie said.

"Happy holidays," Barbara said and put the phone back in the cradle. "Shall I tell the Franks to go away?" she asked Heidi. Heidi put her arms around her mother's neck and her head against Barbara, and Barbara could feel her own hair getting wet with her daughter's hot tears. "I'll be glad to go down and ask them to come over for dinner next week when you're feeling better."

"No, I'm okay. I'll wash my face and come down. I really am glad for Pammy. I want to come down and see her." She stood and walked sniffling into her bathroom.

"Honey," Barbara said, and Heidi stopped and looked at her, her pretty face blotched and scrunchy from the tears shed, "I promise you'll make it through this."

"Thanks, Mom," Heidi said, and went into the bathroom to wash her face.

By the thirtieth of December she and Barbara found an apartment in West Hollywood that Heidi liked and Barbara and Stan could afford to help her keep until she got a job. The last item Barbara moved into the apartment was the old tattered Winnie the Pooh. She had transported it with a few other things from home in her car. While Heidi was talking to the man who had come to install the phone, Barbara took the bear into the bedroom.

"Look after her," she said, hugging the stuffed toy. Then she put it on Heidi's pillow and went to work.

39

ON CHRISTMAS EVE DAY, Ruthie and Shelly went to a big noisy party at the home of a television producer who lived in Santa Monica. "Did you hear about the whale in the San Francisco harbor who got AIDS? He was rear-ended by a ferry!" A bald guy who was standing by the piano told that joke to his girlfriend.

"Let's go," Shelly said to Ruthie. He'd been inside the house at the bar getting a Perrier when he overheard it. Now he came out to the pool area where she was sitting talking to some women writers. He didn't feel like being polite, so without even saying hello to the others, he picked Ruthie's purse up and handed it to her. "Right now."

Sid was having a great time climbing on some play equipment with a group of other kids in which the older ones were tending to the little ones, and Ruthie had been relaxing for the first time in a long time, gabbing away.

Now she was worried about Shelly and the anger in his eyes. "Are you okay?" she asked him.

"Yeah. I just want to get out of here."

"We just got here," she said, wondering what was wrong.

"Then you stay. I'm going."

"What about Sid?"

"He can stay or go. It's up to you."

"Ah, Shel. Why can't we *all* stay?"

"Because I want to leave."

"And do what?"

"Go home."

"Why do you want to go home? It's Christmas Eve, a family time."

"Get ahold of yourself, Ruthie. We're Jewish and we're *not* a family."

The ocean was loud but not loud enough to cover what Shelly said. One of the women saw the pain in Ruthie's face and took her hand, but she pulled it away. "Here's the ticket for the car," she said, yanking it out of her purse. "I'll keep the baby here with me and get a ride home." Shelly took the ticket, turned, walked over to Sid, and with a little kiss good-bye, was gone. Through the large windows of the front of the house Ruthie saw the valet parker pull her Mercedes up, and she watched Shelly get into it and drive away.

According to the doctors, so far he was doing fine. He went to his appointments every month to have his T-cell count checked and to be examined for any symptoms of AIDS, and all was well. But the fear and the stigma tormented him. Sometimes he would wake up and write poetry, which she found around the house. She knew that many nights he would lie in bed, longing to sleep, to cross the threshold into dreams where he was healthy and unafraid, but his anxious mind wouldn't let him. Instead he would find himself filled with heart-pounding panic.

He would hyperventilate and feel nauseated and shaky, so he would get up and walk down the hall and into Ruthie's room. And Ruthie, knowing in her sleep that something was wrong, would wake to find him sitting there. He had come in just to be near her. Once she was awake she would sit up, kneel beside him on the bed, and massage his shoulders, kneading the knots of fear out of his back, saying over and over again, "You're okay. You're okay. Your T-cell count is high, your appetite is good, Sid and I love you, and you're okay." And soon her words and the comforting physical contact of the massage would ground him again, and he would relax.

When Ruthie felt his shoulders lowering and the tension ease, she would get up, put on her robe, and take his hand. "Come on," she would say, leading him down the hallway to the baby's room. And they would stand together in the nursery lit only by the Mickey Mouse night-light and look at the face of their peacefully sleeping son.

"This is why you can't panic. This is why you have to say, 'Everybody's going to die, but they're going to have to take Shelly Milton kicking and screaming out of this world, because I'm hanging in for Sid the Kid.' Are you with that, Shel? We made it through 'Rudy the Poodle,' and love, and death, we made it through frizzy hair and suicide attempts, and we will make it through this one, too." Then she would walk him to his room and watch while he got back into bed, then go to her own room and sit wide awake until she heard him snoring before she could go back to sleep herself. She loved him and she should have gone home from the stupid Christmas party with him, in fact she should leave now and meet him there. One of the women she'd been talking to had walked inside to get something to eat, and the other one was chasing after her own little toddler. Ruthie decided to start asking around to see if she could get a ride home when she spotted Louie Kweller across the crowded backyard.

Louie Kweller was looking a little rounder than he had in the early years, when along with Ruthie and Shelly and all the other comedy writers he had haunted the Comedy Store. But he was still sweet looking, and when he greeted Ruthie with a very warm hug, it felt good and he smelled great. One of the things Ruthie remembered finding so attractive about Louie was that he was well-read. Once they'd had a conversation about a television series which had a lot of simultaneous plot lines and Louie described it as having a "Dickensian multiplicity." Another time he compared the plot of a sitcom they'd all watched together to a Stephen Crane short story.

"No kidding?" Shelly had laughed. "I thought Stephen Crane was the head of miniseries at NBC."

Most of the comedy writers Ruthie knew were funny by feel, instinct, up from pain. Louie Kweller had all of that, but he combined it with an educated overview, and the combination had caused him to become one of the most successful producers in television. He had recently made a highly publicized deal with a studio, giving him what they swore in the trade papers would be a production company with "complete artistic freedom" plus some unheard-of amount of money to do it.

"So you're a hit," Ruthie said to him as he sat on the deck chair next to her. It seemed like forever since the old days when they'd sat for hours in the group of struggling writers at the Hamburger Hamlet on Sunset. When Ruthie and Shelly used to split one bacon cheeseburger between them, because two bacon cheeseburgers were more than they could afford.

"And you're a hit too," he said, smiling. Ruthie found him almost humble for someone who had just been told his every idea was worth millions of dollars.

"But not like you. You could sell your laundry list now for more than I could get for my house."

"Yeah, but you've got a kid," he said, patting her hand. "Is that him in the red shirt over there?" He gestured in the direction of the big wooden structure with a fort at the top where Sid was climbing up the ladder.

"How did you know?" Ruthie asked.

"Because he's so cute," Louie said and looked into her eyes, and Ruthie was shocked when a flame rose in her cheeks the likes of which she hadn't felt in what seemed like a lifetime. Calm down, Zimmerman, she thought. You're losing your mind.

"So what are you working on?" Ruthie asked him, hoping Louie wouldn't notice that something he'd said in passing, probably as a joke, had stirred her. Made her heavyhearted self feel for even a tiny breath of an instant desirable. No. Better than that. Womanly. The party was getting busier and noisier as more and more people arrived.

A very skinny, pretty girl, wearing a spandex dress that was so tight it showed her pelvic bones, spotted Louie and hurried over to remind him that she was on an episode of one of his shows a few weeks ago and that the script was "soooo brilliant." Ruthie liked the way Louie thanked her with seriousness, didn't come on to her, and after she walked away didn't make some snide comment about what an airhead she was. He was an appealing, gentle man.

"You did a good thing, you and Shelly," Louie said now. "By having that baby together. I bumped into Shelly the other day and he's completely changed. Much more serious than I've ever seen him. Is that your observation?''

''That Shelly's more serious? Definitely,'' Ruthie said, feeling really guilty now that she hadn't left with him.

''Are you living together?''

''Yes.''

''Hey, Kweller,'' somebody yelled from the house and Louie waved and Ruthie watched him, impressed by the fact that there was no apparent show of his newfound importance. There was no patronizing air that usually accompanied success in Hollywood.

''So, I mean,'' he said, looking back at Ruthie, and she knew what he was going to ask her. It was a question she'd been asked before. ''I mean, I know this is none of my business, and if it's rude you can say so and I'll shut up, okay? But how does that work?''

She knew exactly what he meant, but she wasn't going to make it easy for him. ''How does *what* work?''

''I mean, is it a love affair, a romance? Anything like that?''

''You're right. It *is* none of your business, but how it works is, he's my best friend. The closest person to me in the world. I love him more than I've ever loved any man or probably ever will, but we each sleep in our own bedroom and we don't have sex.'' Louie Kweller was expressionless. ''And it's okay,'' Ruthie told him.

''Mommeeee,'' Sid shouted suddenly, and Ruthie jumped to her feet and ran over to the play yard where her son was screaming at the bottom of the slide, because he'd just been kicked by a bigger boy. She snatched him up and held him and soothed him and kissed him. After a few minutes he dried his face against her shirt and wriggled away to go back to playing.

''We're going home soon, honey,'' she called after

him. "In a few minutes we'll go home and see Daddy. I'll get us a ride."

"I'll take you home." Ruthie turned to see that Louie Kweller had walked to the play yard too, and was standing behind her.

"Don't you live around *here*?" Ruthie asked. "I mean, wouldn't it be out of your way?"

"Yeah, but that's okay. I feel like taking a ride."

Louie Kweller. He was coming on to her. If he only knew what was going on in her life. That Shelly often woke with night sweats, that no matter what the doctors said about her status and Sid's, she was afraid she'd never stop feeling panicky over every rash, every loose bowel movement.

Louie, oh Louie, she thought, this flirtation is a very nice Christmas present for me and I can use it, but there's no room for anything in my life now. I work for a son of a bitch who I hate, I come home and I raise my kid, and I love Shelly Milton. After that I have nothing left. But when she picked up a protesting Sid, and thanked her host, and Louie Kweller carried the diaper bag over his left shoulder and put his right arm around her to walk her out to the valet parking, it felt very nice.

"You Ruth Zimmerman?" the parking attendant asked.

"Yeah."

"Your husband left the baby's car seat with me so you could use it on the way home," he said, producing it from next to the telephone pole where Shelly had left it. When they brought his Buick sedan, Louie buckled the baby seat into the backseat and Ruthie lifted Sid into the seat and closed the strap around him.

On the console in Louie's car was the box from an audiocassette of William Faulkner reading passages from *As I Lay Dying*. "I guess you don't have *Dinosaur*

Ducks," Ruthie said. "Or *Winnie the Pooh and the Honey Tree*?"

"No," Louie said, smiling in a cute crooked way, "but I'll be glad to order them."

Eastbound traffic was bumper to bumper all along Sunset.

"You still working for Zev Ryder?" Louie asked.

"I'm sorry to say the answer to that is yes."

"He's a no-talent schmuck," Louie said.

"I couldn't have put it better myself."

"He hates women, Jews, and gays. I'm amazed you two have survived there this long."

"You call this surviving? He's already fired Shelly, he's constantly waiting for a reason to fire me. Every day has been a struggle."

"Want to work on one of my shows? Want to date me? Want to fall in love and marry me?"

Louie was kidding, but Ruthie was suddenly uncomfortable that Sid was hearing him say all of that, maybe because it was straight out of her fantasy of what she wished somebody would say. Somebody who would appear and save her from the dread she lived with every day.

"Yeah, sure," she said. They were pulling up outside her house.

"I mean it," he said. "Let's go to dinner one night. I won't jump you. I promise."

"I've got to go, Louie," she told him. "But thanks for the ride."

In the living room, Shelly sat on the sofa with the television on. He stared at it and channel-danced with the remote control. "Who brought you home?" he asked her.

"Louie Kweller."

"What did that rich asshole have to say?"

"He sends *you* his warmest regards."

"Whoopie."

"Daddy, come play."

"I will, honey," Shelly said to Sid, but he didn't move.

"Why don't we open some of our presents now? We don't have to keep the rules," Ruthie said. "As you so aptly pointed out, we're Jewish." Maybe opening presents would cheer Shelly up.

"Daddy! Open presents. We're Jewish," Sid said, climbing onto Shelly's lap. His sweet, innocent face made Shelly grin.

"Do you think we should?" Shelly teased.

"Yaaahhhh!" Sid replied, and climbed down to run to the tree. Ruthie and Shelly followed and watched Sid rip open the paper on his gifts: Talking Big Bird, and an airplane on wheels, the Match Box garage, and the Lego airport, and all of the *Star Wars* characters, and a child's tape player. Then Shelly opened his from Ruthie. An IBM personal computer, and an HP laserjet printer. After he tore off the paper, he pulled the Styrofoam packing out of the boxes and then all of the components.

Since the day they started writing, their style of putting words down had always been first in longhand on legal pads with pencil. When they weren't working on a show where a typist was provided, they typed their own drafts on a very old portable typewriter, then paid a typist to redo the script neatly. Now, staring at them, was the high tech of the 1990s.

"Merry Christmas," Ruthie said, knowing she'd gone a little overboard, but so what? Shelly pulled a manual out of the box and thumbed through it, shaking his head in wonder. "Shel, I know it seems overwhelming and confusing, but the best part of this gift is that I hired someone from the computer store to come over here at night and teach us how to use it. She's a terrific woman who's worked with a lot of writers, and she explains things in plain English, not computerese. She swears that in a few years we'll wonder how we ever lived without it."

Shelly put the thick notebook of a manual down on the coffee table and stood, then he nearly tripped over Sid, who was lying on his stomach running the Match Box cars along the floor and using the coffee table as a tunnel. Ruthie, who still held the first of her unopened gifts in her hand, watched him walk into his bedroom, and she followed him and stood in the doorway.

"What are you thinking?" she asked him. He sat on his bed, looking out of the French doors that opened onto a balcony.

"That in a few years I may not be here. Why do you think that corner of gifts for Sid is three feet high? I bought him stuff he won't be able to play with till he's twelve, because I figured when he was twelve, I wouldn't be around to give them to him. I don't want to take up any of my time learning how to use a computer."

"It won't take long. You learned to work the video camera, and goddamn you, in the time you take worrying about it, you could be learning it, mastering it. By next Christmas you could be Steve Wozniak, for God's sake. And a simple thank you will suffice." She was about to walk angrily out of the room when Sid came running in, carrying the gift he'd just unwrapped on his own, his Ninja Turtle evaporator gun, and he aimed it right at Ruthie. "Yaggggh," he shouted.

"That's what I like to see," Ruthie said. "Another satisfied customer."

In the living room she opened a package from Shelly to her. It was a professionally taken photograph of Sid. The two of them had gone to a studio as a surprise for Ruthie, and Shelly had the picture framed in an antique frame.

"I love you," Shelly said, coming into the living room.

"I love Mommy, too," Sid said and grabbed Ruthie hard around the leg. And Ruthie held the frame to her chest and loved them both so much she wanted to cry. But that didn't stop her from wondering at that same moment what Louie Kweller would be like in bed.

40

ON CHRISTMAS EVE Lainie's health club was open, so first she dropped Rosie off at her mother's house, where the baby went happily, and then she drove over to take an aerobics class. Today as the class started, the rock music was booming so loudly she could feel the floor under her feet vibrating. Because she liked to be able to see herself doing the exercises, she always worked out in the front row.

Today she looked in the mirror at her body, which had been decimated on the inside by illness, and thought how miraculous it was that the exterior still looked good, well-formed, shapely. Thank God, she thought, for good genes. Her mother, who had never owned a pair of tights or sweatpants, never even took a long brisk walk, still had a taut, thin body.

"Arms up and breathe, and exhale. And again, breathe into it, ladies, and feet apart, bend the knees and stretch."

Christmas Eve without Mitch, and all their rituals of the night before Christmas would be wrenching. Last year they bought ornaments that said *Baby's First Christmas*, and took Rosie, who had no idea what was going on, to the May Company to see Santa. This year Lainie hadn't even bought a tree. After class she would pick Rosie up, take her home and feed her, and rock her to sleep. After all I've been through, she thought, that should be enough of a celebration. I am alive and well and I have a baby. Thank heaven for those blessings.

When the heavy aerobic part of the class got under way, the uncomfortable pounding made her want to drop out, to give the teacher a little good-bye wave and just leave. But instead she made herself stay, and after a few minutes the rhythm was getting to her, and her spirits were lifting. Maybe it was endorphins, something she'd read about that was released in the brain during physical exertion. Whatever it was, by the end of the class she felt strong and powerful and ready to handle anything.

"She's been as good as gold," her mother said, opening the door for Lainie. Rosie ignored Lainie's entrance. She was sitting and playing with a musical jack-in-the-box next to her grandmother's two-foot-tall Christmas tree. It was the kind of tree Margaret Dunn had bought for herself over the years since her husband died, as if she were making the statement that a woman alone only needs half a tree.

"Her father called here," Margaret said to Lainie quietly as they stood in the foyer of her Studio City house. "Said he called your place to check on her, but when you weren't there he figured you'd probably be at school, so he tried me. He was in a foul mood."

"Really?" Lainie asked. She knew she was skating on thin ice. That unless she and Mitch put their marriage back together soon, her current custody of Rose was a limited privilege for which she would have to fight if there was a divorce. Mitch could drag her into court and say God knows what about the disposition of custody of the little baby girl he always referred to as "my daughter."

With a nod of her head Margaret invited Lainie into the living room, where she'd been all evening, watching the baby play from her recliner. "Join me?" she asked her daughter, gesturing at a bottle. Lainie rarely drank, because it was dangerous for a diabetic. Now and then she'd sometimes had a glass of champagne with Mitch to relax her in the days when she was trying to conceive, or to celebrate an anniversary.

"No . . . I don't think I can . . ." But the needy look on her mother's face made her reconsider.

"A short one?" Margaret asked.

It was Christmas Eve. Tomorrow Lainie would open gifts with Rosie in the morning, packages friends had sent over, toys she'd bought for the baby. Then Mitch would come to pick up the little angel and take her to one of his sister's houses where his family would be assembled. All of them would be glad, Lainie thought, that *she* was not among them. Then, because she'd promised she would, she would go over to her friend Sharon's Christmas party. It promised to be a time to get through, and move on to the new year. Barbara Singer had warned all the people in the group not to pin any expectations on the holidays. Well, Lainie thought, I should at least stay and have a glass of wine with my mother.

"All right," she said.

"We're both alone now," her mother said as she poured Lainie's wine. "I can only tell you that for me, it's the way I like it."

"I *don't* like it that way, Mother. I just don't know how to change it right now."

"Well, it looks to me as if it's a package deal. You want that baby? You're going to have to take Mitch. Otherwise I can tell you for certain, he's going to pull her away from you."

"Did he say that to you?" Lainie asked, worried.

"Darling, you forget. I work in an office that specializes in divorces. I've seen perfectly nice men turn into fire-breathing maniacs fighting over belongings they didn't even know they had until some lawyer told them they should go after it. Decks of cards, fish forks, we had one pull a gun on his wife until she handed over the papier-mâché napkin rings they bought together in Tijuana. So you can imagine how weird they can get when it comes to what they're going to do about their children."

Lainie took a gulp of wine and it tasted good. She was so unused to the effects of alcohol that after another sip heat flushed through her. When Rosie crawled over to her and into her lap, she kissed the top of the baby's little head, inhaling the sweet baby smell of her, and felt overwhelmingly helpless. All the strength she'd felt after the exercise class was gone.

"Mother," she said. "What are you doing for Christmas Day?"

"Oh, I don't know. Some of the girls at the office invited me to come by. But you know I'm not much for parties, so I'll probably stay put."

"Well, don't do that. I mean, you're right. We're both alone, and we shouldn't be." There was a loud plink, and then a screech of surprise as the jack-in-the-box popped out at Rosie, who slammed the lid of the box shut, and started turning the musical crank again.

"Why don't I stop at the Safeway near my house on my way home and pick up a turkey and some yams, I know you love yams, and tomorrow night you and I will have dinner together at my house. Mitch will bring

Rosie back at about seven-thirty. Please say yes. I don't want to go to any parties with strangers either. Let's do this."

Margaret Dunn was quiet, took another sip of wine as Lainie did too, then finally she answered. "On one condition."

"What's that?"

"That I can make some baked apples for dessert." Baked apples. The one dessert Lainie loved and didn't feel guilty about eating. The dessert her mother started making for her years ago, after Lainie had been diagnosed as a diabetic. A gesture of love.

"It's a deal," Lainie said. She would have company when Rosie and Mitch went off to spend their Christmas without her. And maybe she and her mother could strengthen their relationship. Both those thoughts made it easier for her to gather up Rosie's things and know she was taking her home to a Christmas Eve without Mitch.

She was driving down Ventura Boulevard when she started to feel it. A tingling inside her mouth. My God, she thought, knowing she should stop the car, pull over, and get herself something to take care of it, but the baby was with her and she wasn't sure where to stop. And it was too late because . . . she put her hand up to her hair and her head was soaking wet. Perspiring. Maybe she should turn into one of those side streets and pull over. For some reason the wheel felt hard to turn, but something, probably it was knowing she had the baby in the backseat, made her able to manage. At least get the car around the . . . red light. There was a flashing red light behind her. No. Her foot pushed down on the gas to get away from the red light.

But the red light was staying with her. Following her, and then a loud voice from somewhere said, "Pull over." For a minute she couldn't even remember how to pull over. So she turned the wheel hard and grazed a parked car and put her foot on the brake. And somehow she made her aching hand pull the emergency brake. The looming figure of a policeman was moving toward her. It had to be that he was coming over to save her from whatever was happening because she knew she was slipping away. The policeman stood next to the window now.

"Evening, ma'am. You seem to be having a problem."

Lainie was shaking and leaning against the steering wheel.

"May I please see your driver's license and registration?"

License was where? Purse. Yes.

"Um . . . I . . ."

"Ma'am, can I ask you to step out of the car?"

"Baby" was all she could get out.

"The baby will be all right," the officer said, opening Lainie's door, and Lainie, wobbly-legged, stepped out and fell against the policeman.

"Whoa, easy, lady," he said, steeling her, and a female officer got out of the car and came over to Lainie's car. She turned off the engine and Lainie could hear her talking gently to Rose. Most of what the policeman said to her next was a blur, about standing on one foot, which she knew she couldn't do even if she held on. To close her eyes and touch her finger to her nose. No, Mitch. Mother. Help. An insulin reaction. She should have eaten dinner before the exercise class, that was what the doctor warned her.

The policeman put handcuffs on her and edged her into the back of the police car, and said something to her about the fact that the woman officer was taking Lainie's car with Rosie in it, but Lainie was trembling and still unable to tell him she wasn't drunk, just very close to death.

She didn't remember much about what happened after that except that it was a miracle that they took her to the Van Nuys police station because there was a medic there who knew right away she was having an insulin reaction. He gave her orange juice immediately, which brought her blood sugar back to normal. Not a drunk driver, insulin reaction. Little by little the world came back into focus and when she was feeling as though she was able to get up and walk around, they brought her Rosie, who screamed "Mammmma" when she saw her, then buried her face in Lainie's neck and cried.

For a few minutes she sat holding the baby, trying to decide what to do. Christmas Eve in the police station. All she wanted to do was to be with Mitch. To be with Mitch and Rosie, her family. At the pay telephone she dialed her sister-in-law Betsy's number. When Betsy answered, Lainie heard the sounds of laughter and loud music in the background.

"Betsy," Lainie said from the pay phone of the police station. She was holding her baby on her hip and looking back at three people who were waiting in line to use the phone. "Let me talk to Mitch, please."

"Who *is* this?" Betsy asked with that bitchy edge she always had in her voice.

"It's his wife," Lainie answered.

She listened to the music and laughter in the background at Betsy's as she looked around the police station. A couple of hookers were being booked at the desk. When it took Mitch a very long time to get to the phone, Lainie imagined that his sisters were detaining him on his way to take the call, telling him what to say to her.

"Hello," Mitch said into the phone at last, and Lainie

was so moved by how it felt just hearing his voice that she had to catch her breath so she could talk.

"It's me," she said. "I'm at the Van Nuys police station. I had an insulin reaction which the police who stopped me thought was drunk driving, so they brought me in. Rose's fine, I'm fine. But Mitchie, in those few minutes when I was sure I was dying, all I could think about was that I miss you and I love you and I don't want to spend another minute of my life without you. And all the stuff with Jackie is going to have to be thought out and worked out and made right. But I know we can do it together. So, I think I can get us home from here all right, but what I want is for you to be there too, so we can work it all out."

"Baby," he said, "I'm there."

"Mitchie, I love you," she said.

"Oh, Lainie," he said, "God knows I love you like crazy."

Before Margaret Dunn came for Christmas dinner the next day, Lainie called to warn her that the evening would be a little different than she had described the night before. And that she should make four baked apples, because at dinner there wouldn't just be Lainie and Rosie waiting to see her, but Mitch too. And it would be a special Christmas for all of them.

41

THE AIRPORT NEWSSTAND was decorated for Christmas, and spread across the back wall once again were several magazine covers with pictures of Kate Sullivan in various attire and poses. *Ladies' Home Journal*, *Vanity Fair*, *People*, and *Los Angeles*. On *Los Angeles* she was wearing a red sweater and red tights and a Santa Claus hat. Her photograph was everywhere because she was promoting her new film, *Always a Lady*, the project that had once been Rick's; it was the studio's hot Christmas release. They were putting countless millions in advertising and publicity behind it, and she had directed it herself.

Last night every time Rick flicked the TV remote control, she was there. On CNN, on "Entertainment Tonight." "This is your first time out as a director," Leeza Gibbons was saying, Wendy Tush was saying, Larry King was saying. Kate Sullivan got exactly what she'd wanted all along. Not for Rick to direct her in the film, but to make the situation so intolerable for him that he'd be forced to walk away from it. Then she could say to the studio, "There's no one left to direct this, so I guess I'll have to do it myself."

What does it matter, he thought, knowing that the minute the holiday was over he'd be stepping back into the cold editing room where he'd spent the last few weeks and would spend the next several months cutting his own new film. And the months would only be broken in their intensity by daily visits from the nanny bringing David to visit, or by midnight dinners with Patty, who understood the director's life-style so well from her years with Charlie Fall.

Patty, bless her pretty face, was so solid. Some nights she just showed up at the editing room with a picnic basket of food she'd prepared. And she'd not only cater for Rick, but the editors too. Then she'd slip away, leaving a flower or a funny note. David's nanny said Patty stopped by the house now and then to check on the little boy too.

When the editing process was complete, Rick would have to wait through that agonizing trying-not-to-think-about-it time until his film was released and he learned what the audiences thought of it and what the critics thought of it. What did it matter? This morning he'd spent three hours lying on his stomach on the floor of his living room, setting up an electric train underneath the eight-foot-tall Christmas tree. And *that* was the kind of thing that felt important to him these days.

Then, as David happily watched the train go round and round through the miniature village, clapping and shouting every time it passed, Rick made popcorn and strung all the pieces David hadn't eaten, and soon there was yards of it. Then he held David up high so the little guy could sling the long white strings across each branch of the tree, because that was what Rick's parents had done with him every year when he was small.

After lunch they had a party to attend, so Rick bathed David and dressed him, showered and dressed himself, and pointed his car west toward the address on St. Cloud Road. There were live reindeer in the front yard, and a backyard full of imported snow, which, thanks to the cold wave, wasn't melting. There was an actor in a Santa Claus suit giving gifts to the children, pretty girls dressed as Santa's elves passing hors d'oeuvres, and a lot of familiar people from the business.

David sat in his usual spot on Rick's shoulders looking over the crowd. A few passersby waved to the cute baby as Rick stopped and talked about his latest projects with an agent from CAA and a guy he knew from Disney. Then at one of the buffet tables, without bothering to get a plate, he made himself a roast beef sandwich on a small roll, ate that quickly, and followed it with a ham sandwich, which he munched while he handed pieces of fruit up to David, who put them in his mouth and let their juice roll down his chin and onto Rick's head.

When a strikingly pretty young actress reached past Rick to get a napkin roll filled with silverware, he said to her, "I know it's probably the pineapple juice on my forehead that makes you think I'm attractive, isn't it?"

The girl looked blankly at him, then up at David, then back at Rick and said, "Ahhh, your grandson is really cute."

Rick let out a loud burst of a laugh in appreciation of the joke, then looked around to see who was watching. He was trying to figure out who had set the girl up to say that to him, but there was no one around that he recognized. She wasn't kidding, and certainly he was easily the right age for her to think that. But for some reason it didn't matter to him one bit.

"You know what?" he said to David as the girl strolled away. "I think it's time for you and me to go to the airport."

"And see airplanes!" David said in agreement.

Now the two of them were at the same gate where Rick stood lifetimes ago when he'd waited alone for the pregnant Doreen to arrive. She had been a little pink puff of a girl then, and he was aware that the time which had passed since he last saw her would make a difference in her appearance, but he wasn't prepared for the person who walked through that same door today. Something about her appearance, much more dramatic than the added years, was so different it startled him. It was her entire mien, her posture, the look in her eyes, and it could only be described as beaten.

The sight of Rick brought a nod of acknowledgment as their eyes met, but hers were the eyes of an unhappy woman. Light-years older and wiser than the ones that used to contain an irrepressible twinkle. The sight of David at Rick's side brought first a look of amazement but then a look of pain, filling Rick with instant regret that his hopes for this visit had been foolish, or worse yet, a cruel mistake.

"Hello, you guys," she said, offering her best smile, which was meager, and hugging Rick weakly. David grabbed Rick's pant leg and hid behind it.

"A shy guy, huh?" Doreen said and knelt, and when he peeked around and looked at her and repeated, "A shy guy," she squeaked happily, "He talks like a big boy!"

In the car she sat in the back with David and held his tiny hand, but said very little to Rick. "How's Uncle B.?" she asked at one point, and Rick filled her in on Bobo's life and illnesses and friends at the home, looking in the rearview mirror to see if she reacted, but for the most part she looked blankly out the window.

At the house she unpacked gifts, which she stacked under the tree, and then she walked around the kitchen helping Rick with the dinner preparations while she held David, who never left her arms for hours. He babbled, impressing her with his vocabulary, amusing himself by trying to remove the eyeglasses from her face.

When the last fork was laid on the table and the dinner was bubbling away on the stove, the doorbell rang.

"Yayyy," David shouted, running to the door.

God, they were a beautiful sight to Rick, the whole group of them standing in the doorway. What could make your heart dance like the faces of the people you loved? It was raining so they hurried in. Howard and Mayer and Mayer's billowy blond fiancée, Lisa, were holding brightly wrapped gifts. And Patty, smashing-looking in a bright red coat, was holding Bobo's arm, giving Rick a look he knew meant it had been a near miracle for her to get the old man here. But it was worth it all when David shouted, "Uncle Bobobobobobo!" and Bobo laughed a big hearty laugh, and said, "Hiya, *boychik*."

This is the best night of my life, Rick thought to himself as he took their coats and introduced Doreen to the boys and to Patty. I have a family. A support system, Barbara Singer calls them. Rick looked at Doreen, flushed and wiping her hands self-consciously on the kitchen towel she'd stuck in the waistband of her slacks. She was okay with Bobo, who greeted her warmly, but she seemed awkward with Patty and the boys and Lisa. A few times she called Patty "Mrs. Fall" and Rick overheard Patty say, "Please call me Patty."

Howard was focused on a computer game some friend had given him and he was pushing buttons so it blipped and bleeped. Soon Doreen was sitting next to him on the sofa, and Howard gave her a turn at it, and they were laughing together. Lisa oohed and ahhed over David, and Mayer roughhoused with him. Rick carved the turkey and Patty arranged the plates in the kitchen and brought them to the table. By the time they were eating, Rick was relieved to see Doreen joking with both the boys and Lisa. Yes, she was doing fine, holding her own, seated next to David's high chair, wiping cranberry sauce from his chin.

"This kid's a genius," Howard said. "You know those games where they have all the different shaped holes and then the blocks to put in them? He never misses."

"That's because he has such great genes," Doreen said and laughed.

Bobo and Patty were chatting away too, and the time really felt right for what he wanted to say, so Rick picked up his spoon and tapped gently on his wineglass.

"Attention, please. I know as soon as this meal is over we're rushing over to the Christmas tree to dig into our gifts, but there's one gift I'd like to give separately from the others because this is for someone who has done so much for my life, and I want to acknowledge her with a gift that isn't under the tree."

As he was about to take the gift out of his pocket, he caught sight of Doreen's face and knew by the way she reddened and her half smile that she thought he'd been speaking about her. And that when she realized he wasn't, she might be hurt. When he looked at Patty he could tell by *her* expectant eyes that he had to go on. So he pulled the box out of his shirt pocket, looked at Patty, and said what he'd thought about for weeks. "If you like we can have a very long engagement until you decide how you feel, but I'd like to ask you to marry me and David too."

There was an instant of shocked silence until the two boys laughed and said, "Oh wow!"

"How romantic," Lisa said.

"Thank the good Lord I lived to see it," Bobo said chuckling.

Patty opened the box to see the diamond ring Rick had chosen after endless meetings with a jeweler. When she looked at Rick, her eyes were sparkling brighter than the stone and she said, "This is completely crazy. You're completely crazy, and I should take a long time to decide, like forty or fifty years. But right here in front of God and everybody, I have to admit I really would like to marry you both."

He stood, she stood, and they embraced. Mayer lifted David out of the high chair and squashed the little boy in a happy hug, and it sounded to Rick as if he said, "I've got another brother." Then Patty, visibly shaken, walked over to Bobo's chair and hugged the old man, who was grinning happily. The boys hugged their mother, and Mayer said, "My dad would have been happy about this. He loved you, Uncle Ricky." And Lisa hugged Patty and said, "Maybe we should have a double wedding," and Bobo said, "Just make it soon, will you, I'm a very old man."

Doreen had a smile on her face as she watched it all, as if she were watching a movie, and when Rick went over to hug her he felt her body tense. Maybe, he thought too late, making the announcement tonight when she was here was wrong. He had hoped it would make her happy to see David getting an experienced grown-up woman as a mother. But probably she felt afraid that her own relationship with David would now be threatened.

"She'll be good with him," she said as they all sat back down to eat.

Rick could hardly wait for them to open their gifts. Howard was fascinated with computers but was still using his old Apple II, so Rick bought him a brand-new Macintosh. There was a thirty-five-millimeter camera

Mayer had been longing for and Rick bought that for him with two lenses. Bobo liked to think of himself as a dapper dresser, so both Rick and Patty bought him clothes, including a beautiful robe from Neiman-Marcus. That way he could still look handsome to the ladies at the Motion Picture Home on those days when he was too tired to put on his street clothes.

For David's Christmas, Rick had gone totally berserk. A rocking horse, and a playhouse and a climbing gym for outdoors, a jeep that the boy could get inside and drive with his feet, and a whale he could sit on in the pool. Rick, so full of joy tonight, wondered where Christmas had been for him for so many years. Aside from a dinner with Bobo at some restaurant in the Valley, he had spent most of them at parties like the one he and David had attended that afternoon. Parties populated with people who took each other's hands in their own and with the most sincere expression they could muster looked into each other's eyes and said, "We're family." But not one of them gave a shit about the others, unless there was a deal to be made. Family.

One of Doreen's gifts from Rick was a college guidebook accompanied by a note which said *IOU four years of college tuition*, something he thought would thrill her, but instead he saw her trying to summon enthusiasm. She's a teenager, he thought, they live in the now, she doesn't understand at this moment what that's going to mean to her life. He wasn't surprised when the curling iron and hair dryer and vanity mirror Patty had bought for her got a bigger reaction.

On the last day of her visit, she was quiet, sitting next to David on the trip back to the airport. The baby, who had been chatty and giggly at first, fell asleep in the car seat.

"What have you told Bea about why you ran away?" Rick asked her, breaking the silence.

"Nothing yet."

"You know you have to tell her, don't you? To tell someone."

"Well, I didn't want to spoil everyone's holidays, because it's going to be ugly when I finally do tell. I've been thinking about exactly what I'm going to say," and for the first time since she arrived he heard a lilt in her voice, as if she knew what she was telling him now would please him. "But I'm just trying to figure out when the best time is to say it. I mean, Don and my sister have been fighting a lot. I keep thinking he's going to leave her any day now, and that'll make it easier to do what I have to do." Rick felt assured by the sound of hope in her voice that soon things would work out for the best.

"When you're ready to prosecute, I'll pay the legal bills, no matter how high they are. You're doing the right thing, you know that, don't you?"

"Oh yes" was all she said.

At the airport when her flight was called, she knelt and looked into David's little face, and Rick was amazed at the way the child didn't fidget, didn't move while she talked to him, but seemed to take every word with great seriousness.

"Good-bye, little darling," she said. "I can't tell you how I hate to leave you. But at least I know that you're getting a mother and some big brothers. And even though you may not exactly remember this visit years from now, somewhere inside you you'll know that I was here. Now give me one last hug, and please make it a big one, 'cause it's gonna have to last me for a long, long time."

David must have understood every word because he put his pudgy arms around her neck, his mother's neck, and squeezed very hard, while Rick looked at them together and wished he could stop her from leaving.

Call the police, adopt her too. But there was nothing he could do, until and unless she was willing to reveal what happened to her. He longed for the magical solution that could put him between her and the onslaught of pain she would have to face before things would get better for her.

"I love you," she said to David, then stood and hugged Rick. She was already turned toward the jetway when she tossed the words "And I love you too" over her shoulder, and was gone.

She'll tell Bea, he promised himself. But for weeks he couldn't get the image of the once feisty girl who had walked like a zombie through their Christmas together out of his head.

The day the letter arrived at the office it was opened first, as were all letters to the office, by Andrea, who came in and handed it to him, and without even seeing it he knew by her face who it was from and what it would say. And as he read it, he felt as though he'd been slammed against the wall.

Dear Mr. Reisman,

I am writing this to tell you we lost our sweet Doreen this week, when she took her own life. She didn't leave a note, but for a really long time she seemed sad and scared to me. I know she trusted you a lot and I did too, or I wouldn't have let her come and stay with you at Christmas, so I figured you would want to know.

That little baby was always in her heart. Maybe giving him up was too hard for her to live with, or maybe I was wrong and being able to come and see him wasn't the best thing. I wish I knew, though it wouldn't bring her back. Maybe some boy at school hurt her and broke her heart. My other kids are feeling really awful that she's gone.

Bea Cobb

Andrea sat next to him and they held on to each other. He could feel her trembling, or was that him trembling with rage, and pain, and sorrow? Why didn't he see it or know that when Doreen knelt in the airport and looked at David as if it was for the last time that it *was* the last time? Now he remembered the words she'd said. Somewhere inside you, you'll know that I was here. Rick left the office and went home and held David on his lap all day, reading to him, talking to him, hugging him, noticing more than ever how many of his expressions were Doreen's. Then he called Patty and told her the news, and how glad he was that he had her to love.

42

ON CHRISTMAS EVE Judith's baby, Jody, had an ear infection, and the pediatrician's answering service didn't seem to be able to reach the doctor who was on call. So the baby screamed and Judith walked from room to room, holding her against her chest to try to soothe her. After a while the noise of her little sister's screams woke Jillian, and she climbed out of her crib and followed Judith and the baby around the house and hung on to the hem of her mother's bathrobe.

When the doctor finally called and said he'd be glad to telephone a prescription to the drugstore in her neighborhood if Judith would tell him which one was open, she realized she had no idea which one was open. So with the screaming Jody in her arms and her toddler daughter sitting on the floor tugging her robe so hard it was coming off her shoulders, she pulled out the yellow pages and called around to find an open drugstore. When she found one, after her eighth phone call, she asked the pharmacist to please call the pediatrician, had him give her directions from her house to the drugstore, and told him she was on her way.

Then she dressed herself and picked up the two babies, got each of them as settled as possible in their car seats, and drove toward the north Valley where the drugstore was located. It was miles from her home and the baby screamed all the way there, not quite drowning out the Christmas carols Judith put on the radio in order to calm them. Jillian sat in her car seat directly behind the driver's seat, kicking it to the rhythm of each familiar song, jolting her mother with each kick. In the parking lot of the shopping center, Judith unloaded both little ones from their car seats, sat one on each of her hips, grabbed her purse, and started toward the drugstore. She was hoping their pajamas were warm enough, because it was raining.

The pharmacist was harassed. It was, he announced unhappily and irritably to Judith, his busiest night in years. The round baby-toy rack kept Jillian happy as she spun it and squealed at all the brightly colored bubble-packed toys flashing by her. That was fine with Judith, who had her hands full with the baby, still howling in agonized pain. When the pharmacist mercifully handed Judith the bottle of pink ampicillin, she opened it, and with a little dropper she fed the wincing-at-the-taste baby her first dose immediately.

Within a very few minutes, maybe just the time it took for Judith to pay the pharmacist, the baby seemed better. She was quiet and falling asleep on her mommy's shoulder. But the sudden crash to the floor of the toy rack woke her and caused Jillian to join her in shrill crying, as the pharmacist, assuring Judith he didn't mind picking up the many dozens of fallen toys, walked them to the door and showed them out.

"Merry Christmas," he called out to them as Judith

carried her two crying children to the car through the night rain. By the time she had them back in their car seats and had started the car, they were soaked through and shivering. She turned on the car heat, and hoped that maybe the ride home would put them to sleep. Dear God, she thought driving down Van Nuys Boulevard through the pounding rain, I've been a horrible selfish woman bringing these babies into the world without a daddy.

But then she adjusted her rearview mirror so she could look at the two of them in the backseat. Their little faces looked angelic as the red and green Christmas decorations of the boulevard passed, casting their lights on them. "I love you two," she said, full of emotion at the miracle that had blessed her with them, and she felt good and strong.

At home she changed their clothes and their diapers, tucked baby Jody into her crib, and Jillian into hers. When they were finally asleep, she started a fire in the fireplace. I'm blessed, she thought. I have my babies and that's all I need. I'm not going to sit around feeling sorry for myself or them. We're a happier family than some of the intact ones I know where the parents are fighting and divorcing and cheating on each other.

She had just taped a bow on the box containing the talking teddy bear, when she heard the baby cry out. The pharmacist had told her if Jody woke in the night, she could give her another dose of the medicine, as long as it had been three hours since the first dose. She hurried to the refrigerator where she kept the awful-looking pink liquid and went to comfort her poor little baby girl. After administering another dropperful of medicine, she changed Jody's diaper. Then she scooped her into her arms and rocked her while she sang "Santa Claus Is Coming to Town." And the minute she was asleep and Judith had placed her gently into her crib, Jillian called out to her.

Jillian's diaper was dirty, so Judith put her on the changing table, removed the dirty diaper, and squatted to look on the lower shelf for a new box of premoistened baby wipes. And during that instant Jillian took the open bottle of ampicillin her mother had forgotten to close after she'd diapered the baby, and chugged some incalculable amount of it down. When Judith stood and saw her daughter still holding the bottle to her lips, the pink medicine all over her face, her knees buckled with panic.

"Jillie, no! Did you drink that? Oh, my God. I left it open. Oh no." Clutching Jillian to her, she ran to the phone and dialed the doctor's number again. "This is an emergency!" she said to the doctor's answering service operator. "Please get him on the phone." Why hadn't she learned something about poison control? Who could she call? Maybe she should dial 911. The phone rang almost immediately. "Meet me at the emergency room," the doctor told her, and within seconds she had awakened the baby, stuffed both of the children into their car seats, and was off again into the rainy night.

A nurse held sleepy Jody in her arms at the nurses' station so Judith could stay with Jillian, who screamed and retched while they pumped her stomach, and Judith could hardly keep herself from vomiting. When they were able to leave the hospital it was dawn. Christmas morning. While two nurses watched the babies, Judith went into the little antiseptic ladies' room in the hospital corridor to splash some cold water on her face to prepare for the drive home. As she dabbed her eyes with a harsh paper towel from the cold aluminum dispenser, she looked at what had become of herself, and felt right on that edge of emotion where she could either laugh or cry.

That painful but absurd place where it seems as if anything that might have gone wrong has, and you can either lie down on the floor and kick your feet or dance with relief that you've survived the latest onslaught. "Merry Christmas," she said to her reflection, and that made her laugh. She was wearing an old chenille bathrobe over her flannel nightgown and some fuzzy blue slippers she had ordered from the Norm Thompson catalogue about seven years ago; her usually well-kept red hair was dry and flyaway, and the circles under her eyes were now so long and low they were invading her cheeks. She sighed, and walked into the corridor where one of the nurses stood holding a sleeping Jillian and another stood holding the sleeping Jody.

"Thank you," Judith said to them, so grateful for the tender way they had treated her babies.

"Why don't we walk you out?" one of the nurses asked.

"That would be great."

Judith followed behind as they made their way in an odd little parade down the long hospital corridor. This is all a test, she thought. But I will pass it. At home she put both of the children on her big bed, put herself between them, and they all slept until noon. When they woke, Jody seemed to be one-hundred-percent cured, and Jillian was as chipper as if nothing had happened. So after Jillian had torn into all of her Christmas packages and Jody had rejected all of the toys in favor of the boxes in which they'd been packaged, Judith put them each in a fancy dress and took them out to a party.

"I realized something about myself over the holidays," she said to the group after she'd regaled them with what was now the funny version of her Christmas Eve and Christmas Day. "And what's so interesting to me is that what I got from the whole experience is that I like it this way. Love it this way. Don't want anybody to interfere with the decisions I make for them, don't want to compromise my life-style one bit, and I chose this life-style because I want control. I know it's going to be tough for me on occasion after occasion, but I can do it.

"So what I want to know is, is it okay," she asked Barbara, "for me to be this way? I mean I'm sure we can go deep into my psyche and figure out how my father treated my mother and on and on, but whatever the reason, I know I'm happiest this way. My life, however different it may seem to other people, feels great to me. And now that I really know that, I can stop falling prey to every fix-up, and quit apologizing for the fact that I'm a single mother as if it's just a stopgap on the road to a kind of normalcy I don't want."

"I think," Barbara said, "you just answered your own question, Judith. But also try to give yourself the flexibility to change your mind, when and if that happens."

"Rick," Ruthie said, "you look bad. Are you feeling all right?"

Rick shook his head but didn't speak, looked away from the others and out at David to check on him. Ruthie was right. He was hollow-eyed and gray-faced.

"Doreen is gone," he said, looking at all of them. "It was a suicide. Her mother thinks the reason was her parting with David, maybe even about her coming here for Christmas. I know it had to do with what was going on with her at home, but now with her gone, what can I do . . . ."

"Oh, Rick." The others surrounded him, touching his hands, his shoulders, putting their arms around him.

"And I feel as if in part I contributed to the unhappiness, because right in front of her at Christmas, I proposed to Patty."

Silence.

"So?" Shelly asked.

"So that must have made Doreen afraid that she'd become less important to David. Maybe she would lose her link with him."

"Rick," Barbara said, "the possibility that you would marry was always there whether you thought so or not."

Rick just shook his head.

"I'm so happy for me," he said, "and so god-awful sad for that little girl. Being the parent of that little boy has transformed me, shown me the world through a pair of innocent, loving eyes. Taught me how to need someone and be needed. And most of all taught me about priorities. Now I know that in the final analysis it really is the way we love that matters, and everything else is completely beside the point.

"When I look back at the years I spent before this baby was in my life, sometimes I'm appalled at the time I wasted on so many unimportant endeavors and projects and problems and anxieties. But then I realize that it's okay. That none of that was really for naught, because it was all about teaching me to get here, to this mind-set, to this relationship with Patty."

After a long quiet time Barbara spoke. "Well, it's pretty clear that the De Nardos had a good holiday," she said, looking at Lainie and Mitch, whose chairs were close to each other's and who held tightly on to each other's hands.

Lainie spoke in her quiet way. "I'm starting to feel comfortable with expanding our concept of family to in some ways include Jackie. It doesn't diminish me, and for Rosie, the more people who love her, the better she'll feel about herself. The trick will be getting her to understand all of this when she gets older. But that's when I think the openness is going to pay off the most and make what seems to be the strange part work.''

These people are amazing, Barbara thought. What these babies have done to open up their lives is extraordinary.

''And what about your family? How were your holidays?'' Barbara asked Ruthie and Shelly. Shelly answered.

''We're okay. I hated the parties, but I think Ruthie and Sid had a pretty good time. In fact, as a result of all the socializing, some man is pursuing Ruthie. Calls our house every day.'' It was clear he was kidding Ruthie. A little kidding on the square.

''Oh, Shel, cut it out,'' Ruthie said and gave him a tap on the arm. ''I'm not one bit interested in him.''

''Want to talk about it, Ruth?'' Barbara asked.

''No,'' Ruthie snapped.

''I want you to,'' Shelly said.

''There's nothing to talk about,'' Ruthie said, her eyes angry now. And that was when the little ones came toddling in to have their snack.

43

BARBARA TURNED HER CAR into the parking lot of the Rexall drugstore on Beverly and La Cienega, and looked across the street at the Beverly Center shopping mall. She remembered two decades ago when there had been nothing on that same lot but Beverly Park, an amusement center for children, which had a few toddler rides and a pony ring. It had always been the hands-down favorite spot for both Heidi and Jeff on a Sunday morning. They loved to be taken there and sit proudly on one of the harnessed ponies and ride around and around the ring waving as they passed Barbara and Stan.

An unexpected shadow of sadness moved across her face, and it made her want to cry. For days she hadn't felt well. Maybe it was an ulcer, or a hiatal hernia, or some other digestive problem, but her queasiness wouldn't go away. That was the reason she had stopped at the drugstore, so she could go in and get herself some

Tums or Rolaids to take away that constant feeling of heaviness in her abdomen.

Inside the big bustling drugstore, she was planning to walk straight to the antacid counter, get what she wanted, and leave, but instead she found herself walking to the train of empty shopping carts, extracting one, and steering it toward the beckoning aisles of merchandise. She loved drugstores, the millions of colors, the glossy posters that advertised blushers and nail polish and lipsticks. And the constant barrage of new products. Like a spray to put in a travel case that would remove wrinkles from clothes, or a new kind of diet powder that she had seen advertised in magazines which had already made lots of famous fat people thin.

Feminine hygiene. She slowed the cart down in that aisle, grabbed a box of tampons, and was just about at the end of the aisle when she stopped to look right at what she now had to admit to herself was what she had really come into the drugstore to buy. An EPT. Early pregnancy test. My God, what if what she was fearing was true? Her period was only a little late, and at her age, as Howie Kramer had reminded her more than once, she was premenopausal, so the irregularity was to be expected. But maybe she should buy it as a catalyst. Surely buying one of those tests, wasting the seventeen dollars, would be exactly what she had to do to bring her period on. But she knew she was playing games with herself, because there was no doubt in her mind that she was absolutely, unequivocally, one-thousand-percent pregnant. At age forty-two.

She remembered the feeling from the early stages of both her pregnancies, which now seemed as if they were a million years ago. That bloated, weary, swollen-breasted, full-of-tears, moody feeling, and she didn't need an EPT to tell her it was so. Stan, she imagined herself saying, I'm pregnant. What in the world would he say to that? Hooray? After all, he had suggested the idea of their having another baby not very long ago. But he was kidding when he said it, she reminded herself. He was thinking about buying second homes and traveling and running through the house naked.

How about, Guess what, Heidi, I'm pregnant! That would be the hardest of all. After her own failed engagement and her childhood friend having a new baby girl. A few months ago she was the one who was looking at apartments with room for a nursery. Heidi would look at her, her mouth hanging open in shock, and say, "No way!" She'd be mortified.

Yes, she thought. Maybe if she bought the test she'd get her period. She threw the EPT into her shopping cart and made her way toward the cashier. But before she got there she stopped back at the feminine hygiene aisle, took the big blue box of tampons out of her cart, and put it back on the shelf.

That night at home, she looked at her swollen naked breasts in the full-length mirror on the back of her bathroom door, and then looked down at the body that had carried and brought forth Heidi twenty-four years earlier and Jeff seventeen years earlier. Her body, which was undeniably a little too round in the belly, too wide in the waist, too meaty around the hips, and had no tone whatsoever anywhere else, and she wondered what would become of it after a mid-life pregnancy.

Dear God, she thought, I don't think I can do this. When this child is seven years old, I'll be a fifty-year-old woman. Babies cry all night. Babies feed on demand. Babies require constant care every minute. Am I ready to give up the travel I postponed, first to have kids, then to go to school, and then because I was too busy at work?

Just as I was getting to the point in my life where I could take a big deep breath. Her breasts pulsed with a hot ache from deep inside. So soon into the pregnancy. A baby who will come forcing its way into the world past gray pubic hairs. No! The pubic hairs would be shaved. Oh please. She'd forgotten *that* indignity and the enema that went with it, and the awful itch when the hair started to grow in. And that was the least of the physical discomfort.

Years of no sleep, potty training, the terrible twos. Maybe this is PMS, she thought. Maybe my forty-two-year-old hormones are so out of whack they're causing me to lose my mind. Maybe they're making me imagine that I could actually still be fertile. She took the early pregnancy test out of the bag and looked at the box, opened it, and took out the directions. She had picked this particular test because it didn't require her to use her first morning urine, the way some of them did. This was one she could do at any time. Like right now.

She removed the funny dipstick from the box, watching herself in the mirror as if it were someone else performing this bizarre act. Then she locked the bathroom door so Stan wouldn't pop in on her, and then found that she didn't remotely have any urge to urinate. In fact she was certain she couldn't have squeezed out even a drop. For a long time she stood leaning against the tile counter, staring at herself, wondering what to do.

Pregnant. Mother, I'm pregnant. Gracie would probably laugh at her, then tell her about all the other cultures where older women had babies. No, she wouldn't tell Gracie, or Heidi or Jeff yet. When she found out if she was pregnant, which she knew she was, she would tell Stan and discuss the truth, which was that having a baby at this stage of their lives was probably a big mistake.

Dr. Gwen Phillips was in her late thirties. When Barbara was being escorted from the reception area to an examining room, after a wait that was only as long as it took to fill out a few forms, she passed the young female gynecologist's office and saw the doctor at her desk holding a baby boy.

"That's the doctor's son," the nurse told Barbara.

Maybe I'm lulling myself into a false sense of security here, Barbara thought, feeling defiant and proud of herself for finally breaking the Howie Kramer cycle, but I like this doctor already and I haven't even met her yet. When she'd undressed and was seated on the table, the first thing she noticed was the little knitted bootielike casings around each of the stirrups. Obviously they were put there to make the damn things feel a little softer and warmer. When Gwen Phillips entered, she was carrying a pillow which she gently placed behind Barbara's back.

"Mrs. Singer," she said. "I just checked your urine, and I hope this is good news. You're pregnant."

"I know," Barbara said. "I knew before I did the early pregnancy test. I've been trying to figure out how I got so careless. And frankly I'm not so sure if it's good news or not."

"Tell me your concerns and maybe I can help," the doctor said.

Howie Kramer, Barbara thought, you will never see me again. At least not without my pants on. "My concerns. Well, let's see, where do I start? My daughter is twenty-four and my son is seventeen. When I tell them, they'll probably disown me. I have a full-time career, and clients who really need me. I was recently entertaining the thought of retirement so I could do nothing for a few years. I will probably have to wear glasses to see my own baby. I dye my hair to get rid of the gray and I know for a fact that's unhealthy for pregnancies, and most of all, I don't want to interrupt my sleep on Saturday mornings to watch 'Smurfs.' "

The pretty young doctor was serious. "Are you saying you want to terminate the pregnancy?"

Barbara felt a distant wave of nausea heading in her direction. "I don't know what I'm saying. I mean, I thought I was on my way to being a grandmother. Granted, an early grandmother, but not this. A mommy, again. I mean . . . listen, I wanted to come in just to be sure that I was, but now that I know that I truly am . . . I have to think this through."

"If it helps, I can assure you that I've delivered many healthy babies to women your age and much older too, and with proper prenatal care and testing, the pregnancies and the deliveries have been problem-free."

"Oh, it's not the pregnancy or the delivery, though I'll admit they worry me a little," Barbara said. "It's really the time after the pregnancy and delivery that worries me. The part where they look at you one day and say, 'Mom, get off my case.' "

The doctor smiled. "I understand," she said. "Listen, why don't I give you a prescription for some prenatal vitamins and you can call me in a few days and we can talk about it some more." After she wrote the prescription, the doctor shook Barbara's hand, said to call her at any time day or night if she just needed a sounding board about the pregnancy, and left the room.

"You have great hair," Barbara said to her, but the doctor didn't hear that because she was already out the door and on to put a pillow behind the back of her next patient.

44

RUTHIE WAS ALONE in the Zimmerman and Milton cubbyhole of an office at the network trying to make the script come together, but it wasn't happening. Her face throbbed with exhaustion, and she was wondering if the fluorescent lights were really dimming or if her eyes were going bad from too many hours of close work when she heard someone walking down the hall. Probably it was the night-shift guard checking to see who was left in the building. Maybe she would knock off now, gather her things together and ask the guard to walk her out to her car. It was late and she'd been so engrossed, she'd forgotten to check in at home. Both Shelly and Sid would be asleep by now.

The footsteps stopped and she looked up, sure it was a mirage when she saw Louie Kweller.

"I was already in the parking lot when I spotted your light on up here so I came to say hello," he said. "I guess we're the only two fanatics who work this late."

"Hi," she said, surprised at how happy she was to see him, and worried about how bad she must look, since she'd been sitting in that same spot for the last six hours, and her hair was probably frizzed out to the moon.

"So what's happening?" he asked as if they'd just bumped into each other on a street corner instead of in the back-hall offices at CBS, at what Ruthie, without looking at a clock, knew had to be at least two in the morning.

"What's happening is that I can't figure out how to end the second act," she said.

"Well, let's see," Louie said, and she could tell by his expression that he was searching for something cute to say. "How about if she runs into a guy she knew a long time ago, and she can't believe that she never noticed before what a sexy hunk he is? He's crazy about her, always has been, so she starts dating him and the next thing you know, they get married, and have a few kids together. She already has one kid, and he's so happy to have siblings that he thrives. Then they all live happily ever after, because their life is made into a movie of the week."

"I'll use it," she said. "Have your agent call me to negotiate the fee."

Louie wandered over and sat in Shelly's chair across from her, right under the needlepoint sampler that said DYING IS EASY, COMEDY IS HARD. The night was very black outside and Ruthie looked at the window's reflection of her messy office and Louie leaning back in the chair as he gazed at her. The fluorescent lights hummed like crickets.

"Listen," he said after a while, "I don't want to do something bad to Shelly. He's a terrific man. Talented and smart and a good person. I also think your loyalty to him is awesome. But as far as we know, we each only get one life, and maybe you ought to think about having some romance in yours. Maybe even another baby. I'll make a baby with you, or two or three."

"Louie," she said, looking at his serious face and wishing she didn't feel like crying. "You don't even know me. I'm overwhelming, I'm needy, I crack dumb jokes at all the wrong times. I look ugly in the morning, not just sleepy but like a beast. I go on strange diets that make me cranky, or should I say crankier because I can be a complete bitch, and I may need some expensive dental work coming up in the near future."

"I understand that you feel that way, and I just want to go on record as telling you you're my favorite person in Hollywood. I think you're funnier than Joan Rivers, deeper than Anjelica Huston, sweeter than Melanie Griffith, and—"

"Taller than Danny DeVito," Ruthie said.

"Yeah. That too."

"See, I told you I make dumb jokes."

"Unfortunately for you I happen to like that in a woman. In fact I like it a lot. In the old days at the Comedy Store, I used to have the wildest crush on you. Remember the night a zillion years ago when Frankie Levy did your run about supermarkets?"

Did she remember? "It was the night Shelly and I got our first prime-time television job," she said.

"Well, I wanted to come over to you right after Frankie walked offstage, grab you, and take you away to an island somewhere and jump on you, but Eddie Shindler was doing my stuff next so I had to watch him."

"You mean you put *your* career before *my* sex life?" she teased.

"You and Shelly must have left early that night, because I looked for you, and when you were gone I felt like a jerk and just figured maybe I ought to leave you alone, so here I am, how many years later? Don't answer that, and I'm making another try for you and that island. So what do you say?"

"I say it's a pretty thought, Louie, but I don't think I can accept."

"I'll tell you what. Why don't you ask Shelly about it? Talk to him. I know for a fact that he loves you. So maybe you should ask him if you shouldn't spend some time with me to see if you like me, and I guarantee you he'll say you should go for it. And, Ruthie, I promise you, if it works out with us, when the time comes and Shelly needs you to take care of him, I'll never resent one minute of your doing that. I'll help you do it. I'll support your doing it. Only I'm asking you to not give up your own life now in anticipation of that time."

"Louie, I've trusted too many people who disappointed me. Your speech about the Comedy Store and the island is great. And I mean it as a compliment when I tell you it sounds just like something one of the characters from your show would say. I wish with my soul that you meant it, and maybe you do. But in my repertoire of feelings, the ability to be swept away by romantic love doesn't exist anymore."

"I understand," Louie said softly. "I understand. So why don't I walk you to your car?"

Shelly was having the time of his life with the computer. The woman Ruthie hired from the Writers' Computer Store spent three afternoons with him, and by the time she left after their third session, he was up and running on what had a week earlier been "the dreaded machine." Ruthie could hear him in his room, now and then emitting a "this is incredible," dazzled by his own prowess. Sometimes he would come and get her and make her stand behind him to observe the magic tricks of moving and editing text, telling her that this gift made up for all the toys he never had as a kid.

She no longer went to work fearing she was leaving him at home to watch daytime television. In fact when she called him from the office, he would talk to her in a kind of mindless answering-the-questions-without-listening style that she knew meant he was being distracted by the computer.

After a while he began frequenting the computer store himself to find out what he was missing and found what he called bells and whistles galore. He bought software for screenwriting and tried out the new format by writing funny opening scenes of silly movies to amuse himself and to make Ruthie laugh when she got home.

At the end of five weeks he started writing a real screenplay. Often when Ruthie got home and found her way to his room Sid would be on Shelly's lap where he'd fallen asleep from boredom while Shelly typed madly away in that kind of glazed-over otherworldly writer place inside his brain.

Sometimes he was already sitting there, or still sitting there, in the morning when Ruthie woke to the sounds of Sid stirring in the nursery. This morning it was the clickity clicking of the computer keys that woke her, and she walked into the room where Shelly was working feverishly. For a while she stood in the doorway watching him, then finally she spoke.

"Shel."

"Hmmm."

"What would you say if I told you you were right about Louie Kweller?"

"You mean that he's a rich asshole?"

"No, that I should start dating him."

"I'd say hallelujah." She walked into the room now and looked at his face.

"Hey, I think you should pursue him with everything you've got. Maybe he can pay for Sid's bar mitzvah. By the time the kid is thirteen, the cake alone will cost five hundred thousand."

"You don't mean it. You're pissed off. I know the way your eyes get all bugged out when you're annoyed."

"You're confusing me with Peter Lorre. I'm not annoyed. Can you get him to adopt me and pay my medical bills?"

"Is this your way of saying yes?"

"I don't know why you think you need my permission, but yes. It's a yes. Tell him to come on over."

Louie began by calling her at work every day, and soon he was sending flowers and gifts and cards. One day he sent over an actor in a gorilla suit to her office, and the gorilla brought flowers and serenaded her and the entire writing staff. When the gorilla, paid extra by Louie Kweller to do so, lifted an enraged Zev Ryder above his head and spun him around, all of them laughed out loud.

"I want her to marry him," Shelly said one day in group. "I want her to have a future and I want that for Sid too. I joke around about Louie, but he has a lot of great qualities."

"It sounds as if you're saying that it's okay with you for Ruthie to leave you and be with Louie," Barbara said.

"I'd like to give the bride away," Shelly said, but Barbara detected the fear behind all he was saying. It made sense that he would worry that Louie might take his place, not just as Ruthie's love, but as Sid's.

"Yeah, well, what about Sid?" Judith asked. The group worked in a way that allowed all of them to challenge one another freely, and none of them was afraid to speak out.

"He'll still be our son. And sometimes he'll be with me. And sometimes with them. It's a hell of a lot more amicable than a divorce."

"Louie and I are just dating," Ruthie said. "I'm not getting married so fast."

"Why not?" Shelly flared, and everyone, especially Ruthie, seemed taken aback by his anger. "Don't postpone your life waiting for me to die, Ruthie. Because I refuse to oblige. I *don't* need you to take care of me. I've got a nearly finished screenplay I'm going to sell, and a million other ideas for things to write and do, and I won't have you stop living because you're waiting for me to stop living. If Louie is serious and you love him, it's going to be the best thing for all of us if you goddamned marry the rich bastard. And don't you dare turn me into the reason you're not doing it. I'm calling the caterer the minute we get out of here."

Ruthie, who had been holding tears inside during his tirade, let them go now, and she wept openly, struggling for her words which came out in spurts. "I can't . . . I don't think I can. I don't want to ruin our . . . I can't."

"Well, you'd better figure out why you can't and not put the blame on me," Shelly said tenderly and put an arm around her while she covered her face with her hands, embarrassed to be crying so hard in front of the others.

"Ruthie," Barbara said, "Shelly's right. You need to work on why you're so unsure about how to proceed when it comes to having a relationship with a man who offers you sexual intimacy, and the real possibility of a marriage."

Ruthie shook her head. "I don't know," she said and sniffled, and Lainie handed her a Kleenex. "I think about it all the time. Maybe because when my brothers died it was so painful it made me afraid, or maybe it's because nobody ever really wanted me before the way

Louie does, so I don't believe him, or maybe it's because I wanted to keep up the ruse for Sid that Shelly and I are a conventional couple. I don't . . . I don't . . ." Then she turned in her chair and faced Shelly and took his hand. "I love you so much," she said. "I can never tell you how you are my life and my love, because it was your love for me that gave me a life and a reason to survive."

Shelly smiled at her, holding both of her hands in his, and when their eyes met he said, "Likewise I'm sure. And it's because I feel this way about you that I'm telling you it's time to move on." Then he stood and moved her to her feet and took her in his arms and hugged her. And when the hug broke and Ruthie blew her nose, Rick said, "Yeah, but the real bottom line question is . . . when do *I* get to read the nearly finished screenplay?"

"I'll bring it in next week," Shelly said, and everyone laughed.

45

"YOU OKAY?" Stan asked, curling up next to Barbara, fitting himself against the curve of her back, further warming her already very warm body. She was only half asleep. All evening long she'd been dozing a little, then opening her eyes to peek at the clock and wonder if his plane had landed and how long it would take him to get home. Now she could let herself drift into that unconscious world because he was there and safe. She started to float there, then jumped, remembering in her misty state that she'd been saving the big news to tell him in person.

"I am okay," she said, her voice husky with sleep. "In fact I just happen to be okay enough for two people."

"Well, that's good news," Stan said in a voice she knew meant he was about to get friendly. So she wasn't surprised when he moved his hands under her nightgown and up to her breasts, which were already so large and so sore she wasn't able to lie on her stomach. "My, my," he said. "If I didn't know any better . . ."

"You'd say I was pregnant?" she asked, turning to him slowly and carefully to protect her sore breasts.

"You're joking?" he said looking into her eyes.

"I wouldn't joke about this."

Stan's face filled with wonder and elation. "A baby? You're telling me I'm having a baby?" he said proudly, and pulled her so close that she flinched at the hardness of his chest against her sore breasts.

"Yes," she said, and burst into tears from hurt and hormones and confusion.

"Honey, that's extraordinarily profound news. Have you told the kids?"

"Not yet."

"Why not?"

"Because I wanted to tell you first, and because Jeff's never home, and Heidi doesn't return my calls, and . . ."

"And?"

"Because I'm afraid they'll laugh."

"Laugh? I think this is fabulous news. I'm going right out and getting one of those jogging strollers I've seen dads using all up and down Ocean Avenue. It's a great way to take the baby out for fresh air."

"You don't jog."

"I know, but I'll start. I mean, I'm going to have to get in shape for those late-night feedings, and those early-morning wake-ups, and those soccer practices—"

"Oh, my God," Barbara said, feeling as if her breasts were going to explode, and her bladder was full and she was so tired just thinking about it all. "It sounds awful."

"No, it doesn't," Stan said, as puffed out as he had been the day she told him the news about Heidi, twenty-four years earlier. "It sounds great. I'm so glad, believe me, sweetheart, your hormones are just awry now, but you'll see, you're going to be so glad." He kissed her again and again and tenderly moved down to kiss her throbbing breasts.

At least, she thought as his kisses became heated, I don't have to worry what day of the month it is.

"So am I crazy out of my mind if I go ahead and have this baby? I know as usual you'll tell me the brutal truth, won't you, Mother?"

"When have I not?" Gracie asked, smiling. She and Barbara were walking down San Vicente Boulevard. Gracie loved putting on what she laughingly called her "tracksuit" to make her way along the grassy strip with her daughter, greeting the morning runners and walkers.

"I can't understand why there would even be a shred of doubt in your mind," Gracie said. "Believe me, I wish there was a chance for *me* to do it again. And I say that because it's taken me years to figure out what constitutes being a good mother, and perhaps now in my old age I could do it right. Do as I say, not as I do. Raising a child is the best and most important and most creative act you'll ever perform. Besides, selfishly speaking, I could use another little cherub of a grandchild in my life, so I insist."

Gracie's step faltered for an instant and Barbara held her arm, but then she seemed recovered and they continued. "I was never what you are, good at my work and good at life. My own life was too difficult for me so I lost myself in other people's cultures, values, ways. I guess I was trying to find myself in all of them. But you and your sister, you are without a doubt my greatest accomplishments."

Then she laughed as if she'd just realized something important. "Maybe *that* was my contribution! I was so bitchy it was a character builder just to be related to me. Eh?''

''That must have been it, Mother,'' Barbara said.

''What did your husband say when you told him about the baby?'' Gracie asked, turning down Twenty-sixth Street so they could stop at the outdoor market for breakfast.

''Are you kidding? He now thinks he's the most potent, virile creature on earth, and he wants to go shopping for a jogging stroller.''

Gracie chuckled. ''And the kids?''

''Jeff loved the news. He said he'd feel less guilty leaving for college, knowing I had someone else to hug. Heidi thought about it for a while after I told her, then she laughed and said, 'Go for it, Mom. I'll help.' She's been in very good spirits lately. She has a new job, and she's dating a new young man.''

''Well, now that we've settled the baby issue, what are you going to do about work? You're always threatening to retire but I know you better than that, so how will you handle the baby *and* your clientele?''

They stood together at the coffee counter where Barbara watched the woman steam the milk for Gracie's cappuccino. She couldn't help feeling a little stab of envy because since she'd discovered she was pregnant, she'd given up coffee.

''I don't know. They've all come such a great distance, particularly my group who call themselves the Stork Club. The issues they're going to continue to face with their children makes me think I ought to stay with them forever.''

''So?''

''So, the groups at the hospital are time-limited. They're scheduled from September through June, and there's a long waiting list to get into them. Practicality dictates that nine months is an adequate time period in which to make any necessary intervention. Then we have to say good-bye and good luck to these families and send them out into the world."

"That's preposterous," Gracie said, moving her arm in a way that almost knocked over the coffee cup the woman behind the counter had just set there. "That'll never work. Certainly not for that group of little ones whose parents had them in all those newfangled ways. Their need for an extended family is going to go on endlessly, and those parents are going to have to put their heads together regularly and figure out what to do about it. You *should* run that group forever. There must be other people who are needing to get in there and work out those things too."

"There are," Barbara said. "I've been getting a lot of phone calls."

"Well, I suggest you tell your colleagues you refuse to put a time limit on people's emotions, and if they say no, you'll go ahead and run the groups out of your living room if you have to."

Barbara gripped the counter as a freight train of nausea rushed through her body.

"And what'll they have to say to that?" Gracie asked her, picking up her coffee cup and heading for a table.

"Mother, if I can have morning sickness at this point in my life . . . anything can happen."

Louise Feiffer was especially imposing that morning, taller than Barbara remembered, especially articulate in telling Barbara about the budget problems the program was having and her concerns about the upcoming board of directors meetings. When it was Barbara's turn to explain why she had requested this private meeting, she felt a flutter of nervousness. She tried to keep back the emotion she knew was a result of the way she felt about the group and the hormones in her body, which were doing something akin to the Ritual Fire Dance.

She remembered Ruthie Zimmerman telling her about the times she sat in meetings with all the male writers at work, and had to repeat what she called her mantra, which was "Don't cry. Don't cry. Don't cry." Barbara said those words to herself now as she talked about why she wanted to have an open-ended continuation of the Stork Club. She knew it wasn't the way the hospital's program usually operated, but she wanted the staff to look closely at the possibility that certain groups would benefit from longer terms.

She watched as Louise took a sip of her coffee. And when she thought about coffee the way she'd watched Louise fix hers, with lots of Coffee-mate and sugar, that made her feel so sick that the floor and the ceiling seemed to get closer together. She hadn't yet told anyone at the hospital she was pregnant.

"Barbara," Louise said, "what I think I'm hearing is on two levels. I understand how it feels every year to terminate these groups. You and I have both been doing this for a while and we acknowledge the solitude we as therapists feel as we let these people go. But I think the process of letting the families separate from us, or leave us behind if you will, closely parallels the emotions we feel about our own children leaving us to go out into the world. And I know that in your case it's exactly what you're going through in your own life now.

"So I'm suggesting that perhaps you should examine if your reluctance to let go of this group could be related to your own separation difficulties at home. The issues around your second child going off to college, a situation which doubtlessly is leaving you feeling empty."

"Oh, Louise." Barbara's knuckles were white from clutching the arm of the chair. "If there's one thing I'm *not* right now, it's empty,'' she said, hoping she wasn't going to punctuate that sentence by throwing up all over Louise's desk. Then she took a deep breath, and another, which seemed to steady her insides. ''And my nest won't be either, at least not for another seventeen or eighteen years.''

''Pardon?''

''I'm going to have a baby,'' Barbara announced with enormous pride, commingled with the desire to jump to her feet and run to the bathroom, this time to pee, which she seemed to be doing every few minutes. To say that Louise looked shocked didn't begin to describe her reaction.

''No,'' Barbara said, ''I'm not asking to keep this group going because I can't separate. I'm asking because I learned together with them that every day brings new surprises and questions, and I want to be there to help them answer those questions as time goes on. When the children start school and other kids ask them about who they are. When they're preadolescent and they ask themselves who they are, and when they're adolescent and struggling with their identities. Their unusual genesis will always be an issue. So please consider that it will teach all of us a great deal more about these people if we can follow through. And understand that I believe in this so powerfully that if it can't be done here, I'll want to move it into my private practice.''

''Let me think about this,'' Louise said, ''and we'll talk more by the end of the week.''

The group seemed more subdued this morning than Barbara had seen them so far. ''I want to talk today about the burdens and dangers of secrecy,'' she said to them. ''I don't mean privacy, because what you tell the outside world doesn't concern me as much as what you tell the children and one another. And I used those serious words 'dangers' and 'burdens' because when there are secrets, the out-of-control fantasies that come with not knowing and the gossip that inevitably puts a negative spin on something you did for positive reasons can and will be damaging. Telling your children the right way from the start will keep them from learning the wrong way.

"Again I urge you to keep information you give them simple and age appropriate. Mostly at this time in their lives what they really need to know is that they're safe and loved, but also remember that before there are words for situations, your children will sense what's going on. And eventually the stories will come out. Openness is the healthiest option, and that will mean that the story of their genesis has to become a natural part of their lives."

"Won't it make them feel freaky?" Judith asked.

"Not if it's told in a way that speaks to how much they were wanted and how much they're loved. For example, Judith, share what you know about the donor even if it's not very much. When they get to asking about it all you might say how much you wanted children, but that it takes seeds, or later on you can say sperm from a man to make a baby. But there wasn't a man in your family, so you went to a place where a very generous man gave his sperm so you could have them. And that's when you might say, And he likes reading and music just like you and Jody."

"What if they ask what his name is?"

"You don't know, so tell them that, and you might also tell them that someday they may get to meet him."

Everyone was quiet, thinking about what Barbara had just said.

People usually think we're a married couple," Ruthie

said. "Most of the time I leave it alone. Soon we'll start applying to schools for Sid, and when they find out about his family history, I wonder what to do."

"Sid will find out too, and talking about it early will show him you don't connect anything negative to his family situation. Counteract the myths and neutralize the name-calling by making him know homosexuality isn't bad, or wrong, but part of life. It'll be a long time until the subject of sexual orientation has an impact on him, but when there are homophobic slurs, do the same thing you'd do in the face of any other inappropriate behavior. Tell him, 'We don't like to say hurtful words like that in our family.' "

"I agree with all that you've been saying," Rick said. "I mean, I went on record right away as saying Doreen would always be a part of David's family, but I believe that ultimately it was secrecy that killed her. I think it was keeping the secret inside about David's birth father and the fear of talking about it that finally became too much for her. Maybe if she could have told her mother, told a psychologist, told a friend—but the shame was too deep. I'll always tell David how bright and funny and warm she was. And somehow down the line I'll have to find a way to tell him about her death."

The group, sometimes so boisterous and jovial, was thoughtful and quiet today. Even the children outside in the play yard were occupied with quiet things and only let out an occasional squeal.

"What about your relationship with Jackie?" Barbara asked Lainie and Mitch.

Lainie spoke up. "Well, as you said to us once, being a good parent isn't related to the way we became a parent, and I know I couldn't love Rose more if she'd grown inside me. And I guess it's because I love her that I understand why Jackie has to be in her life. I'm still hurt about Mitch's deception, I still think he handled it poorly, but so does he. We're working on putting our relationship back together, building the trust back, and also trying to figure out the healthiest way to include Jackie in Rose's world.

"The truth is I like and respect Jackie, and I know she'll bring a lot of her joy of life, and sense of humor, and big-heartedness to the situation and to Rose's life. But I'm going to have to work very hard not to resent her. I mean, I know you can't live your life in fear of the future. God knows, I could have died a thousand deaths by now if I had, but if someday Rose looks at me and says, 'I want to go and be with Jackie because I'm like her and not like you,' I don't know how I'll get through it."

"We both know secrets are no good because I nearly destroyed our marriage by trying to keep one," Mitch said, his arm around his wife.

"As you know," Barbara said, "based on the way the programs at this hospital work, this group was scheduled to be over in a few months. But I asked for an unlimited continuation of our work so that we can confront the ongoing issues that will come up for your families from year to year. I thought you'd like to know that, as of this morning, it's been approved."

"Bravo. Hooray!" There was a positive response from all of them. "Thank God," Lainie said, "we're going to need it, because Mitch and I are talking about the possibility of adopting a baby. An unadoptable child this time."

Ruthie announced that she and Shelly and Sid would need more time to talk things out too, because she was engaged. She held up her hand upon which was a ring with a very large sparkling diamond. And Rick reported, just as an aside, that he and Shelly were taking Shelly's screenplay to Universal, hoping to make a deal there.

Soon it was time for the children to come in, but

Barbara signaled to Dana to give her one more moment alone with the grown-ups. "Since we spent some time today talking about *your* secrets, I'd like to tell you one of mine." They all looked at her as she smiled and said, "I'm pregnant."

A whoop went up from the group and everyone ran over to hug her and encircle her with their warm congratulations. She felt flushed and moved and connected to each of them.

"Needless to say, or maybe not so needless, it was a surprise. At first, one that made me furious at myself, but then on reflection, thinking about all of you and your struggles to make and be families, I was inspired, and I realize that I'm very lucky and very blessed."

Now Dana led the children into the room. They all had their snack of grape juice and peanut-butter crackers, and sang "Twinkle Twinkle Little Star" and "Where Is Thumbkin."

Today Barbara said she would read to them. As soon as she located her reading glasses in her purse, she opened a book that was one of her favorites, *The Velveteen Rabbit*. The sweet story seemed to charm the toddlers, who sat quietly.

" ' "What is real?" asked the rabbit. "Real isn't how you are made," said the skin horse. "It's a thing that happens to you. When a child loves you for a long, long time, not just to play with, but really loves you, then you become real." "Does it hurt?" asked the rabbit. "Sometimes," said the skin horse, for he was always truthful. "But when you are real, you don't mind being hurt." ' " For a minute Barbara had to stop, because there was a catch in her voice and the words of the story were making her feel choked up, or maybe, she thought, it's just my hormones going mad. But when she looked up and saw the eyes of all the parents, she knew they were feeling the same way from the message of the book.

When reading time was over, she hugged every child and every parent good-bye, and walked back to her office to return phone calls and open her mail. She smiled to herself as she passed through the corridors, remembering that not so long ago the thought of retirement had actually crossed her mind. Her step was light as she moved past the offices of the other staff members, buzzing with arriving families.

Retirement for a full-of-life woman like me? Full of life, she laughed, and hope and exciting ideas? Ridiculous, she thought, that she'd ever even considered retirement, and she felt joyful and amazed at the wonderful way in which life goes on!